SUICIDE KINGS

The Wild Cards Series

A WILD CARDS MOSAIC NOVEL

SUICIDE KINGS

Edited by
George R. R. Martin

Assisted by
Melinda M. Snodgrass

And written by

Daniel Abraham | S. L. Farrell
Victor Milán | Melinda M. Snodgrass
Caroline Spector | Ian Tregillis

TOR®

A TOM DOHERTY ASSOCIATES BOOK
New York

SUICIDE KINGS

Copyright © 2009 by George R. R. Martin and The Wild Cards Trust

Map by Jon Lansberg

A Tor Book
Published by Tom Doherty Associates, LLC
175 Fifth Avenue
New York, NY 10010

www.tor-forge.com

Tor® is a registered trademark of Tom Doherty Associates, LLC.

Library of Congress Cataloging-in-Publication Data

Suicide kings : a wild cards mosaic novel / edited by George R. R. Martin ; assisted by Melinda M. Snodgrass ; and written by Daniel Abraham . . . [et al.].—1st ed.
    p. cm.
    "A Tom Doherty Associates book."
    ISBN 978-0-7653-1783-4
    I. Martin, George R. R.   II. Snodgrass, Melinda M., 1951–   III. Abraham, Daniel.
    PS648.S3S85 2009
    813'.54—dc22

                                                                    2009034715

First Edition: December 2009

Printed in the United States of America

0 9 8 7 6 5 4 3 2 1

for Wanda June Alexander
and all the English teachers everywhere

without you, there would be no readers

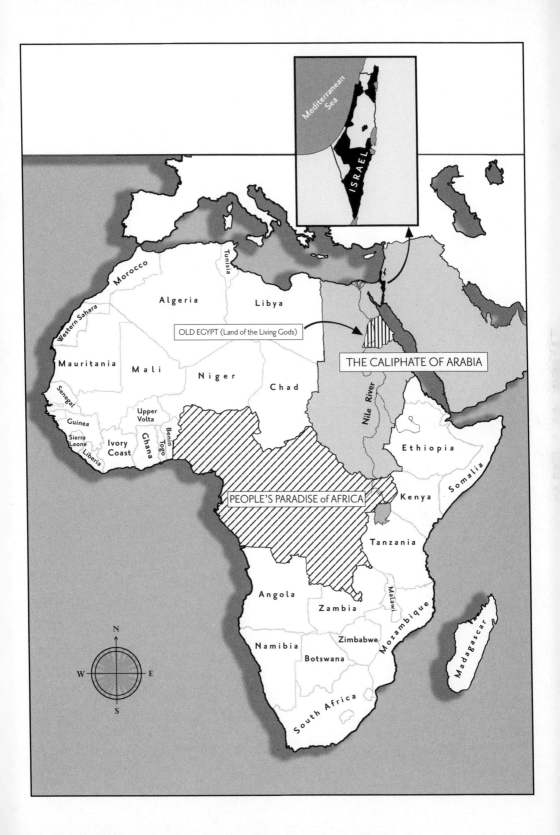

Mediterranean Sea

ISRAEL

Morocco

Tunisia

Algeria

Libya

Western Sahara

OLD EGYPT (Land of the Living Gods)

Mauritania

Mali

Niger

Chad

THE CALIPHATE OF ARABIA

Senegal

Upper Volta

Guinea

Benin
Togo

Ghana

Ethiopia

Sierra
Leone

Ivory
Coast

Nile River

Somalia

Liberia

PEOPLE'S PARADISE of AFRICA

Kenya

Tanzania

Angola

Zambia

Malawi

Zimbabwe

Mozambique

Namibia

Botswana

Madagascar

N

W   E

S

South Africa

SUICIDE KINGS

Thursday, November 26

THANKSGIVING DAY

Guit District
The Sudd, Sudan
The Caliphate of Arabia

FROM WAY UP HERE it was all so clear.

Over here on the left were the Simba Brigades, the armed forces of the People's Paradise of Africa. They had foolishly deployed in an area, a couple square miles in extent, which were among the very few in the southern Sudanese papyrus swamp called the Sudd. They had armor, glittering dully in the sullen southern Sudan morning sun, dug in by bulldozers and concealed in clumps of brush and stands of trees: mostly Indian Vijayanta tanks and British-made Nigerian Mark IIIs, which were almost the same thing. They were enhanced unevenly by upgrades provided by the PPA's Chinese patrons.

Dug in alongside them were armored cars, light tanks, and several thousand mechanized infantry. They were long-term veterans of the war that had liberated and unified Central Africa, leavened by Nigerians trained to a fare-thee-well. Advised by Indian army officers, they had made a stab at catching their enemies debarking from the evanescent and nameless tributary or strand of the Nile onto ground where they could maneuver. Now with small arms and rockets they fought a desperate battle against superior numbers of Caliphate tanks and men.

Tank main guns cracked like thunder. Rockets sprang away, drawing lines of cottony white smoke behind them that settled and dissipated slowly in air so humid and heavy the flying man almost felt he could walk on it. Vehicles blossomed in sudden fire, the ripples of their fatal detonations propagating outward, the shock waves punching at the bare pale skin of the man's face. On columns of black smoke and red fire the smell of fuel combusting mounted upward, momentarily overcoming the hot reek of vegetation rotting in the endless swamps, the acrid stink of spent propellant giving way to the deceptive barbecue aroma of burning human flesh.

Up here was too high to hear the screams. Not that they carried far under the colossal head-crushing din of modern war.

The Caliphate forces rolled forward from barges guarded by Russian-made armored riverboats flying green banners that stirred like the shit-brown surface of the river in a sluggish breeze. Their fighting vehicles were mostly Russian made. Flat T-72s and a few more modern T-90s led the wave. Following came Echelons of BMP-2 and -3 personnel carriers with 30-millimeter machine cannon snarling from their turrets and laser-guided antitank missiles leaping away from rails mounted on the low turrets.

After the PPA's initial shatter of success, superior Caliphate numbers began to tell. Betrayed by their own fire, defending tanks and rocket nests were rapidly destroyed in turn. Adopting the classic Muslim crescent fighting formation, the attacking armor winged out to either side to envelop their foes. Then their infantry could dismount from the BMPs and dig them out and kill them. Despite spiking casualties the PPA's camouflage-clad black veterans held tenaciously and fought.

Up above the world so high, skimming in and out of a cloud in the sky, the man didn't much care if he was seen or not. It would be better if he wasn't, of course; it'd make for a better surprise. Not that *surprise* mattered. Not in the military sense. The people like ants down there on the green and murk-brown ground couldn't change what was about to happen.

But nobody looked. In a world where flying humans weren't unknown, they still weren't anything anybody, y'know, expected to *see*.

A roaring filled the sky, growing in the north. He heard it even above the anvils-of-the-gods racket of modern war. Looking around, the flying man saw two spots appear in the blue sky, just above the flat swamp horizon.

"My turn," he told the wind aloud. He dove.

They flashed past on his right: two Russian-made ground-attack SU-25s, as squat and unlovely as their NATO nickname of "Frogfoot." The PPA fighters, always deficient in combat aircraft—expensive to buy, crew, and maintain—had little answer except man-portable surface-to-air missiles, already arcing up from below and already chasing the dazzling foolish fires of the flares the Caliph's pilots seeded behind them. Even a single pair of attack planes, with Gatling cannon, antitank rockets, and armor-piercing bombs, could torch tanks like a kid with a magnifying glass plus ants.

Except just before they passed him by the man flung his right arm out. A white beam flashed from his palm that made the flares look dim. It punched a neat hole through both aircraft.

They stumbled in yellow flames as fuel and munitions blew up, and fell like disgraced stars.

It was a Sign. A beat after the planes exploded a darkness came upon the land. Like a wave it mounted and rolled forward, across the overmatched PPA defenses toward the triumphantly advancing Muslim army.

The flying man laughed again. He imagined the green-flagged enemy below: confidence faltering, turning quickly to sheer existential terror. It must seem to them that their Allah had forsaken them in spades.

But the liberators hadn't won the battle. Not yet. Their night-vision gear was as helpless in this unnatural Dark as the Caliphate's. All the enemy need do was roll forward blind and they'd smash the defenders to jam in their holes. *Time for Leucrotta to do his thing.* And, of course, the flying man, who swatted multimillion-dollar aircraft like mosquitoes.

It was good to be an ace. And more: an ace with nearly the powers of a god. A god of retribution. A god of Revolution.

He was the *Radical*. And it was cool to be him.

Into the Darkness he dropped. It clutched him like the fingers of a man drowned in some cold ocean, enwrapped him in fog blacker than a banker's heart. But he could see: the girl had touched his eyes with her cool slim fingers. It was like threaded twilight that leached away all colors. To announce his advent he loosed a sunbeam, another. Two of the leading T-90s flared up in response. The turret of one rose up ten feet on a geyser of white fire as its ammo stores exploded. The massive turret dropped back, not entirely in place, so that the red glare of the hell unleashed within shown clearly even to eyes blinded by the Dark.

The Caliphate tankers were totally freaking. Most had stopped when they quit being able to see outside their armored monstrosities. Others continued to plunge on, crashing into each other or crushing smaller AFVs like roaches. A T-72 fired its main gun, torching a brother tank forty feet ahead.

Despite the poison smoke that threatened to choke him, Tom threw back his golden head and laughed.

In terror Arab and Sudanese troops began to spill out of their personnel carriers. Some fell as more Caliphate gunners panicked and cut loose with machine guns. More tanks shot blindly. Others flared up like monster firework fountains.

Rockets buzzed past from behind him. The Darkness had walked among the front-line antitank pits and picked tanks and anointed their crews, too. They could see to slaughter blind foes.

Tom looked back toward the PPA lines. Through the murk surged a big four-footed form, a slope-backed high-shouldered avalanche of spotted fur and massive muscles. Saliva streamed from huge black jaws. It was a spotted hyena, *Crocuta crocuta*. But not a normal animal: a giant, four feet high at the shoulders and four hundred pounds easy. It was a were, a shape-shifter. The third ace the PPA had brought to the battle.

Behind it ran a dozen naked men. Even as Tom watched, their dark, sweat-glistening bodies began to flow and change. They became leopards, four melanistic, the rest tawny and spotted.

No aces, these. The innermost circle of the mystic Leopard Society, who had in horrific secret rituals accepted the bite of Alicia Nshombo. Even their fellow Leopard Men—the PPA's shock troops and secret police—feared them.

The snarl of a twelve-cylinder diesel filled Tom's ears, driving out even the near continuous explosions. He sprang upward. For a moment he hung in orbit. The stars shone down. He lingered a heartbeat, enough to feel the sting of the naked sun and the pressing of his eyeballs and blood outward against the vacuum. He didn't explode in vacuum: no one did. It was just a single atmosphere's difference in pressure: deal.

Then he was back, hovering two meters above a T-90 whose driver had decided or been ordered to charge straight ahead toward the infidels, in hopes of escaping the blackness, or at least getting to grips with the foe. Heat belching from the topside vents of the 1,100-horsepower engine enveloped him like dragon's breath. He dropped to the deck behind the turret.

Squatting, Tom gripped. Grunting, he stood. He deadlifted the heavy turret right out of its ring. Spinning in place, he hurled it like a colossal discus toward a nearby T-72. It struck the side of its turret. A violent white flash momentarily obscured both as ammo stowed in both turrets went off.

Tom dropped to the ground on the first tank's far side. Still massive despite the loss of turret and gun, it heeled perceptibly toward him as the blast fronts from multiple explosions slammed into it. High-velocity fragments cracked like bullets overhead.

The driver's hatch fell open with a ring as the last remaining crewman sought to abandon ship. Suddenly a giant bristling shape hunched on the truncated tank's low-sloped bow armor plate. Sensing danger the driver, half out of his hatch, froze.

Then he screamed as Leucrotta's immense jaws slammed shut with a terrible crunch, biting the driver's face off the front of his skull.

Tom took in the situation. The whole Caliphate armored force milled in utter confusion. At least the parts that weren't burning. Leucrotta and the were-leopards ran freely and killed dismounted soldiers like rabbits. The Darkness-touched PPA gunners continued to pour fire and steel into their enemies. The whole Muslim army was finished as a coherent force; it was now a stampede seeking in all directions for an exit.

All that remained was to slaughter everything in reach. Tom Weathers *really liked* that part.

Jackson Square
New Orleans, Louisiana

MICHELLE IS LYING ON a beach letting the sun bake her.

The outline of a boy blocks out the sun. "Who are you?" she asks.

He opens his mouth, but words don't come out. Light and fire spew forth.

Michelle wants to run away, but she knows she can't escape. Fire and light and power surge into her. Her body expands, opening to the overwhelming force. The power goes on and on and then the weight is crushing her, bearing her down into the ground. The earth groans beneath her. And the power inside her is thick, overwhelming, brutal. It's running through her veins. It wants out.

It wants to bubble.

Just as she feels the bubbles start to flow, she hears Juliet.

"I don't know how much longer I can do this," Juliet says. She's sitting on the edge of the bed petting a small rabbit.

When did we end up in bed? Michelle wonders. *And where did the bunny come from?*

"Ink, you don't have to fucking be here all the time," says Joey. Joey is sitting on the other side of Michelle. A cold worm burrows into her stomach. Does Juliet know about that night with Joey in the hurricane?

"What else can I do?" A tear rolls down Juliet's cheek and Michelle reaches out to wipe it away. But her hand comes in contact not with Juliet's warm face, but with cold, rubbery flesh.

She jerks her hand back, but it connects with more dead skin.

"Jesus," she says. But Jesus isn't here. It's just her alone.

It's dark, but not impenetrable darkness. She's lying inside a tangle of corpses piled up on one another.

Is this another Behatu camp nightmare? But it doesn't feel right. The colors are wrong. The light is off. And, it smells. It smells like rotting flesh. She's never had a sense of smell in a dream before.

Michelle tries to turn over, but she can't feel her legs. Her arms are useless weight, too. The light filtering through the dead limbs around her is greenish. And the air is thick and humid.

Panic begins to crawl into her throat. She's alive, but no one knows it. No one knows she's here. "Help me!" she screams.

"You know, we're her parents, and if we say she's dead, she's dead." Mommy? What was she doing here?

"You people are even worse than Michelle said you were." What was Ink saying? Now they were all sitting on the bed in Juliet and Michelle's apartment. The sheets were a pretty floral pattern that Michelle bought because Ink liked flowers.

"I don't care if you and Michelle are involved in some sickening relationship," Daddy said. "We have rights."

"The fuck you do," said Hoodoo Mama.

Oh, God, Michelle thought. *Joey will kill them.*

"Best as I can tell, you fuckers have no cocksucking rights regarding Bubbles here 't'all. Selfish pieces of sticky brown . . ."

"Joey!" Ink again.

"My goodness," her mother says. How could her mother's voice send a knife of pain through Michelle while at the same time she still wanted to curl up in her mother's arms?

But her mother is gone now. Michelle is back in the pile of bodies. Down in the twilight of dead flesh.

"Help me," she whispers.

A spider slides down a fine silk filament and dangles in front of her. It puts its front legs under its chin and studies her. Then it points up.

Michelle rolls awkwardly onto her back to look in the direction its foot is pointing.

Peering over the edge of the pit is a leopard. Its eyes glow phosphorescent yellow. Cold sweat breaks out on Michelle's brow. Her fear is coppery in her mouth. Another leopard joins the first. Soon the entire edge of the pit is rimmed with them.

The leopards exchange glances, occasionally yawning, revealing sharp, ivory-colored teeth. Then they begin to growl. Low guttural sounds like they're talking to each other.

Her heart is pounding. They must know she's down here. They must know she's alive. They must smell the fear on her. She can smell it herself now, along with the heavy feral odor of the cats. Tears burn her eyes. She tries to blink them away, but they slip out and slide down her cheeks, leaving an itchy trail.

What the hell? Michelle thinks. *I'm the Amazing Bubbles. I don't lie in a pit crying because some damn leopards are looking at me like I'm lunch. They can't do anything to me.*

And she tries to bubble, but she can't. *No hands,* she thinks. *If I had hands, I could bubble.*

"You're not so fucking special, Michelle," Joey says. "And zombies are not disgusting."

Michelle looks down at herself. She's turned a greyish color and her clothes are in tatters. Black mold is growing on her skin. She holds her hand up in front of her face. At least now she has a hand. Bones peek out between the rotted parts of her fingers.

"This is so wrong," she says.

Barataria Basin
New Orleans, Louisiana

JERUSHA CARTER GAZED OUT over a mile-wide expanse of open water. White egrets floated overhead like quick, noisy clouds; blue herons waded in the nearby shallows, and an alligator's tail sluiced through the brackish water not far from her boat.

The scene wasn't entirely idyllic; the sun was merciless, drawing wet circles under her armpits and beading her forehead. Midges, mosquitoes, and huge black flies tormented her. The muck had managed to overtop her high boots and slither down both legs. A storm front was coming in from the Gulf: thunderheads white above and slate grey below piled on the horizon, and the mutter of distant thunder grumbled in the afternoon heat.

The Barataria Basin was a marsh south of the city of New Orleans, one of the several such natural buffers for the city and St. Bernard Parish in the event of a hurricane. It was Jerusha's job to help restore it. Once, she'd been told, before the levees had been built, this entire area had been marshland, not a lake. Since the 1930s, the area around New Orleans had lost two thousand square miles of coastal wetlands. According to the experts who had briefed Jerusha, for every 2.7 miles of wetland, hurricane storm surge could be reduced by one foot. Therefore, to protect the city from future disasters, it was vital that the wetlands be restored.

That was backbreaking, hard work. Silt had to be hauled in to be dumped in the open water to make it shallow enough to allow the plants that had once flourished here to grow again. Jerusha's part came when the silt had been dumped and the margins of the lake were ready to be replanted. There, her wild card gift could make short work of what would otherwise take months or years.

Yesterday, it had been bulwhip; today Jerusha was spreading cordgrass— *Spartina spartinae,* specifically, Gulf cordgrass, with its ability to grow rapidly and to thrive in water of varying salinity. Without Jerusha, teams of volunteers would have been brought in to plant mats of seedlings in the mud and silt, which in time would grow into dense, tough plants high enough to hide a person entirely.

Today was also Thanksgiving. There were no teams out here today. Jerusha was working alone. Everyone else had somewhere to go, somewhere to be: with family, with friends. She tried not to think about that, tried to forget the frozen Swanson turkey dinner waiting for her back at the empty apartment or the call to her parents she'd make while she was eating, listening to their voices and their good wishes and the laughter of their friends in the background, which would only make her feel more alone. Jerusha's seed belt was full of cordgrass seed, and it needed to be planted. Today.

She stepped out into the knee-deep muck of newly dumped silt, her boots squelching loudly as the mud sucked at them. She plunged her hand into one of the pouches on her belt and tossed handfuls of the tiny seeds onto the ground in a wide arc in front of her. She closed her eyes momentarily: she could feel the seeds and the pulsing of nascent life within them.

She drew on the wild card power within her, Gardener's power, funneling it from her mind into the seeds. She could feel them responding: growing and bursting, tiny coils of green springing from them, roots digging into the soft mud, tender shoots reaching for the sun. She led the cordgrass, feeding the power slowly and carefully.

She *was* the cordgrass, taking in the nutrients of sun and water and earth and using it, her cells bursting and growing at an impossible rate, forming and re-forming, new shoots birthing every second. She could see the grass rising in front of her, writhing and twisting, a year's growth taking place in a few moments. As the grass lifted higher, Jerusha laughed, a throaty sound that held a deep, strange satisfaction. There were a few people who might recognize that laugh—it was the same laugh she sometimes gave, involuntarily, in the midst of sex: a vocal, joyous call that came from her core.

Gardening as orgasm.

The cordgrass lifted, writhing and twisting—and atop a cluster of stalks a few feet away something floppy and brown was snagged, bending the grass under its weight.

She let the power fall from her. She felt her shoulders sag: using the ability the wild card had given her always tired her. Usually, after a day out here, she would go back to her apartment and just fall into bed to sleep twelve hours or more. That was most of her days: wake up early, come out here and spread seeds to restore the marshland until near sundown, then back to the city for a quick bite in a restaurant or in her apartment (but alone, always alone), then sleep. Rinse and repeat. Over and over.

Jerusha waded through the mud to the new cordgrass. She pulled the sopping wet piece of felt from the stalks. It took a moment for Jerusha to unfold it and see that it was a hat—a battered, moldy, and filthy fedora, the lining torn and mostly missing, the band gone entirely. A mussel shell clung stubbornly to the fabric; it reeked of the swamp.

She shook her head: *Another fedora. We've sent Cameo at least a dozen hats we've found out here, hoping it was the one she lost.* The only way to know for certain was to send this one to her also: a Thanksgiving present. She'd do that when she got back.

Jerusha sighed, glancing at the sun and the clouds. The storm was rolling in. It was time to head back unless she wanted to be caught in the weather, which would only make an already miserable Thanksgiving more miserable.

Holding the sodden hat by the brim, she made her way back to where she'd tied up her boat.

The Winslow Household
Boston, Massachusetts

"SON OF A *BITCH*! I can't believe he dropped that pass!"

Noel Matthews was jerked back to his surroundings by the shout from his father-in-law. *He* couldn't believe he was sitting in front of an entertainment center that looked like it should be the command deck of an aircraft carrier while his American in-laws watched football and shouted at the bigscreen television.

Of course it wasn't really football. It was that turgidly slow American game where extremely large men dressed in padding and tight pants jumped on each other and patted each other's asses. For a country that was so uptight about fags this seemed an odd sport to be the national pasttime.

Noel reached for his bourbon and soda, and groaned faintly as he shifted on the couch to reach the glass. It felt like a cannonball had replaced his gut, and he surreptitiously undid the button on his slacks. It was Thanksgiving— that peculiar American holiday that seemed to be a celebration of gluttony and taking advantage of the Indians.

But there had been no choice. He and Niobe were living in New York because of fertility treatments at the Jokertown Clinic. Her parents were close by in Massachusetts. And Niobe was determined to show off her famous and successful husband to the old money society that had shunned her when her wild card expressed and she became a joker. Noel had consented to be displayed like a prize Scottish salmon because they had treated Niobe so shabbily, and gloating was a perfectly acceptable response.

Murmuring about "needing the lavatory," Noel made his escape from the company of men to go in search of his wife. In the kitchen he discovered hired help busily washing up the dishes and packaging the leftovers into plastic containers. Noel was rich now, but he hadn't been raised rich. They had lived modestly on his mother's salary as a Cambridge professor. In his house there was no hired help.

He paused in the hallway and listened. The soprano piping of women's voices in the living room vied with the basso shouts and bellows from the den. As he walked down the long hall, past a rather impressive modern art collection, he buttoned his pants and suit coat.

The living room was done in shades of gold and green, and a fire in the large marble hearth made the room seem cozy and warm. Outside, the big pines in the front yard groaned in the wind. It would snow by morning. Thank God they had a way home from this circle of family hell even if they closed the airport.

Arranging his features into a pleasant smile, he approached the women seated on sofas surrounding a low table that held a silver tea and coffee set. The scent added to the feeling of conviviality, as did the staccato of conversation. He was pleased to see that Niobe was chattering with the best of them, and that her chic equaled or excelled the other women.

It was amazing what a year of contentment—and the tender care of hairdressers in New York, spas on the Dead Sea, and couture in Paris—had done for her hair, skin, and wardrobe. The only jarring note was the thick tail that wrapped around his darling's feet. At least the laser treatments had removed the bristles.

Their eyes met, and Noel was pleased to see the triumph brimming in hers. He came around behind the sofa, leaned down, kissed her on the cheek, and made a single white rose appear. Niobe blushed, and he was pleased to see her cousin Phoebe look down and frown into her tea. The woman had spent the afternoon placing her fingertips on his forearm, leaning forward so her breasts would be displayed, and generally making a fool of herself.

"You're not watching?" his mother-in-law said.

"Forgive me, but they're fools. They're watching large men grunting and falling down in the mud. I, however, am no fool. I would rather spend my time with the ladies."

Their laughter fell like ice around him. Niobe wasn't laughing. He knew her husky little chuckle. She was looking at him, wide-eyed and questioning. He gave her a reassuring smile.

He studied his mother-in-law's profile, and briefly regretted he'd abandoned his previous profession. If ever a person deserved killing it was Rachel Winslow. When Niobe's wild card had turned, she had tried to pass her off as a cousin's child, and when Niobe had been driven to attempt suicide her parents had sent her away to a facility where she was treated like a cross between a lab rat and a sex toy.

His wife handed him a cup of tea. The china was so thin and fragile that it felt like a cricket's wing in his hand. He looked down and realized she'd already doctored it with a dollop of cream. It squeezed his heart to know that there was someone in the world who knew how he took his tea, and liked his eggs, the temperature of his bathwater. And he returned the favor. They were bonded physically, emotionally, and mentally, and she had helped to close the hole in his heart left after the death of his father a little over a year ago.

He settled onto the sofa next to Niobe and sipped his tea. Noel found himself reaching for one of the cheese crackers. God knew he wasn't hungry, but nerves made him want to do something with his hands, and he wasn't allowed to smoke in his in-laws' house. He was saved from more calories when he felt the cell phone in his left pocket begin to vibrate.

He set aside his cup, pulled out the phone, murmured an apology, and retreated to stand by the window. The caller ID offered only UNKNOWN CALLER, but he recognized the foreign exchange number—*Baghdad!*

He knew a lot of people in Baghdad, but they only knew his identity as the Muslim ace, Bahir. Only one person knew that Noel was Bahir—his onetime Cambridge housemate, now head of the Caliphate and implacable enemy, Prince Siraj of Jordan.

This was a clean phone. The fact that Siraj had the number meant the Caliphate's intelligence services had been working overtime. Looking for him and finding him. Tension buzzed along every nerve as Noel considered his options.

Better to know what he's up to. Noel answered the phone.

"I didn't know if you'd take the call," came that familiar baritone.

"I almost didn't." Silence stretched between them. Noel pulled out his cigarette case.

Finally Siraj spoke. "I need your help. Will you come to Baghdad, now?" Anxiety roughened his fruity BBC vowels.

It was the last thing Noel had expected. He fumbled out a cigarette and thrust it between his lips. "Ah, well . . . let me see . . . the last time we met you had your guards shoot me. The time before that you had me thrown into an Egyptian prison. I think I'll skip the third time. It might be the charm for you."

"I give you my word I won't make a move against you. I really do need your help."

Siraj suddenly sounded very young, like the friend who'd gotten into trouble with a professor's daughter and come to Noel for help, or the friend who'd loaned him the money to pay off his gambling debts when Noel had become fascinated with the ponies in his sophomore year.

But there was no place for sentimentality. "Why?"

"Half of my armor's been destroyed in the Sudd. This is my last army, Noel, and it's all that stands between the Caliphate and the People's Paradise of Africa. And you in the West do not want Nshombo and Tom Weathers controlling the oil. Trust me."

"Well, that really is the crux of the problem. I *don't* trust you. Sorry about your army, but I'm out of the game. For good. Just an average citizen now. Lovely talking to you." Noel hung up the phone, and rejoined Niobe.

She looked up at him, and he was struck again by her beautiful green eyes. "Was that Kevin?" she said, referring to his agent.

"Yes," Noel lied.

"You have a cigarette *in your mouth!*" his tanned and brittle mother-in-law said, forcing the words past clenched teeth.

"Yes, but it's not lit. I'll go outside and rectify that."

Stellar
Manhattan, New York

WALLY TUGGED ON THE collar of his tuxedo. The tailor had insisted the tux fit him perfectly. As perfectly as anything could fit a man with iron skin and rivets, anyway. But it sure didn't feel right.

He stopped fiddling with the bow tie. He didn't know how to tie it; it would be embarrassing if he had to ask a waiter to help him fix it.

The elevator glided to a stop. It jounced slightly as Wally stepped out.

"Hey, Rusty! Get over here, you."

Ana Cortez stood outside Stellar with a phone to her ear. It looked like she had stepped outside to take a call. She smiled and waved to Wally as he clanked out of the elevator lobby.

His footwear, like his tuxedo, had been specially tailored for him. The fancy Italian shoes looked nice, but they were pretty flimsy; they did little to lessen the pounding of iron feet on a marble floor. Wally would have preferred a less formal Thanksgiving.

Back home, denim overalls and work boots were perfectly acceptable holiday attire. He'd considered going home to Minnesota for the holiday, but in spite of the growing loneliness and homesickness that hovered over him like a cloud these days, he'd decided against it. Every visit home felt more awkward than the last one.

It wasn't that he didn't want to see Mom, Dad, and Pete. He missed them pretty bad. More than anything he wanted to go back home to the days before *American Hero*. He wanted to spend one more Saturday afternoon watching TV with his brother, while their dad snored in his easy chair.

Thing was, Pete had never traveled farther from home than Duluth. His folks had been born and raised on the Iron Range. It was their whole world. Sometimes Wally wished he could go back to being that way, too.

His family imagined Wally's life was glamorous. Exciting. Full of adventure. And it made them so happy, thinking that. The last time he went home, he thought his folks were going to burst with pride. Wally Gunderson, the hero. Wally Gunderson, international traveler. Wally Gunderson, troubleshooter for the United Nations. Pete always questioned him about the places he visited for the Committee, all the people he worked with, all the good deeds he'd done.

Every visit, it got harder and harder to tell them what they wanted to hear. To avoid telling them about the boredom, the loneliness, the dread and fear he felt every time the Committee sent him someplace new, the sense of confusion about what he was doing and why he was doing it, the sense that he'd stopped being heroic a long time ago.

Wally hadn't spent much time at home after his trip to the Caliphate.

"Rusty's here," Ana said into her phone. She cupped her hand over it. "Kate says hi."

"Howdy, Ana. Howdy, Kate."

Into the phone, Ana said, "He says howdy back . . . uh-huh . . . uh-huh." She laughed. "I doubt it . . . I should go. Happy Thanksgiving to you, too. Call me later and we'll compare notes." Ana shut her phone with a snap. "I'm glad to see you. You look good."

"You too, Ana." Her dress looked expensive. It even matched the blue in her earrings.

She reached up to give him a quick hug. Wally dwarfed her. "Gosh," he said. He returned the hug, gently.

He looked into the restaurant, where white-coated waiters carried trays, pitchers, and bottles between the tables. They looked like photo-negatives of Wally, except not as large. Inside, the clink of cutlery chirped through the murmur of conversation. Unfamiliar faces, unfamiliar voices. A sad feeling crept over Wally.

He went inside with Ana. The maître d' greeted them. He didn't bother to ask if they were on the guest list; everybody knew Rustbelt and Earth Witch, two of the Committee's founding members. He paused in the act of ushering them toward the hors d'oeuvres when he noted the gouges Wally's heels left in the floor. The pencil-thin mustache quivered on his lip. He sniffed. But he didn't raise a fuss. His establishment was full of aces.

Not that Wally knew many of them. The Committee wasn't like it had been in the beginning. It was much bigger nowadays. Which was good, really, since it was becoming more international. No longer just a bunch of kids from some dumb TV show. It felt more professional, but also more sterile. He'd met a few of the newer members in passing at other Committee functions—Garou, Noppera-bo, the Strangelets. One of the new guys, Glassteel, nodded companionably at Wally as he passed; they'd worked together in Haiti. They made a pretty okay team, though Wally had liked working with DB the best, and DB was gone now.

Most of the guests had congregated around the long tables where the appetizers had been laid out, near the windows overlooking the Manhattan skyline. Wally munched on miniature hot dogs bathed in fancy ketchup while eavesdropping, trying to find a conversation he could join. The battle in the Sudd dominated most of the conversations. Wally had seen a blurb about it on one of those big stock-ticker things in Times Square during the cab ride to the Empire State Building.

"The PPA has overstretched itself," declared Snowblind in her elegant French-Canadian accent. If silk could talk, thought Wally, it would sound like Snowblind. "There's no need for the Committee to involve itself. Once the Caliphate regroups, this will be over quickly."

Brave Hawk shook his head. "Not if Ra gets involved. Old Egypt doesn't have much use for the Caliphate."

Wally didn't have much of a head for political discussions, and truth be told he wasn't all that keen on Brave Hawk anyway. So he wandered farther down the table, where the hors d'oeuvres included grapes, smelly cheese, and pear slices marinated in port wine. Those were pretty good.

Tinker and Burrowing Owl argued about the World Court. The pending war crimes trials of Captain Flint and the Highwayman were almost as divisive an issue as the fighting in Sudan. Burrowing Owl thought it was a meaningless show trial; Tinker thought both men deserved to be tried before the world. "Oy, Rusty," said Tinker. "What do you think?"

Wally shrugged. "Um . . ." What *did* he think? "I think they did a real bad thing, killing all those folks. But I think they did an even worse thing by making that poor little boy do it."

Burrowing Owl frowned. "Yes, but what about sovereignty and jurisdiction?"

Wally sighed, wishing it was time to sit down and eat.

Jerusha Carter's Apartment
Garden District
New Orleans, Louisiana

HER CELL PHONE CHIRPED before the bell on the microwave went off. That puzzled her, since it was an hour earlier where her parents were, and they would usually still be sitting at the Thanksgiving table at this point. She picked up the cell from the entrance-hall table, glancing at the number on the front.

It wasn't her parents; it was Juliet Summers. *Ink.* Strange. She knew Ink, of course, but they certainly weren't close.

"Hey," she answered. "Ink. What's up?"

"Jerusha? I need your help." There was someone shouting, no, *cursing* in the background. A woman. "That's Joey. Those scumbag LaFleurs convinced a judge to give them that court order. They're gonna pull the plug on Michelle."

Jerusha was shocked. Michelle Pond—the Amazing Bubbles—had been lying comatose in Jackson Square for more than a year, since the day she saved New Orleans from destruction by absorbing the blast of a nuclear explosion. For the past six months, her estranged parents had been fighting in court to obtain a court order allowing them to terminate their daughter's nutrition and hydration.

Jerusha could not believe they had actually won. "If they do this, what do the doctors say will happen to Bubbles?"

"No one's certain," said Ink, "but their best guess is that given the massive amounts of nutrients that Michelle has been consuming every hour, and with a body as dense and heavy as hers, the results would be very quick. Her bodily processes could begin to deteriorate almost immediately—increased heart rate, blood pressure, organ failure. Death in no more than three hours, maybe sooner." Ink sighed. "Or maybe she'll just starve to death."

On Thanksgiving. The LaFleurs had a ghastly sense of irony, Jerusha thought. "What can I do?" She was no lawyer. The Committee had no legal standing within the United States.

"You can help me stop Joey," Ink replied. "She's gone crazy. She's pulled up every halfway fresh corpse in the city, and some that aren't so fresh. She says she's going to kill the LaFleurs as soon as they show their faces in Jackson Square."

Hoodoo Mama. I should have known. Joey Hebert had been born angry, as far as she could tell, and being turned down by the Committee had not improved her disposition.

"She won't listen to me," Ink was saying, "and you're the only one in New Orleans who might have the power to stop her before someone gets hurt. But you gotta get down there quick. You hear me?"

The shouting in the background continued. *Joey,* Jerusha realized. Then Ink was yelling back. "*Damn it,* Joey. Calm down, girl. You're gonna bust an artery."

The phone went dead. "Ink?" Jerusha said.

Nothing.

She flipped the phone shut. The microwave bell rang in the kitchen. She could smell the turkey.

Jerusha put her phone in the pocket of her jeans and grabbed her keys.

The Clarke Household
Barlow's Landing, Massachusetts

"I SEE," MARGARET TIPTON-CLARKE said, in a voice that meant she didn't see at all. "So you're . . . dead?"

Jonathan Tipton-Clarke, or Jonathan Hive, but most often Bugsy, had known that bringing his girlfriend to Thanksgiving dinner was going to be tricky. He hadn't appreciated the full depth of the issue. His mother kept asking difficult questions. His older brother Robert and sister-in-law Norma were scowling over their plates of cranberry sauce and turkey like sour-faced bookends without the books. The twin sisters were grinning with near cannibalistic delight. It just wasn't going to be a good night.

Ellen was very pretty—thin, blond, dressed in a dark charcoal item that clung in all the right places without seeming slutty. It, like all of Ellen's best dresses, had been designed especially for her by the ghost of Coco Chanel. The cameo she wore at her neck looked like it had been picked to go with the outfit more than the other way around. Just to look at her, she fit perfectly with the Tipton-Clarke family decor. Classy, expensive without having neon "nouveau riche" on her forehead. The earring was maybe a little bit off, but that was really nonoptional.

True, she was almost two decades older than Jonathan, which would have been a little weird all on its own. More the issue was that she wasn't exactly his girlfriend. She was the ace who could channel the spirits of the dead. The dead like his girlfriend.

Aliyah didn't wear Ellen with quite the same style that Ellen wore the dress.

"Yeah," she said, using Ellen's mouth. "I . . . I died back when the Caliphate army was attacking the jokers in Egypt, right before they formed the Committee? If you read about it, they might have called me Simoon. That was my ace name on *American Hero*. There was an ace on the other side called the Righteous Djinn? In Egypt, I mean. Not on the show."

When Aliyah got nervous, she ran her sentences together and everything she said turned into a question. When Jonathan got nervous, bits of his body broke off as small, green, wasplike insects, so it was hard to really fault her. He took a bite of stuffing. It was a little on the salty side, as usual, but if he kept his mouth full he wouldn't have to talk to anyone. That seemed the best strategy.

"That must have been terrible for you, dear," his mother said.

"Oh, I don't remember it," Aliyah said. "I wasn't wearing my earring. At the time. I mean, I was a sandstorm when it happened, so it's not like I had any clothes on."

One of the twins, Charlotte he thought, leaned forward on her elbows. Her smile was vulpine. "That's just *fascinating*," she said.

"Well, Ellen can only pull me back from the last time I was wearing my earring."

"No," Charlotte (or maybe Denise) said. "I mean you fought *naked?*"

Aliyah blushed and stammered, her hands moving like they weren't sure where they were supposed to be. With a small internal sigh, Jonathan decided it was time to go ahead and lose his temper. "She was a sandstorm," he said. "Big whirly scour-your-flesh-to-the-bone sandstorm. The kind that could kill you."

Charlotte's smile turned to him. There was a little victory in it. *I could kill you, too*, he thought, and Charlotte yelped and slapped her thigh. She pulled up a small, acid-green body with crumpled wings.

"Oops," Bugsy said. "Sorry."

"You act like you can't control those things," Charlotte said. Or maybe Denise. "You aren't fooling anyone."

"Is it possible," Bugsy's older brother said in a strangled voice, "to have a simple, calm, normal family meal without going into detail about the naked dead women with whom my brother is sleeping?"

"Spirit of the season," Jonathan said. "I mean, unless there's something *else* to be thankful for."

"Excuse me," Aliyah said, stood up, and walked unsteadily from the room.

"So, Robert," Jonathan said. "Have you and Norma gotten knocked up yet, or have the doctors decided there's no lead in the old Wooster pencil after all?"

"That is none of your—"

"Oh, Robert, he didn't mean anything by—" their mother said.

"*Norma!*" Denise (or maybe Charlotte) said. "I've been so worried but I didn't dare—"

With his brother's penis squarely on the chopping block, Jonathan pushed his plate aside and followed Ellen to the den. The room glowed in the festal candlelight. Two wide sofas in leather the color of chocolate seemed cozy, looking out through the glass-wall picture window at the angry Atlantic Ocean. Ellen sat on one, legs tucked up under her. He could tell by the way she held herself that the earring wasn't in.

"I told you so," he said.

"You really did," Ellen said. "I'm sorry I didn't believe you."

"The nice thing about Jerry Springer is that you get to throw chairs. I never get to throw chairs."

"And your mother," Ellen said. "She's the worst of all."

"There is that Demon-Queen-Directing-Her-Monstrous-Horde quality to her. It was more fun when Aunt Ida was still around. She was *much* worse."

"Aliyah felt awful. I told her I'd apologize for her."

"For getting beaten up by my family? Doesn't that usually go the other way?"

"It usually does," Ellen said coolly.

Before Jonathan could think of a good answer, his cell phone started the ring tone he'd set aside for the United Nations. Committee business calling. He dug it out of his jacket pocket, held up a single finger to Ellen, and said hello.

"Bugsy! I hope I'm not interrupting," Lohengrin said.

"Not at all," Jonathan said. "What's up?"

Ellen rose, shaking her head slightly, and headed back toward the ongoing train wreck of the Tipton-Clarke Thanksgiving. Jonathan put one hand over his ear to block out the voices.

"Can you come to New York?" Lohengrin asked. "There's something we need to discuss. An assignment."

Jonathan nodded. Truth to tell, it was moments like these that made working with the United Nations fun. "You bet, buddy. I'll be there with bells on," he said. Then, "You know, I could probably have fit about three more b's in that if I tried. Betcha buddy, I'll be by with bells on my—"

"Jonathan? Are you okay?"

"I may be a wee teensy drunk," Jonathan said. "Or I might hate my family. Hard to tell the difference. I'll be in New York tomorrow. Don't worry."

Lohengrin dropped the line, and Jonathan put his cell phone away. The voices in the dining room had changed. With a sick curiosity, he made his way back to the table.

"You *always* did that, Maggie, ever since you were a little girl," Ellen said, pointing an antique silver butter knife in his mother's direction. "Salt, salt, salt. You'd think God never gave you taste buds."

His mother's cheeks had flushed and her lips pressed white and bloodless. Ellen turned to consider Jonathan, except whoever she was, it wasn't Ellen. The familiar eyes surveyed him slowly. She snorted.

"Aunt Ida?" he said.

"I like this Ellen of yours, Johnny," Ida said. "I'm surprised she puts up with you. Sit, sit, sit. I feel like I'm at the bottom of a well with you just looming there."

"How did—?" he began as he sat.

Ida held up the silverware. "I always said this set was mine, and now I've proven it, haven't I? Robert, dear? Pass the potatoes, and let's see if she's oversalted them, too. Maggie, stop looking at me like that. I was right, you were wrong, and no one is in the least surprised. Thanksgiving is a time for family. *Try* not to ruin it."

Stellar
Manhattan, New York

"ANA?" WALLY WHISPERED. "CAN I sit with you?"

"Sure."

Wally followed her through a maze of round tables draped in billowing tablecloths. The lights were set low; candlelight and the glow from the skyline glinted on wineglasses and silverware. He nodded or waved at the few folks he recognized.

Ana led him to a table near the middle of the room. Wally's own chair creaked precariously. He sat between Ana and the Llama. They'd never worked together, but Wally had met the South American ace at other Committee events. Wally always thought he looked a little like a giraffe, what with his long neck and all, but never mentioned it. "Hey, how ya doin', fella? Happy Thanksgiving."

"Hi," said the Llama, chewing on something. That seemed strange, since the waiters hadn't brought any food out yet. They didn't even have bread on the table.

The Llama seemed distracted. Wally realized he was busy glaring across the room at the Lama.

Wally turned to Ana. "So how's Kate these days?"

"Good, I guess. She's glad to be back in school, but it's probably kinda weird. I think she misses us. She doesn't miss this stuff, though." She pointed to the cyan United Nations banner hanging over the head table where Lohengrin, Babel, and a few others sat.

"Yeah." The Committee had lost much of its allure for Wally over the past couple of years. For some reason he kept sticking with it, even though he'd found better ways to make a difference in people's lives. A *real* difference. Plus, these shindigs weren't the same without the old crew.

As if reading Wally's mind, Ana asked, "Do you still keep in touch with DB?"

"Sure do." They'd gone to war together, Wally and the rock star. Twice. They'd been through a lot.

He looked around the room. Except for Ana, none of the people he knew best were around. In addition to Kate and DB, Wally missed Michelle, who was still down in New Orleans and apparently not doing too good. King Cobalt, his first friend from *American Hero*, had died in Egypt. So had Simoon, who had been pretty nice to Wally.

Except that she wasn't entirely dead, not all the time, anyway. Bugsy and Simoon were going out, which Wally couldn't begin to understand. All he knew was that Bugsy spent most of his time these days with Cameo, who had joined the Committee last year in New Orleans, before she lost her old-time hat. They were having their own Thanksgiving.

Thanksgiving was a time to be with family. But what family? More and more, his visits home to Minnesota made him feel lonely and isolated. He thought he'd found a family, of sorts, with the Committee. And that had even been true for a short time. But he didn't feel at home with the Committee any longer. And so Wally had tried to help other families, on his own, but now even that seemed to be going away.

A little cheer went up throughout the room when a stream of servers emerged from the kitchen. They brought out turkey, chicken, goose, sweet potatoes, mashed potatoes, stuffing, three kinds of gravy, cranberries, corn bread, spinach salad, fruit salad, and pumpkin, pecan, apple, and cherry pie. They even brought out a turducken. Wally wouldn't have known what that was if he hadn't heard Holy Roller and Toad Man discussing it once, back before the big preacher had left the Committee to return to his church in Mississippi. Wally missed him.

He couldn't imagine anybody eating so much food. And that made him think of Lucien, his little pen pal. A single table here probably held more food than his entire family saw in a month.

"You're looking glum," said Ana.

"Just missing folks, I guess."

"Yeah," she said.

"Like, see, I got these pen pals. It happened because I saw a commercial late at night during a Frankie Yankovic marathon. You know, for one of those setups where you send in a few dollars to help out a kid somewhere?"

Ana smiled. She took a drumstick from the platter at the center of the table. "That's great, Rusty."

"Well, I got a few of them. But this one kid, his name's Lucien, and me and he got to be pretty good friends, writing letters back and forth. But his last letter said—"

Babel started tapping her wineglass with a butter knife. It chimed through the dining room.

Lohengrin stood. He waited for a hush to fall over the room before speaking. The kitchen clamor ebbed and flowed as servers passed through double doors to the dining room.

"*Ja, ja.* Welcome. My friends, we are the United Nations Committee for Extraordinary Interventions." Polite applause. "Today we gather to celebrate our achievements and be thankful for the opportunities we've been given. And the world has much to be thankful for since our inception, no?" His laughter actually sounded like ho-ho-ho. Like Santa Claus, if Santa wore magical armor. Before meeting Lohengrin, Wally had never known anybody who laughed like that for real.

If Lucien and his family had much to be thankful for, it had nothing to do with the Committee. In fact, it seemed to be the only thing Rusty had done in the past couple of years that actually improved somebody's life. But it didn't even begin to make up for what he and DB had done in Iraq.

The German ace droned on and on, peppering his remarks with references to "my predecessor," as though there had been some kind of special ceremony to transfer the reins of power when he took over the Committee. Everybody knew that John Fortune had bowed out quietly but quickly after becoming a nat for the second time. Rumor had it he was traveling the world, though to what end, nobody could say.

But thinking about John Fortune and his travels gave Wally an idea.

Jackson Square
New Orleans, Louisiana

THE MOOD WAS UGLY in Jackson Square. The triple spires of St. Louis Cathedral glistened in their spotlights; nearby, Andrew Jackson waved his hat atop his rearing horse. That was normal enough, but as Jerusha approached, she realized that the crowd ahead of her was . . . wrong. The stench of death hung around them, and their faces were stiff and unresponsive.

Zombies.

There were at least a couple dozen, more than she'd seen Hoodoo Mama raise up for a long time. At least with Thanksgiving the usual crowds in Jackson Square were sparse, though there were still enough onlookers watching from a wary distance to make Jerusha nervous.

Joey and Juliet were standing at the makeshift wooden "shrine" that enclosed Bubbles, its planks adorned with ribbons and handwritten testimonials. The thick pipes of Michelle's feeding tubes stabbed into the white cloth that covered her body, which had sunk so deeply into the soft ground that pumps had to remove the water that would otherwise have flooded the depression. Jerusha could hear Joey shouting into the night. "Fuck them. Goddamn leeches. They stole her fucking money. Now they want to kill her, too? Well, *fuck* that."

Ink was standing next to Joey, an arm around her, her voice so quiet that Jerusha couldn't hear it. Whatever she was saying, Joey didn't like it. Her zombies muttered and groaned. "I ain't gonna let that that cocksucker of a father and her cunt mother screw Michelle again. I ain't." Her lips were pressed into a tight line. A hardness came over her thin face. She ran a hand through the tangled shock of brown hair, ruffling the bright red streak. "I'll fucking rip them both into a hundred fucking pieces. I swear."

"Ink, Joey," Jerusha said loudly, skirting the edge of the zombie crowd. "Listen, you can't . . ."

She stopped at the sound of sirens, cutting through the low whine of the pumps driving Michelle's feeding tubes. Along Decatur Street, a small motorcade pulled into the square, pulling up on the far side of Bubbles's shrine, near a large grey electrical box. Jerusha plunged a hand into the open zipper of the pouch at her waist, fingering the seeds inside.

NOLA SWAT police officers piled out of the first three black vans, their faces masked by riot helmets, armed with what looked to be shotguns. Ira and Sharon LaFleur emerged from a limousine, accompanied by another phalanx of policemen.

Jerusha had always pictured them as villains, monsters who would steal money from their child. She'd expected their sins to be written on their faces, but they weren't. Ira was balding and overweight, looking pudgy and ineffectual; Sharon's face was drawn and haggard and thin, but the lines were those of a model: like her daughter's face, what Bubbles might look like in another quarter century. They looked *ordinary*.

"*Motherfuckers!*" Hoodoo Mama shrieked, and her zombies howled with her. Ink had both arms around Joey, clinging to her desperately. Joey pointed at the LaFleurs. "You miserable cocksuckers! You stay the fuck away from her, you hear me!"

Sharon LaFleur looked at them, hand over mouth. The zombies started to shamble toward them. The cops shuffled nervously, weapons up and ready. "Joey, you can't!" Jerusha shouted.

Joey shook her head. "You kill her," she screamed at the LaFleurs, "and I'll just raise her up again. She'll be the biggest fucking zombie in the whole goddamn world. You hear me, you cocksuckers?"

Ira LaFleur nodded to the officers nearest the grey box, which now had a panel open. The low whine of the pumps driving Bubbles's feeding tubes suddenly vanished. The silence was more terrible than any sound could have been.

The zombies screamed as one, wordless. They advanced.

"Damn it." Jerusha pulled her hand from the pouch, fisted around the contents there. She flung them wide. As soon as the seeds hit the ground, they were rising, a wriggling carpet of vines that tore through the pavement of Jackson Square. Kudzu. Jerusha guided the growth in her mind, snarling the vines around the zombies' legs, bodies, and arms, encasing them in living green chains. She coiled them around Joey and Ink for good measure. Hoodoo Mama glared at her, cursing wildly.

The SWAT officers were piling back into the vans, hustling the LaFleurs back to their limo. With a scream of sirens, the cars backed away and sped off again.

"*Stop them!*" Joey screeched. Spittle was flying from her mouth. "God damn it, Gardener, you're a fucker just like them. Just like them. You're letting them kill her."

Jerusha had no answer. "I'm sorry," she told them.

"Fuck you're sorry," said Hoodoo Mama. "And fuck you, too, cunt. You better hope that Bubbles doesn't die. 'Cause if she does, you're next."

Stellar
Manhattan, New York

AFTER THE MEAL—AFTER the clink of silverware and the random chorus of burps and satisfied *mmmmm*'s died down, after the last slice of pumpkin pie had been tucked away (Wally had two pieces), when most of the conversation in the room was a hushed murmur as people slipped collectively into a digestive stupor—Wally excused himself and went over to Lohengrin's table.

Klaus was deep in conversation with Babel when Wally clanked up to their table. They must have been discussing something pretty intense because it took them a few seconds to notice Wally. He caught something about New Orleans, Sudan, and the Caliphate before they tapered off to look up at him. Babel grinned. "Happy Thanksgiving, Rustbelt."

Wally said, "Thanks. Um, you, too." He didn't know her very well, but she made him uncomfortable. He remembered how she'd sabotaged DB when he split with the Committee, and wondered if she'd do the same thing to him, since he and DB were friends.

Lohengrin yawned. Two empty wine bottles rattled on the table when he stretched his legs. He motioned for Wally to sit and join them. "A good feast, *ja?*"

"Oh, you bet," said Wally, taking a chair. "I like them sweet potatoes with the marshmallows on top. Real tasty." He nodded, and patted his stomach. His cummerbund muted, ever so slightly, the *clang* of iron against iron. "Hey, I have a question."

Lohengrin sat a little straighter. "What troubles you, my mighty friend?"

"Well, see, I was wondering if we'd be doing anything in Africa sometime soon. I mean, you know, the Committee."

Babel assumed the tone that people did so frequently around Wally. The tone that spoke volumes about what they thought of him and his faculties. "Well, Rustbelt, it's a very complicated situation. The Committee's involvement with Noel Matthews in New Orleans put us on precarious footing with Tom Weathers, and by extension the Nshombos."

"Oh, sure. Sure. But I didn't mean about any of that. It's just, see, I have this pen pal. My friend Lucien. He and his family live up in the Congo thereabouts."

Babel cocked an eyebrow. "Pen pal?"

"I sponsor him. I send a few dollars every month and it pays for his school and medicine and stuff."

"Ah." Lohengrin nodded. He approved of noble causes.

"Anyway, his last letter kind of worried me. He was real excited because he'd been chosen to attend a brand-new school. But he said that the soldiers who picked him told him he wouldn't be allowed to write to me no more. And that when Sister Julie tried to stop them from taking the last bunch of kids to the school—Sister Julie is a nun in his village, you see—well, he said they hurt her. And I thought, that doesn't sound right. I mean, what the heck kind of school has soldiers? So I figured, maybe the next time I go somewhere, you could send me to Congo and I could check in on him."

Babel said, "I don't think that's a good idea, Rustbelt. There's no telling how Weathers and the PPA would react if they believed the Committee was encroaching on their territory."

"But I wouldn't be, not really. I'd just be visiting Lucien and making sure the little guy is okay."

Again, that tone. "Yes, certainly. You know that, and we know that, but the Nshombos would never believe it. And, let's face it, you aren't inconspicuous. They'd know you were there. Ostensibly on Committee business."

Lohengrin yawned again. "Frau Baden is correct that the situation is complicated. We must be careful with the Nshombos." Wally slumped in his chair. "But," Lohengrin continued, solemnly putting a hand on Wally's shoulder, "your cause is just. I promise to do what I can to help your missing friend."

"Well, gosh. That's swell, Lohengrin." Wally practically leaped out of his chair, grinning. The Committee would help him go find Lucien! "I can't wait."

"Yes. I believe that if I ask him, Jayewardene will make careful inquiries through diplomatic channels."

Inquiries? Oh. Wally tried to hide his disappointment. "Right. That'll be a big help, no doubt. I sure do appreciate it."

He returned to his table, just long enough to say good night to Ana; the Llama had already left. Wally didn't much feel like hopping in a taxi when he got down to the street, so he started walking in the general direction of Jokertown.

A thin dusting of snow covered the sidewalks. It fell in large flakes that drifted slowly to the ground like cotton. The clouds overhead and the snow underfoot reflected the soft glow of the city in all its colors, making everything look like a Christmas tree decoration.

Back home, Wally and his brother Pete used to make snow forts during Christmas vacation. He remembered countless snowball fights on winter mornings, too, waiting for the school bus. Lucien had loved hearing about stuff like that; to him, snow was the white stuff on distant mountains. Wally had secretly hoped he'd get to take him to the mountains someday, so he could see the snow firsthand.

But Lohengrin and Babel had been pretty clear. If he wanted to go to Africa, he'd have to go privately.

The Winslow Household
Boston, Massachusetts

THEY FINISHED OFF THE evening playing bridge and eating another round of pie before retiring to Niobe's old bedroom. Niobe found this embarrassing and Noel found it charming. He investigated her bookcase filled with a collection of late Victorian and early twentieth-century children's books—*The Bird's Christmas Carol*, *The Secret Garden*, *The Little Princess*, *Little Lord Fauntleroy*. He rooted through the closet and discovered a stuffed animal collection (now consigned to the top shelf), and picked out a few choice specimens to take home to New York. *For our baby*, he thought, but neither of them gave voice to that. This was the fourth try, and they were both too superstitious to invoke the child out loud lest it lead to another miscarriage.

Noel read aloud from *Fauntleroy* until Niobe's eyelids dropped and her breathing slowed. "He had a cruel tongue and a bitter nature, and he took pleasure in sneering at people and making them feel uncomfortable. . . ." Noel's voice died away. He slowly slipped his arm from beneath her, snapped off the light, and settled down to sleep.

It took a long time because he kept replaying the conversation with Siraj, and wondering what it all meant.

Rusty's Hotel Room
Jokertown
Manhattan, New York

"UM, HI? DB?"

The phone receiver compressed the noise of a raucous party into a dull roar. "What? Who is this?"

"It's me, Wally."

A long pause. "Ollie?" DB sounded distracted. Then, more muffled, he shouted, "Hey! Leave that fucker for me!" This was followed by peals of high-pitched laughter. Wally had looked online; it was a little after eleven in Mumbai.

"No, *Wally*. You know, Rustbelt?"

Another pause. Then: "Rusty! How the hell are ya? Great to hear ya. Hey, guys, it's Rusty!"

This provoked a chorus of greetings from the other members of Joker Plague.

"Same to you, fella. Look, I was wondering—"

"You need tickets to the show? No problem! You've got a permanent backstage pass, you know that." Something shattered, followed by more groupie laughter. Bottom shouted something that Rusty couldn't quite make out. "Wait. You're in India?"

"What? No. But I was wondering, since your tour is winding up soon—"

"—Yeah, one more month, then we're back in the States. God damn it, S'Live, I told you to leave it—"

"—if you'd wanna go to the Congo—"

"—bongo drums? We don't play much world music—"

"—no, I said Congo, like the country—"

"—country? Yeah, I hate that shit, too. What the hell is that? Hey, Rusty, I gotta go, I think I smell smoke. Take care of yourself, pal!" *Click.*

Well, cripes. Wally had figured that if anybody would join him on a trip to Africa, it would be Drummer Boy. They'd been comrades in arms (and arms, and arms) more than once. But it seemed that DB was busy with his old life.

Wally thought about other folks he knew. Kate was real nice, but it sounded from Ana like she'd had enough of traveling for a while. He would have asked Ana, too, but she'd told him the Committee was sending her to China. The government there had specifically requested Ana's consultations on a series of giant dams they were building.

He toyed with the idea of contacting Jamal Norwood. Stuntman had probably learned a whole lot about finding missing people while working for SCARE. Plus, he was real tough. And he sorta owed Wally for all that stuff he said back on *American Hero*. But Jamal would never agree to help him. Plus, Wally didn't want to travel with somebody who disliked him so much. Even he could foresee an awkward and unpleasant conversation.

One more name sprang to mind: Jerusha Carter. Gardener's ace couldn't be better suited to traveling through Africa. She was perfect for the trip in just about every way. He even knew her, a little bit.

It took some calling around to other Committee members before he got

Jerusha's cell number. Wally reclined on the bed in his hotel room. The mattress groaned; somewhere halfway across the country, a telephone rang.

"Hello?" A weary voice, thick with fatigue. Behind it, what sounded like voices raised in quiet song, like they were singing hymns or something. Not like in church, though. It sounded more like a vigil.

"Um, hi. Jerusha?"

"Yes." Her voice got distant, and the background noise got louder, as if she was holding the phone away from her face to look at the caller ID. "Who is this?"

"It's me, Wally. Gunderson. You know, Rustbelt? We worked together when the Committee sent us to Timor."

"Oh, *Wally*. I thought I recognized your voice." A pause. "What's up?"

"I was wondering—um, are you okay? You sound real tired. No offense or anything."

"Uh . . . it's been a tough few days down here. Did you hear about Michelle? Her parents?"

"Yeah. It's a bad deal." The thought of Bubbles helpless like that—at the mercy of others—made him think of Lucien, and brought on another pang of anxiety.

"Really bad." Jerusha sighed, loudly. "Anyway. What's up?"

Wally didn't know the best way to broach the subject. He plunged ahead: "Do you wanna go to Africa with me?"

"Why is Lohengrin sending you to Africa?"

"He's not," said Wally.

Another pause. "Huh?"

Wally explained the situation.

"So . . . you want me to go to the PPA to help you find your pen pal?"

"Yep. Well, no, I mean, I thought we'd go to the Congo, where Lucien's from."

Jerusha said, "That's *in* the PPA."

"Oh."

"Ugh, Wally . . ." Wally recognized that tone. It was the sound of somebody cradling her head in her hands. "Say. Why did you ask me?"

Oops. "Well, you're real smart. And you know about jungles and stuff. And you're, um . . ."

"I'm what?"

"Black."

"Uh-huh." Jerusha's tone here was a little harder to read. Maybe he shouldn't have said that. "Look. What you're trying to do is very sweet. But I think you're biting off more than you can chew. Even with that giant jaw of yours. Besides, I have my hands full down here."

"What if I came and helped out?"

"That's nice of you, but it wouldn't change my answer."

"Oh."

"Sorry, Wally. Don't do anything rash, okay?"

"You bet."

Wally stared at the ceiling. *That's in the PPA.* He hadn't put that together before. He knew a little about the PPA; that whole mess down in New Orleans, Bubbles and all, was tied up with the PPA. He knew that much. But until she'd said it, he hadn't associated Tom Weathers and Dr. Nshombo and the PPA with Lucien's Congo.

All the more reason to go to Africa, and the sooner the better. All the more reason to find a traveling companion. But the more he thought about it, the more Jerusha seemed the best choice.

♣

Friday,
November 27

The Winslow Household
Boston, Massachusetts

A LEGACY OF NOEL'S previous profession was an inability to sleep any deeper than a doze. He awakened when the mattress shifted as Niobe left the bed. Cold grey dawn seeped around the edges of the blue velvet drapes, and Noel could hear snow pecking at the windows. He snuggled deeper under the down comforter, and was headed back to sleep when a tiny whimper of fear from the bathroom sent him leaping out of bed. "Niobe!"

At the same moment she called out, "Noel!" The panic in her voice squeezed his heart.

He ran to the bathroom, the legs of his pajamas whipping at his ankles. She was sitting on the toilet with her arms wrapped around her stomach. He dropped to his knees in front of her.

"I'm cramping."

"Bad?" he asked.

"Not as bad as last time," she replied through white lips.

Oddly she was staring at a point where the tile met the porcelain side of the bathtub rather than at him. Noel had a sudden memory as they had stood on the rocky beach of a distant Scottish island, and she had told him how she had tried to cut off the damning mark of her jokerdom, and win back her parents' love. He glanced at the thick white scars that twisted across her tail. She had nearly bled to death in the bathroom of her family home. Noel realized this was the room. *And that bitch put us in here.* He again felt that shaking desire to kill his mother-in-law. "I'm taking you to the clinic."

"We can't just run off," Niobe called out as he ran back into the bedroom. "They'll be so angry."

"Watch me. And fuck them."

Noel pulled her long, fur-lined suede coat and his overcoat out of the closet. He returned to Niobe, got slippers on her feet, and tucked her into her coat. The hood framed her face. She looked like a figure on a Russian icon box. He slipped on his own slippers and guided her back into the bedroom.

He pulled back the blinds so he could map the sun's progress. *Come on, come on!* They couldn't lose another. Niobe couldn't take much more. He wasn't sure he could, either.

It was another four minutes before he could make the transformation to Bahir. The pajamas cut into his crotch, and the overcoat strained across Bahir's broad chest. It didn't matter. He would transform back once they reached the Jokertown Clinic.

Jackson Square
New Orleans, Louisiana

MICHELLE OPENED HER EYES.

Juliet, Joey, her mother and father, and a couple of people dressed in hospital scrubs were ringed around her. Her throat was raw, like when she had strep throat. She tried to speak, but she had no voice.

"She's alive!" Juliet said.

"You don't know that," snapped Michelle's mother.

"It could be a reaction to the feeding tube being pulled," said the woman in baby-blue scrubs.

Michelle tried to look around, but she couldn't move her head much. Behind her mother, there was a table crammed with flowers and candles. The floor under the table was thick with store-bought bouquets. She looked up. The ceiling was bare plywood and had water stains.

A TV hung from the far corner with the sound turned off. It was tuned to a news channel, and there were bulletins scrolling across the bottom of the screen. She caught the last bit of one story: ". . . and the latest contestant voted off Season Three of *American Hero* is . . ."

She blinked. It couldn't be Season Three. They hadn't even finished Season Two. She was supposed to do a guest shot on Season Two.

She looked down at herself.

She was huge. Bigger than huge. Enormous. Bigger. Humongous. What was bigger than humongous? She didn't even look like a girl anymore. They had draped something over her. A parachute maybe? She could feel the rolls of fat that rippled down her front. It was impossible for her to be this big.

It came back to her then. A spinning golden necklace. Drake grabbing his chest. His eyes. His eyes were white and glowed and burned. She had embraced him and—

No. No. No. No. NO!

Blythe van Rennsaeler
Memorial Clinic, Jokertown
Manhattan, New York

THE DARKNESS AND THE cold lasted the briefest second, and then they were standing just outside the emergency room of the Jokertown Clinic. Noel willed his body to shift back into his normal form. It felt like the muscles were crawling across his bones, and there was an ache in the bones themselves as he was returned to his normal height.

Niobe had already gone in ahead of him, and was talking to the joker receptionist. The clinic was relatively quiet at 7:00 A.M. There was only a wino sleeping in a corner and a joker mother clutching her four-year-old as he alternated between sobs and hacking coughs.

Niobe gazed at the little fellow with naked longing in her green eyes. Unlike his mother, he was completely normal though to Noel's mind the green snot crusting his upper lip and his beet-red face made him a more unlovely sight than her.

The receptionist made a call, and he and Niobe settled into chairs to wait. A television hung on the wall was set to MSNBC. Noel's attention was caught by the heading—THE SUDD. A helicopter shot was panning across an expanse of reeds and water. On bits of dry ground that humped like the backs of prehistoric water beasts hiding in the swamp, destroyed tanks belched smoke into the air. Bodies, doll-like at this height, floated in pools and bled onto the ground.

Noel read the scrolling subtitles. *The Sudanese government had voted to join with the Caliphate. Dr. Nshombo, leader of the People's Paradise of Africa, has charged the Sudanese with genocide against the non-Muslim black tribesmen of the south, and moved into the Sudan to protect them. Clearly a major battle between PPA and Caliphate forces has occurred.*

Noel turned away from the lure of the flicking box. It wasn't his problem. He was done with political games on a world stage. A pox on both of them.

But there was no way that Prince Siraj could be compared to the madman who led the armies of the PPA. Siraj was a cunning politician, and killed when expedient. Dr. Nshombo was a cold ideological killer. Tom Weathers was just a killer. *And they all hate you. Why not take one of them off the table? Make Siraj an ally rather than an enemy? You were close friends once.*

Because I don't know if I can trust him now. Those boys of Cambridge are dead, Noel replied to that part of himself that sometimes missed the excitement of the game and that sense of serving a greater cause.

Fifteen minutes later the centaur doctor came clattering through the door. Dr. Finn took Niobe's wrist in his hand, feeling for her pulse. "Worse or better?"

"Better," she said.

"That's good."

"If . . . if something were to go wrong . . . I won't try again. I can't watch any more of my children die."

Niobe wasn't just talking about the miscarriages. She was thinking of the hundreds of "kids" born from her ace power. Her "tail" was actually an ovipositor. Within minutes of sex, two to five eggs would move through the tail, be laid, and hatch into tiny children. They were usually aces, and their powers seemed to be linked to Niobe's needs at a given moment.

They were the primary reason she had been able to escape from a secure facility and help free the young boy whose nuclear ace had endangered them all. But these children only lived for a few hours or a few days. Their homes were filled with photographs of the kids. Niobe grieved for every one of them. The last four had been Noel's. He grieved for them.

One of the reasons Niobe—or Genetrix as they had called her at BICC—had been studied was her ability to reverse the wild card odds. Instead of ninety percent black queens, her clutches were ninety percent aces. She and Noel had hoped that those odds would continue when they tried to conceive a normal baby.

Unfortunately that hadn't been the case.

Like every other ace and joker/ace trying to have a baby, they had the same devastating odds of a black queen. Add to that the fact that Noel was a hermaphrodite and functionally sterile, and the odds of Niobe every achieving her dream of motherhood seemed remote . . . until they came to the Jokertown Clinic, where more authorities on the wild card practiced than in any other place in the world. Dr. Clara van Rennsaeler had designed an ingenious plan of treatment, which her husband Dr. Bradley Finn was implementing.

First he pumped Niobe full of hormones so her ovaries produced multiple eggs. Then Finn had combined the nucleus from one of Niobe's wild card ovipositor eggs with Noel's barely mobile sperm and a real egg from her womb. By Noel's count they'd discarded forty-three zygotes. Sad little creatures who had begun and ended their lives in petri dishes when they turned out to be black queens or jokers. Four had been viable, but they'd lost three to miscarriages.

And now this one. They knew the sex—male. They knew he would be an ace. Finn told them that if they reached sixteen weeks they were home free. But now . . .

"Let's see what we've got." The centaur doctor led them out of the waiting room and into the examination room. Noel waited just beyond the screening curtains while Finn and a female nurse examined Niobe. A few moments later the steel rings chattered as Finn pulled back the curtain.

Niobe was beaming.

"We're good," the joker doctor said. "Thirteen weeks and counting. We're not going to lose this little guy." He made it sound like a vow.

Noel stepped up to the bed, and was surprised when Niobe took his hand and pulled him down. "Sit down before you fall down," she said.

Noel realized that relief had left him limp. "What caused the cramping?"

"Just a little gas," Finn replied.

Niobe hung her head, taking refuge behind her mane of chestnut hair. "I'm sorry."

"No problem. I understand why you're jumpy as a cat," Finn said.

"Can you blame us?" Noel snapped. Niobe shushed him, and stroked her hand down his arm.

"No, of course not. Not after three miscarriages," Finn soothed. "But we're in good shape."

Noel looked at his wife's wan face, and suddenly hugged her tight.

Finn cleared his throat. "I know you don't want to take anything," he said. "But I can prescribe a mild sedative."

Niobe was already shaking her head.

"Just to take the edge off."

A more emphatic shake.

Finn sighed. "All right." He tapped Noel on the shoulder. "Take her home and keep her happy, okay?"

Noel nodded, and acknowledged to himself that going off to Baghdad would definitely not keep her happy.

Louis B. Armstrong
International Airport
New Orleans, Louisiana

THE FIRST THING WALLY noticed as he tromped down the jetway was the smell.

New Orleans smelled different from Manhattan. It didn't smell like sidewalk garbage and truck exhaust; it smelled, faintly, of earth and water. There was humidity in the air, too, which along with the wet smell reminded him of summers at the lake cabin, back home in Minnesota. It had been that way the first time he came here, too, back when Bubbles saved the city.

Thinking about Michelle saddened him. Part of him had never wanted to come back here, and part of him felt badly for not visiting Michelle.

He waited in the airport, watching people buff the floors for an hour, before calling Jerusha. He figured she might not be that happy to hear from him again, and that would only be worse if he woke her up. Was she an early riser? They hadn't shared a tent in Timor, like he and DB had done a number of times, so he had no idea. DB snored.

"Hello?" Her voice didn't sound gravelly, like most people when awakened by the phone. *Whew.*

"Jerusha? This is Wally."

"Oh, hey, Wally. Look, I hope you're not upset about yesterday—"

"Nah, I understand. I did sorta spring the whole thing on you outta the blue."

"Well, yeah. I'm glad you understand."

"Sure. But hey, can I show you something? It'll be real quick, I promise." Farther down the terminal, a buzzer launched into a series of short, loud bursts. A baggage carousel creaked to life.

Jerusha heard it, too. "Where are you right now?"

"I'm at the airport. I caught a flight."

"Wally . . ." She was doing it again—cradling her head. He could tell.

He said, "It won't take long."

A sigh. And then: "I don't know why, but I spent a lot of time yesterday thinking about your trip. So, I do have some advice for you."

Wally sat up straighter. "Wow! That's great!" His voice echoed through the carousels. A few heads turned among the people waiting for their bags to come tumbling down the conveyor belt. "Um, where should I meet ya?"

"I'm with Michelle right now, in Jackson Square. Any taxi driver can take you here."

Wally thanked her and rang off. He hiked his backpack over his shoulder and tromped off in search of a taxi stand.

As often happened when Wally used a taxi, the driver heard his accent and immediately assumed Wally was an easy way to make a few extra bucks. Wally's taxi drivers tended to take long, circuitous routes that ran up the meter. Usually he didn't mind; he liked seeing the sights in unfamiliar places. He'd been here before, so he got impatient when the driver tried pointing out some of the sights in the French Quarter. But the driver waived the fare when he learned that Wally knew Michelle.

Jackson Square was a little different than he'd last seen it. For one thing, it looked like they'd had a pretty bad kudzu infestation not too long ago. Most of it had been cut away, but he could see tendrils here and there on the sides of booths and poking up through cracks in the pavement. *Weird.*

But the main change was the wooden enclosure beneath the statue in the center of the square. It was covered with flowers, candles, cards, and home-made signs. Prayers and thank yous. The flowers and signs fluttered in the breeze; Wally caught a whiff of magnolias. The wind rattled the slats of the shrine where a pair of nails had come loose. Wally peered through the gap. He glimpsed something pale. It took a few seconds before he realized that he was staring at the white cloth draped over Michelle's body. That made him want to cry.

Wally strolled around the shrine, reading signs and cards until he found the entrance. A cop waved him through the gate. Jerusha must have told her he was coming.

If the tiny glimpse he'd had of Michelle from outside made him feel sad, what he saw inside made him feel rotten. Her body—she wasn't recognizable, but who else would it be?—quivered beneath bolts of cloth, like the biggest dress he'd ever seen. She smelled . . . not good. A water pump hummed to itself, sucking away the water that continually seeped into Michelle's crater.

There were bundles of pipes, too, draped across her. Feeding tubes, he realized. They were still. Silent.

"Hey, Wally. Over here." Jerusha waved at him from halfway around the enclosure.

Wally waved back. He trotted over to her, his iron feet echoing on what had once been a sidewalk and was now the floor of Michelle's shrine. "Holy cripes," he said. "Poor Michelle. How is she?"

Jerusha frowned at him. "She's still alive, if that's what you mean. But she's still unresponsive, too."

"I wish there was something we could do," he said.

"I like to think that deep down she knows we're here."

Huh. "Hey, Michelle," he said. "Hang in there."

Jerusha looked at him sideways, a funny look in her eye. "Come on. Let's get something to eat," she said.

She led him across Decatur Street, to a place called Café du Monde. It smelled like chicory and fresh doughnuts. They took a seat outside, at a small round table that gave them a clear view of Michelle's enclosure. There wasn't room for his legs under their table, so he sat sideways. Wally ordered hot chocolate and a plate of fancy French doughnuts heaped with powdered sugar. Jerusha got coffee.

"Okay," she said, after they'd settled in. "What's so important you had to fly all the way down here to show me?"

Powdered sugar from Wally's lips snowed into his backpack as he fumbled with the zipper. He pulled out the three-ring binder where he kept the letters from his pen pals. Wally chanted off their names as he flipped through the binder. "Marcel, Antoinette, Nicolas . . ." He found the first page of Lucien's section, and held it out to Jerusha. "This is my friend Lucien," he said. In the photo, a little boy treated the camera to a wide, gaptoothed grin. He wore a brown-and-white-striped T-shirt that was easily three sizes too big for him. He had knobby knees, and his shaved head made his ears look ridiculously large. He was giving the camera a thumbs-up.

Jerusha looked at the photo. She asked, "Did you put this binder together just for the purpose of coming down here and showing it to me?" She sounded surprised, but not in a bad way. Almost like he'd done something good but he didn't know what. If anything, she'd sounded a little bit annoyed when he'd said he was in town.

"Nah. I didn't want to lose any letters." Wally turned the page. "This is the first one I received from Lucien." Like the photo, he kept the letter in a laminated sheet protector. He mentally recited the letter while Jerusha read the scrawly handwriting. *Dear Wally, My name is Lucien I am ate years old. I live in Kalemie . . .*

Quietly, almost to herself, Jerusha said, "Huh. Smart kid." She asked, "When did you start doing all this?"

"A while back. After me and DB went to the Caliphate."

A memory grabbed him. Instead of sitting in a café, he was on the deck of an aircraft carrier, drinking beer with DB while the sun set over the Persian Gulf.

Hey, Rusty.

Bad deal, huh.

Yeah. The fucking worst.

Kids. I don't want to fight kids.

None of us should have had to.

Jerusha's voice brought him back to the present. "Okay, I'll bite. Can I see the last letter he sent?"

Wally found the page for her. Jerusha read it, looking thoughtful.

"So, what are you thinkin'?" he asked.

♠

"So, what are you thinkin'?" Rusty—Wally—asked.

Jerusha had never seen the Café du Monde so quiet and empty, especially this early in the morning. People were drifting in from the street to buy their paper bags of beignets and café au lait. A few of the other tables were occupied, but no one sat near them. Perhaps it was Wally's bulk and his appearance. Certainly it wasn't Jerusha—she wondered how many of the patrons recognized her at all, an ordinary-looking black woman except for the belt with many pouches around her waist. The flashes of tourist cameras were constant, though, and the staff kept eyeing their table uneasily.

What are *you thinking?*

Now that she'd listened to Wally, now that she'd seen his binder, she wasn't quite so certain anymore. She'd come here with the intention of giving Wally a firm "no" and trying to talk him out of this entirely. Now . . .

The picture of Lucien stared up at her. She could see the scratches on the plastic sheet protector from Wally's metal fingers; there were a *lot* of scratches. He pawed through that binder frequently, then. And his mouth had been moving as she had read the boy's poorly scrawled letter—he'd obviously memorized it.

Wally's simple tenderness and compassion made her want to hug him. She just wasn't sure it made her want to go with him.

Jerusha sipped at her coffee. The cup rattled on the table as she set it down. "I've been looking at maps, and I called Babel and talked to her a bit after your phone call." Jerusha saw the hope rising in Wally's eyes with her statement, and she frowned in an effort to quash it. *You're not doing this. You're not.* "Wally, she's really not happy with the idea of you going to Africa, and she's doubly not happy with you taking another Committee member with you. . . ." Jerusha paused, wondering if she really wanted to say the next words. "*If* I did this," she said, with heavy emphasis on the first word and a long pause after the phrase, "or no matter *who* ends up going with you, Wally, I agree with Babel that you don't want to go directly into the PPA. What looks best to me would be flying into Tanzania and crossing over Lake Tanganyika, especially since you say that Lucien's in Kalemie, right on the lake."

The hope in Wally's face was now transcendent and obvious. "So . . . you're coming with me?"

Sure. I'm black, aren't I? she wanted to retort angrily, but she only shook her head. "I still have work here. All the marshlands that need to be reclaimed before the next big storm hits here . . ." *Alone. Out in the swamp. Alone.*

Wally looked down at the table, dusted with the remnants of beignets. "I guess you make the plants grow a lot faster . . ." She saw him start to rise, his shoulders lifting. "Well, thanks for looking at those maps. That will help." His face scrunched up stiffly, the stiff iron skin over his eyes furrowing. "So where's this Tanzania place?"

Jerusha sighed. "Tanzania is . . ." she began. Stopped. *He won't last five minutes out there on his own.* She realized that somewhere in the midst of this, she'd made the decision. *What's here for you? You've nothing. No friends, just Committee work. And when Michelle dies, now you'll get the blame for that, not the Committee. You have a chance to save a life. . . .*

"Oh, hell," she said. "I'll show you on a map on the way over."

Jackson Square
New Orleans, Louisiana

MICHELLE REACHES A HAND out in front of her face. Five fingers. *That's good.* She pulls her legs up to her chest, reaches down, feels her feet. "That's better," she says. Even though she's in the pit again, she's happy about her feet and hands being back.

The spider pops down in front of her, points up to the edge of the pit. "Yeah, leopards, I know. I'm really the wrong person to try and scare with kitties."

The spider grabs Michelle's hair. Its body lengthens and grows and the four middle legs shrink into its torso. The mandibles slide back into its head and the eight eyes move toward each other until there are only two.

Sitting on Michelle's lap is a little girl, maybe eight or nine. She wears a threadbare dress. The pattern is faded, and in the dim light of the pit it's a mottled grey. The girl places her hand over Michelle's mouth, then leans forward and whispers in her ear.

Michelle whispers back, "I can't understand you."

The girl pulls away from her, and a tear slides down her cheek. Michelle reaches up and wipes it away. "I'm sorry," she says.

The girl puts her hands on either side of Michelle's temples. The girl shuts her eyes and suddenly Michelle is slammed by a barrage of images.

Trees limbs whip her face as she runs. Vines grab at her legs, but she can't stop. She can hear her own harsh breathing. Are they closer now? Close enough that they can reach out and . . . a claw rips open her back.

She shrieks. Warm blood wells up and burns. She trips and begins to fall.

Wait a minute, Michelle thinks. *Claws don't do anything to me.* She reaches up and gently pulls the girl's hands away.

The girl gazes at Michelle with such longing and pain it makes her want to cry. Michelle reaches out and touches her own hands to the girl's temples, imagines pointing at herself, whispers, "Michelle."

An image blossoms in Michelle's mind. It's the girl in her lap, but now she's wearing a pale blue checkered dress. Her hair is plaited with a pretty pink headband. The girl points to herself and says, *"Adesina."*

United Nations
Manhattan, New York

THE UNITED NATIONS PERCHED at the edge of Manhattan like the guest at a party who really needs to leave now, but has just one more very important thing to say.

Bugsy showed his ID to the guards at the front who all knew him anyway, and took the brushed steel elevator up to the seventh floor. In the brief time that the Committee had existed, they had commandeered much more space than Bugsy would have expected the international bureaucracy to permit. Having a lot of superhuman powers probably helped with that.

Lohengrin's office was on the western side, its windows facing out toward the skyscraper mosh pit of uptown. The hallways were filled with people in thousand-dollar suits looking harried. He nodded at the people who nodded to him and ignored the ones that didn't.

It was getting harder and harder to keep track of who exactly was with the Committee. It seemed like every time he turned around, it was *Let me introduce Glassteel. He can shatter anything made from hard metal. Or Noppera-bo here can mimic anyone's appearance.* Then Bugsy would shake hands (with Noppera-bo it had been particularly creepy since she'd taken on his face as soon as their fingers touched), exchange some pleasantries, and scurry off to someplace he could add their names into his database. Even so, he forgot the newbies more often than he remembered them.

Lohengrin, at least, was familiar. The long, blond hair actually looked really good with a dark grey power suit. Maybe a little tired around the eyes, but that went with the suit, too.

Bugsy closed the office door behind him and plopped down on the couch while the Teutonic God finished his phone call. "No," he said. "I have nothing to do with the prosecution on a day-to-day basis. You'll have to call the World Court. At the Hague." He put down the handset with a sigh.

"Highwayman's lawyers still giving you shit?" Bugsy asked.

"Captain Flint today," Lohengrin said. *CAHptain flEHnt*. No one could do round vowel sounds like the Germans. Except maybe the Austrians. And the Dutch. "There was a time, my friend, that I believed this would be fulfilling work. There are weeks I spend fighting and fighting and fighting and at the end, I think I might just as well have stayed at home."

It had been a long time since they'd gotten drunk and burned Peregrine's house down. There weren't many people Bugsy had actually known that long. Not that were still alive, anyway.

"Brokering world peace keeping you busy," he said, his tone making it an offer of sympathy.

"Water rights. Human rights abuses. The slave trade. I come in every morning, and I find something new and terrible. And every afternoon, I find why we can do nothing direct. Nothing final. I am becoming tired," Lohengrin said, then sighed. "What do you know about the Sudd?"

"Their second album sucked."

Someone in the next office ran their shredder for a second. "You don't know what I'm talking about, do you?" Lohengrin said.

"Yeah, not really. No."

Lohengrin nodded like he'd just won a bet with himself and leaned forward over his desk. "The Muslim government of the Sudan has taken steps to join their nation to the Caliphate."

"Ah," Bugsy said. "That's a bad thing."

"No," Lohengrin said. "That's the background."

"That's not the problem?"

"No."

"Ok-ay."

"The People's Paradise of Africa," Lohengrin said, "under the leadership of Dr. Kitengi Nshombo, has accused Khartoum of enacting a policy of genocide against the black tribal population of the south and west Sudan."

"Got it. Genocide. Problem."

"No," Lohengrin said.

"Genocide not a problem?"

"Genocide isn't happening. It is an excuse. The PPA has manufactured evidence and generated propaganda to make a case for the invasion of the Sudan. Its forces are making incursions across the border, and the Caliphate has mobilized to defend Sudanese national territory. Yesterday there was a battle in the Sudd. A terrible battle."

"And that's the problem, right?"

"Yes," Lohengrin said. "In the bigger picture, that is the problem. But it gets worse. The PPA forces are being led by Tom Weathers. The Radical."

Bugsy sat up straighter. "Hold it," he said. "Same guy who tried to set off Little Fat Boy and nuke New Orleans last year?"

"Same guy, *ja*."

"I don't like him much, you know. He tried to kill me. I mean, I don't like the Caliphate much either. They tried to kill me too."

"Tom Weathers tried to kill many hundreds of thousands of people," Lohengrin said.

"Yeah. And I was one of them."

"The PPA has been a destabilizing influence for years. Now they have begun to use aces to further their own political agenda."

The silence was a hum of climate-controlled heating and the distant ringing of phones. Lohengrin looked serious and waited for Bugsy to work through the implications.

"World war," Bugsy said. "Only fought with aces. Meaning probably the Committee."

"And a great many dead people," Lohengrin said.

"What about getting Little Fat Boy back in play? A fourteen-year-old nuke with a personal grudge against Weathers should rein the PPA in, right?"

"*Ra,*" Lohengrin said. "His name is Ra now, and no. So long as Old Egypt is not attacked, the Living Gods are determined to stay out of the conflict."

"How very Swiss of them."

"There is a further problem with Tom Weathers. We've always known that Weathers had more powers than most aces. Insubstantiality. Strength. Ultraflight. Heat beams. We know he was involved in the battle in part because these powers were in play. But other powers have been reported as well. The wave of darkness? The terrible mauling of the bodies?"

"You think he's like the Djinn?" Bugsy said, sitting forward on the couch. Nothing took the humor out of a situation like the Djinn. "You think Weathers is picking up new powers."

"I do not know," Lohengrin said. "New powers. Or new allies. We know little about the man himself. Where he comes from, how he drew the wild card, what his weaknesses might be. What exactly his powers are. That is what I want you to uncover, Jonathan. Tom Weathers is likely the most powerful ace in the world, he is starting a war, and I know nothing substantial about him."

"And so," Bugsy said, "who the fuck is the Radical?"

Unnamed Island
Aegean Sea, Greece

"DADDY!"

The woman who came flying at him across rocky soil tufted with pale green grass was tall and slender. Despite the fact her handsome face was clearly middle-aged, it showed few lines. Her hair, long and blond, had begun by slowly evident degrees to turn to silver. Yet her manner was that of a seven-year-old girl.

A very happy one. She caught him in a hug that for all his superhuman strength still almost overbalanced him. She was just four inches shorter than his six-two.

He kissed her. "Sprout. Hey, sweetie." He tousled the long straight hair. "I missed you."

"I missed you, too. Can we go to the park soon?"

"Aye, that's a good idea," said Mrs. Clark, emerging from the modest fieldstone cottage behind her. "It's not fit for her to spend all her days cooped up here alone, with no one for company but an iPod and a dried-up old biddy like me."

"I wouldn't call you dried up, Mrs. Clark," he said, past the woman's cheek, wet with happy tears.

"You'd not dare."

"You got that right."

This was true. The caretaker was a middle-aged to elderly New Zealander, half Maori with a crisp Scots brogue. Her coloration and build were those of a brick wall; her tight bun of curly hair was nearly the same hue. Sprout loved her. She treated Sprout with patient cheerful firmness and took absolutely not ounce one of shit from anybody else. Not even Tom.

Which was fine. It was what he paid her for. Fantastically well, he vaguely gathered. Unlike most of the self-proclaimed socialist revolutionaries he met, Tom had no interest in money whatsoever; it was one of the reasons he always wound up getting pissed off at the posers, and then there was trouble. Dr. Nshombo—more often Alicia—always gave him whatever he asked for. Most, in fact, went toward keeping his daughter well cared for and as happy as possible in a succession of the remotest locations Earth provided.

It was the only way he knew of keeping her safe from that teleporting puke. Until he hunted him down and killed him, of course.

"I could use a day's shopping as well, I admit," Mrs. Clark said. "Time to myself and a few necessities for the child and me. Maybe tomorrow, Mr. L?"

She didn't even try to pronounce the name he gave her, which was Karl Liebknecht. Among the things he paid her so well for was not to wonder about such things as why his daughter sometimes called herself by the last name Weathers, and other times Meadows. Or why the daughter looked older than her father. Her main concern was that there was no funny business between her employer and her charge. Once he had convinced her of that, she was content to live in isolation with her charge, so long as she got the occasional day off in civilization. And in between had a sufficient supply of mystery novels.

"Tomorrow?" his daughter said, blue eyes shining eagerly. "You promise?"

He nodded. "I promise."

Sprout hugged him fiercely. "I wish I could stay with you, Daddy."

"Someday you can, sweetie. Someday. But I got some things to *take care of* first."

Noel Matthews's Apartment
Manhattan, New York

NIOBE WAS SLEEPING, WORN-OUT by the emotional upheaval of the past few hours. Noel wandered around the apartment they had rented while they underwent the fertility treatments. It had come furnished with sofas and chairs designed more for magazine covers than the human body. They had tried to personalize an impersonal space by putting up lots of framed photos—most of them of Niobe's "children"—the little aces who had lived and died like mayflies. Noel found the pictures depressing, but they were important to Niobe so he never said a word. His own efforts had consisted of leaving magazines piled on the glass coffee table and used teacups on the side tables. Niobe had also crocheted an afghan to throw across the black leather and chrome sofa.

Three more weeks and we can really go home. Noel entered the kitchen and set about brewing a pot of tea. He realized he was hungry and set out a muffin. His back felt tight. He hadn't worked out in weeks and hadn't attended a karate class in months. The fact that he had been complacent suddenly alarmed him, and he decided to get back to the gym.

He snapped on the TV in the kitchen, headed to CNBC for the latest financial news, and found himself passing through CNN. He caught a quick flash of the Presidential Palace in Baghdad and a grim-faced Prince Siraj surrounded by security rushing up the steps. Siraj looked old. Shockingly old.

I need your help. . . . I really do need your help.

His old friend's words echoed filled with sadness, reproach, and might-have-beens.

Noel pulled out his phone and dialed. "What exactly do you want me to do?" he said.

Jackson Square
New Orleans, Louisiana

MICHELLE WAS IN THAT strange room again. Juliet and Joey were there. But her mother and father were gone now.

Her throat was still brutally raw. She could barely swallow, much less try to speak. Her arms and legs were as useless as her throat.

And the power was like napalm in her veins. *Drake*, she thought. *Oh, God, Drake. What happened? Did I kill him? Did Sekhmet kill him? Tom Weathers? Was that wound from the medallion worse than it seemed? And how am I not dead? How are we all not dead?*

"Wha . . ." Her voice was a rusty hinge. Her throat felt as if it were being stabbed by a knife when she swallowed.

Juliet started crying, and Michelle wanted to comfort her. To tell her it was all right. Whatever had happened to Michelle had clearly hurt Juliet. Juliet didn't even have any tats scrolling across her body.

Michelle closed her eyes. Maybe if she went back to sleep, she'd wake up later and everything would be all right.

◆

Saturday, November 28

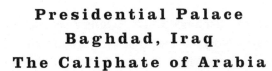

Presidential Palace
Baghdad, Iraq
The Caliphate of Arabia

THE SCENT OF DUST, dried lemons, and saffron seemed to pierce not only his sinuses, but his heart.

Noel staggered, and rested his hand against the stone wall. It was hot to the touch. He drew in another deep breath and more scents were added—kerosene from countless cookstoves, the wet smell of donkey, incense from the nearby mosque. The sun beat down on his head and warmed his shoulders. He could almost feel the cold fogs of New York and England leaching from his pores. *Yes,* he thought somewhat ruefully as he stepped out of the alley, the hem of his robe brushing at his heels. *I am one of those desert-loving Englishmen.*

The music of spoken Arabic fell like glittering notes all around him, but the point of the conversations were dark and somber. Too many fathers, brothers, husbands, and sons had marched off to the Sudd, and too few had been heard from again. Speculation ran wild in the streets.

As he walked by the palace he kept touching the dark glasses that disguised his swirling golden eyes, and he kept the tail of his *keffiyeh* across his face. Not that he expected to be recognized. When he'd developed his new male avatar he had made certain that Etienne was clean-shaven. But golden eyes were always going to be a problem.

Noel knew this city almost as well as he knew London. He had lived a second life here as Bahir, the Sword of Allah, the Caliph's ace assassin. He had even taken a wife, whom he'd put aside for barrenness last year. It had been entirely his fault. He was a hermaphrodite, and basically sterile. It hadn't been easy for Finn to find a few viable sperm. Luckily the little fellows hadn't had to make their way upstream all on their own.

What would have happened if he and Gamal had undergone the fertility treatments? But thank God they hadn't. She had been just another pawn as he served as an agent for the British Secret Service. That was another life, a life he'd left behind.

Except here he was, armed with three pistols and four knives and scouting out the lay of the land. He had told Siraj he would come. He had even told him when, but Noel wouldn't keep that appointment. He would arrive earlier, at a time of his choosing. A time when every good Muslim would be at prayer.

The call from the minarets began. Achingly beautiful, it was an echo across the centuries. Noel reflected that the Catholic Church should never have abandoned the Latin Mass. They had lost that link to history.

The streets emptied. Noel ducked behind a parked truck, stared narrowly at the palace, pictured Siraj's office, and teleported. There was the faintest *pop* as his arriving body displaced air. The man kneeling on his prayer rug, forehead pressed to the floor, didn't react.

Noel studied Siraj's vulnerable back. It would be so easy to remove this threat forever. One shot. Done.

But was Siraj actually the worst of his problems? Tom Weathers was a far more dangerous enemy, and Siraj and Weathers were locked in a bitter war. *The enemy of my enemy.*

Noel pulled out a pistol, moved quickly to Siraj's side, and joined him on the floor, while at the same time pressing the barrel of the gun into the other man's side.

Siraj gasped. His expression was both angry and amused. After a moment he looked back down at the floor and resumed his prayers. Noel joined in. They finished, and both pushed up until they were sitting on their heels.

Siraj looked again at the gun. "Are you going to kill me?"

"Not today."

"That's probably wise. You see, I've prepared a number of packets with information regarding England's crack assassin and his family connections."

At this oblique reference to Niobe, fury seemed to claw across the inside of Noel's skull. His finger began to tighten on the trigger.

Siraj sensed Noel's rage for he added quickly, "And if I die by assassination those packets will be sent. To the World Court, to the press . . ." He paused for maximum effect. "To Tom Weathers."

Noel forced himself to relax.

"That's better. Would you like a drink?" Siraj moved to a table and lifted a carafe out of an ice bucket.

"What is it?" Noel asked.

"Fruit juice."

"Still being a good Muslim, I see."

The sigh seemed to shake the prince's body. "On days like this, it isn't easy." Siraj set the carafe back into the ice. He paced the office, clasping and unclasping his hands. "What happened to the boys of Cambridge?"

"They grew up." Noel paused. "And discovered the world was complicated."

"We thought we could save it."

"Yes . . . well . . . my goals are more modest now."

"Yes, I heard you got married. Congratulations."

"Thank you."

"A very different look," Siraj said. "How do you do it?"

He seemed reluctant to get to the point. Noel was willing to wait for a little while. He had told Niobe he was going to England to talk with his manager. "Simple redistribution of mass," he answered. "Etienne is taller and thinner than Bahir. Losing the beard and mustache is easy." Noel touched the frame of his dark glasses. "The eyes are harder. They never change."

Siraj walked behind his desk, randomly moved a few papers, turned, and gazed out the window. The hands clasped behind his back were still writhing as if he were choking something.

"So, what do you want?" Noel finally asked.

"I need to see what happened. I need you to take me to the Sudd."

"You don't have a helicopter?"

"You're more subtle than a helicopter," came the dry reply. "Why are you so reluctant? This is a small thing when compared to the actions you took to put me here."

Noel briefly closed his eyes and remembered the night of chaos and death when he'd killed the Nur, clearing the way for Siraj to take control of the Caliphate. He was supposed to have been a compliant puppet for Britain's ambitions.

It hadn't worked out that way.

"That was another life. I'm different now. I'm married. I'm going to be a father. I do my shows. I don't concern myself with politics."

Noel felt a blaze of anger when Siraj's lips curled into a smile. "You must be bored stiff," the prince said, and Noel's anger was swept away by a sudden cascade of laughter.

Suddenly they were whooping, struggling to catch their breaths. Siraj wiped away tears of laughter. "Well?" he asked.

"Oh, all right. One last adventure before staid middle age overtakes me. But remember, I can still kill you."

"And I can still ruin you."

Jackson Square
New Orleans, Louisiana

A FLASH OF FIRE. The smell of bacon.

Not bacon—searing flesh. And it isn't fire, either. It's raw power right before it transforms into something else—something more specific.

And now there's a bunny.

"Fuck the damn bunny."

Michelle doesn't need to look to know who it is.

"Hey there, Joey," she says. "Are we going to have zombies, too? 'Cause you know I love me some zombies."

Hoodoo Mama crouches down in front of her. "This is no way to run a fucking railroad, Bubbles. Cocksuckers out here want you gone, baby, gone. You can't stay like this."

Michelle can't look at Joey. Not after what they did.

"What? After we fucked?" Joey says. A group of zombies appears behind her. *Damn it,* Michelle thinks. *It's my dream and there are still zombies.*

"Shit, Bubbles, if you get like this every time you tear off a piece . . ."

"Okay, that is so not what happened!" Michelle yells. But she remembers what went on between them and feels ashamed and aroused.

"Don't you understand?" Michelle wails. "I betrayed Juliet. Why did I do that? And I'm now the size of a elephant and, apparently, too large to move or be moved. Oh, and if I'm not mistaken, I think I have the power of a nuclear explosion in me."

The zombies vanish. Joey stands alone on a blighted landscape. She's frail, tiny, and anyone could hurt her.

Then Michelle is back in the pit. Adesina is there. Her face is obscured by her hair come undone from its braids. She isn't wearing the faded dress anymore. Her body is barely covered by rags.

"Adesina," she says softly. Michelle crawls to her. She tries not to think about the corpses. She brushes the hair from Adesina's face. A dark bruise swells on the girl's left cheek. There are half-healed cuts on her chin and on her forehead.

"Why are you in my dreams?" she asks. Michelle puts her hands on Adesina's temples. She allows images to flow through her mind, trying to connect.

Adesina pulls away. It hurts. Dreams aren't supposed to hurt. Nothing hurts Michelle. And dreams don't smell. And there is a definite lack of bunnies here. *If there aren't bunnies, then this isn't a dream. But if this isn't a dream, then what is it?*

There are bodies piled up in the pit. They're in different stages of decomposition. And it reeks. A stench so bad she can barely keep from gagging.

"Adesina, are you really down here?"

And as she says it, a shriek explodes in her mind and Michelle runs to the only place far enough away that she can't hear it anymore.

The Sudd, Sudan
The Caliphate of Arabia

THE SUDD WAS A stinking swamp.

The bloated bodies, already rotting in the sun, didn't help. Siraj gasped, gagged, dug a handkerchief out of his pocket, but the rising vomit couldn't be stopped. He turned aside and puked. The bile and chunks pattered in the standing water. A breeze hissed through the papyrus, carrying away the scent of vomit, but bringing more stench of death and blood, overlaid with cordite and gunpowder. Smells Noel knew well.

They picked their way through the reeds and papyrus, seeking reasonably dry ground. Bodies floated in the waters to either side. There were more on the solid ground. Noel paused over one corpse. The man's face was gone. He squatted down, and inspected the raw wound at the top of the corpse's skull and beneath his jaw. "No bullet did that," Siraj said.

"No. His face has been bitten off." Noel pointed at the raw edges. "Those are teeth marks." He stood and looked around. Now that he knew what to look for he saw many more faceless corpses.

"What does that?" Siraj asked.

"Probably not your average soldier in the Simba Brigade."

They broke through the reeds to a relatively open, dry patch of ground. Ruined tanks sat smoldering like Easter Island monuments to some forgotten war god. Several of the tanks were tossed aside, as if a giant's child had thrown them in a fit of massive pique.

"I think we can safely assume that Tom Weathers was here." Noel scanned the tank graveyard and spotted a human figure leaning against the shattered treads of one reasonably intact tank.

He and Siraj ran to the man. His face was smoke-blackened, and blood had turned his shirt into caked armor. He was in his early forties, and he recognized Siraj. "Mr. President. I'm sorry." He coughed, a wet sound that Noel didn't like. "We were winning. We outnumbered the Simbas. But then a darkness came. Unnatural, horrible. Our troops were blind, but somehow the blacks could see. They massacred us. There was something else in the darkness. Not human. A demon." His head lolled forward onto his chest.

"Those are not among Weathers's known powers," Noel mused.

"We need to get this man to a hospital," Siraj snapped.

"We'll drop him in Cairo on our way to Paris."

"Why are we going to Paris?" Siraj slid his arm beneath the soldier's. He gave a grunt as he lifted him.

"Because you need a drink," Noel said.

Offices of *Aces* Magazine
Manhattan, New York

"THIS," BUGSY SAID TO himself, "is why print media is dead."

The offices of *Aces* magazine had once been in the hippest, happeningest part of Manhattan. They hadn't moved, but the neighborhood had changed.

The tides of years had eroded all the cool out from under the fashion and finance, leaving the streets decent but unexceptional, and tacitly on its way down. Like the magazine.

Bugsy leaned against the door, squinting through thick security glass into the darkness beyond. He'd only met Digger Downs a few times before during Bugsy's somewhat foreshortened run on *American Hero*. It seemed like a lifetime ago. Three years, it had been. The guy had seemed sort of an asshole, as much as you could tell when he was at the big desk and you were singing your heart out to make your big break in showbiz. But he'd been picked by the Hollywood types for exactly the reason Bugsy was there now. He was old school. He knew where the bodies were buried. In a lot of ways, Digger Downs was the history of the wild card.

But the history of the wild card clearly didn't work weekends. So screw it.

Bugsy shrugged his laptop case back up onto his shoulder and checked the time on his phone: 2:30. Still at least three hours before Ellen would be back at her place. He had some time to kill, and there were about half a billion Starbucks to choose from within an eight-block radius. He picked the third one he came to because it had the FREE WIRELESS sign up in the window and the barista smiled at him when he paused outside the window.

Double-shot tall dry cappuccino firmly in hand, he staked out a tall chair by the front window that afforded a view of the street, popped open the laptop, quietly cursed Windows Vista again, rebooted the laptop, and spent fifteen minutes checking e-mail and catching up on a couple news blogs. He cracked his knuckles and the joints in his neck, then pulled up Google and dug through the largest single machine ever built by humanity for traces of the Radical.

Wikipedia gave a decent overview. Tom Weathers, the Radical, had first appeared in China in 1993. That was actually a lot more recent than he'd thought. He followed some of the reference links at the bottom of the entry.

> As long as the fascists, the capitalists, and the willing collaborators hold the reigns of power, it is the duty of the people to oppose them. When the last landlord in the world is strangled with the intestines of the last banker, the work of peace can begin. Until that, any discussion of peace is treason against the people.

Bugsy figured the guy probably meant "reins," but whatever. He read on for another few sentences, muttered "yadda yadda blah blah blah" under his breath, and went to a different site. There were a long series of small wars, guerrilla resistances, police actions, and freedom-fighting brotherhoods that Weathers had gotten himself involved in over the years. Burma, Indonesia, Colombia, Turkmenistan, Afghanistan . . . Yadda yadda blah blah blah.

A wild cards discussion board had a thread on him. It hadn't been updated in a couple of years, but the archived conversation painted the same picture. The Radical was against the Man in all His forms, fighting for whomever he was fighting for and against whatever he decided was fascist or oppressive. He had a bunch of powers, real charisma, and a bad habit of deciding his allies weren't politically pure enough. There were half a dozen sites that sold T-shirts with his face, many with slogans in alphabets Bugsy didn't recognize right off.

"Need anything?" the barista asked. She was maybe twenty-two, blond, with the black tips of a tattoo sneaking out from her shirt near her collarbone.

"Freedom from the oppressors," he said cheerfully.

"Word," she replied in the whitest, most middle-class voice imaginable.

It would have been funnier if Bugsy hadn't thought the Radical would have killed both of them, just for joking about it.

The willing collaborators. It sounded like a garage band.

Tuileries Garden
Paris, France

"IF WEATHERS DOESN'T HAVE these powers, then what killed my soldiers?" Siraj gripped the stem of his champagne glass like a man hugging a life preserver.

"Other aces. *Aces* plural." Noel sipped his Hendricks gin martini and savored the cool/hot smoothness on the back of his tongue.

Siraj knocked back his champagne in a single gulp and waved his glass at a passing waiter. He got the usual Gallic sniff, frown, and shrug, but the man did head toward the bar. Noel looked out the window at the Tuileries Garden across the street. He had wanted to sit outside, but the late November rain made that impossible. The furled umbrellas in the metal tables looked like hunched, skeletal men in dripping coats.

"Then the PPA has multiple aces." Siraj's voice was heavy with despair.

"How can that be? The release of the virus was localized over New York. The preponderance of aces has always been in America. I had one . . . Bahir . . . you. Now I have none. Unless . . . ?" The implicit question hung in the air between.

Noel held up a restraining hand. "Oh, no, no, no, no. Weathers has sworn to kill Bahir."

"I've got to have aces. If the PPA is recruiting them, then so can I."

There was something about that that struck Noel as wrong. He contemplated Tom Weathers—charismatic, arrogant, impatient, always questioning the purity of one's commitment to The Movement. "I can't imagine Weathers ever accepting a mercenary ace into his army."

"You've now taken two contradictory positions," Siraj snapped. "Which is it?"

"Oh, they're using aces. The question is where they came from." Noel remembered Weathers's dossier. The man had been thrown out of every revolutionary movement prior to the PPA because the other members always turned against him. The glimmering of an idea began to coalesce.

Siraj was speaking again. "Look, if you won't fight for me will you at least help me recruit some aces? You have contacts from the Silver Helix."

Noel gave an emphatic head shake. "If you field your own aces, Weathers will move directly on Baghdad. I have a better idea. One relying more on cunning, guile, and manipulation rather than brute force. The things at which I excel—"

"Yes, yes, yes, you're a genius. Move on."

"Remove the Nshombos. The PPA will collapse. The armies will pull back from the Sudan to join in the inevitable power struggle—"

"Which Weathers will win."

"No, he has neither the personality or the force of character to hold it together. And he's a white man. There are too many colonial memories to allow that to happen."

"Yes, there are a lot of colonial memories." Siraj smiled thinly. "So you're going to kill the Nshombos."

"That seems very crude. The last thing you want is to make a tin-pot dictator a martyr. It may come to that, but let's try something more elegant and subtle first."

"I suppose you use those same terms when referring to me," Siraj said, and again smiled thinly.

"Oh, no, you're not a *tin-pot* dictator." Noel's smile matched Siraj's in thinness. "I know you actually want to help your people. I respected you for that, and that's one of the reasons we selected you to replace the Nur."

"Please, spare me your smug British approval." The waiter returned with a bottle of champagne and an ice bucket. Siraj poured himself another glass. "I want this done by the end of the year. If it isn't, I'll release my little dossier on you to the World Court, the press, and Tom Weathers."

There were times when remonstrating was pointless. This was one of them. Noel shrugged. "All right, but we need to postpone the march of the PPA on Baghdad. Let's buy some time."

"And how would you suggest I do that?"

"Ask Dr. Nshombo for a peace conference. If Nshombo refuses he'll look like the aggressor. All these dictators like to think of themselves as the hero of their own three-penny opera. He won't want the bad press."

Siraj took another long swallow of champagne. "And if I involve the UN it will only add to the pressure on Nshombo to accept."

"It will take time to arrange the conference, and you can spool out the talks for weeks, if necessary."

"Five, to be precise." Siraj filled up Noel's empty martini glass with champagne. Their eyes met over the rim of their glasses and Noel saw no warmth in Siraj's.

His old housemate would follow through on the threat.

Jackson Square
New Orleans, Louisiana

MICHELLE HAD BEEN AWAKE for several hours when Juliet and Joey showed up. The security guard let the girls in, and when the door opened Michelle could smell the olive trees, the heavy scent of the Mississippi, and beignets cooking at Café du Monde.

"Oh, honey," Juliet said. "You're awake again!"

Michelle opened her mouth, but only managed a hoarse croak. She swallowed and said, "Oil can."

"Oil can?" Juliet asked.

"Fuck all. It's a stupid joke, Ink," Hoodoo Mama said. "'Member? *Wizard of* Fucking *Oz*? She needs some water."

"Of course," Juliet said. "You had that tube down your throat for so long." She hurried out, then came back a moment later with a cup and a straw. Michelle drank and she felt as if there wasn't enough water in the world to quench her thirst.

"Don't drink too much, baby," Juliet said. "The doctor said it could make you sick."

Michelle dropped the straw. "I'm almost indestructible," she said. "I doubt a little water will hurt me."

Adesina hasn't had water in God-only-knows how long, Michelle thought. *She was just a little girl. Even a few days without water could . . .* Michelle felt something warm and wet drop onto her cheek. Juliet was crying.

"Oh, God, Juliet . . . don't."

Juliet just cried harder. Michelle glanced at Hoodoo Mama—she felt guilty doing so with Juliet's hot tears dropping on her. She shoved her guilt away and a stab of anger rose up in her.

It was Tom Weathers's fault that she was here and that she couldn't bubble even though she'd spent the last couple of hours trying to. There was this insane power in her and she couldn't figure out how to get rid of it.

And that scared her so much she thought she might lose her mind. And then none of it mattered because Adesina was still stuck in that pit and Michelle couldn't help her as long as she was trapped in her fat.

Another of Juliet's tears fell on Michelle's head and brought her back to New Orleans. The last time she had seen Juliet, she'd gone corporate for her job with Billy Ray. Now her hair was short and spiky again. But her tats weren't the pretty Mayan ones she'd favored in her punk days. Now they were black and tribal and aggressive.

And then Michelle noticed that Joey and Juliet were dressed alike: both of them wore Joker Plague T-shirts and ratty jeans. What had happened to change Juliet back into a punk chick, and what had made Joey a fan of Joker Plague? Michelle knew the signs of girls who had hung out too long together. They'd gone all hive-mind. "What's happening, Joey?" she asked. It was getting easier to talk. "Where am I? This is still New Orleans, isn't it?"

"Jackson Fucking Square," said Joey. "After you ate that fucking nuke you got really big and really, really, really, really heavy. The cocksuckers couldn't move you, so, for a while, they just put up a tent around you."

Michelle shook her head. Or at least she tried to. "How long have I been here?"

"A year and change."

Michelle was staggered. *A year. A year. A YEAR?* She was cold, then hot, and then cold again. Her hands started shaking. How was she even alive after a year?

"I know it sounds like a long time . . ." Juliet said.

Joey interrupted her. "You just missed Thanksgiving. The city erected this temple thing over you after they couldn't keep the tourists and grateful citizens away from your massive ass. You're a cocksucking saint to most of the dumbasses on this planet. Except your shit-stain parents, who got you taken off life support so they could get their hands on your money again.

"Oh, and fuck me sideways, but Tiffani's been coming down here every chance she gets to read to you all night long. She told us you weren't dead. Fuck me if she wasn't right about that one."

Michelle tried to take a deep breath, but it didn't work. It felt like someone had punched her in the gut. Except that *that* usually felt pretty good. This felt horrible. Her parents had tried to kill her.

"You okay, Michelle?" Juliet asked. "You're looking pale. Should we get the doctor?"

Joey threw up her arms. "Jesus H. Motherfucking Christ on a pogo stick, Ink. She's not dying. She just heard that her dick-lickin' parents tried to kill her to get at her money. No one would take that good."

Michelle closed her eyes. She wanted to throw up. She wanted to run away. She wanted to scream. She wanted to cry. Was she just going to be some kind of freak for the rest of her life? A mound of flesh with so much power inside her that it hurt?

Tears stung her eyes. She hoped that Juliet wouldn't notice. She hated being this repulsive and she hated being so helpless.

♥

Sunday, November 29

Paraguaçu River
Bahia State, Brazil

BIG CROCS SWAM THE muddy river around him. As the dolphin slid through the water with near effortless undulations of his sleek and powerful body, driven by his tail flukes, he sensed them with sonic sprays emitted from his jaw, processing the echoes with the liquid mass that gave the distinctive bulge to his forehead.

He felt no fear. For he was the baddest motherfucker in the Paraguaçu River. A dolphin had a rostrum—a beak—capable of killing great white sharks. What were overgrown aquatic river lizards to him?

The warm fresh water had a land taste, an oleaginous feel. He reveled in it anyway. Almost reluctantly, he steered toward the island.

As he began to break water he saw the hut waiting among mangroves, the woman on its porch, as blurs in sundry shades. Greater detail emerged as he approached, but what were mere eyes, especially in the desiccating air, against the sensory richness of sound in water?

On his last arcing lunge he left the river's embrace completely. The sandy silt of the bottom caressed his belly when he splashed down. It took an effort of will to will the change. When he emerged from the water, dripping water from his leanly muscled, naked bipedal form, he was Tom Weathers again.

"Hoo," he said, shaking water from his golden hair. "And to think that just a moment ago I was thinking of this air as *dry*. *There's* a perspective change." To his human nostrils the air smelled so ripely of tannin-rich water and wet-leaved mangrove forest it almost made his head swim.

The woman laughed. His human eyes made her out clearly. Forty-something or not, a naked Sun Hei-lian was well worth seeing. "I can never get over that particular power of yours," she called as he trudged up the gravel-paved trail from the water's edge to the rough plank steps with the slanting late-afternoon spring sun stinging his skin from upriver. "How'd you ever get the ability to do something like that?"

The question made his nut-sac tense up as if to crawl back in his belly. "There's no limit to what the power of world revolution can do," he said. "You should know that, *Shang Xiao*."

It meant "Colonel." The world at large knew Hei-lian as an intrepid trouble telejournalist for Chinese Central Television's English-language news service. The intelligence community knew her as a top agent of China's well-feared Ministry of State Security: the Guojia Anquan Bu, or Guoanbu for short. Beijing had set her to seduce the PPA's superpotent and mercurial Western ace.

She'd succeeded so well she was now the People's Republic's chief advisor to its ally Nshombo, the hard-core male chauvinism of her communist gerontocrat bosses notwithstanding. And in the process she'd fallen in love with her chief subject.

"If you say so," she said.

As he clomped up the steps beneath the thatch overhang of the roof she handed him an open bottle of almost self-luminous green fluid. It chilled his palm, meaning it came straight from the cooler they'd brought with them from Salvador, capital of Brazil's Bahia state, about thirty miles downstream where the river emptied into the Atlantic. The little shack had no electricity or running water or any modern conveniences.

Which didn't seem to impair its popularity as a weekend retreat for urban *baianos*; getting it hadn't been easy. Especially since Tom couldn't exactly flash his ace powers to impress the booking agent. This was supposed to be a *hideout*, after all: he never spent the night in the same place twice running. That running-dog teleport Bahir was still on his case, too, and he had to sleep sometime.

More and more he was growing reluctant to let himself sleep at all, for reasons having nothing to do with the golden-eyed Arab ace.

Tom twisted off the cap and took a hit. The coolness suffusing outward from his throat was welcome relief after walking a mere thirty feet. Although it was "cool" only by comparison to the mind-blowing tropic heat.

Holding a half-full beer, Hei-lian leaned against the side of the doorway, an oblong cut through warped wood to the darkness of the interior. Her long black hair was pulled back in a ponytail. Her skin, normally ivory tinged pink, glowed gold in the angled light.

She wasn't his usual type. He'd be the first to admit that. It wasn't that he went for the big-boobed blond cheerleader types, especially not with augments out to *here*: fake tits symbolized capitalism's obsession with conspicuous consumption. But he usually did like his women fuller-figured.

Not to mention *younger*. Sun Hei-lian wore her years lightly, although he knew they'd been spent in hard service. She kept herself in remarkable shape, gymnast shape, martial-artist shape. She'd been taught *taijiquan* and internal martial arts by her Daoist-priest father, and more violent applications by her employers.

She claimed he made her feel years younger. She'd laughed more in the last year, she said, their year together, than in her entire life previously. As serious as she still normally was, he believed that.

She was the most beautiful woman he'd ever met, not despite her years but because of them. And she was *smart,* fierce smart, a trait he respected. More than a skilled, and now passionate, lover, Hei-lian was something the Radical had never known in his brief years of freedom: a confidante.

"You seem thoughtful, lover," Sun said.

He turned and leaned on the rail. Sun-heated wood stung his arms. "I miss Sprout," he said softly. "I miss being able to have her with me."

"You could've brought her along."

"Would you be running around like that?"

"Of course not," Sun said in mock outrage. "Not in front of a *child*." She came up to put her chin on his shoulder and tousle his hair. He felt the heat and yielding firmness of her body on his back and buttocks, skin on skin, the slight rasp of her bush. Unlike a lot of chicks these days she didn't shave her pussy. Her pubic hair was on the sparse and wispy side anyway.

As sunset approached, vast flocks of scarlet ibises, pink-pale from their season in the north and long flight back to southern summer, fell on sandbanks and overgrown islands and the dense *mangal* on either bank like cotton-candy rain, to feed on mangrove crabs among the tough, gnarly roots knuckling down into black water. Their cries bubbled into a sky being overtaken by bands of orange and yellow.

With a sloshing of syrupy water a crocodile, what the locals called a *jacaré*, emerged from the water by the little dock. No boat was tied there now: no need for one. The *jacaré* was a big fucker, maybe twelve feet long. It dragged itself up by the gravel path and stared insolently at the humans from gelatinous armor-lidded eyes, as if laying claim on them for supper.

Tom pointed. A pencil of fire stabbed from his finger and crisped a tuft of grass a couple of inches in front of the croc's sharp snout. Moisture in plant and mud flashed to steam, scorching the animal's nose and shooting grains of dirt against it. Opening its yellow-pink mouth to roar surprise, displaying impressive teeth, the beast wigwagged its fat tail hastily backward into the water and was gone.

"Arrogant prick," Tom said. He raised the finger and blew away imaginary gunsmoke.

Hei-lian laughed. "That's more like it. I was wondering why you brought us here to this rustic tropic paradise for the night. Other than the usual security considerations, of course. I didn't think you went in much for that whole hippie back-to-nature thing."

Supernova anger burst inside him. He spun. Hei-lian leapt back like a startled cat. "What the fuck is that supposed to mean?" he shouted in her face. "What the *fuck*?"

There was more surprise than fear in those wide black eyes. But there still was fear. Colonel Sun, consecrated to service of Guoanbu and country since prepubescence, survivor of decades of full-contact play in some of the world's most blood-soaked open sores, did not scare easily.

But Tom was the most powerful ace on Earth, except maybe for Ra. He swatted fifty-ton main battle tanks like bugs. She knew far too well what he could do with *her*. "Nothing," she said. She managed to keep her voice almost steady. "I was just making a joke. Trying. Failing."

The stricken look on her face stabbed through him like that Kalashnikov slug through the back. He let out a big breath. The anger had already vanished, as quickly as it had lit. It left behind a kind of clammy, shaky emptiness.

"I'm sorry, man," he mumbled. "Didn't mean to rattle you like that." *You got to* maintain, *man,* he told himself. *You can find another woman. But there's way more at stake here than that.* More than he dared let anyone suspect. Not Hei-lian. Not even Sprout. More than he cared to let himself think about. *Everything.*

Shaking his head, he turned back to the rail and the river and the gathering birds and evening. "I'm just a little uptight these days."

She was back, pressed against him, stroking him soothingly. Mingling sweat made a slick membrane between them. He respected the nerve it took her to approach him.

"The Sudan?" she said.

"Yeah," he said, leaning heavily on the rail. "Wrong war, wrong place, wrong time." Tom picked up the soda, now past tepid to near hot, chugged half of it. He wished he dared let himself have even one beer to take the edge off. But he didn't. Hadn't in the almost decade and a half since he'd . . . come into his own. Nor had he gotten stoned. He couldn't allow himself to alter his brain chemistry. "Nshombo's always been hung up on Muslims, especially Arabs. He remembers it was always the Arabs who encouraged the slave trade, thinks they mean to bring all that back." He shrugged. "Shit. They even might. In South Sudan we found some local Muslims—they call themselves Arabs, even though they don't look any different from their neighbors—keeping animist tribesmen as slaves. We gave the slave owners to their own slaves. Perfect propaganda by deed. This Caliph's just a puppet, and Siraj is a Western wannabe. I'm cool with putting him up against the wall. But in ten years. Maybe five. When we've shown the world the revolution works, made this place the People's Paradise in reality as it is in name. It's too early. Way too fucking early." Tom turned away to lean on the rail. "And Alicia's pet aces . . . they're too big a risk. Look at what happened with the last one."

"Dolores." She laid a hand cool on his shoulder. "Butcher Dagon killed her."

Tom turned away. "Alicia's first success story, and look how that turned out." The sun poured in crosswise beneath the thatch awning as it sank toward the *mangal* and the big river's origin in the Chapada Diamantina in the middle of Bahia state. The light had softened, lost some of its sting. But the air stayed still and hot, the humidity thick enough to swim in. The bugs, ever-present, had gone from busy to frenetic.

Tom blew out his lips in a sigh and turned to Sun with a lopsided grin. "What say we go inside and get, you know, horizontal?"

Jackson Square
New Orleans, Louisiana

AND THEN SHE'S BACK in the pit.

Adesina is crouched down. Her hair has come undone from its braids and is a tangled cloud around her face. She looks feral.

Michelle glances around. *Corpses. Check. Leopards. Check. Adesina. Check. No bunnies. Check.*

She closes her eyes hard and wills herself back to New Orleans.

Juliet and Joey were staring at her. "What was that you were saying?" Juliet asked.

"I wasn't saying anything," Michelle replied.

"Hell you weren't," Joey said. "That was some fucked-up shit, Bubbles. You were talkin' in tongues."

Michelle wanted to shake her head, but she only managed to move it a little. "No. That was Adesina."

Ink and Hoodoo Mama glanced at each other.

"Hey!" Michelle exclaimed. "I saw that!"

Juliet stroked Michelle's forehead. "Sweetie, you've been in a coma for a year. You're probably tired."

"I am *not* tired," Michelle snapped. "Hello? *Coma?* I am plenty rested. And I've been having these weird dreams that I'm pretty sure aren't dreams. No bunnies." Michelle glowered up at them. "You can stop with the looking. I can *see* the two of you."

But then they weren't looking at each other. They were staring at her. Any other time she might have laughed at the expressions on their faces. "What the hell? I swear I didn't fart."

Juliet pointed at Michelle. "You're bubbling."

Michelle looked down at her hand. A large bubble was forming on it. It glistened, iridescent and beautiful, and it felt as if it could go on for days.

She released the bubble, and it drifted up to the ceiling. Then her hand was shaking and she thought she would lose control. A horrible nausea flowed through her again. And then the power was tearing at her. Fire in her veins. But she could *bubble*.

Somewhere Over the Atlantic Ocean

FROM NEW ORLEANS THEY flew to New York. From New York they'd fly to Rome. There they would transfer to a smaller plane bound for Addis Ababa, where they would board an even smaller plane bound for Dar es Salaam.

Wally shook the foil packet the flight attendant had handed him a couple of hours earlier. He leaned across the aisle (Wally needed an aisle seat; people complained about sharing an armrest with a metal guy) and said, over the rumble of the engines, "Want my peanuts?"

Jerusha shook her head, still studying the maps spread over her tray table. She'd been studying them since they left New York. She studied a lot. "No, thanks."

It was dark in the cabin. The flight attendants had dimmed the lights, to help people sleep away the time zones. Wally had traveled a lot since joining the Committee, but he still hadn't learned how to sleep on an airplane.

He yawned; his jaw hinges creaked. Wally stretched until the metal in his seat groaned. He made another attempt to focus on the guidebooks they'd purchased, but they were full of stuff he didn't understand. He figured it would all make more sense once he got there.

The in-flight movie looked good; it even had a couple folks laughing. But the headphones didn't fit him.

"Hey, Jerusha?"

"Uh-huh?"

"What do you think we'll find over there? In Congo?"

In a stage whisper, Jerusha said, "The horror. The horror." She grinned, as if she'd just made a joke.

Wally stared at her.

"Maybe we'll find an ivory dealer."

Wally shook his head, slowly.

"Joseph Conrad? *Heart of Darkness*?"

Wally shrugged.

"It's a book."

"Oh. I don't read much." He shrugged, but inwardly he cringed. This was the sort of admission that attracted cutting remarks the way magnets attracted iron filings. He braced himself for the inevitable sneer.

But something strange happened: she shrugged, too. "You're not missing anything. I had to read it in high school. Royally hated it, too."

"We had to read *The Great Gatsby*. That's the longest book I've ever read. I had to ask Mr. Schwandt for an extra week, but I finished it."

"Good for you." Weird—it sounded like she meant it. No sarcasm. "Oh, I know. Do you see many movies?"

"Oh, sure. Lots."

"Ever see *Apocalypse Now*? It's based on *Heart of Darkness*."

"Yeah, I saw that one. I liked it pretty good when I saw it." Thinking about war movies reminded him of what he'd seen and done in the past couple of years. More quietly, he said, "I don't think I'd like it so much now."

Wally was quiet for a long time. When he looked up again, he found Jerusha still looking at him.

"Wally? How many kids do you sponsor?"

"Seven. Counting Lucien." Again, that pang of worry. "We're gonna find him, right?"

"You know what I think? I think we'll get all the way over there, and find out that Lucien is a little boy."

"What does that mean?"

"It means he's a kid. Kids are forgetful. They play and make up games and forget to do the things their parents tell them. That's what kids are supposed to do."

"I never thought about it like that. I hope so."

In a lighter tone, Jerusha asked, "So. How's it coming with those guidebooks?"

"Oh, good. Real good." She looked at the unopened books on his tray table, then cocked an eyebrow at him.

Wally's sigh sounded like the release valve on an overheated boiler. "I don't read much," he confessed.

"Did you do any preparation at all for this trip before you called me?"

"Well, I have all of Lucien's letters. And on Saturdays back home my brother and I used to watch those old Tarzan movies on TV. I've probably seen them all."

"Tarzan." Jerusha rubbed her eyes. "Great."

"I can even do a pretty good Tarzan yell."

Quickly she said, "Please don't."

"You're not mad, are ya?"

"I'm not mad at *you*, Wally. I'm mad at . . ." She gave him a wan little smile. "I'm just a little tired, that's all. I haven't slept since yesterday."

Wally didn't know what to say, so he said, "Thanks."

He picked up a guidebook. And when he woke up, they were in Rome.

Headquarters of Silver Helix
London, England

NOEL SAT ON THE floor of the file room, sucking on a Tootsie Roll Pop (part of the leftover Halloween candy stash, another peculiar American custom) and reading through the agency's files on the Nshombos. He had quit the Silver Helix last year, and he and the organization had a fragile peace.

Noel's statements to the Hague had led to the arrest of John Bruckner, aka the Highwayman, and Brigadier Kenneth Foxworthy, aka Captain Flint, for war crimes. A year ago, Flint and Bruckner had broken into his parents' house, killed the ace "kids" Noel had sired with Niobe, and kidnapped an American boy whose uncontrolled nuclear power had governments all over the world trying to kill him or control him. Bruckner had delivered Drake to Nigeria, to stop the advance of the PPA army into that oil-rich nation. Thousands had died in the detonation, and ultimately Nigeria had fallen to the PPA anyway.

Foxworthy and Bruckner were now in custody in Holland. Bruckner was gobbling about how he was "just following orders," but Flint had fallen on his sword for crown and country by taking all the blame. The Silver Helix knew that Noel had a huge file about the assassinations he had undertaken on behalf of the British government just waiting to be released if they made any move against him. Noel didn't see why the "MAD" agreement couldn't be extended to making use of the resources of the Silver Helix.

He scanned quickly through the pages, searching for something he could use to discredit the brother and sister. The brother was an abstemious man—no mistresses, no drugs, no alcohol. The sister was more sybaritic—she overindulged in food and sex. It was believed she slept with most of the men recruited into her Leopard Society. But she wasn't the head of the state—exposing her excesses would do little.

Noel flipped up another page. The heading on the one below read ASSETS. The Nshombos had three Swiss bank accounts—one guess who had two and who had one—but the numbers were unknown. In addition to the palace in Kongoville there was an apartment in Paris and a home on the Dalmatian coast. There was a yacht. A line caught his eye. *The national treasury appears to consist of a mixture of gold bullion, platinum bars, and uncut diamonds held in the Central Bank of the Congo.*

Suddenly the door opened.

Noel cursed himself for being so focused on his reading that he had missed the approaching footsteps. He glanced at his watch: 4:42 P.M. Outside, the winter sun was dropping into the fogs and fumes of Old London Town. But it wasn't full night yet, and Noel was trapped in his real body and unable to teleport. The headshrinkers with the Silver Helix had never been able to help him overcome his psychological glitch so Noel himself could teleport like his avatars.

He reached under his jacket for his pistol. He really didn't want to shoot one of his former comrades, so he just rested his hand on the butt.

"Noel, what the hell are you doing here, man?"

It was Devlin Pear, aka Ha'Penny. Since Noel was seated on the floor they were actually nose to nose. Dev was a midget. He could get smaller, a lot smaller.

Noel held up the file. "Just a bit of intel."

"You can't do this. Lady Margaret's on the desk tonight. She'd have your balls if she knew you were here."

And that was most certainly true. Lady Margaret, aka Titania, had nursed a desperate crush on the former head of the Silver Helix for years. Now Captain Flint was awaiting his war crimes trial, and Noel had put him there. "Well then, don't tell her."

"I've got to. You can't just pop in here—"

Noel laid a hand on the file. "Look, I'm doing God's work. Or at least England's, which is almost the same thing." He gave Dev a smile, but the little ace continued to look worried. "I'm looking for a way to remove the Nshombos that won't have Western fingerprints on it. That can only help British interests in the area, right?"

"Why would you do that? You left the service."

"I don't give a tinker's damn about the Silver Helix, but I'm still an Englishman. I just wanted some information."

"That's really all you want?"

"I swear."

"All right, but don't do this again." The little ace hesitated. "Call me instead."

They shook hands, Noel put away the files, stood, and checked his watch. It was still three minutes until full night.

"Wish you hadn't left us," Devlin said.

"I had to. I didn't like what I'd become."

Ha'Penny considered Noel's role in the Silver Helix—assassin—and nodded slowly. "I can see that."

It was time. Noel made the transition to Lilith. "The PPA's the danger, Dev," she said. "I just want to help." And she teleported away.

♣

Monday,
November 30

Paraguaçu River
Bahia State, Brazil

HIS EYES SNAPPED OPEN to darkness.

The humid air remained hot long after midnight. Sweat rolled ticklingly into armpits that felt at once familiar and utterly alien. Insects buzzed like power-saw choirs. Poison-arrow frogs trilled to advertise their killer beauty. The river sighed and gurgled through the mangrove roots. The smell of the water, like strong tea and death, overwhelmed even the smell of sweat-soaked bedding.

Starlight through the open window confirmed his memory, still vague with transition, that the blur beside him was the sleeping face of Sun Hei-lian. Details of her incredibly fine features resolved slowly as his mind and vision focused. The lines that living left in her face somehow made her even more beautiful to Mark Meadows's eyes.

Good thing she's close, he thought. He'd always been nearsighted. And for the last fourteen years he had seen through eagle-perfect eyes.

It took him three breaths to dare to try to move his eyeballs. There was little left to see: the bed, the rough room with its few and deliberately raw furnishings of wood and coarse rope, the Coleman lantern they'd brought from Salvador, now dark. And the rest of the woman herself, pale and slender and exquisite.

That was a favor, anyway. If as much torment as pleasure. He knew that body's every contour. Yet she had never known his touch. Only the touch of this body he inhabited. *Isn't that just my luck?* he thought. *I fall in love with a lethal lady Chinese spy. And she falls in love with the evil alter ego who's taken over my body. Perfect.*

It wasn't the first time he'd made himself a fool for love. His obsession with his first love, Sunflower, had led him into the obsessive quest that resulted in his body being usurped by the Radical. Long after the love he'd felt for her had ended in divorce, acrimony, and Sprout.

Sprout—it was Hei-lian's treatment of Mark's daughter that made him fall in love with her. She had begun with coldness, almost loathing. Now she showed every sign of loving her. It was as if Sprout had awakened a capacity for kindness in a woman who had lived virtually her entire life professionally coldhearted.

Hei-lian possessed a razor-keen intellect and a will so fierce it had forced her hidebound bosses to acknowledge her excellence. Years of witnessing— and yes, no doubt working—brutality had never crushed her spirit. Yet it was her unexpected capacity for *warmth* that won him.

I love you, he wanted to tell her. *I know the Radical's seductive power. Far too well. And it's a lie.*

He ached to warn her. Warn the world. *The man you think you love is changing into something that* isn't human. *If he isn't stopped he'll destroy everything. He—*

Mark felt himself swirl away from the world, down into old accustomed darkness. He uttered a vast and desolate cry that his throat could never voice.

"Aaaahh!"

The scream snapped Tom awake and upright. Sweat soaked his hair and face and body as if a tropical downpour had busted loose inside the cabin. The rough canvas covering of the bed under his butt was a mess, more sodden than the relentless heat could account for.

Fingers trailed down his arm. "Are you all right?" Hei-lian asked, sitting up beside him.

He drew in a huge breath and palmed hair back from his forehead so it would stop stinging his eyes with sweat.

"Yeah," he said hoarsely. "Just a nightmare."

Ellen Allworth's Apartment
Manhattan, New York

IT WAS STILL DARK outside when Bugsy woke up. The alarm clock blazed 6:22 in numbers of fire. He groaned and rolled to his side, pulling the covers with him. The woman beside him made an impatient sound and pulled the blankets back. He sat up, watching her sleep in the dim light filtering in from the window.

She was beautiful, especially when she was asleep and wasn't Ellen or Aliyah. Her naked body was familiar now. Known territory, and still fascinating. The way her small breasts rose and fell with her breath. The nameless fold where her thigh stopped being thigh and turned into body. The mole on her spine. When she wasn't anyone and her face went slack like that, she looked young. She looked his age. He sighed.

The room still smelled like sex and liquor. His head hurt a little, but not enough to bother with. The soft buzz of a few stray wasps made a white noise that seemed like silence. Still, he gathered them up, folding the insects back into himself. She slept better when it was quiet.

He rose, showered, nuked some scrambled eggs and coffee. The apartment was like a really high-class junk shop or a really cheap museum. All around him were artifacts of other people's lives. The cameo that Ellen wore and sometimes channeled her mother with. The pen that brought back a dead investment banker that she used when she was planning out her budget. A pair of scissors. A pair of glasses. A hundred dead people, all of them there for Ellen when and if she needed them. He was dating a republic.

When he snuck back into the bedroom to get some real clothes, her eyes were open. Until she moved, he didn't know which one she was.

"Aliyah," he said. "You sleep okay?"

She nodded gently.

"Ellen?"

"Still asleep," Aliyah said, touching the earring gently. "It's kind of weird, not having her back there. I guess I'm really used to it now, huh?"

"Yeah," he said.

"It means I'm real, though," Aliyah said. "I mean if I can be here when she's not, that means I'm really me and not just . . . I don't know. An echo. I'm not just her wild card if I'm awake and she's asleep. I'm not just a *dream*."

"That's what it means," he agreed, because it was what she needed to hear.

She lay back with an exhalation, watching the ceiling go from black to grey, grey to blue, blue to white. On his way back toward the kitchen, he caught himself humming something. Louis Armstrong was in his head.

Say nighty-night and kiss me
Just hold me tight and tell me you'll miss me
While I'm alone and blue as can be
Dream a little dream of me

He stopped humming.

The FedEx guy came while Ellen and Aliyah were in the shower. Bugsy signed for the box and dropped it on the counter, then picked it up and checked the return address. New Orleans. Jerusha Carter, his old teammate from Team Hearts. Somehow invoking hearts seemed like an omen, but he couldn't say whether it was good or bad. Probably it was just the hangover talking.

Ellen walked in from the back, still toweling off her short hair. "Who was it?" she asked.

"Christmas in November," he said, nodding to the package. Ellen picked it up, turned it over, then got a steak knife out of the drawer and slit the tape. Something in bubble wrap, and a note. "What is it?" Bugsy asked.

"Another hat," Ellen said with a sigh that meant another lottery ticket. Another chance that maybe this was the one she'd lost. Nick. Will-o'-Wisp. Her lost love, carried away by the wild winds of New Orleans. In the year since she'd lost him, they'd gotten hundreds, and not just fedoras. Baseball caps. Kangols. Two leather ten-gallon cowboy hats. A straw porkpie.

Ellen tore the bubble wrap open with her fingers, the popping sound like distant gunfire. The thing nestled in its center was a nasty green-brown, smelled of rot and river water, and had once been a fedora. "Hey," Bugsy said. "That one even looks kind of like—"

She had already scooped the hat up, cramming it over her still wet hair. Her body went still. Bugsy held his breath, and Nick opened her eyes for her.

Well, Bugsy thought, *fuck me sideways. Things just got more complicated again.*

"What happened?" Nick asked.

"You blew off in a hurricane. Ellen'll fill you in on the details," Bugsy said. "I'd hang out, but I've got a thing I've got to get to. Anyway, you two lovebirds probably want to catch up, right?"

Nick looked stunned, his attention focused inward, where Ellen was probably talking with him. *Another dead guy in the house.* When Bugsy slipped out the front door, there were tears in her eyes, and he couldn't tell if they were Nick's or Ellen's.

His three-way was a foursome again. Being in love with dead people was probably the only thing he and Ellen really had in common. Nick was going to be some hard explaining come Christmas dinner with the Tipton-Clarkes.

The offices of *Aces* magazine were open when he got there. He waited in the lobby drinking stale coffee from a paper cup until Digger Downs came out, shook his hand, and led him to the back office. "Sorry to keep you waiting," Digger said. "We're just about to put this issue to bed. You still doing any writing?"

"Not much," Bugsy said, with a little twinge of longing. A phantom itch on an amputated career. "Saving it up for the memoir, I guess."

Digger chuckled, gestured to a chair, and leaned against his desk, arms folded. He looked older, up close. More wrinkles around the eyes, more white in the hair.

"What can I do for you?" he asked.

"I'm doing some background work on the Radical. When he first came on the scene. Who his friends are."

"Should any of them still be alive," Downs said.

"That's the guy I'm talking about," Bugsy said. "I have him first showing up in China in 1993, but he's clearly a westerner since—"

"Sixty-nine."

Bugsy tilted his head.

"Nineteen sixty-nine," Downs said. "San Francisco. Right after they shot those kids at Kent State. The Radical was in the People's Park riot when the Lizard King fought Hardhat."

"Ah. Was T. T. even alive in the sixties?" Bugsy said.

"Who?"

"Todd Taszycki. Hardhat."

"No no no," Digger Downs said. "Not that one. There was another guy who used that name back then. Very blue-collar. Didn't have much use for the hippies."

"So when you say the Lizard King," Bugsy said, "you mean Thomas Marion Douglas? Lead singer for Destiny?"

"I sure do," Downs said. "The Holy Trinity. Jimi, Janis, and the Lizard King. He was . . . he was amazing. I saw him in concert once. When he died, we really lost someone. That was a little before your time, though."

"*Ninety-four* was before my time," Bugsy said. "Sixty-nine was the end of the Napoleonic wars. What was Weathers doing in San Francisco in the sixties? And where was he for those twenty-five years in the middle?"

"Got me," Digger said.

Jackson Square
New Orleans, Louisiana

"**AND HOW DO YOU** feel today, Miss Pond?"

Michelle opened one eye. A middle-aged woman wearing hospital scrubs was standing over her. "Like someone I don't know just woke me up." Her voice was still rough. And she was thirsty. Really thirsty. "Can you get me something to drink?"

"I imagine so. I'm Mary. I'm supposed to check your vitals."

"I'm not dead."

"That's pretty clear." The woman moved out of her line of sight. Michelle wanted to crank her head around, but the fat made it impossible. When Mary walked back into Michelle's sight, she had an Aquafina bottle in her hand. The water was sweet and cold, and Michelle drank almost the full bottle before gasping for breath.

Then Michelle became aware of a noise. It sounded like a flock of birds, but she'd never seen big flocks of birds in Jackson Square. "What's making that sound?"

"That? Oh, that's the faithful talking, honey."

"The faithful?"

As she pulled a stethoscope from her bag, Mary nodded. "They're the bunch of folks who've been bringing you these flowers, praying over you, making you the focus of their lives."

Michelle tried to move her leg, but couldn't. It pissed her off to no end. "That's insane."

Mary shrugged and stuck the stethoscope in her ears. "Honey, you'd be amazed. And, just to be fair, you did prevent a lot of them from dying horribly."

"I was trying to save my friends."

Mary put her hand on Michelle's wrist and popped the business end of the stethoscope onto Michelle's chest. "Doesn't matter why you did it. Just matters that you did. Now be quiet for a minute."

Michelle ignored Mary as she poked around. There wouldn't be any blood drawn. Needles broke when they came in contact with her skin. That had been happening ever since her card had turned.

"Everything sounds good," Mary said. "Same as it has for the last year."

Michelle wasn't listening to her. Her attention was focused on the TV. The volume was still turned off, but there were images of herself flashing behind the blond anchor. One showed her at the height of her modeling career. Then there were publicity shots from *American Hero*. And finally there were pictures of her lying in Jackson Square after . . . after.

Michelle had grown to love her fat. It was power and control, and it meant nothing could hurt her. But seeing herself . . . Bile rose in her throat. The whole world had seen her like *that*.

Her body was a distorted mass. Rolls and rolls of fat rippled across each other. The cement under her had shattered. Most of her body was naked. Her pale flesh mortified by the summer sun. And everyone had seen it. Hot tears stung in her eyes.

"Oh, damn it, honey," said Mary. "They should have turned that off." She walked to the set and punched the red button.

"Why are they showing that now?" Michelle asked.

"Because you're awake now. You didn't die when they took you off life support. You're a miracle."

"I'm not a miracle. I've got a virus that changed me. It could have happened to anyone. Are people really that thick?"

"Would you like to meet them?" Mary asked.

"Oh, yeah, 'cause I'm definitely at my best," said Michelle. "I love the idea of loads of strangers looking at me gape-mouthed while thinking I rescued them." She shut her eyes. Why was she being such a bitch? "I'm sorry."

"It's okay, honey," Mary said, puttering around the room throwing dead flowers out and putting the empty vases in a box. "I imagine it's something of a shock. Losing a year. That thing with your parents. And finding yourself, well . . . different."

It was impossible for Michelle not to giggle. *Different*. Yeah, she was different all right.

Noel Matthews's Apartment
Manhattan, New York

"THOSE ARE ZLOTYS. WHAT are you doing with zlotys? You don't have a show in Poland."

He'd heard the phone ring, and thought Niobe was safely ensconced in a conversation, so he'd pulled out the zlotys and began preparing for his fast trip to Poland. Now, busted, Noel tried to scrabble the bills, and—more incriminating—a passport photo of his new male avatar form, under a book, but it was way, way too late.

Niobe stood in the door of the bedroom he'd turned into an office. The desk was littered with decks of cards, linked metal rings, scarves, handcuffs, and padlocks. In a cage by the window a pair of doves billed and cooed, heads bobbing in that particularly silly fashion unique to doves. The tools of his trade.

Right now the doves' soft calls didn't seem to be having a soothing effect on Niobe. Her thick tail was lashing, hitting the floor with heavy thumps as she stared at him with a look that was two parts angry and one part worry.

"It's nothing," Noel mumbled. "I didn't want to worry you. In your condi—"

"Do not patronize me! I am not made of glass. I escaped from a federal facility and managed to elude every ace the government sent."

"Well, I helped a little," he protested.

"Granted, but either we're a team or I'm out of here."

And even just the threat made his heart stutter. He gave her the truth. "There's a man in Warsaw who makes the best forged papers in the business."

"And why do you need forged papers?"

"It's a little thing I'm doing for Siraj."

Niobe folded her arms across her chest. "Are you going to be in danger?"

"A little. But I'm always in danger. From my former associates . . ."

"And Tom Weathers."

"Him, too."

"And once you have these papers what are you going to do with them?"

"Travel with them."

"Where?" Noel squinted, pulled at his lower lip. Niobe stormed forward until she stood right in front of him. "I will not be treated like a goddamn mushroom!"

"Are we having our first fight?" Noel asked lightly.

"You only wish. If you think this is me angry . . . well, you've got a lot to learn. Now where are you going?"

"Kongoville."

"The place where Tom Weathers lives. The man who vowed to kill you."

"Well, he vowed to kill Bahir."

"And if he kills Bahir, won't *you be dead, too?*"

And suddenly Noel had to acknowledge that that loose feeling in the depths of his bowels was fear. He stood up, wrapped his arms around Niobe, and buried his face against her shoulder. The tension in her shoulders dissolved as she stroked his hair.

"The PPA is dangerous, viciously dangerous," Noel murmured into her hair.

"Oh, my dearest, don't do this. Let somebody else handle the PPA. The Silver Helix, SCARE, the Committee . . ."

Noel smiled down into her face. "Those idiots? You eluded SCARE, I ran rings around the Committee, and the Silver Helix is hamstrung with Flint and John facing trial. It has to be me."

Her hand went to her belly, fingers spread protectively. "Don't you dare get killed."

"And have you really angry with me? Not a chance." Her mouth tasted so sweet and he wished he didn't have to leave.

She broke the embrace and asked, "Do you have time to take me to New Orleans?"

"Why on Earth do you want to go to New Orleans?"

"Bubbles has woken from her coma." Niobe's eyes were glowing. "She's my friend and I want to see her." She touched her stomach again. "And I want to tell her about the baby."

"I thought we were keeping it secret until . . . we were sure. . . ."

"Not from my closest friends."

Noel sighed, and while Niobe went off to change into something cooler he phoned Bazyli to tell him he'd be delayed.

♠

Tuesday,
December 1

Mwalimu J. K. Nyerere
International Airport
Dar es Salaam, Tanzania

DAR ES SALAAM. THE name translated as "safe harbor"—at least, that's what the guidebooks Jerusha had read claimed. Jerusha hoped they were right.

They flew into Mwalimu J. K. Nyerere International Airport. An aide from the American Embassy was there waiting for them—that was certainly the Committee's doing—and he walked them through Customs. Jerusha didn't attract much notice as they walked through the airport, but Wally certainly did. She saw people pointing and whispering, heard them chattering and calling to each other. A crowd followed at a judicious distance as the aide shepherded them from the airport lobby and out to the waiting limo.

The heat and humidity of the outside air hit them like a physical blow as the doors opened. "Cripes," Wally said. "It's hot here."

The aide was openly grinning. "Welcome to Africa," Jerusha told Wally. "We both need to get used to it."

As they drove eastward back toward the city, she stared out from the darkly tinted windows. The area directly around the airport was dominated by industry: warehouses and businesses served by a double-lane divided highway. The landscape was rather barren: between the buildings there was bare, brown earth punctuated with scrub brush. It reminded Jerusha of the American Southwest and the parks her parents had worked, except that the Southwest was never this humid.

The driver turned north off the divided highway after a bit, though, and they were driving among houses. There were lots of kids: laughing, running after each other, huddled in groups around adults or parents, playing ball. The aide was rattling on as he had been since they'd left the airport, talking about how proud they were to be hosting two such famous *American Hero* members as the famous Rustbelt and Gardener, how they believed in good relations with the United Nations, how Ms. Baden had called the embassy herself.

Jerusha listened to him and answered with polite nods and short replies, but Wally stared out toward all those kids. She watched him watching them, as if he were looking at each face hoping to see his precious Lucien there. She wondered what he was thinking.

They drove past a winding river heading toward the sea. Here the trees were thick and dense, more like what Jerusha imagined Conrad's "Africa" might have been. They caught a glimpse of deep blue water running out to the horizon: the Zanzibar Channel. The limousine pulled onto another large divided road and continued north. Wally's eyes were closed and he was snoring softly; Jerusha envied him. The jet lag was pulling at her and she wished the aide would stop talking. She leaned her head against the window, staring out at the strange world drifting by.

Then she lifted her head again. "What is *that*?" she asked, pointing. The aide turned in his seat.

"Oh—that's a baobab tree," he said. "Lots of native tales about them. The baobabs are one of the symbols of Tanzania—of Africa in general, in fact. We have one of the oldest baobabs in Dar es Salaam on our compound grounds."

The baobab loomed in the central divider, as if a divine hand had ripped a gigantic tree from the ground and rammed it upside down back into the hole with the root system dangling from the top and overhanging both sides of the highway. The trunk was enormous and thick, furrowed with deep ridges, and green leaves fringed the branches here and there. The tree *looked* powerful and ancient, at home here like an ancient, gnarled oak might dominate a forest back in the States.

Jerusha stared at it and touched her seed pouch. "A baobab, eh?" She would remember that. "Listen," she said to the aide. "I—we—appreciate your taking us to the embassy, but it's important that we get to Lake Tanganyika as soon as possible. We're . . ." Jerusha didn't know what Barbara had told the ambassador, but it didn't seem wise to mention that they were intending to cross over into the People's Paradise. ". . . we're supposed to meet someone there. It's Committee business. We have to keep it quiet."

"Ahh." The aide pursed his lips, tapping them with a forefinger. "There's a man," he said. "A joker, Denys Finch. He's a bush pilot flying out of a little airport a few miles north of the embassy. Sometimes we have him courier for us, or take dignitaries out to the national parks or up toward Kilimanjaro."

"Could you take us to him?" Jerusha asked. Wally was still snoring. "Now?"

A shrug. "The ambassador wishes to have dinner with you, but that's not for a few hours." He tapped on the window separating their compartment from the driver and gave the man directions. Jerusha heard the word "Kawi." Then the aide turned back to her with a smile.

"We'll go there now," he said.

Jackson Square
New Orleans, Louisiana

THERE ARE MORE CORPSES in the pile this time. Adesina is curled into a fetal position on top of the pile. Michelle crawls toward her. The limbs slide as she puts her weight on them. Some of them feel squishier. She can't see the bodies clearly. All she can see is Adesina—who is still curled in a ball, but rocking back and forth. Her hand trembles as she reaches out and touches Adesina's temple. And as soon as she touches, images explode in her mind.

Adesina runs through the forest. The leopards give chase. Clothes tear on branches and thorns.

She's in a village. There are ugly little houses made of concrete blocks and corrugated tin roofs, painted in bright colors: yellow, blue, and green. Children play in the unpaved street, their feet kick up puffs of dirt that hover in the still air.

Michelle sees Adesina among them. She's wearing the same blue-and-white checkered dress. Her feet are bare. Her hair is braided, and someone has wrapped the braids around her head so they look like a crown.

The children are laughing. In the shaded doorways of the houses, women gossip while they watch the kids. It's warm and the air smells heavy with rain.

Bursting into the town come a trio of jeeps. Each has three men riding in it. The men are armed and shots ring out. The women grab the children and cover them with their bodies. Michelle wants to bubble—wants to do something to help. But she knows she would be useless. This memory is stuck in Adesina's head.

The men are dressed in green camouflage uniforms. Their heads are shaved and some of them wear leopard-skin fezzes. Machine guns are slung over their shoulders. They train the weapons on the women and children, then start shouting orders in French. Michelle understands about half of what they're saying. She tries not to feel afraid—it's difficult. She's in the well of Adesina's fear.

Michelle looks around the village, trying not to let the fear distract her. There are tires piled up at one end of the street. A couple of thick-wheeled bicycles lean against the tires. No help there.

The guns go off again. The women and children moan and cry. Michelle looks at the soldiers. Some have their guns pointed in the air. The rest have their guns trained on the villagers.

And then she knows it's time to go. It doesn't matter what happens next in the dream or vision or memory or whatever this is.

Adesina woke Michelle from her coma. And now it's time for Michelle to repay the favor. But she can't do it trapped in her fat and afraid to use her power.

Kawi
Dar es Salaam, Tanzania

"WALLY." JERUSHA NUDGED HIM. "We're here."

Wally jerked awake, and accidentally scratched the window glass with his ear. *Nuts.* He looked around, ready to apologize to that nice fella from the embassy, but he had already stepped out of the car. Jerusha looked like she was trying not to laugh. They shared a look and shrugged at each other.

Wally followed Jerusha from the cool, air-conditioned cocoon of the embassy limousine into an equatorial steam bath. He'd first felt it when they landed, but he'd been so comfortable dozing in the car that he'd almost forgotten where he was.

When he and his brother were kids, before his card turned, one of Wally's favorite things was visiting their aunt Karen and uncle Bert up in Ely, Minnesota. Bert had built a sauna into their basement. A proper sauna, lined with spruce, and an exterior door that opened just a few dozen feet from their dock. Wally loved the smell of the spruce, the tingle in his nose, the sizzle of the stones.

He and his brother used to take turns pouring water on the stones, until the sauna was so steamy it hurt to breathe. They'd stoop lower and lower as the steam rose, until it was unbearable. Then they'd dare each other to run down and dive in the lake in their skivvies. It wasn't cold at all, even in October and November, if you were fast enough. On a crisp, still night you could see the steam rising from your skin when you stepped out of the sauna.

Tanzania in December felt a little bit like that sauna. Except you couldn't control the temperature, and saying "uncle" didn't make your brother stop pouring water on the stones. Wally didn't handle humidity as well as he had before his card turned.

It was the rainy season here. The shorter of two, Jerusha said. That meant it was ninety degrees every day, with three inches of rain in both November and December.

They were parked on a patch of hard-packed red earth, along a road bounded by dense greenery on both sides. Wally made a mental note to ask Jerusha about the trees; everything was so green. Across the road, a handful of temporary huts clustered around a large, open-ended corrugated steel Quonset hut. Part wood, part metal, the huts looked like they'd gone up quickly and wouldn't be around very long. Wally could just make out an airplane in the shadows of the Quonset, and what might have been a landing strip in a clearing through the trees. They weren't too far from the ocean; Wally could smell it, on the strongest gusts. Mostly, though, he smelled humidity and what might have been the stink of burning garbage.

A trio of kids ran past them, laughing and shouting to each other. They were kicking a ball down the street. It appeared to be a crushed-up plastic water bottle wrapped with tape. Wally wondered what they were saying, if their game had any rules, and if Lucien played something similar.

"Uh, Jerusha?" said Wally. "Where's here?"

She said, "I think this is a town called Kawi. We're just a few miles north of the embassy. There's a bush pilot here who can fly us to Lake Tanganyika." Her voice dropped to a whisper. "I told him"—she nodded her head in the direction of the aide, who was knocking on a door next to the hangar across the street—"that we're on Committee business, meeting somebody at the lake. If anybody asks, I sort of implied that it's all very hush-hush. So just play along and we should be fine."

"Okeydokey. That sounds real good," he said. "Way to go, Jerusha!" He gave her a thumbs-up and a smile.

She didn't respond. Instead, she stared at his shoulder. Her eyebrows rose. "Wally? Did you know you're . . . rusting?"

Wally craned his neck to peer over his shoulder. Little splotches of orange dusted his skin. Sure, it was wet here, but he'd hoped this wouldn't have started quite so fast. "Awww, heck."

"Does that hurt?"

Huh. Nobody had ever asked him that before.

"Nah," said Wally. "Not when it's just on the surface like that." He fumbled through his pockets until he found some steel wool. A few quick rubs turned the splotches into a red dust. The slightest of breezes carried it away.

Jerusha still looked upset. She was frowning. "Does that happen a lot?"

"Sometimes. When it's humid outside."

"Humid? We're heading into the jungle. During the rainy season."

"Don't worry. I got lots of S.O.S pads with me."

Jerusha frowned, looking doubtful. She started to say something, but stopped when the sound of raised voices echoed across the street.

They turned. The aide was talking to a fellow with grey skin, dark little eyes deep in his round face, and a snout topped with a thick horn. He was a big guy, too, built like a fire hydrant. Wally remembered the Living Gods, jokers that had taken the forms of the gods of ancient Egypt. Kinda like the way Wally had grown up around open-pit iron mines and ended up with iron skin. This fella seemed to be something similar, only here in Africa his jokerism had taken the form of a rhinoceros.

The aide waved Jerusha and Wally over. They joined him. To the rhino guy, he said, "Here they are. Jerusha Carter and Wally Gunderson." To Wally and Jerusha, he said, "This is Denys Finch. He's the pilot I mentioned."

"Best pilot in the bush," said Finch.

Wally held out his hand. "Pleased to meetcha, guy."

Finch looked him up and down, his stubby little ears twitching like crazy. He did the same to Jerusha, then looked at the aide again. "Oh, no," he said. "Not this time. I've had it with your bloody tourists."

The aide looked embarrassed. "Not tourists, Mr. Finch. I told you, they're here on business for the Committee. The United Nations."

"Yeah, you and your so-called dignitaries." Finch spat in the dirt. "Comin' all the way to Tanzania, askin' me to fly them around. 'Ooh, Mr. Finch, show us Kilimanjaro. Ooh, Mr. Finch, show us the lakes, show us elephants and hippos and the real bloody Africa so we can take a few holiday snaps before going home to brag about our safari adventure.' Then it's thank-you-Mister-Finch-good-job and before you know it they're headed back to their proper Western hotels for proper Western food and proper Western air-conditioning." He spat again. "Wankers."

The embassy aide tugged at his collar, blushing. Wally understood the gist of Finch's tirade, if not every word.

"Hey, fella, we're not tourists," he said. "Not like that. Promise. We might be here awhile."

"Is that so? Then where's your kit?"

Wally frowned. "Kit?"

Finch rolled his eyes. It looked like he was mad enough to hit somebody with that sharp horn of his. Wally sidled in front of Jerusha.

"Yes, kit," said Finch. "Provisions. Gear. Tents and the rest."

"Actually," Wally said, "we were kinda hoping you'd help us with that."

Jackson Square
New Orleans, Louisiana

THE WOMAN WAS DISGUSTING, a mass of flesh draped in a light, silky material. Noel wondered if they'd used a circus tent. They had to have something covering her for modesty's sake, but it had to be light given the sultry heat.

Michelle and Niobe were deep in conversation. Ink hovered at the edges of the conversation, and the terrifying Hoodoo Mama stalked the edges like a protective rottweiler.

"We've been married almost a year, and . . . I'm pregnant," Niobe trilled. Then all of the females let out that peculiar shrill squeal reserved for news of an impending whelping. Even Noel's large, no-nonsense, horse-faced English mother had produced *the sound* when they'd relayed the news to her.

Michelle rolled her head toward him. "I didn't know you had it in you."

"I might surprise you."

"I doubt it."

"Oh, Michelle, be nice. Though we did have to try real hard," Niobe added, and Noel closed his eyes as peals of female laughter rolled past his ears. He wondered if he would have understood these tribal responses if his mother had chosen to raise him as a girl rather than a boy.

But if she had he wouldn't have Niobe, which indicated his brain wiring was male even if his parts were confused.

Michelle smiled at Niobe. "Would you get me a cup of lemonade? Ink can help you."

Both Niobe and Ink looked startled. Noel gave Michelle a cynical know-ing smile. As the two women walked away he moved in close to her. He no-ticed that she lay in a crater formed by her massive weight in the moist soil of New Orleans.

"That was a little in-artful," he said. "So, what is it you want to say to me?"

"Are you out of the spy business?"

"I left the Silver Helix, yes."

"That didn't answer the question."

"That's all the answer you're getting."

"So you *are* up to something. I thought Niobe looked worried. She's try-ing to hide it, but she's upset."

Noel found himself just glaring at the woman, hating to admit that she was perceptive.

"Tell me or I may just have to get a message to Jayewardene and the Committee."

"I'm getting very tired of being blackmailed," Noel said.

"Tough."

He hesitated, but realized he had no choice. "Very well, I'm engineering a little regime change in the Congo."

He thought he saw something flash in the back of Bubbles's eyes when he said Congo. "Oh, great, that worked out so well the last time." And her scorn and disdain drove away all thoughts about her reaction.

"If all goes well the final act will be taken by Tom Weathers," Noel gritted.

"When I hear the phrase 'all goes well' in conjunction with you I immediately get hives."

"I'd say that's the least of your problems."

Jackson Square
New Orleans, Louisiana

"OKAY, SO WHY IS it you can't stand Noel?" asked Juliet, when he and Niobe finally took their leave.

"I met enough self-aggrandizing dickweeds when I was a model," Michelle replied. "Every time Noel pops in, he spends the entire time looking down his nose at everyone."

Joey laughed. "He thinks his shit don't stink. Yeah. Not to mention he was the fucker who stole that Sprout kid and got that cocksucker Weathers all pissed off."

"People rarely change who they are at their core," Michelle said. "Sure, occasionally, someone stops doing all the crappy stuff they used to, but most folks will revert to form if given the chance. Noel's got responsibilities now. He's got a wife and a baby on the way, but he's still playing spy. The more he screws around with Tom Weathers, the more he puts himself, Niobe, and the baby in harm's way."

"He seems to make Niobe happy," said Ink.

Joey shrugged. "He knocked her up, you mean?"

"Looks like," Michelle replied. "I confess, it's giving me the hard-core willies, but it's what she wants. I don't care if they used a spatula and a turkey baster."

Juliet nodded, then changed the subject. "Have you had any more dreams?"

"They're not dreams. And yes, every night, just about. I've got to get to her . . ."

"You're assuming she's a real person."

"I know the difference between dream real and real real. These dreams about Adesina are real. They *smell*, for crying out loud. When was the last time you had a dream that smells?"

"Never. But how is she even alive if she's really in that pit?"

And how long will she stay alive? That was a question Michelle hadn't wanted to ask, even in her own thoughts.

"Time to tear the roof off the temple," she announced. "Has the square been cleared?"

"The police have it cordoned off."

"Then let's do it."

"About fucking time." Hoodoo Mama hopped up, grinning. "One roof, coming the fuck off."

Michelle smiled at Joey, but only for a second. The guilt of what they'd done still ate at her.

Then there was a loud snapping noise, like cheap firecrackers. The midnight sky appeared above her. She could see the blue-white light of the stars. There were zombies walking across the joists, some carrying plywood, others grabbing chunks of the roof and pulling it off.

Michelle told Ink and Hoodoo Mama to leave. Juliet started crying. "*Bbbbbut*, I want to be with you." Her nose was red.

Michelle wished she had a Kleenex to dry her tears. At the same time, she felt irritated with Juliet. There were worse things happening in the world.

"And I wish I had a pony," Michelle said. "But I don't know how this is going to work. I just want you safe when I start."

Joey put her arm around Juliet. "C'mon, Ink. Bubbles is a dick-flavored pain-in-the-ass, but she's right about being careful. She swallowed a nuke, remember?"

"You do know I didn't actually eat that nuke, right?"

Juliet gave Michelle a kiss on her forehead. "I love you," she whispered. A wave of stomach-churning guilt poured through Michelle as they left.

She waited until she couldn't hear them anymore. Then she waited longer. Above her she saw a sparrow fly down and perch on one of the joists.

"*Joey, get that goddamn zombie bird off my temple,*" Michelle said. The sparrow gave a nasty squeak, then flew off. Some of its moldy feathers drifted down to her.

It was time to get down to it.

For a moment, she was terrified, but then the thought of bubbling again zinged through her body. It wasn't as good as sex, but it was damn close.

Michelle flexed the fingers of her hand, and then opened them to the sky. *One first*, she thought. *See how it goes.*

Liquid heat slid down her arm into her palm. She watched as the bubble grew. It wavered slightly, and she let it go. It drifted up and bounced against the wooden beams, then rose toward the pale stars.

◆

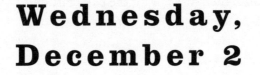

Wednesday, December 2

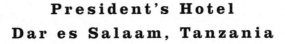

President's Hotel
Dar es Salaam, Tanzania

JERUSHA WOKE IN HER room at the President's Hotel at what the room clock insisted was 5:30 A.M., but to her body felt more like the middle of the night. She could hear Wally snoring in the adjoining room like a venting steam locomotive. She lay there for several minutes trying to will herself back to sleep, but her mind was racing with all that she needed to do, with worry about the plane flight with Finch, with even more worry about how they'd cross Lake Tanganyika and what might be waiting for them in the PPA.

Judging by Wally's snoring, he was worrying about nothing at all. She envied him that.

Jerusha threw aside the covers. Twenty minutes later, she was showered and dressed and striding out the lobby doors onto the embassy campus. The American Embassy compound was a dreary fortress: a series of rectilinear concrete buildings set behind a high security wall. To Jerusha it looked more like a prison than anything else. The ambassador had told them at dinner that this was the third embassy site they'd had in Dar es Salaam, that the campus sat on the site of what had been called the Old Drive-In Cinema, and droned on how the land gave them so much more room to expand at need.

The desk clerk had told her where the baobab tree was on the grounds; she headed in that direction. Rain had soaked the grounds overnight, and the grass was steaming as the day's heat rose, but for the moment, the air was cool enough that the humidity wasn't a bother.

She found the baobab easily. Up close, the tree was even more impressive than the one she'd glimpsed on the street, and even stranger. The trunk was massive—it would have taken a dozen people holding outstretched arms to encircle it. The trunk was furrowed and dented, branching above into nearly leafless main branches that diverged quickly into a tangled maze of branches and twigs. Birds were nesting in the hollows of the tree: several burst up into the air as she stroked the trunk. She saw a lizard sliding quickly around the trunk away from her, and dark squirrels chattered angrily at her from above.

There were pods hanging down from some of the branches, and a few on the ground at Jerusha's feet. She picked one up: a gourd roughly the size and shape of a football, the outside covering leathery and hard. It was heavy in her hands.

"Monkey fruit," someone said, and Jerusha turned to see a man in the uniform of the embassy staff stepping out of an electric golf cart a few yards away, the back stuffed not with clubs but with spades and rakes and trimmers. "That's what some people call it." His voice was heavily accented with Kiswahili or one of the other local languages, a lilt that Jerusha found charming. "Baobab fruit is very nourishing. The animals love to eat it: monkeys, baboons, elephants, even antelopes. They break open the gourds to eat the fruit and the seeds are discarded or end up in their droppings, and so new baobabs come up."

"The seeds are in here?" Jerusha hefted the gourd.

The man nodded. His skin was the color of thick cocoa, but the black hair was liberally salted with grey. "You're the one grows plants?" he asked.

It was Jerusha's turn to nod. "My name's Jerusha Carter," she said. "Sometimes they call me Gardener."

"I'm Ibada. I keep the grounds for the embassy. Toss that here." He held out his hand, and Jerusha underhanded the gourd to him. He slid a long knife from a sheath in his belt and pressed the heavy blade into the gourd, splitting it open. Jerusha could see pulpy fruit inside, laced with large seeds. "The baobab is the Tree of Life in Swahili," he said as he cut the fruit open. "That one there, it's an old, old one. It's been growing since before the birth of your Christ."

Jerusha looked at the tree again, trying to imagine all that history that had passed since it first sprouted. It was impossible. "They look so . . . strange."

"One tale says that the gods gave each of the animals a seed to plant. Poor baobab was the last, and it was given to the stupid jackal, who planted the seed upside down so that the roots came out on top." He laughed, and Jerusha had to laugh with him. He was pulling seeds from the pulp, gathering them into one large palm. "Tree of life, remember? You'll find the leaves used as a vegetable. *Kuka*, they're called—my mother used to make *kuka* soup. Here, look . . ."

He handed one of the halves of the gourd to Jerusha and poked a finger into the pulp. "You know cream of tartar? That originally came from this fruit. Down in the market, you can buy dried pulp covered with sugar; it's called *bungha*. Or you can mix it with milk or porridge. Very versatile." He took the gourd from her again, took her hands, and poured a dozen of the seeds into her cupped palms. "Those—grind them down and you can use them to thicken soup, or roast them, or grind them to get oil. But I think you will use them for growing, eh?" He smiled at her.

"Thank you, Ibada," she said. The seeds were cool and wet, and she could feel the great trees inside them, waiting to spring forth. "Later," she whispered to them. She opened a pouch of her seed belt and let them fall inside. The pouch felt heavy and comforting.

"This is why you came to the tree, no?" he asked. "You could feel the call of the Great Mother in her?"

"Yes." Jerusha brushed a hand over the thick trunk. A heat seemed to answer her, welling up from the ground below. "I think I could."

"Hey, Jerusha!" The call was a loud bellow. Both of them looked back toward the buildings of the embassy. Wally was striding toward them, waving.

Ibada nodded, grinning again. "I feel that call too, sometimes. You and the metal man, you're not here just to see the animals or take pretty pictures of Kilimanjaro?"

"No."

"Then you might need the baobab," he said. "Use the seeds well, Gardener."

"I will."

Ibada lowered his head, almost as if he were bowing to her. He began walking back to the electric cart. Wally passed him with a suspicious glance. "He bothering you?"

"No. And I can take care of myself."

Wally had the grace to look abashed. "Sorry," he said. The cart whined as Ibada left with a wave. "They said the car would be ready in an hour to take us to that Finch feller. I knocked on your door to tell you, but you didn't answer. The feller at the desk said you were out here, so . . ." His voice trailed off into silence. He was looking up at the baobab behind Jerusha. "Cripes, that's one big tree," he said. There was a distinct note of awe in his voice. Somehow that made Jerusha feel better.

"Yes, it is," Jerusha told him. "C'mon, we should get ready."

Kawi Airport
Dar es Salaam, Tanzania

FINCH HAD SAID IT would take at least a couple of hours to get them properly provisioned; they wanted to leave for Lake Tanganyika in the early afternoon. He took them to a . . . well, it wasn't really a store. Not that Wally could tell. It seemed more like a depot, or small warehouse, not far from the hangar where Finch kept his plane.

A stuffy, mildewy smell wafted out of the mud-brick building when Finch unlocked the door. Wally and Jerusha followed him inside. There was no electricity; the only illumination was the mustard-colored light leaking through grimy windows, except in places where the windowpanes were broken. Rows of shelves and piles of crates filled the space. Many shelves were empty, but those that weren't amounted to lots of gear. Camping gear, by the look of it.

"Wow!" said Wally. "This is all yours?"

"Finders keepers," said Finch. "Been flying in and outta the bush for thirty years. People get lost, people leave things behind, people get one glimpse of the jungle and go screamin' back to their hotel. I find it, take it here, and then sell it to lucky blokes like you."

Jerusha said, "This stuff isn't stolen, is it?"

"Bite your tongue!" Air whooshed through the pilot's flared nostrils. "I'm an honest businessman."

Wally edged in front of Jerusha again, just in case. "Hey, she's just asking, is all."

"Just so we're clear, mate. I don't steal, but I don't run a charity here, either."

"Huh?"

Finch rolled those tiny little eyes again. "You're gonna pay for what you take, right?"

"Oh, sure, you betcha."

"Thing is," said Finch, "I'm sure the Committee is good for it, but I can't wait around six months for a check to arrive from the United States. Not many banks around here that would honor it anyway, right?" He chortled, slapped Wally on the back. Most people flinched after doing that, but not Finch; it looked like he had pretty thick skin. The *clang* echoed through the warehouse.

"Right, I guess. So, um, what does that mean?"

"It means I run an honest *cash-only* business."

Wally looked at Jerusha. She shrugged. What else could they do?

The outfitting trip turned out to be an expedition in its own right. Though she'd offended him with her question, Jerusha won a bit of grudging respect from Finch once they got down to business. She had done her homework, and had compiled a list on the way over from New York. Wally knew they were doing this on the spur of the moment, but he had no idea just how unprepared they'd been.

He'd been camping up in the Boundary Waters Canoe Area. Preparing for a trip like that was nothing compared to this.

It was one heck of a list: Packs. Safari vests (with extra pockets). Biological water filtration bottles. Chlorine tablets. Painkillers; antibiotics; antidiarrhea medicine; rehydration salts. Pocketknives; machetes, for hacking through brush; compasses; toilet paper; rope. Flashlights; electric lanterns; a handheld GPS unit. Lots of batteries. Sleeping bags. Tents.

For Jerusha they also bought insect repellent, mosquito netting, and antimalarial tablets. Wally hadn't been bitten by a bug since his card turned. Jerusha got a wide-brimmed hat, too. Sunburn wasn't much of a danger for Wally, but he bought a pith helmet for the fun of it. He'd always wanted a pith helmet, ever since watching *Tarzan the Ape Man* (the original, not the remake). It would keep the sweat and rain out of his eyes.

Finch made a big deal about footwear. It had to be comfortable, he said, but it also had to let your feet breathe. Wally decided to go barefoot. It would be more comfortable than anything else, and besides, Finch didn't have any secondhand boots or hiking sandals that wouldn't get shredded by Wally's iron feet. As long as he was extra careful about rust, going barefoot wouldn't be a problem.

Finch made an even bigger deal about the satellite phone. "Don't lose this bloody phone," he said, shaking it in their faces. "This is your lifeline to the outside world. Your cell phones will be worthless in the jungle." He gave them a long lecture explaining how to use the phone. Wally tried to follow as best he could, but he secretly hoped Jerusha was getting it.

They unrolled one sleeping bag after another, trying to find a pair that hadn't been afflicted with mildew. Finch asked Wally, "Committee does this to you a lot, does it?"

"Does what?"

"Sends you off to the arse end of the world without any provisions." Finch's ears twitched. "Seems like a bloody awful group to work for, if you ask me."

"Uh, no. I mean, it happens sometimes. But not all the time."

Jerusha chimed in. "Our trip to the lake is an emergency. There wasn't time to get properly outfitted back in the States. We had to get here as quickly as we could."

"Ah, right. Right. So you said, so you said." Finch didn't sound entirely convinced.

After two hours, they had almost everything they needed. Jerusha haggled with Finch, so in the end it cost them just under half of the cash they'd pooled.

Then it was time to leave. They bundled up their gear and followed Finch outside. Wally offered to carry Jerusha's pack for her, but she didn't seem to like that.

Finch disappeared into the hangar. Wally lingered outside with Jerusha. "I don't think he believes us," he said. "What should we do?"

Jerusha frowned. She looked tired. "What can we do? Stick to our story until he gets us to the lake."

"Oy, tin man!" Finch pointed at Wally. "Get over here. Help me push her out."

Wally set his pack down next to Jerusha. Little eddies of red earth swirled around him as he clanged over to the hangar. The dust clung to the sweat on his legs; it looked like the worst case of rust he'd ever had.

Wally had never flown in such a small airplane, even back in Egypt. He'd flown in helicopters, but those were UN things, and still larger than this plane. He cupped his hands to a window glass and peered inside. It looked like it could seat maybe four or five, or fewer with gear.

"Grab her like this," said Finch, "gently." He leaned on the diagonal strut that braced the wing to the fuselage. Looking at Wally's hands, he added, "And don't scratch her."

Together they eased the plane outside. Finch made a musky smell when he exerted himself. Wally could have moved the plane himself, but it looked kinda fragile.

Actually . . . once they got it outside, in the sunlight, it looked *really* fragile. Long cracks spiderwebbed a couple of the windows; the fuselage had silvery gouges where the white paint had been scraped away; the wings had pits and dings and one thing that looked like a homemade *patch*. And the huge landing gear appeared to be more patch than tire.

"Hey, Mr. Finch? Is this safe?"

Finch's nostrils flared again. "Tourists," he muttered.

Jackson Square
New Orleans, Louisiana

CNN WAS BROADCASTING IT live. So was every other major news outlet. Juliet told Michelle it was being streamed live on the Internet.

Michelle had been bubbling for almost twelve hours now. She was still as huge as she had been, but she could tell she was getting lighter.

The bubbles were pouring from her hands. As many bubbles as she could release. She kept them dense enough that they didn't just pop, but light enough to float away. Just making a bunch of soap bubbles wouldn't do, and every other variation she had thought of had risks. She'd tried to make the bubbles somewhat pop-able; it was impossible to have the kind of control over them that she wanted. Even now, even hours since she'd begun bubbling, the power was still clawing through her. It was exhausting trying to keep it in check.

On the TV there was a long shot of the temple with the stream of bubbles rising from it. Then there were overhead shots, but these were on a loop since they'd shut down the Louis B. Armstrong Airport and closed New Orleans to all air traffic. Now they were cutting away to viewer video.

In every frame they showed, pretty, iridescent bubbles floated and bobbed like a child's playthings. They went up, up, up and then floated here and there, carried by the prevailing winds, until they slowly started to fall back to earth.

It was raining bubbles in New Orleans.

The TV showed a long shot of a young man in front of the Super Dome, preening for the camera. "Yeah, I know she saved the city, but damn, couldn't she have done this bubble thing somewhere else?"

The camera cut to another shot. A harried-looking woman held a toddler on her hip.

"I've got babies to think about. You don't know what's in those things. Oh, they look pretty enough, but have you tried to keep a baby away from one of them? They put everything in their mouths. I saw *American Hero*. She can make those things blow up."

Michelle yelled at the TV. "*These* aren't blowing up! They're not supposed to!"

"See, that's part of your damn problem, Bubbles." Joey turned down the TV sound. "You worry about what fuckers think about you. Me? I don't care."

"Did you tell Juliet about us?" Michelle blurted. *Stupid, stupid, stupid,* she thought.

Joey gave her an annoyed look. "Fuck no. Christ on a crutch, why would I do somethin' like that?"

"I don't know. Maybe you wanted to unburden yourself. Feel less guilty."

"I don't feel guilty about nothin' I do."

"Then why didn't you tell her?"

"You know why," Joey replied. "She sat here for a *year* waiting for you to wake up. She kept your parents away long as she fucking could, considerin' she don't have no rights. And she did it expecting nothin'." Joey shook her head. "You and me, we're alike. We're used to having to look out for ourselves. Juliet, she don't know how to do that. She loves you and that means putting everything else aside to take care of you."

"I suppose you know more about my girlfriend than I do," Michelle snapped.

"Yeah, I do." Joey slouched down in her chair. Juliet had gone out for coffee and beignets and it was the first time Michelle and Joey had been alone.

"Oh, my God. You're sleeping with her!"

"Jesus, you are one crazy bitch. No, but it ain't because I didn't want to. You just don't know a thing about Ink, do you? Fuck me all to hell." Joey jumped up from her chair and grabbed her gimme cap. "I'm gonna go see if she needs some help with those doughnuts."

Michelle fumed. She wanted to run after Joey. To tell her she was wrong. That she did *so* understand Juliet. But she was still too big. And then there were those damn bubbles. They went on and on and on . . .

Jokertown
Manhattan, New York

THE FAMOUS BOWERY WILD Card Dime Museum was a short ride on the subway. Ellen spent the time looking out the windows at the speed-blurred concrete and the darkness. She had a slight smile on her face, and a sense of peace that was almost postcoital, though Bugsy knew for a fact it wasn't.

He knew what it was. "How's Nick?" he asked.

Ellen took a deep breath and let it out slowly. "The hat itself is a little the worse for wear. It's strange having him back again. I still can't quite . . ."

Ellen's voice got thick for a moment. She hadn't expected to get Nick back. He'd died before she'd met him, and with the physical locus she used to channel him gone, she'd thought he was gone again. She'd been in the middle of mourning him.

Now he was back, and she had spent most of the last day communing with him—bringing him up-to-date, sharing confidences, no doubt telling funny stories about Bugsy and Aliyah and that one time when the FedEx guy opened the apartment door when they were in flagrante in the kitchen.

There was something basically unnerving about hearing the same mouth you kissed when you were making time with your girl laughing about you in a man's voice.

The subway reached their station, and Bugsy and Cameo ascended into the light.

Jokertown made up a section of Manhattan small enough to walk across in half a morning. It was also a different world. In the pale sun of early morning, two jokers jogged slowly down the street, one half mastodon half insect, the other with the body of a beautiful woman and the head of an oversized horsefly. But they were talking about Tara Reid's latest fashion blunder, so maybe it wasn't such a different world after all.

On one of the city buses that stopped to let out its cargo of freaks and misfits, a teenage girl was weeping. The cell phone pressed to her ear let out squeaks and buzzes, making words in no known language. An old man still drunk from the previous night urinated in an alley, his penis talking in a high, gargling voice of its own about imagined sexual conquests. A bat the size of a rottweiler with the face of a twelve-year-old Chinese girl flapped desperately, trying to catch up with a distant school bus. The coffee shops filled with the morning press of men, women, and who-the-hell-knew all grabbing a cup of joe and a corn muffin on their way to work while a neon-blue man in the back booth sucked down eight breakfasts, the plates stacking up beside him higher than his head.

Bugsy and Cameo crossed in front of a slow-moving delivery truck and went into the museum. The place smelled like old french fries and mildew, but it looked like the best secondhand shop ever. Display cases were filled with oddments and curios. A waxwork Peregrine stood in the corner in the same pose and outfit as the copy of *Aces* framed behind her. The joker at the counter could have been a man or a woman. The long face was something between a melted candle and road rash. Thick, ropey arms spilled out of a Yankees jersey. "Cameo!" it said.

"Jason," Ellen said, smiling. "It's been a while. How's Annie?"

"The same," the joker said, spreading his splayed, tumor-budding hands in a gesture that meant *Women. Whatcha gonna do?* "What can we do you for today?"

"My friend here is doing some research. People's Park riot."

"The what?"

"Apparently there was a riot in People's Park in 1969," Bugsy said.

"Could have been," the joker agreed. "I was two, so chances are I wouldn't remember."

"Thomas Marion Douglas was there," Ellen said.

"The Lizard King? Oh, fuck yeah. We've got crates of stuff on him." The joker squinted, scratched himself, and nodded. "None of that's on display anymore. The whole sixties rock thing we don't put up unless there's a revival or something going on. But . . . yeah. I think we've maybe got something back in the newsreels, too."

"Anything you've got would be great," Ellen said.

The joker held up a disjointed finger. One minute. He disappeared into the shadowy back of the museum. Bugsy walked around slowly, taking in the hundreds of small items and pictures. A poster for *Golden Boy*, the movie where the ace had gotten his name back before he got tangled up with McCarthy. Weird to think it was the same guy Bugsy had seen in Hollywood two years before. He looked just the same. Still pictures from the Rox War. A cheesy pot-metal action figure of The Great and Powerful Turtle, the grooves in the top making it look like a hand grenade cut along its length.

"I love this place," Ellen said.

A dress Water Lily had worn. A copy of an arrest warrant for Fortunato. A metallic green feather off one of Dr. Tachyon's hats. A solid two dozen pictures along one wall, each of them different, and all of them Croyd Crenson. "It's a trip," Bugsy said.

The joker stepped out of the shadows and motioned them in. The dim back office was stuffed to the ceiling with cardboard boxes and piles of paper. A ten-inch color monitor perched on the desk. It showed an image of a newscaster in the pale, washed-out colors that Bugsy associated with 1970s television.

"That's the footage I was thinking about," the joker said. "I've got a wash towel from his last concert in the box there. We got it off eBay a couple years ago, so it might be bullshit, but it's the only thing I'm sure he'd have worn after the People's Park thing."

"You're great, Jason," Ellen said.

"I try," the joker said with a sloping, awkward grin.

Bugsy squatted down, found the remote, and started the video playing. There he was. Thomas Marion Douglas. He was shouting at a crowd, exhorting them. A line of National Guardsmen stood shoulder to shoulder, facing him. This was before the advent of the mirrored face guard, so Bugsy could make out the nervous expressions on the soldiers.

Something loud happened. The reporter ducked, and the camera spun. A Volkswagen Bug was in flames. The camera pulled back to an armored personnel carrier, Thomas Marion Douglas on the upper deck, twisting the barrel as if it were nothing. The Browning came off the APC, and Douglas held it up over his head, bending it almost double.

"Watch this part," the joker said. "This is great."

The Lizard King bent down and hauled someone in a uniform out of the carrier. The poor nat kicked his legs in the air, and the Lizard King went down.

"Wait!" Bugsy said, poking at the buttons on the remote. "What happened?"

The joker lifted the remote from his hands and the images streamed backward. Frame by frame, they went through it. The burning car. The broken APC. The captain plucked out like the good bits of an oyster. And then the blurred arc of something moving fast. Thomas Marion Douglas's head flew forward and to the right, and he went down like he was boneless.

The man who stood where the Lizard King had been wore work overalls and a hard hat. A long iron wrench was in his hand. The guy was huge, but seemed to be shrinking. "Go home!" the previous generation's Hardhat called. "Go home now. Is over. You must not fight no more."

It looked like the big guy was weeping. Someone shouted something Bugsy couldn't make out, and the previous Hardhat went from maudlin to enraged in under a second.

"That's not good," Jason the joker said. But just as the guy with the big wrench was about to start in on the crowd, he went down too, tripped by Thomas Marion Douglas. The Lizard King got up as Hardhat regained his feet. The picture was jumping back and forth now, the cameraman torn between a great story and the threat of becoming collateral damage. Bugsy leaned forward. The Lizard King, blood running down his forehead and into his eyes, took a solid swing straight to the ribs and went down again. Hardhat stood over him, ready to crush the man's skull. The wrench rose, and then something—a chain, maybe—wrapped around it and spun Hardhat to face a new enemy.

Tom Weathers. Bugsy stopped the frame.

He looked familiar, but not quite the same. Slender, with blond hair down to his shoulders, wearing only a pair of blue jeans and a saucer-sized peace medallion on a chain, but this was absolutely unquestionably the Radical. The man who had threatened New Orleans, who had killed enemy and ally alike for almost two decades.

But Bugsy couldn't help thinking that the Tom Weathers on the screen looked . . . not younger, precisely. Softer. Kinder. Less ravingly homicidal.

He started the tape again. Hardhat, the Radical, and the Lizard King carried on their battle until it ended with Hardhat on the ground, reduced to merely human size and weeping, the Radical and the Lizard King in a victory embrace that was almost sexual.

"That's all we've got," Jason said.

"Okay," Cameo said. "Ready to meet the Lizard King?"

Bugsy nodded. Cameo took the old grey terry-cloth hand towel from Jason the joker's outstretched hand, settled it around her neck like a prize-fighter, and closed her eyes. Bugsy could see the change almost at once. She slouched into her chair, the angle of her shoulders changing, her head slipping back on her neck like a petulant schoolboy. He knew that Thomas Marion Douglas would be the one to open her eyes.

Apparently Ellen spent the two or three silent minutes prepping the Lizard King, because he didn't seem surprised.

"I have risen, man," Tom Douglas said in a slow, theatrical drawl. "That is not dead which can eternal lie, and in strange eons, even death may die."

"Yeah, okay. So my name's Jonathan," Bugsy said. "I was wondering if you could tell me a little bit about the Radical. From the People's Park riot?"

Tom Douglas shook his head as if he expected his hair to be longer and leaned even farther back and lower in his chair. Arrogance and contempt came off him in waves. "He's still fighting the good fight, is he? Cool for him, man. He was righteous."

"How well did you know him?" Bugsy asked.

The Lizard King shook his head. The movement was languorous, as if designed to stall just for the joy of stalling. "Just that one night, man. Just that one bright, shining moment. We showed the Man that we would not be intimidated. The people would not be pushed down. We stood the National Guard and their aces on their asses, man. And afterward, it was love, sweet love until the dawn."

Bugsy blinked, mentally recalculating. "So you and the Radical were . . . ah . . . lovers?"

"That make you uptight, man?" the Lizard King asked with a smile.

"Well, not in a queers-are-yucky way. I just never really thought of Tom Weathers as a sexual object."

"Everyone was with everyone, man. No jealousy, no possessiveness, no hang-ups. We were free and wild and full of love, man. But no, Radical and me were the power and the light. People were drawn to us. There was too much of us not to share around. Radical, he spent most of his night with a chick called Saffron . . . no, no. Sunflower. That was it. Seemed really into her."

"And after that night," Bugsy said. "Did he keep hanging out with her in particular?"

"There was no after that night, man. There was that one authentic moment, and then nothing. Dude came when he was needed and vanished with the dawn."

"You never saw him again?"

"Before or since."

"Great," Bugsy said.

Thomas Marion Douglas leaned forward, shaping Ellen's face into a smoky glower that Bugsy recognized from the covers of classic rock albums. "The thing was, we weren't afraid of death, man. We *embraced* it. We became free, and everything around us was transformed by our power. After us, nothing was the same. Nothing."

"Two words," Bugsy said.

The Lizard King lifted his chin, accepting the implicit dare.

"Britney Spears," Bugsy said, and then while the Thomas Marion Douglas looked confused, he lifted the towel from Ellen's neck and returned her to herself.

"Well," she said. "That could have been more useful."

"We've got Sunflower to work with, at least."

"Couldn't have been more than eight or nine million girls called that in sixty-nine," Ellen said.

"It's something," he said. Then, looking at the limp towel in his hand, "So that guy was the edgy, dangerous sex symbol of a generation, huh?"

"Apparently so," Ellen said.

"Guess you had to be there."

Kawi Airfield
Tanzania

THE PLANE HAD CREAKED as Wally stepped aboard, the suspension visibly sagging. Jerusha eyed the rust-spotted and patched fuselage with suspicion. "How old *is* this plane?" she asked Finch.

He grinned. "Ah, this crate's as old as me, and just as mean," he said. "She's a Cessna 206, made in 1964—a good year, all around. We're both perfectly serviceable, lady, if you catch my drift." He winked one tiny eye at her, and his glance drifted down the length of her body.

"Can it carry Wally?"

"Your metal man, you mean? Sure. How much can the bloke weigh?"

She said nothing, but climbed into the plane and took one of the four seats in the cabin, in front of a pile of boxes and crates lashed in with webbing and straps. Finch climbed into the pilot's seat, and the propeller on the plane's nose spun into invisibility as the engine coughed, sputtered, and roared. They clattered down the dirt runway, bouncing as Jerusha held tightly to the seat arms. As the plane finally lifted into the air and began to climb, Jerusha could see the sapphire water of the Zanzibar Strait, and off the horizon, the distance-blued green hump of the island itself. Below, the port city spread out, revealing all of its complexity and life.

"Where's Mount Kilimanjaro?" Wally asked, shouting against the roar of the plane's engine as they lifted from the airstrip, wings dipping left as Finch set them on a westerly course. "That's in Tanzania too, right?"

Finch snorted. He pointed out the right window of the aircraft. "Kilimanjaro's that way about six hundred kilometers: north, not west."

"Nuts," Wally said. He looked disappointed.

"Maybe on the way back we can make a detour," Jerusha told him. "With Lucien."

Wally brightened a little. "That'd be swell," he said. "I hope we can."

"So do I," she told him, but the churning of her stomach belied her confidence.

As they slid westward under the high sun, the shadow of the plane below moved initially across well-greened land, but as they moved farther from the coast, the landscape below became more arid, tan earth dotted with the green of occasional stands of trees and brush, interrupted at intervals by the winding paths of streams. An hour or so into the flight, the ground began to rise and crinkle underneath them, steep green-clad mountains and deep valleys sliding underneath their wings. "Mongoro Region," Finch called out, pointing down. "Beautiful, if you like mountains."

Jerusha nodded. Staring down, she realized that it would have taken long days to cross Tanzania by car as she'd first planned, following the winding, rough roads carved into this wild land. The mountains eventually drifted off behind them, and they were flying over flat savannah plain. Finch pointed out herds of wildebeest, and buzzed low above elephants and giraffes. Wally was entranced, staring out the windows of the cabin and pointing.

In the late afternoon, Finch set the plane down near a small village. "Delivery," he said, jerking a thumb back toward the crates. "We'll be spending the night here . . ."

The village—a Masai *boma*, according to Finch—was a collection of mudbrick adobe huts. The children hung behind the adults at first, staring at Wally mostly. By the time they'd off-loaded the plane, the kids had overcome their shyness: they darted out to tap Wally's metallic skin and dart away again, coming back to hit him harder and laugh at the sound. They plucked at Jerusha's clothes too, but it was Wally who intrigued them, and

Wally seemed to enjoy their attention. He'd make false lunges toward them, roaring when they ran away shrieking and enduring their pestering. He showed them Lucien's picture, telling them (in English that they couldn't understand) how he was going to visit Lucien, who was his friend. One of them kicked a soccer ball in Wally's direction, and he booted it high and long, the children exclaiming and shouting as they ran after it.

Jerusha watched, laughing with them. She reached into her seed pack and found an orange seed; she let it drop, drawing on the life within so that in a few minutes an orange tree had bloomed, with ripe fruit hanging on the branches.

The village smelled of orange rinds that night.

Special Camp Mulele
Guit District, South Sudan
The Caliphate of Arabia

"HEY!" TOM SHOUTED. "HEY! Knock that shit off!"

The two ignored him. One was the stocky kid Leucrotta, the other the Lagos guttersnipe with the Brit accent, Charles Abidemi, the one called the Wrecker, or sometimes ASBO, after some incomprehensible Limey bullshit.

Tom already knew who started it. Poor skinny Charlie wouldn't start shit with anybody, although he might make your Austin Mini explode a one-kilogram chunk matter at a time once he got clear of you. But Leucrotta was your typical adolescent male: a dick with legs. Which, given that he was an ace, was a very dangerous dick indeed.

Tom hauled Leucrotta off by the collar of his outsized Simba Brigade camo blouse just as it quit being outsized anymore. As a giant hyena-form chest exploded all the buttons off the front and blew out the sleeves, Tom tossed the rampaging were-beast up just far enough to transfer his grip from a collar that had just turned into a ribbon to bristly scruff.

"What the hell is *wrong* with you little shits? Don't you know there's a revolution on?" Tom spoke French. After spending six or seven years in the Congo, he could speak it just about as well as he chose to. He found that *slangy* with a deliberately nasty *américain* accent usually had the best effect. It wasn't like anybody was going to mouth off to him about his bad pronunciation. Not twice.

Of course, then he had to repeat it in his native tongue. Son of an Igbo soldier who immediately abandoned his Yoruba mum in a Lagos slum, Charlie had spent most of his short, miserable life in a housing estate in a not-so-trendy part of the London suburb of Brixton, getting his narrow ass kicked by Pakistani Muslim gangs, poor white gangs, Yardie gangs, and gangs of England-born blacks who despised immigrant Africans. He understood nothing but English. When the Limeys deported them Charlie's single mother hauled him back to Lagos, which got promptly overrun by the Simba Brigades. She'd jumped at the chance to sell her troublesome son to Alicia Nshombo's recruiters for a couple hundred bucks. But *he* wasn't the fucking problem.

As if to prove the point Leucrotta snapped at Tom. Only his ace reflexes let Tom shove him out to arm's length as drooling black jaws clacked shut. They'd have taken his face off as cleanly as any sad-sack Egyptian tanker's, *Über*-ace or no. "You little *fuck*," he shouted. "Try that shit on *me?* You need to cool off, man." And he flicked the four hundred pounds of spotted furious monster a casual two hundred yards through the air with a flip of his wrist. Trailing a howl of despair, Leucrotta landed in the middle of a swamp channel with a colossal brown splash.

About half the couple dozen kids hanging around by the tents broke out clapping. Tom gave them a sour smile and stomped off to confront the supposed *authority figures* who had made themselves oh-so-scarce during the dustup.

The special-unit camp, set well apart from the rest of the PPA army in the Bahr al-Ghazal and surrounded with coils of razor tape that glittered evilly in the white-hot sun, was as depressing a patch of perpetually soggy alkali clay, barbed-wire scrub, sorry-ass grass, and hyperactive mosquitoes as Tom had encountered in all his years spent knocking around the very least desirable real estate in the whole Third World. *What the hell possessed me to take my day off in fucking Brazil, anyway?* he asked himself furiously. *Next time I'm going to goddamn Greenland.*

The adult supervisors on duty stood aside in a clump: four surly overfed Congolese nurses from the National Health Service and a pair of Leopard Men commandos in their spotted cammies. All wore web belts with Tasers and Mace prominently displayed. The commandos wore holsters with 9mm SIG P226 handguns, too.

"What the *fuck?*" Tom said, spreading his hands palm up. "That asshole Leucrotta is throwing his weight around. You can't be dumb enough not to know how that's gonna fly: either he's gonna waste somebody or somebody's gonna waste him. Either way the People's Paradise loses a valuable asset. You need to keep these kids in line. They're freaked out and pissed off. They're gonna tear each other apart without Siraj having to lift his little finger!"

"They are like animals anyway," one of the nurses said. "Let them settle their pecking order themselves."

"At least exercise some adult moral guidance," he said in exasperation. "Try persuasion. Lead by example."

"If the great leader will show us the way," the shorter of the Leopard Men, Achille, said.

Tom walked two steps back into the sun. Then he swung back around and jabbed a finger at the handlers. "All right. I'll do that. I'll do that little thing. *Hey, kids.* Listen up."

Back came Leucrotta from his bath, human, slouching, and squelching. Tom favored him with a hot blue glare.

"Got control of yourself now, Fido?"

The boy glared. "Uh-huh."

"If you *ever* pull shit like that again with me I'll take you up for a nice little visit to orbit. For about five minutes. Do you understand? Say yes."

"*Oui,*" said Leucrotta sullenly.

Tom nodded. "Smart answer. Let's hope that means you're *getting* smart." He turned to the others. They stared at him wide-eyed. He saw awe on some faces and dread on others, but no hint of hostility. That was a relief; some of them could threaten even him. *I'm Hell's scoutmaster, here*, he thought. *Fuck me.* He drew a deep breath. "All right. Just what are we doing here in the middle of the nastiest swamp God never made? Can anybody tell me that?"

"We're helping liberate the oppressed people of the South Sudan," a boy said.

"Yeah," Tom said, nodding. "That's the official line, isn't it? And hey, that's true. That is what you're doing. Don't forget it. And what else?"

"We're trying to keep from dying." The speaker was a stick-thin girl in ridiculously baggy Simba BDUs. She was about thirteen, extremely dark-skinned and threatening to become pretty one day. Her hair was cut short to her head. Despite strict embargoes on "unnecessary" personal possessions she sported a pair of huge red plastic hoop earrings and matching glasses with big round lenses.

"You show some respect to your betters, little freak," bellowed the stoutest of the Health Service matrons, a slab-faced woman with wire glasses named Monique.

Tom opened his mouth to invite Monique to butt the hell out. Before he could speak, inky Darkness began to dance around the skinny girl like black flames, then leaped suddenly toward the matron. Screeching, she turned and fled as her fellow matrons stampeded out of the way.

"Now, that wasn't nice, was it, Candace?" Tom asked.

The Darkness shot her nonexistent hips and stuck out her underlip in a cute prepubescent pout. "We're not here to be nice, *non?* And anyway, she oppresses us. Or are we not meant to share in the Liberation?"

Candace Sessou was a bright and sassy teenybopper girl from a middle-class neighborhood of the city of Kinkala, near the former Brazzaville part of Kongoville in the southwest of what had been the Republic of the Congo before Nshombo and Tom liberated it. He was constantly surprised she'd survived to make it out of the labs alive. She had a problem with authority.

So did Tom.

"You are," he told the group. "The Revolution is for everybody. It's about liberating everybody. The people of the world. The people of the South Sudan. You."

The handlers shot him barbed looks, as if he were giving the children license to eat them all alive. None of them had the guts to say anything. They were bullies, all of them. But he couldn't very well let the kid aces go all Lord of the Flies on them, either. Time to try getting their twisted little minds right.

"But the Revolution is all about discipline, too," he told the children. "About putting aside your selfish little ego trips and squabbles. See, the way the Man keeps the people down is divide and conquer. So what you need to do is pull together. Do your parts for the Revolution, for all the other kids suffering oppression around the world, and most of all, for each other. Can you dig it?"

"Yeah!" They shot to their feet, throwing their little fists up in the air on skinny arms.

"That's the spirit. That's my brothers and sisters. The Man can't stand against commitment like that. You kids will save the world!" He let them soak that up. Then he said, "Now listen up. We got a job to do. And this time you kids are gonna make all the adults in the *world* sit up and take notice."

♥

Thursday,
December 3

Near Lake Tanganyika
Tanzania

THE CESSNA BOBBED AND weaved through the air, tossing them violently from side to side. Wally clenched the seat in front of him so hard that the metal frame dented. Finch grinned back at them from the pilot's seat, his stubby rhino ears twitching. Whenever he glanced at Jerusha, his gaze seemed to drift down to her chest and linger there. At least she'd worn an athletic support bra. "Bit of a rough ride, eh?" he said. "But we're almost there."

The turbulence grew brutal, and Finch paid more attention to the plane than to Jerusha. They skirted purple-grey thunderheads tossing lightning down toward the savannah and occasionally passed through rain showers. Tanzania glided slowly underneath them, and finally ahead, Jerusha could see an immense stretch of blue water. Finch spoke over a crackling radio as he circled the aircraft as they neared the lake's shore. "We're setting down there," he said, pointing to a tiny airfield.

Ten minutes later, in a cloud of brown dust, they were down and taxiing up to a long Quonset hut. Finch cut the motor—the silence was deafening, the roar still echoing in Jerusha's ears. Finch opened the doors and gestured. The air outside was sweltering and humid; she could see the orange spots beginning to dot Wally's skin again. Huge mountains loomed to the east, but Jerusha could glimpse the lake to the west, beyond the buildings of the town. "Welcome to Kasoge," Finch said.

There was a squad of a half-dozen soldiers leaning against the hut. As Jerusha stepped from the plane, they began to saunter over toward them. When Wally followed her, they stopped. One of them snapped something, and the muzzles of their rifles suddenly came up.

"Hang on now, mates," Finch called out, his hands lifted and open. Jerusha followed his example, but Wally only raised an eyebrow. Deliberately, he stepped in front of Jerusha. The gesture was touching, but it meant she couldn't see. She moved around him. Finch was talking to the soldiers in what Jerusha assumed was Kiswahili.

Their voices were loud and strident at first, and Jerusha's hand drifted to her seed belt, her fingers curling around kudzu seeds. A quick toss, and she could entangle them. . . .

She took a step to Wally's side. The soldiers were still staring at them, but their weapons had dropped back to their sides. Finch was still talking, waving his hands. "I need your passports," he said. Jerusha handed them to him.

The squad's officer glanced through the documents, finally passing them back to Finch. The soldiers went back to the hut, conversing among themselves and still watching them. "Those blokes are looking for PPA incursions, or for refugees from there," Finch told them. "I told them we'd come from Dar es Salaam, not the Congo. I told them you had no interest in the PPA. I *think* they believe me." He sniffed, the horn on his snout tossing. "So—was that true?"

Jerusha didn't answer; Wally just shrugged. If there were soldiers patrolling the shores of Tanganyika, they were going to have to be very careful. "If Wally and I would like to take a boat ride on the lake tomorrow," she said to Finch, "would you be able to negotiate that for us? We could pay you. . . ."

♣

"Boat ride, eh?" Finch scowled, tiny ears fluttering while he fixed Wally and Jerusha with a scowl. "A nice, leisurely sightseeing ride?"

"Yep. That's right," said Wally. "Sightseeing."

Behind him, Jerusha sighed.

Finch scratched at the base of his horn with one long, blackened finger-nail. *Scritch. Scritch. Scritch.* He narrowed his little eyes, taking a long, hard look at Wally and Jerusha. He seemed to spend more time looking at Jerusha. His gaze was a little less angry when he looked at her, too; he never seemed to have much to say to Wally.

"Well, I expect that since you're just a pair of innocent tourists with no interest in the People's Paradise of Africa you'll not know that the border between Tanzania and the PPA runs straight down the middle of the lake." Finch hacked up something dark and wet. He spat it in the dirt, adding, "And you do not want to find yourselves on the wrong side of that line."

Jerusha said, quietly, "What would happen if we did? What would we find? Just out of curiosity."

"Rebels and Leopard Men. If you're lucky."

Leopard Men? Rebels? What the heck was going on over there? What the heck had happened to Lucien? Wally couldn't help it: "Holy cow! Leopard Men?" The soldiers over by the Quonset hut looked up from their private conversation. Worrying about Lucien had got him worked up; he'd asked a little more loudly than he'd intended.

"It doesn't bloody matter, does it? Since you're not going over there." Finch had a strange look in his eye, like he was saying one thing but meant something else. "All you need to know is that they'd shoot you dead the moment they noticed you." He punctuated the last with a sharp jerk of his head, pointing his horn toward the lake and, by extension, the PPA.

"Well, look, buddy, bullets don't—"

Jerusha clapped a hand on Wally's arm. "Thanks for the warning. We wouldn't want any misunderstandings." She emphasized "misunderstand-ings." Then she tugged at Wally. "We'll trust you to hire a boat for us."

Once out of earshot from Finch, Wally asked her, "What if he gets a boat that won't go across the lake?"

"I don't think that will be a problem, Wally. I think Finch had our num-ber the minute he laid eyes on us. He thinks we're on a secret mission for the Committee."

They followed the road to a narrow bend. In one direction, from where they'd walked, Finch unloaded more crates from his battered Cessna. In the other direction, around the bend, Wally got his first glimpse of the outskirts of Kasoge.

It wasn't all that different from the other villages they'd visited. The buildings he saw were a random assortment of wood, mud-brick, and some-times metal siding. They gave the impression of having been built, or re-built, from whatever was handy at the time. Wind sighed through the trees that grasped at a bright tropical sky. It carried with it the earthy smell of jungle, the dead-fish-and-fresh-water scent of the lakeshore, and the stink of the garbage fires. The smoke stung Wally's eyes.

From above, in Finch's plane, Africa had seemed like a paradise that stretched from horizon to horizon. But down on the ground, Wally noticed different things. Like the garbage fires. People just collected their trash into piles on the street. When the piles grew large enough, they were burned. He figured that was because they didn't have a city dump and regular garbage collection like back home. It made sense. They did what they could.

Still, Wally had been real disappointed when he'd discovered that the smoke from the garbage fires obscured his view of the stars. He'd figured that being in Africa would mean he could see all sorts of stars. And different from the ones he knew.

For all the beauty, Africa sure wasn't a paradise. Even here, in Tanzania. And Finch's warnings about the PPA hadn't done anything to make Wally feel better about Lucien. He wished he could just grab a boat and get over to Kalemie.

Wally and Jerusha stepped off the road, out of the way of a truck. When it passed, he saw that a long board had been nailed to the back of the truck, and several bicyclists coasted along by gripping the board. One fellow had fixed his bike chain with lengths of wire.

They stopped at a pavilion built from irregular panels of corrugated alu-minum fastened atop brick stanchions. Like he had at the last village, where they'd stopped the night before, Wally drew a lot of attention. He plopped down on a bench and zipped open his pack.

"Want a snack?"

"Yeah, actually." Jerusha looked at his pack. "What do you have in there?"

"I brought some peanut butter. It's good on bananas."

A funny little smile blossomed on Jerusha's face. "Hold on a sec," she said. She wandered over to a spot near the tree line, upwind of the fires. There she dug into her pouch and dropped something on the ground. She returned to the pavilion a few moments later, carrying a golden yellow thing a little larger than a pear.

"What's that?"

"It's a mango." Jerusha took the knife from her sack and deftly skinned the fruit in long, wide strips.

"Oh. I've never had a mango before."

Again, that smile. She didn't look up from peeling the mango, but she said, "Yes you have. And you liked it, too."

"I have?"

"At the embassy. Remember? All the fruit on the table at breakfast?"

"I remember some pineapple and bananas, because I like those, and some orange stuff, too. It was pretty good."

"That orange stuff was a mango. And I could tell you liked it, because you ate an entire bowl of mango slices."

"Oh." Wally felt himself blushing. "You saw that?"

"Yep." After skinning the mango, she sliced it, neatly excising a large pit from the center. She dried the pit and put it in a pocket of her belt.

Childish laughter echoed across the street. A pair of kids not much older than Lucien ran down the street, trailing a homemade kite: a plastic garbage bag, two long sticks, and about a million little scraps of string tied together into one long string. The kids had two shoes between them; one wore the left shoe, the other the right.

Wally wondered if Lucien had ever flown a kite. Maybe Wally could show him.

They ate in companionable silence, watching the kids.

"Jerusha?"

"Yeah?"

Wally looked at his feet, not wanting to embarrass her. "I'm real glad you decided to come along."

Jackson Square
New Orleans, Louisiana

THERE'S A SHOT OF the French Quarter on TV. At first, it looks like there's been a freak snowstorm. But as the camera zooms in closer, you can see that there are bubbles everywhere. People are wading knee-deep through them, kicking them up in the air. Sometimes they pop and everyone laughs.

"I've never seen anything like it," the reporter says. "It's been raining bubbles here for three days now. We've been trying to talk to Michelle Pond, the Amazing Bubbles, to find out when this will end."

Michelle rolled her eyes. She'd refused interviews because she really didn't *know* how much longer it would go on. She was definitely lighter, and she thought she was getting smaller, but there was still so much energy in her. She looked up at the TV again.

The next shot was of a playground. Kids were shrieking and laughing as they slid into the masses of iridescent bubbles. They picked up bubbles and threw them at each other. Some popped immediately, but most bounced harmlessly off their targets.

Then another shower of bubbles began, and the children held out their arms and let the bubbles rain down on them.

♠

Friday,
December 4

Lake Tanganyika
Tanzania

"CROSSING OVER INTO THE PPA would be very unwise," Barbara
Baden said, line static hissing underneath her voice. "Don't. Things are getting very dicey there. The war, the Leopard Society, Tom Weathers . . ."

"Don't worry about us," Jerusha told her, standing on the dock where the
boat they'd hired was moored. Mist was rising from the lake, and the jungle
around them was noisy with stirring life. "I'm just helping Wally nose around
a bit."

"Good," Barbara said. "Be very careful, and stay in touch."

"Sure will," Jerusha told her and snapped the phone shut.

"Sure will what?" Wally asked. He was scrubbing furiously at his left
shoulder with an S.O.S pad. Finch was a few feet away, talking to the boat's
owner. Their kit sat in bundles around them, looking heavy in the dawn
light, but Wally seemed barely able to stand still now that they were so close
to Lucien.

Jerusha lifted a shoulder. "Nothing important." She wondered whether
she should tell him what Barbara was saying about the PPA, but she was certain it wouldn't change Wally's mind. If she refused to go with him, he'd

just go alone. Jerusha wasn't quite sure why, but she knew she couldn't let him do that. *He needs you, and you . . .*

Finch interrupted the thought. "Hamisi here doesn't much like the idea of going over to the PPA side of the lake," he said. "He's saying he needs another hundred dollars. For the risk."

"You already negotiated the price. We've already paid him fifty."

Finch shrugged. "Now he wants more. Or, he says, he won't do it. Can't say I blame the bloke. The PPA's not a place I want to get too near myself, with the things I've been hearing. You're lucky to have found anyone who's foolish enough to ferry you across." He waved at Hamisi, who stood watching them from where the boat was tied up. "You want to talk to him yourself?"

"I'll pay you back when we get home, Jerusha," Wally interjected. His foot was tapping on the pier, shaking the wooden planks, which already bowed under his weight.

Jerusha sighed. "Offer him another fifty," she told Finch. The man shrugged and went back to Hamisi. After a heated exchange, he came back. "Got him to agree to an additional seventy. Best I can do. Or the two of you can try to find someone else, or better yet, stay here. Your call."

Jerusha looked at Wally. "All right," she said. "Seventy."

Ten minutes later, Finch had tossed the rope from the pier into the boat where they were sitting. The boat smelled equally of old fish and grimy diesel oil; the deck was filthy and slick, the bench seats only slightly less so. Hamisi fiddled with the controls in the small cabin; the engine snorted blue exhaust and bubbles churned at the rear of the boat. "Good luck to the both of you," Finch called as the bow began to cut through the dark water of the lake. "You're going to bloody need it."

Jerusha tried to put that last bit out of her mind as she watched Finch's body dwindle into the distance and mist.

Thirty miles across—that's what Finch said it was—a trip that would take at least three hours, according to Hamisi, who didn't understand English but could converse—haltingly—in Jerusha's French. The Congo had always used French as an official, tribally neutral official language, a practice retained by the PPA, and Hamisi had originally come from the PPA, long ago. *Three hours . . .*

The lake water seemed to drift slowly past the hull as the mist lifted in the rising sun, but there was no sign of the other side of the lake. She could see other boats out on the water: schooners with white sails, distant fishing boats with their snarls of nets, pleasure craft lifting bows high out of the water. The horizon ahead of them was unbroken water seeming eternally fixed despite their own movement. The landscape was beautiful, though: the deep lake, the walls of green mountains behind them and parading off into the distance, a rain squall spreading darkness well to the north, and thunderheads looming in the distance. It reminded her of the wild beauty of Conrad's description of the Congo.

Wally didn't glance around at the scenery. He sat in the exact middle of the boat, staying very still and looking out at the water apprehensively. "Wally, you okay?"

He gave a shrug and worked his steam-shovel mouth. "All this water," he said. "Cripes, I used to love swimming, back before my card turned. But now . . ." He tapped his chest with his fist, a sound like a trash can colliding with a Dumpster. "Can't swim. Don't like water."

"It'll be over soon. Just hang on." She rubbed at the back of her neck with her hand, kneading the ache that threatened to become a headache. *And then there's the jungle, and the rains, and the rivers we'll probably have to cross there, and getting across Lake Tanganyika again afterward . . .*

After a time, Jerusha realized that she could finally see the smudge of the PPA coastline. The blue-hazed humps there crawled toward them, far too slowly for Jerusha's comfort, but reachable now. The boat puttered steadily forward, and Jerusha was beginning to think that the crossing was, despite Finch's pessimism, to be uneventful.

"Hey, what's that?" Wally said.

He was pointing northward. A black dot was slicing through the water: a patrol boat, with a white wake tracing its path. At about the same time that they noticed it, the boat shifted course toward them. Hamisi, at the wheel, cursed.

"Can't you beat them to the shore?" Wally asked hopefully. He pointed to where the trees reached the lake. Hamisi scowled. He spat a long, loud harangue in what Jerusha assumed was Kiswahili. "What'd he say?" Wally asked Jerusha. She could only shake her head.

Someone on the patrol gunboat was shouting through a megaphone in French. "Shut off your engine!"

Hamisi looked at Jerusha. She didn't know what to tell the man. The command was repeated, and this time the machine gun mounted on the craft sent a long white line spattering into the lake just ahead of them. White smoke drifted away from the muzzle, the noise echoing back at them belatedly from the shore. Hamisi slapped at the key; the engine went silent as the waves swayed the boat from side to side.

Wally grabbed at the gunwale for balance as the patrol boat circled them at twenty yards or so. "Jerusha," he said, "just stay behind me if they start firing, and I'll . . . I'll . . ."

"You'll what? Swim over to get to them?" The crestfallen apology on his face made her regret the words even as she said them. Her hands slid over her seed belt, her fingers slipping into the enclosures to touch the seeds there. Out here, there was nowhere to hide. If they wanted them dead, all they need do was pepper their sorry little craft with holes and watch them sink. They could capture them just as easily.

Jerusha had no intention of seeing what a PPA prison might be like. Wally's strength meant little here, if there was no ground on which to stand. Hamisi was already backing away from the wheel of the boat, his hands up.

"Wally," Jerusha said. "Hands up."

He looked surprised at that. "We can't just give up."

"*They* have to think we will," she told him, nodding toward the gunboat. She lifted her own hands. "Go on," she said, and reluctantly Wally raised his own huge arms; there were large orange spots on his underarms.

The gunboat circled once more, then moved in toward them. When it passed in front of Jerusha, only an arm's length from their boat, she threw the seeds in her hand and opened her mind to her wild card power.

Kudzu vines were already sprouting wildly from the seeds before they even hit the gunboat's deck and the water near the hull. Some curled rapidly around the crew members as they tried to draw guns, while others fouled the twin propellers of the craft. Jerusha could hear the groan of the patrol boat's engine as it tried to force the props to turn. Then—with a whine and a cloud of white smoke—the engine cut off entirely.

"*Hamisi!*" Jerusha shouted in French. "Let's go! *Hâte!*"

Hamisi pressed the starter and water gurgled as they started to move, slowly, along the length of the patrol boat. The crew members were shouting, tearing kudzu from around themselves. Jerusha had been unable to toss the small seeds far enough to reach the machine-gun mount—it swung around to follow them and she heard the man ratchet a slide back. She took a baobab seed from her pouch: she wasn't certain she could toss it that far. "Rusty!" she said. "Here. Throw this onto the boat."

Wally took the seed from her, tossed it high and long. The seed rang on the deck as the baobab sprouted roots and its strange crown—a dozen years' growth done in a breath. The deck plates groaned metallically as the thick roots plunged downward seeking water and earth. One branch tipped the machine gun's barrel up, and tracers laced the sky as it chattered.

Jerusha bent the tree with her mind, tilting it so that the gunboat began to lean. Water suddenly burst around the new baobab's girth. The gunboat listed over entirely in the space of a few breaths, the half-dozen crew members beginning to scream. Jerusha had the vines fling them overboard, releasing them at the same time.

"Go!" she shouted to Hamisi. *"Allez! Au rivage! Rapidement!"* She pushed him toward the cabin of their boat as the gunboat crew flailed at the water, grasping for the baobab's branches even as the gunboat turned entirely on its side, the hull now facing them. The baobab floated low in the water as Hamisi's engine coughed and roared. They moved away from the men, who were waving their arms and calling out to them.

"Good toss," Jerusha told Rusty.

He grinned. She thought that if he could have blushed, he would have. "It was nothin'," Wally said. "But cripes, that was pretty terrific, Jerusha."

She gave him a quick, fading smile. She could feel the baobab dying in the water, drowning without earth to sustain it. The crew of the gunboat was still shouting, their voices fainter now; the tree would serve as a raft until someone noticed them. *I'm sorry*, she whispered to it. *I'm sorry.* "Let's get to the shore before reinforcements show up." She stared at the slopes there, pointing to the nearest point of land. "There," she told Hamisi. "Take us there. . . ."

Jackson Square
New Orleans, Louisiana

FOR ONCE, MICHELLE ISN'T in the pit.

This is a nice looking place. But she's still afraid. No, Michelle thinks. *Adesina is afraid.*

There are small buildings in a circular layout. They're nicer than any of the houses in Adesina's village. These are sturdy, built from concrete blocks and are painted in bright primary colors and all the roofs are brick red. They have glass in the windows and she sees power lines running from generators to each building. There's gravel laid out on the ground so the walkways won't turn to mud when it rains. There's even a pretty painted sign: Kisa . . . something Hospital for Children. Michelle can't quite make it out.

Even though she's frightened, Adesina is awed by this place. She's never been anywhere so nice before. A woman comes out of the red building. She wears a white coat and carries a clipboard. Something about her frightens Adesina and she cowers with the other children. The woman walks by each child, pointing at each one, then gesturing to one side of the path or the other.

After the children are divided, they're taken to different buildings. Adesina goes into the green building. She likes the color green, but not today. Today she hates it. She's crying and she wants her mother and father. One of the other children pinches her and tells her to stop being such a baby. But Adesina doesn't care. She doesn't mind being a baby now.

Another woman in a white coat comes into the room. She carries a tray covered by a white cloth. Adesina cries harder, and soon all the children are crying. The woman ignores their tears.

The woman opens the door to another room and then steps inside. Before she closes the door, she makes a quick gesture to one of the children's captors. He grabs the boy who pinched Adesina and drags him inside.

One by one, the children are taken into the small back room. The children don't come out again. When Adesina's turn finally comes, she sees why. There's a door leading out the back of the building.

The woman in the white coat speaks sharply to Adesina. Michelle doesn't understand the words, but she grasps the intent. Adesina stops crying, but snuffles as she tries to contain herself.

The woman pulls the cloth back from the silver tray. There's a row of needles. Adesina doesn't know what they're for, but they look sharp and hurty. She starts crying again. The woman grabs her arm and before Adesina can squirm away, the needle sinks into her flesh.

For a moment, nothing happens. Adesina's so surprised she stops crying. Then the fire roars through her. It tears at her mind and pulls her apart. She looks down at her hands and sees that they're changing. And that's when she begins to scream. Then the world goes dark.

Khartoum, Sudan
The Caliphate of Arabia

THE LITTLE GIRL WAS unnaturally still in his arms as they hung for a breathless instant in orbit. The bandages wrapped around her wizened little body felt rough. Tom took quick stock: for once his objective was marked by a terrain feature—the confluence of the Blue Nile from Ethiopia and the White Nile from Uganda, becoming then just the plain old Nile everybody knew. Supposedly the ancients thought it looked like an elephant's trunk. How they could tell, given that the country here was every bit as stomped-down flat as the Sudd not so far south, he had no clue. But the alleged resemblance had given the place its name: *al-Khartum*, the Elephant's Trunk.

Khartoum. Capital of the former Republic of Sudan. Now just the capital of the newest province of the Caliphate.

They called the girl the Mummy, for the bandages that covered her whole little body and big head to protect her sensitive skin from the blistering African sun. The docs said she was eleven, though she was the size of a four-year-old, and a none too healthy one at that. The Simbas had found her wandering in drought-stricken northeast Uganda during that country's recent liberation.

Downward like a beam of light—

And here, see, was where the plans ran a bit off-rail. Tom and his charge found themselves on a dais decked with festive bunting in the Sudanese colors of red and black and white and the obligatory Muslim green. It stood in the courtyard of the Defense Ministry: a blinding white colonial-era wedding cake, like a smaller version of the nearby Presidential Palace, almost on the Blue Nile bank.

The courtyard, partially shaded by trees planted by those same long-gone English colonialists, was packed with martyrs of the Sudan's wars. The living ones, of course: the merely wounded, who could look forward to life on the leavings of a rat-poor state, propped on a wheeled platform that kind of replaced your legs, and in constant pain that even the rare morphine dose could never really ease.

A mustached man in an extravagantly medaled blue uniform stood behind the podium, staring at the impossible apparition of a tall Western man and a tiny girl completely swathed in bandages *right beside him*. But he wasn't the Sudanese president, Omar Hasan Ahmad al-Bashir. And he was *supposed* to be.

Hell knew where Bashir was. Maybe he was held up taking a call from one of his wives (he had two). Or maybe he had just shone the vets on. They weren't any more use to him except for PR, after all. Instead, the dude in blue was Major General Abdel Rahim Mohammad Hussein, Sudan's Minister of Defense. He'd been accused of assorted lurid war crimes in Darfur and South Sudan.

He'll do just fine. Tom pointed at him. "Do your thing, honey," he said.

The Mummy never spoke. Probably she only understood a little English. But she went where she was pointed and did what she was told. Which was all Tom needed now.

Beyond the minister was a fat man with a blue scholar's gown and a bunch of bristling grey beard whose extravagant eyebrows were trying to crawl up under his sacklike hat to hide. He was another prize target, the Sunni Imam al-Bushehri of Iraq, the Caliph's advisor to the Sudanese. He promptly hitched up his robe and ran with surprising hippo speed for the Ministry's portico.

Tom grinned and blinked out. He was just as happy to miss the rest of the strangled squawks and *squelching* sounds that had begun to emerge from the Defense Minister.

Up; then back down to the camp in the Sudd.

His next passenger was a small boy, underfed-looking but otherwise a lot more normal than the Mummy. But his eyes were spooky. Tom didn't know his story and wasn't sure he wanted to. And he made sure to keep his parts well clear of his mouth. Just, y'know, *in case.*

He landed on the podium again. It was the one spot in the courtyard the guards were unlikely to spray with frantic fire from their Kalashnikovs, packed as it was with Sudanese brass. The Minister of Defense had shrunk, although still upright and clinging to the podium with sticklike fingers. The Mummy had ballooned *way* out. Fortunately they had learned to wrap her in elastic bandages, loose and with lots of give.

The imam, now—his fat ass and billowing robes were just vanishing through the front door between two astonished-looking guards. Still clutching the boy, Tom flew right through the open doors. Fastball fast, not photon fast. But faster than the guards could react.

The imam's slippers made soft thumping sounds on immaculately polished hardwood floors. Smelling whole *generations* of varnish Tom flashed past the wheezing man. Ten feet ahead of al-Bushehri he set the boy down.

The bearded cleric labored to a stop. "Here," Tom said in English. "There's someone I'd like you to meet. Wanjala, Imam. Imam, Wanjala."

"Go ahead and kill me, *Mokèlé-mbèmbé*," al-Bushehri said. "I die a martyr."

The Iraqi had balls of brass. Tom had to give him that. Not like it mattered. "I'm not going to kill you," Tom said as the skinny boy fixed the huge man with a feral stare, then darted toward him. "The Hunger will."

"A child? What's—*ow*! He bit me!"

"Shit happens, *effendi*. Gotta book." He grabbed Wanjala up by the back of his camouflage T-shirt—fuck knew he didn't want the kid biting *him*—and dashed past the fat man, who was clutching his soft brown hand and staring at the blood welling up from the tooth marks on the back of it.

The guards at the entrance had wheeled to aim their rifles down the echoing hall. They hesitated to shoot for fear of hitting the imam. Tom didn't hesitate. Crimson plasma jetted twice from his palm. The two guards reeled away as torches, falling in flames on the Ministry steps. Both were dead on the instant; but superheated air venting from their lungs made them scream as if they felt the fire that consumed them.

Even before Tom cleared the door he saw that confusion still reigned outside. The Mummy was almost globular now. General Hussein lay beside her like a bundle of brown sticks in a gaudy blue sack. The other Sudanese war pigs stood gaping, too confused and horror-stricken even to run the fuck away. Tom reckoned the girl had at least a few seconds' grace before anyone thought to shoot her. As soon as he got clear sky Tom was gone to orbit, swapping Wanjala for Charlie Abidemi in a single drop and grab.

This time Tom lit on the edge of the Ministry roof overlooking the courtyard o' chaos. He let Charlie drop to the hot tarred gravel beside him, then gave a quick pulse of sunbeam to the grass right in front of the first rank of martyrs, who fell out of their wheelchairs. That was tough luck; he didn't have anything against them. But he didn't hurt them, either.

Fact was, he couldn't afford to fry too many guards: all this rapid hypertripping and flying had about worn him out. He just wanted to make the guys with guns *flinch*.

They did. He turned to the boy he'd just deposited on the roof. "All right, Wrecker, start wrecking. You got two minutes. Have fun."

As a guard lined his sights up on the Mummy his Kalashnikov's receiver exploded in his face. He shrieked. There was no flash, no flame, no fragments larger than dissociated molecules. But the shock of the bonds that held all those molecules together simultaneously bursting—*that* stripped cloth, skin, and muscle from torso and arm and the front of his skull. Howling out of a red mask the guard fell over backward.

Other similar cracks rang out around the courtyard, each followed by fresh screams. Charlie Abidemi's ace only worked on inorganic matter, and had a range of only about fifty feet. But all he had to do was look at something made of stone or metal and snap his fingers, and about two pounds of it went *poof*.

Tom jumped down beside the Mummy. Smiling down at the obsidian eyes that glittered impassively from the stretched-out bandages, and trying his best to ignore the yellow pool around her feet as her kidneys desperately processed the extravagant overload of water she'd sucked into her tissues, he put an arm around her. "No offense, honey," he said, "but you're gonna be a load."

Around the corner of the building, invisible to Tom, past high white walls but clearly not from the roof, something big blew up. Like a Russian-made BTR armored car. Wrecker was definitely living up to his name.

Tom grinned. Was gone.

♦

Saturday, December 5

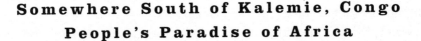

Somewhere South of Kalemie, Congo
People's Paradise of Africa

IT WOULD HAVE BEEN easier to keep to the shore as they moved north, but after the run-in with the PPA gunboat, Wally suggested they stay inland so as not to be seen from the lake. Jerusha agreed. It did hide them from the lake, but since they also had to avoid the roads, it meant slow going as they trudged through a solid wall of vegetation.

Wally took the lead. He tried to hack his way through the thickest bits. It wasn't as easy as it looked in the Tarzan movies. He hadn't realized that swinging a machete took so much technique. The hardest part was turning his wrist to make another slash on the backswing. And every swing had to be coordinated with a step of just the right size, so that he didn't overextend the next swing. A few times he even managed to hit himself on the follow-through.

He made up for the lack of technique with brute strength. His knife hand went numb from the constant *smack* and vibration of mistimed or misplaced swings.

Wally ignored the growing tingle in his hand. Kalemie was so close. Just a few more miles to Lucien, and then everything would be okay.

Hack. Rip. Slash. Rip. Hack. They hadn't been going more than half an hour before his face, chest, and forearms were splattered with little bits and pieces of green vegetable matter.

Here he was, adventuring in the middle of Africa, complete with pith helmet and machete—just like the games he and his brother had played as kids. But it wasn't very fun. In fact, it wasn't fun at all.

TV couldn't convey just how wet, how humid, it was in the jungle. That wasn't counting the rain, which, as Wally had quickly learned, sometimes came down so hard and so fast that it hurt. He wondered how Jerusha put up with it. Nor did the old movies convey the sickly sweet smell of constant decay that enveloped him like a fog. Not to mention how sticky it made a guy, cutting through all these plants.

And in the movies, Tarzan always rescued his friends in the nick of time. But if Wally had learned one thing from his time with the Committee, it was that real life offered no such guarantees. *Rebels and Leopard Men . . . What happened, Lucien? What's going on at that school of yours?*

Wally glanced over his shoulder. Jerusha had fallen back a respectable distance, to avoid the rain of debris. She didn't say anything, but he wondered if it upset her that he was hurting so many plants.

He fell into a meditative rhythm, replaying the lake crossing over and over again. Wally hadn't entirely understood just how far out of his depth he was on this trip until the gunboat showed up. In fact, he wouldn't have made it that far if not for Jerusha.

Wild card powers aside, she at least could talk to folks in French. He couldn't even do that. It hadn't occurred to him that communication might be a problem; all of his foreign travel experiences had been carried out through the Committee, where he and DB were always surrounded either by translators or folks who spoke English. Plus, Lucien had pretty good English for a little guy, so Wally had figured everybody here did.

And then, when the PPA boat had shown up, Wally had done . . . nothing. He'd been no help at all. Jerusha had taken care of the whole thing in a few seconds. Even her aim was great. Almost as good as Kate's.

She didn't need his help at all. But he sure as heck needed her.

New York Public Library
Manhattan, New York

"**YES! OH, YES YES** yes yes yes! Fucking A, *yes!*"

The inhabitants of the reading room raised their collective heads, considered the young man capering wildly at his carrel with amusement or uneasiness or disgust, and then went back to their business. Bugsy nodded apologetically to the guard, and sat back down. "I am too cool," he said under his breath. "I am the man. Oh, yes. Oh, yes. Ain't nobody better than me."

Three huge bound volumes were stacked before him. The first was a volume of ancient arrest records dating from the end of 1970 to the beginning of seventy-one. The second were summaries of small claims court proceedings from the same period. The last, bound in black leather like an ancient grimoire, were the documents for the New York City Family Court for the eighties.

The ruling that Bugsy was poring over, that had inspired his delight, was a custody battle between one Kimberly Ann Cordayne and her estranged husband Mark Meadows. He shifted in his seat, his grin almost ached. He took a legal pad and a pen, marked DO NOT RESHELVE—I'LL BE RIGHT BACK on the top page, and laid it across the opened book. Then, just to be sure, he popped half a dozen wasps free and set up a little perimeter guard on the books before skipping out of the reading room and pulling out his cell.

Ellen wasn't answering, so he called Lohengrin's office number. The man's secretary said he wasn't in, but offered to take a message or drop Bugsy to voice mail. He opted for voice mail.

"Lohengrin!" he said, grinning. "Lohengrin, you great quasi-Nordic war god! You huge example of German technology run amok! I am the coolest guy you know. Seriously. I have plucked the Sunflower out of a haystack. Kimberly Ann Cordayne, aka Sunflower. Arrest record like a small-town phone book starting with petty crap in the late sixties and going up—I shit you not—to suspected membership in the Symbionese Liberation Army. Married some poor schlub named Mark Meadows back in seventy-five, got divorced in eighty-one. Knock-down, drag-out custody battle over a retarded kid goes through eighty-nine. Wound up with the judge ruling both parents unfit and giving the kid to the state. And the girl was named . . . wait for it . . . Sprout!

"So unless there's a bunch of other Special Olympians named Sprout born right around seventy-seven, this is the same one Tom Weathers got his panties in a bunch about last year when he tried to nuke New Orleans. Now I don't know if this Meadows creature is the bio-dad, or Sunflower was bumping uglies with the Radical all through the seventies or what, but I am on the case. *On it.*

"So . . . *yeah.*

"Um. I get anything else, I'll call you back." Bugsy dropped the connection, smiled a little less widely at the cell phone, and went back to the reading room.

The next seven hours brought little information about Sunflower Cordayne, but Mark Meadows turned out to have a fair paper trail. The implication from press clippings and court documents was that he was some kind of ace with the *nom de virus* "Cap'n Trips," but what exactly his alleged powers were was never made explicit. Instead, he ran the Cosmic Pumpkin Head Shop and Organic Deli (renamed the New Dawn Wellness Center sometime in the late eighties) on the border between Jokertown and the Village and hung out with a raft of better-known aces. Jumping Jack Flash. Moonchild. Aquarius.

When Moonchild got herself elected the president of South Vietnam, Meadows got himself named chancellor, only to bite the big burrito when the presidential palace went up in a fireball. And supposedly his daughter Sprout died with him. Right about the time Tom Weathers showed up in East Asia, kicking ass and taking names in a list that was still growing today.

Bugsy closed the books and rubbed his eyes. The windows were all dark now, and the breeze coming in from the east smelled like taxicabs and the Atlantic.

There were a number of good scenarios. Tom Weathers shows up in sixty-nine, hooks up with Sunflower. Maybe he's living underground this whole time, getting crazier and more political right along with Sunflower.

And then . . . and then something happens, and Sunflower hooks up with Cap'n Trips. Someone gets her knocked up—Meadows or Weathers— and things go south. She's locked up in a psycho ward where she might be moldering even now. Meadows gets a long, colorful career as illegal pharmacist, fugitive from the law, minor Southeast Asian politico, and dead guy.

Then the Radical comes in from the cold, with the daughter at his side. Could Tom Weathers really have been the one who killed Moonchild? It was looking more and more plausible.

Back at Ellen's place, the scent of curry and coconut milk filled the air.

Ellen was sitting on the kitchen counter, a fork in one hand, a white take-away box in the other. She raised her eyebrows in query as he dropped onto the couch. "You see the news?" she asked.

"Not the recent stuff," he said. "Something happen?"

"The Radical led a raid in Khartoum. Killed a bunch of Sudanese officials and a few delegates from the Caliphate," Ellen said. "Things are getting worse."

"Well, small victory here. Good old-fashioned legwork paid off," Bugsy said. "It was all in the stacks."

"No database?"

"Nope. Internet doesn't know everything after all."

"Good to know."

"Ellen? Look, I don't know what your plans are tonight, but . . . ?"

She looked at him, smiling softly. He felt a small biological urge. "You want to see her?" she said.

He'd actually intended to ask for Nick. The guy was an ass, but he was a damned good detective, and he'd know better than Bugsy how to track down Sunflower. On the other hand, it looked very much like an offer of sex might be accepted, and Nick and his swamp-soaked hat would be around in the morning.

"Yeah," he said. "If that's okay."

Kalemie, Congo
People's Paradise of Africa

KALEMIE WAS WORSE THAN anything Jerusha had yet witnessed.

The city had been flattened. There were ruins everywhere—a massacre had taken place here, and much of Kalemie had burned. In the pelting rain, there were sodden black timbers marking the place where houses and buildings had stood, with vines and green shoots already poking up through them. Occasionally, they had glimpsed the white curve of rib cages protruding from the rubble.

Worse were the people who had survived: emaciated and starving, lost souls with eyes peering in shock from deep in the hollows of their faces, stretching out arms with the ropes of ligaments and muscles plainly visible, their bellies distended from hunger, fly-infested open wounds on their skin.

The school where Lucien had lived hadn't been spared. Most of the tale they received from Sister Julie, whom they found trying to salvage books in the ruined main building. "They came two weeks ago now," she said in her perfect French as she nibbled at the final crumbs of the energy bar Jerusha had given her. "Leopard Men. They said Kalemie was a haven for the rebels fighting Nshombo, and they would clean it out. They took the children, and then they . . ." She stopped, her lips pressed tightly together. "They did things I will not tell you."

"Ask her about Lucien." Wally pushed the picture of the boy forward in his thick-fingered hand, tapping at it as he placed it under the nun's nose. "Ask her if she knows him."

The nun didn't understand English, but she had taken the photo from Wally's hand. "That's Lucien," she said, and the sorrow deepened in her eyes. She looked at Wally. "You were his sponsor, weren't you? They took him with the others," she told Jerusha in French. "They took them all."

"Where?" Jerusha asked. "Where did they take them?"

The nun shook her head. "Up the river. Into the jungle. To the bad place where they *change* them. Nyunzu, they say." She began to weep then, a wracking sorrow that gathered and broke, as if everything dammed inside her had suddenly broken loose.

Jerusha started toward her but Wally was faster. He took the picture of Lucien from her with surprising gentleness, then he gathered Sister Julie in his great iron arms, holding her. "It's okay now," he told her, and Jerusha could see tears in Wally's eyes. "It's okay."

It wasn't, though. Jerusha suspected that for many of those in Kalemie, it might never be. She left Wally, stepping out into the courtyard that bordered the street. The rain had dwindled to a persistent drizzle. The school was set on a slope, overlooking the curving shore of Kalemie and the rain-swept opening where the many-armed Lukuga River exited the lake on its journey into the heart of the jungle and the headwaters of the Congo River. There were people there, scavenging through the tumbled foundations of what must have once been lovely houses, soaked clothing clinging to skeletal forms. They were pulling at whatever scraps they could find—she saw a woman fling a rock eagerly at a rat, then go scrambling after it in the mud.

Jerusha heard Wally coming up alongside her, his bare feet squelching in the muck. *He'll need S.O.S pads for his feet tonight.* The thought was strange and irreverent. "I'm sorry," she told him. "I know you were hoping to find Lucien."

"I'm still going to find him."

"Wally—"

"I'm going to *find* him," Wally said firmly. "You don't have to come."

"I'll come," she told him. The words came easily, somehow, without thought. Wally said nothing for a time; like her, watching the people picking through the ruins of their city. *He needs you. And you . . . you care about him. You like him.*

"They need food." He slid the backpack from his shoulders and set it down, opening the zipper. "This stuff we brought . . ."

"Wait," Jerusha told him. "There's another way." She reached into her seed belt. There were still orange seeds, and apples, and corn. And—there, heavy and large—the baobabs.

Jerusha took a variety of seeds in her hands. She closed her eyes, feeling them, feeling the vibrancy inside. She let herself become part of them, the gift of the wild card letting her fall inside them. She tossed the seeds wide with a cry: the oranges and apples and corn, and two of the baobabs. They hit the mud, and up sprang the trees, thrusting high and branching out, the seasons passing in the blink of an eye: a momentary flowering and a fall of petals, then the fruit growing and ripening, heavy on the branches. The flurry of cornstalks were higher than Wally's head, and golden. The baobabs especially bloomed, thick, heavy presences on either side of what had once been the road, their trunks ten feet around and the pods hanging full and ripe.

The people around them were shouting and pointing. They sidled forward, shyly, whispering among themselves. "Go on," Jerusha told them. "All of this—it's for you."

They looked at her, at Wally, as if afraid that in the next instant, all of the bounty would disappear as quickly as it had come. Then the closest of them plucked an apple from a branch and bit into its firm skin. Juice sprayed, and she laughed.

And they all came running forward.

♥

Sunday,
December 6

On the Lukuga River, Congo
People's Paradise of Africa

THE RESIDENTS OF KALEMIE gave Wally and Gardener a well-used motorboat and filled the outboard engine with gasoline, but none of them would guide them, not when they realized that the two of them were intending to go to Nyunzu. There were mutterings, curse-wardings, and prayers at that statement.

Jerusha wondered if they shouldn't have taken that as a sign.

The Lukuga River, just north of Kalemie, flowed out from Lake Tanganyika, winding and turning as its slow current slid westward into the jungle. They very quickly left behind the houses that gathered on the hills near the lakeshore, and then there was no sign of humankind at all, only unbroken jungle to either side. Jerusha felt that she was truly caught in Conrad's story, drifting down the river into an emerald-shaded, hidden world where people were more intruders than conquerors.

Away from the lake, the river narrowed to the width of a football field. A few crocodiles lounged on the banks, sunning themselves and lifting great, heavy heads to watch them as they passed. Shrikes, hornbills, herons, and storks brooded in the shallows or flickered in the branches and vanished; strange and unidentifiable animals gurgled and yowled and screeched in the shadows, monkeys chased each other high in the trees, shrieking. The mosquitoes were relentless and hungry . . . though that was a problem only for Jerusha. They left Wally entirely alone.

Once they passed a pod of hippos, steering carefully away from them. The green hummocks of islands blocked their way, and the river would split abruptly into branches where they would need to decide which one to follow—they would choose the larger of two, hoping to remain in the main flow of the river. The dense foliage was made up of trees and plants that Jerusha often didn't recognize; there were no bare-branched baobabs here, not in the jungle, nor the ubiquitous acacias of the savannah. The understory of the forest canopy loomed fifty to a hundred feet up; the floor was dense with ferns, parasitical vines, and other large-leafed plants.

The air was heavy and thick; even without the rain, Jerusha's clothing was soaked within a few hours from sweat and mist and humidity. Wally's skin was almost visibly growing orange rust spots as she watched. "I'd give a thousand bucks to be in an air-conditioned room for two minutes right now," Jerusha commented.

Wally glanced at her quizzically. "I didn't think . . ." he said, then seemed to think better of continuing. His mouth clanged shut with a sound like two cast-iron skillets striking together.

Jerusha cocked her head at him. "I *really* hope that you weren't about to suggest that because I'm black and some distant generations ago my ancestors lived somewhere on this godforsaken continent, you thought I should be perfectly comfortable here."

Wally looked away, down, to the side. He didn't speak.

"I didn't think so." Jerusha pulled her sodden shirt away from her shoulders; it clung stubbornly to her skin. She smiled inwardly at Wally's discomfiture.

Every so often, a village would appear on one bank or the other, and people would stare at them as they drifted past or watch silently from their fishing craft. No one approached them, no one called out to them, no one challenged them. They only stared. Jerusha saw almost no children in those villages, and few young men: this area, from what they could see, was inhabited largely by adult women and old people.

Once, passing one of the larger settlements, they watched as a group of older men dressed in business suits and carrying briefcases walked into an open-walled grass hut as if going to a corporate meeting: the juxtaposition was startling. The men watched them too, and one of them reached into the breast pocket of his suit jacket and spoke rapidly into a cell phone, staring at them as he did so.

"Nuts," Wally muttered. "I don't like that."

Jerusha could only agree.

They continued down the river. Around noon, a swarm of bees crossed the stream just ahead of them, a thick, snarling dark arm that twisted and churned up from yet another river island and wriggled its way toward the nearest bank. Jerusha turned off the boat's motor to avoid running into the swarm. The silence was pleasant as they watched the tail of the swarm vanish into the trees.

"That was a *lot* of bees," Wally said.

Jerusha nodded. "Biggest swarm I've seen. Not even those in Yosemite . . . Umm, what's that?"

Wally's head had also swiveled at the same time. They both heard the throaty whine coming from farther down the river and growing louder. "Another boat," Jerusha whispered. Few of the boats they'd passed so far were motorized; those that were had been, like their own boat, using single-stroke gas engines. This was something far more powerful: low, growling, sinister. "Come on," she said to Wally. "Let's take the boat into the island. . . ."

They used the paddles in the boat to maneuver to the rocks at the edge of the island. Jerusha jumped out of the boat, steadying it as Wally came ashore. Wally grabbed the rope at the bow in one massive hand and dragged the boat fully ashore into the foliage. They both hunkered down near it, watching the river through the fronds. A few minutes later, the roar of the engine increased as a patrol boat similar to the one they'd encountered on the lake rounded the nearest bend. It was moving slowly upriver, and the men aboard . . .

Several of them *weren't* men; they were boys who looked to be somewhere between twelve and fifteen, holding semiautomatic weapons strapped around their necks and wearing uniforms. What chilled the blood in Jerusha's body, though, was the man standing near the boat's cabin: a tall man in a military uniform, dark aviator sunglasses over his eyes, and a leopard-skin fez on his head.

A Leopard Man. Babs had told her about Alicia Nshombo's Leopard Society. So had Finch.

"Down!" she whispered harshly to Wally as the boat slid closer to their island. Wally collapsed like a falling tower, hard and loudly. Jerusha grimaced as she pressed herself down into the weeds and rushes, her hands on her seed belt in case they were spotted. Wally had dropped to the mud and stones of the low island, but Jerusha was afraid that his color would show through. She stripped a seed pod from one of the rushes and cast the seeds around him, pulling up the fronds carefully as a screen between Wally's body and the boat, shaping the plants carefully so that their rustling movement wouldn't be noticed.

The motor roared close by. Jerusha put her head down, one hand on Wally's body and the other at her seed belt, listening for any change in the sound and ready to move. The sound grew, too close, then finally began to recede. She could hear the chattering of the child soldiers on the boat, heard the Leopard Man grunt a command. She lifted her head carefully.

The boat had passed them, continuing on upriver, the Leopard Man and the others scanning the riverbank ahead of them, their backs now to Wally and Jerusha.

They waited until the patrol boat had passed around the next bend and they could no longer hear its motor before they stood up. "I think we just got lucky," Wally said. Jerusha nodded. Wally pushed himself up. "Uh-oh," he said.

"Uh-oh?" Jerusha repeated.

Wally's hand was on the large satellite phone case on his belt. "The phone," he said. "It was underneath me . . ." He reached into the pouch and brought out an antenna trailing wires and shattered plastic. "Cripes, it's kinda broken. I'm really sorry, Jerusha. I shoulda been more careful."

He looked so sad that Jerusha couldn't do more than shake her head. "Nothing we can do about it now. Maybe we can find a landline somewhere in one of the villages, or maybe there'll be a cell tower somewhere. Right now, there are other things for us to worry about."

"There could be more boats," Rusty agreed. "So we have to leave the river now, right?"

"If we stay on the river, we know we'll get to Nyunzu," Jerusha told him. "If we try to go overland, it'll take longer and we could easily get lost, even with our GPS unit. We still have that—it's on *my* belt."

His face sagged at that, and she regretted the comment. *You don't have to be mean to him. He wouldn't have said a thing if you'd lost the GPS.* She smiled belatedly in an attempt to soften the comment; she wasn't certain that it helped.

Wally sighed. He dropped the remnants of the phone back in its pouch.

He scratched at his arm with a fingernail. Orange flakes scattered. Silently, he pushed the boat back into the brown waters of the Lukuga.

Ellen Allworth's Apartment
Manhattan, New York

NICK MOVED DIFFERENTLY THAN Ellen. Where Ellen seemed to view the world from about three degrees back, Nick leaned five degrees forward. Where she was always just a little touched by melancholy, he was all about anger.

Or maybe he wasn't. Maybe he just didn't like Bugsy.

"All right," Nick said into his telephone. "I owe you one."

"Well?" Bugsy said.

Nick hung up the phone, kicked Ellen's legs up to rest on the coffee table, and shrugged. "She was in treatment until the mid-nineties. The big reform movement that shut down all the asylums was the end of that. She was supposed to get treatment through a local clinic, but it never happened."

"So what? She just vanished into the air? Where does that leave me?"

Nick considered Bugsy with silent impatience. In Ellen's spare bedroom/office, the fax machine rang twice. Bugsy looked over his shoulder, and when he looked back, Nick was smiling.

"That," he said, "leaves you on the couch."

Bugsy struggled for a comeback as Nick rose from the couch and walked to the back of the apartment. He even walked like a guy. It was creepy.

Nick's voice came from the back, low and conversational. He laughed twice. Bugsy looked at the room. It still smelled of old curry. The earring was in the bedroom, laid gently by the book Ellen was reading before she fell asleep. He rose to his feet, paced a little, then sat down and turned on the television.

CNN was all about New Orleans. The visuals were astounding. Thousands of bright, soft-looking bubbles rising through the air, floating in the Gulf Coast breeze. Now and then, a detonation would set off a chain reaction, bright cascades of light that made the most glorious fireworks look tame. The news anchor was talking about the airspace over the city being shut down, about the travelers stuck in the city, about the cost and inconvenience. The Amazing Bubbles was coming back to life, and Bugsy found himself both surprised and delighted. All that energy floating in the Louisiana sky had once been a nuclear fireball, and now it was coming out slowly, over hours and days, as something beautiful. Mardi Gras in December. The biggest, loudest, least convenient celebration ever of the simple fact that New Orleans still lived.

He forgot the business of the Sudd and the Caliphate and angled back toward the office to get Ellen. Nick was in her chair, leaning forward, telephone handset pressed between shoulder and ear. Bugsy, his mind still on the news channel, was almost surprised to see him.

". . . with the Internal Revenue Service," he said. "I'm trying to get in touch with Kimberly Ann Goodwin. Or possibly Meadows or Cordayne, the records aren't clear, but I have her social . . . oh, did she? Well, that makes sense. Do you have that? Of course."

Nick looked up. "Declared bankruptcy and changed her name five years ago," he said. "I'm getting the new . . . Hello? Yes, that's right. Thank you." Nick patted the desk, then looked up at Bugsy, miming the act of writing. Bugsy pulled a notepad and pen from the storage closet and handed them over. "All right. Great. Yeah, and do you have a good contact number for her?" Nick went silent. "You're kidding," he said. He shook his head and wrote something on the paper. "Okay. That's great. You have one, too."

Maybe Nick was trying not to look smug as he passed the notepad back. If so, it wasn't his best effort. Bugsy took the pad. Kimberly Joy Christopher, it said. Then a phone number with a 541 area code, and block letters: RISEN SAVIOR SPIRITUAL CENTER.

"She's found Jesus," Nick said. "Apparently, they're living together."

"You rock," Bugsy said, stuffing the paper into his pocket. "But come look at the news. You've got to see this."

Kongoville, Congo
People's Paradise of Africa

"WE ARE A GREAT people. A great people," the taxi driver said in rapid-fire French. "Africa held many great kingdoms long before the whites came out of their caves."

The traffic in Kongoville was manic, with three and four lanes being formed by jostling cars on a two-lane road. Cranes loomed over the city like contemplative dinosaurs. There were vast piles of rubble where shanties and older buildings had been razed in preparation for another The People—The People's Theater, The People's Hall of Justice, The People's department store, laundrette . . .

Even in early December the air-conditioning in the car was blowing full blast. Add that to the music pouring from the radio and the driver's commentary, and it was hard for Noel to gather his thoughts for his upcoming meeting with President-for-Life Dr. Nshombo. Noel wore a perfectly tailored Italian suit, an opal and diamond ring on his little finger. He didn't want Etienne Pelletier to seem *too* upscale. He hid the avatar's golden eyes behind dark glasses.

Noel found the taxi driver's assertion of lost African kingdoms both understandable and sad. He had spent a lot of time in the Middle East, and the populace there shared the same sense of racial, national, and geographic pride, completely at odds with their actual situations. In the Middle East you heard how Baghdad had streetlights when Europe was mired in the Dark Ages. In Africa it was the lost kingdoms.

They were all the dreams of conquered and economically depressed people reacting against Western might. Noel contemplated how Prince Siraj's three-hundred-dollar-a-barrel oil had almost brought Europe and America to their knees, and how the PPA's conquests in Africa were denying the West vital resources. *Payback's a bitch*, he thought.

A large stone structure caught his attention. That was new since his last visit to Kongoville. Whatever it was it shared that Albert Speer style of architecture that was favored by the good Doctor. "What's that?" Noel pointed.

The driver turned down the radio, and said quietly and respectfully, "That is the tomb of Our Lady of Pain."

Noel pulled back a cuff and glanced at his watch. He had time. "I would like to see that."

The driver pulled over and parked. Noel walked up the stone steps. They had already begun to wear. There must have been literally thousands of people through the door, he thought.

The single room was high and cavernous. High above him Noel heard the squeaking of bats that turned the tomb into a cave. The center of the room was lit by a powerful spotlight that shone down on a crystal bier. Inside lay a beautiful young woman. The embalming job had been exquisite. Her burnished black skin seemed soft and pliable, no one had forced a false smile onto her mouth, and the way her lashes brushed at her cheeks gave the impression she was only sleeping. Around her neck hung an enormous gold medal suspended by a purple velvet ribbon.

For a moment Noel reflected on this desperate need of dictatorships to worship their dead. *Lenin, Mao, this child. The English never did such a thing. No one kept Victoria on display. Even the Americans aren't so crass.*

"A people's hero," the driver murmured.

"What did she do?" Noel asked.

"She took our pain into herself and healed us." The man bowed his head.

Jackson Square
New Orleans, Louisiana

AND ON DAY FIVE, Michelle rested.

She'd been able to stand up yesterday. It felt weird and she was a little wobbly, but it wasn't impossible.

Today she was almost as thin as she'd been when she was modeling. There was still energy in her. She felt heavier, even though she looked skinny. That seemed to be the legacy of what had happened. She was heavier all the time now. With no mirror, she couldn't tell how she looked, but the jeans and T-shirt Juliet had bought for her felt like they fit.

The temple seemed sad. The flowers had dried up and Juliet and Joey had thrown them out. The girls were waiting outside for her in the soft drizzle.

Michelle knew what she had to do next.

There was a loud murmur outside. If she hadn't known better, she would have thought it was the faithful. But they had evaporated during the rain of bubbles. What awaited her outside were reporters.

Michelle let a tiny bubble form on the tip of her finger. It was hard and bright and she shot it to the night sky. It burst high above the temple—a small pop that no one would notice. Then she turned and walked out the door.

On the Lukuga River, Congo
People's Paradise of Africa

THEY WENDED THEIR WAY downriver. Every bend in the river took Wally a little closer to Nyunzu. And, he hoped, Lucien.

Now he understood what Lucien had been referring to in his last letter, about the soldiers who hurt Sister Julie. But it had been worse than he'd feared. Lucien's village, Kalemie . . . it was one of the worst things he'd ever seen, even counting all the stuff he saw and did for the Committee. He hated himself for waiting so long before he came to Africa. "Jerusha?"

"Yeah?"

"What do you think she meant, back in Kalemie? The nun, I mean. Sister Julie."

"Meant about what?"

"About them taking the kids. About changing them."

Jerusha was quiet for a long time. The boat bobbed and swayed when he glanced over his shoulder, looking for hippos and crocs. Up front, Jerusha kept one hand on the wheel and both eyes on the river, watching for the same dangers. Finally, she said, "I don't know, Wally. I wish I did."

The *putt-putt-putt* sound of their little motor echoed up and down the river, bouncing between the dense jungle to either side. Water gurgled quietly beneath the prow, where their boat gently peeled back the murky waters of the Lukuga. Not like the patrol boats. Those things cut through the water like a knife.

"That patrol boat had kids on it. Kids with guns." It reminded him of Iraq. *Kids . . . I don't want to fight kids.*

"Yeah," said Jerusha. "It did." He didn't need to look at her to know how she felt. She was sad. Wally was getting to know her moods, the nuances of her emotions, just from the tone of her voice. Somehow that felt like a small bright spot in what was otherwise turning into a pretty bad deal all around.

"Do you think that's what she meant? Turning the kids into soldiers? Like maybe they're gonna do that to Lucien?"

"I don't . . . Ouch." She slapped at her neck, then flicked a squashed bug into the river. The sharp *slap* ricocheted down the river. "I'm afraid it might, Wally."

"Me, too. I figure Nyunzu must be where they're doing it. It's where they've got Lucien at. But he'll be okay once we get there. They all will, all those kids."

"I hope you're right."

Wally fell silent, thinking. The river forked again. As always, Jerusha took the wider branch. A small island, just a sliver of brush and trees, separated them from the other branch. Wally could see the water on the other side. All around them, the jungle chattered, shrieked, and sang with life. "I'm sorry about what I said earlier. Or, I mean, you know, what I almost said."

She was silent again. This time, he knew, she was cocking an eyebrow at him. An expression halfway between bemusement and irritation. He could picture it.

"Sometimes I say dumb stuff. But I don't mean anything by it, okay?" As soon as the words came out, Wally realized this was a dumb thing to say, too. It could give her the wrong idea. Then she'd hate him, and he really, *really* didn't want Jerusha to hate him. They were partners now, and had to work together. He needed her help. But that wasn't all of it. He just . . . wanted Jerusha to like him.

"I mean, I don't always say dumb stuff. Sometimes people think . . . aw, heck. Remember that thing with me and Stuntman? Back when we were all on TV?"

Guardedly: "Yyyyyeeeeeessss."

"I didn't say that stuff."

Jerusha laughed. Not a real gut-busting laugh, but it was still the most he'd heard her laugh since they started traveling together. "I know, Wally. Everybody knows it."

Wally sighed. That was a small relief. "Well, okay. That's good. I just wanted to . . ."

He trailed off again as they passed the last bit of island. The two branches of the river rejoined behind them. Neat. It reminded him of canoe camping trips, back home.

Wally turned around just in time to see the boy on the prow of the hidden patrol boat leveling his rifle. "*Get down!*" he yelled. Jerusha must have seen his expression, because she was out of the pilot's chair and diving under the gunwale almost before the warning passed his lips.

Tat-tat-tat. Tat-ping-tat. The boy squeezed off two bursts. One round *cracked* off Wally's bicep and sent up a white spray from the river. Another shattered the windscreen. "Jerusha?"

"I'm okay," she said. "I—"

But then Wally couldn't hear anything except the howl of a motor. A big motor. Jerusha reached up from her hiding spot to wrench the wheel, aiming for the riverbank.

The Leopard Man yelled something. The patrol boat roared out of its hiding spot. It streaked like an arrow toward where they would make land. More bullets whizzed past them. Wally stood. Their boat rocked precariously, but he tried his best to shield Jerusha.

Ping-ping-ping. Hailstones falling on a tin roof.

Twenty feet to shore. Ten feet.

"Jerusha, stay behind me!"

At the last second, she wrenched the wheel again and killed the motor. They swung around, keeping Wally between her and the patrol boat as they bumped up against the roots of a massive mahogany tree leaning out over the water.

Pingpingpingpingpingping.

He crossed the boat in one stride, bullets pattering harmlessly against his back, and grabbed Jerusha under the arms. "Hold on," he said. And then, as gently as he could, he hurled her into the jungle.

It nearly capsized the boat. Water slopped over the gunwales. A *crash* and an *oof!* emanated from somewhere in the brush. Wally spun to face their attackers, hoping to heck that Jerusha wasn't hurt.

The Leopard Man shouted another order. The soldier at the wheel—the only other adult on the patrol boat—gunned the engine, wedging them between Wally and the shore. Two kids stood up front, along with the Leopard Man. The driver was in the middle; another kid stood in the stern.

Wally jumped onto the prow of the other boat, to keep them from going after Jerusha. The Leopard Man scrambled backward, out of the reach of Wally's arms, yelling another order. All three kids (*they're just kids!*) opened up with their rifles. All Wally could think about through the cacophony of gunfire was putting an end to this before a deadly ricochet killed one of the kids, just like what had happened to poor King Cobalt back in Egypt.

Wally called up his wild card power and lunged forward, reaching for a rifle with both hands. The kids tried to scoot out of reach. One barrel crumpled in his fist. The second rifle he didn't quite manage to grab, but he grazed it with a finger, which was all he needed to command the iron inside the gun to disintegrate. It crumbled.

The third kid stopped firing, but the driver pulled his sidearm and extended his arm toward Wally's head.

Cripes! Don't you guys pay any attention? You could shoot one of these kids! Wally pushed the two disarmed boys into the river. It wasn't entirely safe there, but it was a lot safer than standing next to Wally while people shot at him. Then he spun, grabbed the gun in the driver's outstretched hand, and squeezed.

The driver screamed. Wally flipped him halfway across the river.

The third boy darted past him and jumped to shore, followed closely by the Leopard Man.

"Hey! Leave her alone!" Wally charged after them.

The kid hadn't gone a dozen yards when the earth under his feet erupted in a mass of vines. They enveloped him in seconds. *Right on, Jerusha!*

The Leopard Man skidded to a halt. He spun to face Wally, and melted.

No, he didn't melt. But his body flowed like soft wax, becoming low and sleek while the yellow-and-black spotted pattern on his fez oozed down, covering his body with fur.

The big cat snarled, revealing a mouthful of fangs. Muscles rippled under the fur with deadly grace as it prowled back and forth, growling. Then, like a spring uncoiling, it leapt. Fangs clicked against Wally's throat. Inch-long claws scrabbled ineffectually at his shoulders and chest. The leopard fell off him and collected itself for another try.

"Aw, come on, fella. Give it a rest, would ya?"

The leopard lunged again. Wally caught it in midair with a punch to the nose. He heard a *crack*. The big cat dropped to the earth like a sack of potatoes. It wobbled to its feet, and crawled off into the jungle, mewling.

Wally called into the jungle. "Jerusha? You okay?"

Please, please, please . . .

"I'm okay." She emerged from behind a dense screen of foliage, rubbing her armpits. "Just a little bruised."

"Oh, cripes, did I hurt you? I'm real sorry."

Jerusha shook her head. "Don't sweat it. I'm pretty sure they didn't expect you to fling me into the jungle like that." The corners of her mouth twisted into a wry half smile. "Neither did I." She touched his arm. "It was good thinking, Wally. But next time, try to give me some warning, okay?"

Wally blushed. "Okay."

She nodded toward the rustling kudzu vines where the kid from the patrol boat struggled to free himself. "Well. Let's see what he has to say, huh?"

♣

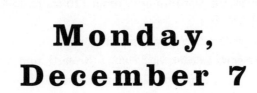

Monday, December 7

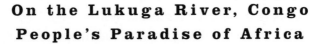

On the Lukuga River, Congo
People's Paradise of Africa

NYUNZU. NYUNZU. NYUNZU.

Wally rapped his fingers on the gunwale, wishing their boat had a larger engine, the river a stronger current. He'd already pushed the throttle as far as it could go. *Crack.* Another hairline fracture appeared in the sun-rotted wood under his hand. He stopped tapping. But he couldn't contain the anxiety; his leg bounced up and down, almost of its own accord. Soon the boat bobbed in time with the rhythm of his impatience.

"Hey, Wally." Jerusha turned. "You're gonna give me seasickness. River sickness." Her smile didn't touch her eyes. She was worried, too.

"Sorry." Wally directed his attention to the river, turning the wheel slightly to keep them in the center of a mild bend. Jerusha went back to watching for surprises: patrol boats, submerged logs, hippos, crocodiles . . .

Lucien was in Nyunzu. He had to be. That's where the PPA was taking all the children. That's what the kid they'd caught (whom *Jerusha* had caught) had said, more or less.

To change them. To turn them into soldiers. Little kids, like Lucien, given guns and taught to kill.

In the end, Jerusha had disarmed the kid she'd caught while Wally fished the other two up from the riverbank. Then they loaded up the patrol boat with a couple days' worth of food and let them go. What else could they do? They were just kids.

Motoring around the bend, they passed a crocodile sunning itself on a sandbar. Wally tensed. But the giant reptile didn't react to their presence. It just lay there with its mouth open and its eyes closed. Jerusha said that was how they sweated—they panted, like dogs. And that a logy croc was often a well-fed croc.

Half an hour later, they passed another croc. And another. "Huh." Jerusha dug out her guidebook. She flipped through it. Wally watched how the breeze from the pages lifted stray hairs from her sweat-glistened fore-head. A stirring sight, but somehow comforting, too.

"Yeah, that's what I remembered." She tapped the page with her finger. "African crocodiles don't tend to congregate. Except," she added, with another tap to the page, "during mating season, or if there's food to be found. They'll travel miles if there's a good carcass to eat."

Wally watched the crocodiles warily. He kept glancing at the sandbar until it passed out of sight around another bend. So did Jerusha.

"Lots of crocs," said Wally.

"Lots of *well-fed* crocs," said Jerusha.

"Tarzan wrestled with a crocodile once. *Tarzan and His Mate.* Johnny Weissmuller and Maureen O'Sullivan."

"That was a movie."

"Yeah, but it was pretty neat. He even—"

"Wally, look out!" Jerusha dropped the book and jumped to her feet, pointing at something in the river.

Wally spun the wheel; the engine died. *Please, not a hippopotamus.* Finch had warned them about the hippos: "Roit nasty buggers. They'll flip your boat and bite your head off just for spite. Even yours, mate," he'd said, jab-bing his horn in Wally's direction.

Behind him, Jerusha braced for impact. Wally clenched his eyes shut and hunched his shoulders.

Bump. Something brushed gently against the boat.

Wally opened one eye, then the other. They were still afloat. He released the breath he'd been holding. He looked at Jerusha.

She shrugged. "I saw something floating low in the water. I couldn't tell what it was. I thought it might have been a log, or an animal."

Wally could see it now, too, just a couple of feet off the side of the boat.

They must have nudged it when he turned the boat broadside. Weird. It was a piece of pale driftwood, draped in tatters of cloth.

No, not cloth. Clothes. A sun-bleached pair of cargo pants.

On a body.

United Nations
Manhattan, New York

THE ELEVATOR DOORS SNICKED open. Lohengrin stepped out. Out of his shimmering white armor he looked like a regular guy. Big and blond and good-looking, but chunkier than she remembered. *Too much time behind a desk.*

"Bubbles. It has been too long." His accent was still heavy. He pulled her into a hug, then kissed her on the cheek. "Who is this?"

Michelle introduced Joey and Juliet. Lohengrin nodded as he shook Joey's hand. "I remember this one. You raise the dead. Hoodoo Mama, *ja?*"

"Yeah. And I remember how y'all didn't like my background. Prissy motherfuckers."

Klaus reddened. "Ah, you are so young, you do not understand. The world watches us, all the time. The Committee must be above reproach."

"I'm not that much younger than you, asshat," Joey snapped. "Reproach my ass. Don't you shine me on."

"Joey, please." Michelle wanted to throttle the brat. The last thing she needed was Hoodoo Mama screwing things up with the Committee. "I'm sorry, Klaus." Michelle slipped her arm into his and drew him away.

Lohengrin shrugged. "Things are more complicated than before, Bubbles. Jayewardene does what he can, but we must be so careful. He is waiting for you upstairs. Come."

The hallway leading to Secretary-General Jayewardene's office was lined with photographs of Committee members. Michelle smiled as she passed Jonathan Hive, Rustbelt, and Gardener, but instead of the shots she remembered of Curveball, Drummer Boy, John Fortune, and Holy Roller, there were photos of people she didn't know. It made her uncomfortable. She'd spent a lot of time walking these halls. *A year,* she thought. Still, it wasn't right that so many of her friends were gone.

Lohengrin opened the door to Jayewardene's office and then followed the girls inside.

"Michelle, my dear, it's good to see you looking so well." G. C. Jayewardene rose from his chair, came around the desk, and crossed the room to embrace her. One of the perks of his position was having the largest office in the UN building. A wall of windows faced the East River. There was enough room for a sitting area with a couple of couches and an area for Jayewardene's desk and several sleek, modern leather chairs. It was larger than most apartments on the Lower East Side.

Jayewardene was a small man, but it never seemed to bother him that Michelle towered over him. That was one of the many reasons that she'd grown so fond of him. He also had an old-fashioned, courtly side to him that she liked.

"I see you've brought Miss Summers and Miss Hebert," he said. Both girls looked surprised. And, Michelle noted, he even pronounced Joey's name right. "How are you feeling, my dear?" Jayewardene asked as he walked back to his chair.

Michelle smiled at him. "I'm certain you already know, Mr. Jayewardene. Given what happened, I'm surprisingly well."

"You know that we want you to come back to duty as soon as possible."

The door to Jayewardene's office opened. A plump, dark-haired woman came into the room carrying a folder. She was pretty enough, but something in the way she carried herself made Michelle suspect she didn't feel pretty all of the time. "Oh, Mr. Jayewardene," she said. "I didn't realize you had guests. . . ."

Jayewardene rose from his chair. "These are old friends of mine, Barbara. Have you met? This is Miss Pond, Miss Summers, and Miss Hebert. Miss Barbara Baden."

"We've met."

Michelle remembered that Barbara had only recently joined the Committee. Just before New Orleans. Her ace name was the Translator, but some called her Babel. "It's nice to see you again, Barbara," Michelle said.

Lohengrin stepped forward. "Babs is our vice chairman now, Michelle. You must know that John left us after New Orleans . . . after he lost his powers." From the way his voice softened when he said her name, Michelle had the sneaking suspicion that there was more than translating going on between Klaus and Babel.

"Are you coming back to the Committee?" Barbara asked. "We could certainly use an ace of your power."

Michelle stuck her hands in her pockets. "I don't know. I've only been awake for a week." She turned back toward Jayewardene. "I was just about to tell the secretary-general about these dreams I've been having."

"Dreams?" Babel looked incredulous.

Michelle felt another shot of annoyance. This . . . *translator* was starting to piss her off.

"Yes, dreams. They brought me out of my coma. They weren't really dreams. They were things that had really happened to this little girl. She needs me to help her."

"Telepathy?" mused Jayewardene. "It would not surprise me that such a thing had happened. Tell us of this child."

Michelle stepped back so she could see their faces. "She's in a pit of dead bodies. And she's a little girl—maybe six or seven. It's horrible."

Babel's expression was one of complete disbelief.

Michelle ignored her. "I owe this little girl. I need to find her."

Jayewardene got up and walked to one of the tall windows overlooking the harbor. "Do you have any idea where this pit is?"

"Not exactly," Michelle said, "but I think I have it narrowed down." She just wanted him to give her the damn Committee. "There were soldiers wearing uniforms and these leopard-skin fezzes. I recognized the uniforms from our training. They were Congolese. I confess, the fezzes confuse me, but it may have been part of Adesina's trauma. She's obsessed with leopards in her dreams."

"Yes," he said softly. "Leopards."

"In her dreams, she's being captured by these soldiers and taken away from her home. It's almost like she's calling me—pulling me to her."

Jayewardene turned back from the window. "Dreams can be a powerful thing, Michelle. If you are certain that you must find her, then I suppose you must go to the Congo."

Barbara blinked in surprise.

"Sir," she said. "The Amazing Bubbles is one of the best-known and best-loved aces in the world right now. After New Orleans, she's almost a legend. If she sets foot in the People's Paradise, the Radical will . . . Klaus, *talk* to her."

Lohengrin looked very unhappy. "Babs, if this child is in danger . . . what is the Committee for, if not for things like that?"

Babel threw her hands up in dismay. "She can't just go waltzing around in the PPA. Not with Rustbelt and Gardener already in Africa, doing God knows what. This could provoke Weathers to a fresh round of atrocities."

Michelle flinched when Babs said Weathers's name. It had been a long time since anyone had scared her, but Weathers had done his best to nuke New Orleans.

All she could think about was the fire running through her veins. "Mr. Jayewardene," she said. "I know it sounds stupid, but Adesina is stuck there in a pit filled with corpses. I'm going to her. With the Committee's help or without it."

"I cannot give you the Committee." Jayewardene sounded sad. "You must do what you must do, but Barbara is correct. The Nshombos keep a careful watch on who crosses their borders. These men in the leopard-skin hats that you have seen in your dream are Alicia Nshombo's secret police, the Leopard Society. They would arrest you as soon as you entered the country."

They could try, Michelle thought. She glanced at Joey and Juliet. Neither of them looked very happy. Joey was fidgeting in her chair as if she had sand in her underwear.

"Fuck it," Joey blurted out. "Are you cocksuckers deaf, or what? Didn't you hear what she said? The little fucker in her dreams is just a *kid*!"

Dr. Nshombo's Yacht
Kongoville, Congo
People's Paradise of Africa

THE RECEPTION WAS ON the Nshombo yacht. Supposedly it was "the people's yacht," but the burly Leopard Men in their leopard-skin fezzes guarded the gangway, making damn sure none of the people actually came aboard. The word in the streets was that Alicia's crack troops could actually turn into leopards, but how much of that was clever manipulation and how much was truth Noel had no way to know.

As the fiberglass gangway bowed slightly beneath his foot, Noel realized he had better prepare for the masquerade. He was entering the lion . . . leopard's . . . den, and he needed to concentrate. Monsieur Pelletier presented his invitation to a grim-faced guard, and was waved aboard.

The hip beat of a jazz quartet, the chink of ice in glasses, and the roar of conversation led him to the party. He touched his dark glasses to reassure himself that Etienne's golden eyes were obscured. He also checked his watch to verify exactly how long until sundown. He had one hour, seventeen minutes, and forty-two seconds.

Dr. Nshombo stood by the rail discussing Marxist theory with a pair of engineers from Kenya. The two men were looking longingly toward the bar and the attractive young women who wove through the crowds offering canapés and champagne off silver trays. Noel extended his hand. "Ah, Monsieur President, so kind to include me. The yacht, so *ravissant*, and the river, like a mighty heart through your great nation," he said in French. Actually he thought the Congo smelled like an open sewer as vegetation, human waste, and probably bodies provided by the ever-helpful secret police rotted in the dark waters.

The engineers made a quick and tactical retreat. Noel joined Dr. Nshombo at the rail. The spare little man with his expressionless ebony face snapped his fingers, and one of the servers hurried over. Noel accepted a flute of champagne. Nshombo waved her off—he neither smoked nor drank. Personally Noel had always preferred the whoring, boozing, gambling variety of dictator over the abstemious, self-righteous variety. The hedonists were easier to bring down.

"Monsieur Pelletier, have you located a site for your factory?" Dr. Nshombo asked.

"Not yet, sir, but I've seen several promising locations."

"You will find my people are good workers. They will build excellent cars."

"And be able to afford them with the wages they'll earn," Noel said.

He realized his error the instant the words left his lips as Nshombo's face closed into a tight, hard mask. "Are you suggesting my people do not earn a decent wage without the actions of a white man?"

"No—"

Nshombo ran over the start of Noel's apology. "Before I founded the People's Paradise of Africa, that would have been the case. Corrupt leaders working with Western flacks sucked away the fruits of their labor, but I changed that. Through me flows the wealth of a continent, and it all goes into the hands of my people."

"Yes, yes, quite. And that was what I meant to imply, but was, alas, inartful. It is due to your prescience that you are allowing me to found this Peugeot factory. Your people will benefit from your wisdom and hard work."

"Dear, Mr. Pelletier, please ignore my brother." Alicia Nshombo flowed around him like the storm bands of a hurricane. First there was the overpowering scent of her gardenia perfume, then the salty, musky scent of a heavy woman exerting herself in the stifling Congo heat. Next the folds of her brightly colored, floral print robe/muumuu/tent tangled at his legs and torso, and finally her heavy, plump arms wrapped around Noel's shoulders. "He's still thinking it's the old days when we were not treated with respect, when the Western countries viewed us as just another set of black oppressors. You are one of the first white businessmen to see the potential in the PPA."

Noel gave Alicia a small bow, and bestowed a Gallic kiss on the back of her hand. "I'm sure I'm only the first of many. Your hospitality and willingness to assist in my little venture has been overwhelming."

Noel straightened and found himself almost mesmerized by the flat stares of the three security officers who surrounded her. He considered the motorized patrols that raced through the streets near the river, the snipers positioned on the roofs of surrounding buildings, and decided that the PPA armed forces offered a great opportunity for employment and promotion.

Alicia gave him a hug that left him breathless. "You French, always so gracious. Now, please, come and meet a few more of our illustrious citizens."

Noel followed, feeling like a wood chip caught in the wake of a carrier. As they moved across the polished oak deck Alicia continued. "In a few weeks these decks will be draped with beautiful girls. I arranged with *Jalouse* for them to hold the swimsuit shoot in Kongoville aboard our yacht. You should time your return trip to coincide with that." She gave him a wink, then tucked his arm through hers and pressed it against her side. "Though why you men prefer these skinny rails . . . African men are wiser. They like a woman of substance." She leered at him.

Noel suppressed a shudder and gave her a Gallic pinch on the tips of her fingers. Alicia giggled, her breasts jiggled, and she patted Noel on the crotch. He tried to will a reaction, but even he wasn't that good an actor.

She led him up a short flight of stairs and onto a small upper deck. "So nice to watch the sunset from up here," she crooned.

"Alas, madam, I need to return to the hotel to take part in a conference call with some American backers. The Americans have no taste, but a vast amount of money."

Alicia giggled again, an incongruous sound from so large a woman.

"Alicia, you bawdy broad, there you are." The words were delivered with a boyish lilt. Noel felt his genitals trying to retreat deeper into his belly.

He turned to find Tom Weathers bounding up the stairs. He had the face of an aging model. Handsome, but his expression was too young for the wrinkles, as if he hadn't realized that time marches on, and even the golden youth must grow up.

A few steps behind him walked a middle-aged but still beautiful Chinese woman. When Noel had last seen Sun Hei-lian her face had been shiny with Lilith's juices, as Sun had eaten pussy while Tom Weathers boned her from behind. *The things I did for crown and king.* Noel knew from her dossier in the files of the Silver Helix that she was a Chinese agent, very smart and very deadly. Today she seemed oddly subdued, her head bent, eyes on the polished wood deck. Occasionally she glanced up at Tom's back, and her expression was an odd combination of fear, frustration, and grief.

So, Noel thought, *maybe this isn't just an agent running a useful asset. She might actually care for Weathers. If he cared for her she might offer a decent substitute for Sprout. Or she's an agent who knows her asset has gone rogue, and she's trying to decide how to liquidate him. Either way she might prove useful.*

Noel's attention was so tightly focused on Sun Hei-lian that he didn't notice the arc of Alicia's arms as she threw them wide to accept Weathers's embrace. One of her heavy bracelets caught Noel's sunglasses and swept them from his face. Noel spun away, covered his eyes, and bent to snatch them up.

"Oh, Monsieur Pelletier, I'm so sorry," Alicia cooed.

"Hey, man, let me help you."

Noel seized the glasses just before Weathers did, and slammed them back over his eyes. *Had he seen? Did he see? Oh, Niobe, I'm sorry.* "Cataracts," he muttered, his voice breathless with fear. "I'm trying to avoid surgery."

Suspicion melted away into concern, though Noel read it as calculated as his own performances. "Oh, man, I'm sorry. That sucks. Aren't you a little young?"

"A genetic propensity. It blinded my father," Noel lied glibly.

"Wow, sucks," Weathers repeated.

"Monsieur Pelletier, I would like to introduce our dear Tom, and his lovely lady Sun Hei-lian."

"So pleased to meet you." They shook hands, and Tom played boy games with an overly strong handshake. Noel kept his deliberately weak, quickly pulled his hand away, and gave it a surreptitious shake . . . though not *too* surreptitious. Weathers noticed, grinned, and dismissed him as a weakling, and therefore not worthy of attention. Noel turned his attention to Sun, and gave her one of Monsieur Pelletier's flourishing greetings. She didn't respond to it half as well as Alicia.

Noel decided that engaging in small talk with Tom Weathers and a Chinese agent known for her brains and deadly abilities didn't make a lot of sense. "My champagne is empty," he said. "I'll leave you all to talk."

And he hurried away down the stairs, only to stop halfway down. He kept walking in place as he tried to overhear.

A shadow fell across the hatch. Someone was coming.

It was too late to move farther down the stairs. Noel set aside his glass, and bent quickly to tie his shoe. He always wore wing tips for just this reason. Retying a shoe was always an excuse for loitering.

Sun appeared at the top of the steps and stared down at him. Noel straightened, recovered his glass, smiled, nodded at her, and continued his descent.

Manhattan, New York

THEY WERE ALL QUIET on the way back to the apartment.

They came out from the subway at Fourteenth Street, the closest stop to Michelle's apartment. The first snow of winter was falling in thick, wet, white flakes. Most of the people exiting the subway turned up their collars against the cold, hunching down in their coats.

"Snow," Joey said in an awed voice Michelle had never heard before. She held out her hand and stared at the flakes hitting her palm. "Cool. I've never seen snow before." Her face was full of wonder.

Michelle just wanted to get inside and figure out what to do next. But Juliet took her hand and that made her stop walking.

And so Michelle and Joey and Juliet stood on the sidewalk and let the snow fall on them until they were damp and cold.

♠

Tuesday,
December 8

On the Lukuga River, Congo
People's Paradise of Africa

THE BODIES IN THE river were becoming more numerous; they'd passed three of them in just the last hour, and one of the floating corpses was that of a child. Wally had stared at the bloated form, at the distorted face, trying to see if it might be Lucien. Jerusha could feel his silent anguish, and she could do nothing more than put a hand on his shoulder. "It's not him, Wally. It's not."

The worry and fear on his face was a torment to her. She found tears gathering in her own eyes as she saw the anguish in Wally's face. She hugged him, wishing there were something she could say that would comfort him, wanting to be able to reassure him that it would be all right in the end.

But she didn't believe that. She couldn't believe that. They needed help; they needed it quickly. If the babbling of the frightened child soldier they'd captured was even halfway true, then the Committee *had* to know. Now.

Jerusha hardly believed it herself: a prison where hundreds of children had been injected with the wild card virus, where hundreds more had already died in order to produce two or three aces for the PPA. The thought sickened and infuriated her. She wanted to see the place razed and burned, wanted to see the Nshombos and Tom Weathers tried and executed for what they were doing here. And Wally . . .

Poor Wally. She didn't know what to say to him. He glared downriver as if his gaze alone could drive them toward Nyunzu and his precious Lucien. All she could do was stay close to him, to stroke his shoulders, to whisper ineffective comforts that yes, they would still find Lucien alive. They would . . .

Their satellite phone was useless, and her cell didn't work—no bars, no service—and the battery was nearly dead to boot. Jerusha sighed and thrust the phone back into one of the pockets of her cargo pants. Squinting into the sunlight, she could see a village set in the hollow of the next bend.

Wally crowded into the tiny cabin of the craft as they passed the village, and Jerusha avoided looking at the people staring as they motored past, facing forward as if confident and unworried about their presence on the river.

As soon as the bend put the village out of sight, she extended a hand to help Wally clamber out again. "Put us in here, Wally," Jerusha said. "We really need to find a way to tell Lohengrin what's going on down here. Maybe there's a landline in that village I can use."

Wally's face stiffened. "That's too dangerous."

The roiling in her stomach agreed with him. "I don't see another choice. Some of these people may not like the Nshombos any more than we do; they're scared, but they might be willing to let me make a phone call."

"And what if there's a PPA fella there? It would only take one of them."

She'd been thinking the same, but she tried to shrug as nonchalantly as she could. "It's a chance we gotta take. I'm not sure we can do this alone, Wally. There's something awful going on here, something big—something Lucien looks to be caught up in."

Wally vented a breath through his nostrils. The boat puttered toward the bank and Jerusha cut the engine; Wally jumped out, knee-deep in the water, to drag the boat out of the river into the cover of leaves.

Jerusha gave him another hug. "Be right back," she said.

"I'm going with you."

She shook her head. "I'm black, remember?" she said with a brief flash of a smile. "Wally, it's one thing if a woman who looks mostly like them shows up in the village. I'm not visibly an ace and not visibly threatening. It's another thing entirely if a big guy made out of iron is with me. Then they'd *know* we're up to something." She slid a hand along his arm. She could *feel* the rust spots, like patches of dry, scaly skin. "Stay here—hey, use those S.O.S pads you brought along."

"I don't like it."

"I don't either," she admitted. "I'll tell you what: if you hear me yell, you come running, okay?"

A grimace. "Okay."

She hugged him once more, then headed back upriver along the bank, pushing through the thick vegetation toward the settlement as stealthily as she could. If anything looked wrong with the village, she promised herself, she would head immediately back to Wally and the boat.

As she approached, she could see through the fronds and leaves a cultivated field between her and the village: corn, soybeans, and other crops rising straggling from the poor jungle earth. A woman worked the field, walking along the rows with a cloth sack from which protruded a few corn husks. The woman was only a dozen feet away. Jerusha parted the leaves at the edge of the field and called out softly to the woman in French. *"Bon-jour."*

The woman glanced up, startled, and backed up a few steps. "No," Jerusha called out, showing her hands. "I'm not going to hurt you. I need a telephone. A landline. Do you have one here?"

The woman glanced over her shoulder, and Jerusha looked in the same direction. A man was standing at the end of the small field nearest the village. He had a semiautomatic weapon of some sort strapped around him, though he was looking out toward the river, not toward Jerusha.

"No," the woman answered in heavily accented French, quickly and softly. Her eyes were wide and frightened. "You should go. There's nothing here. Nothing."

"I have to make a call," Jerusha persisted. "It's urgent. Please. If there's any way . . ."

"There's no phone here. What the rebels didn't destroy, the Leopard Men smashed. No phone. No electricity. Not for months." She gestured. "Go! You can't be here!"

The armed man called out to the women, though not in French—he was looking their way. Jerusha slid back toward the brush but it was already too late. He began to run toward them, bringing up the blackened muzzle of his weapon. Jerusha plunged a hand into her seed belt as the man shouted again, words that Jerusha couldn't understand. The woman screamed and flung herself to the ground.

Something dark and heavy slammed into Jerusha from behind and she went down just as the weapon loosed its deadly staccato clamor. She heard the bullets whining away, tearing harmlessly into the leaves, and ricocheting off iron. Wally was standing in front of her.

Gardener threw the seed she'd plucked from the seed belt as if it were a hand grenade: one of the remaining baobab seeds. It rolled to the ground at the attacker's feet and he glanced down, scowling as Jerusha sent her power plunging hard into the seed. It seemed to explode: roots plunging down, branches shooting skyward. One snagged the weapon and ripped it away from him as others wrapped around him. Soon he was encased in a snare of branches fifteen feet off the ground.

Wally plucked Jerusha up from the ground. The village woman lay in a fetal curl. Wally stared upward at the new baobab and its captive.

"You were supposed to stay with the boat," Jerusha told him.

Wally grinned. "Sorry."

The man shouted from his wooden cage, and people were beginning to look toward the field from the village.

"We should go, Jerusha," Wally said.

"Yeah," she told him. "I think maybe we should."

Wally turned and plunged into the jungle, tearing the foliage apart and crushing it underneath his massive feet. Jerusha followed his orange-spotted back.

People's Bank
Kongoville, Congo
People's Paradise of Africa

THE BANK HAD BEEN built during the colonial era, so it had some grace and charm as opposed to the proletariat grandeur (an oxymoron if Noel had ever heard one) of the Nshombos' People's Palace, Palace of the Arts, People's Defense Headquarters, Justice Center, etc.

His guide for the day was supposed to be the Economics Minister, but at the last minute he had been replaced with Alicia. Noel looked over at the woman as they sat in the backseat of a Mercedes limo. "What an . . . ah . . . incongruous building," he said, not wanting to call it beautiful in case the sister loved proletariat grandeur.

Alicia made a face. "I think it's beautiful. I wish we had emulated this building, but my brother has strong attitudes about Western culture. I think we should embrace all the West has to offer." And she stretched out an arm, and dragged her fingertips across the back of Noel's neck and down his arm.

Just as Lilith's sexuality could arouse men, his male avatar had the same effect on women. This was one time when Noel wished he could have appeared as a middling height, very average Englishman.

Noel leaned in close to Alicia's ear and whispered confidingly, "I too love French architecture. But then we French love many things."

Alicia turned to face him. They were only an inch apart. Every line in her body and the softness of her lips said she was waiting to be kissed. Noel knew he had to oblige her.

As he pulled back from the snog he thought, *God, I hope it doesn't go past this*. Noel knew Alicia had a taste for torture . . . no, *more* than a taste, a veritable *passion* for torture. And he also had Niobe waiting at home. He wanted to be done with killing and fucking for crown and country.

Realizing the silence was going on a little too long, Noel said, "I do hope the security has been upgraded since 1920. On your recommendation I'll be depositing a great deal of cash rather than using electronic transfers."

Alicia made a soothing gesture with her plump but perfectly manicured hands. "Not to worry. The president put in place state-of-the-art security measures."

"May I have a hint as to what they are?" Noel asked.

"I'll tell you a few, but I must keep some secrets," Alicia said with a suggestive smile.

Noel returned the smile. "Thank you, I am reassured."

The driver parked illegally in front of the bank, and they climbed out. Noel glanced back at the not-so-subtle unmarked security car that rolled slowly past them. The three men inside were so large it looked like a college prank or a clown car at the circus. Monsieur Pelletier would not notice a tail, no matter how obvious, so Noel said nothing.

The bank manager held open the etched-and-frosted glass-and-brass front doors and bowed them into the marble interior. Art Nouveau nymphs held up brass lamps, carved pediments showed a Classical Greek influence, a pair of gigantic chandeliers illuminated every corner of the lobby. Their heels rapped sharply against the marble and echoed in every corner. What with all the brass, glass, and stone, Noel expected it to be cool inside, but the moist, breathless Congo heat still held sway. The Europeans could bring their architecture, insist on their own cuisine, wear wool, corsets, and cravats, and die, but they could not defeat the jungle. Ultimately it won. It always won.

"Monsieur Pelletier is going to be building a Peugeot factory that will employ three thousand people," Alicia said to the manager. "You know how my beloved brother prefers to do business in cash, so that the Western powers cannot steal our wealth."

The manager's head bobbed up and down so energetically that all Noel could picture was the man's head set on a dashboard instead of a hula girl or a bobble-headed dog.

"I would like to see the vault, just to reassure myself," Noel said.

The manager looked to Alicia for guidance. She nodded, and he said, "But of course."

Two of the men from the car strode into the bank and began pushing patrons aside. This, as well as the slung Uzis, were so obvious that Noel felt he could comment. "There seems to be a great deal of . . . er . . . security around you. I'm concerned. Are you in danger?"

"Oh, no, no, no, monsieur. There is no problem *inside* the country." Alicia frowned. "The problem is counterrevolutionaries who seek to stop the march of our glorious country. One of these aces actually came into the country and killed our beloved Tom. Shot him dead as he stood inspiring the troops."

That wasn't actually how it had been. Bahir had unloaded a clip from a machine gun into Tom Weathers's back as he took a piss into a latrine trench. Noel put on an appropriately horrified expression. "But I met him yesterday. How did he survive?"

"Our Lady of Pain brought him back to life before she was killed by those same wicked elements."

Ah, mystery solved, Noel thought. *I'd wondered about that. But as one of those "evil elements" I know I didn't kill her, and I didn't hear of any other Western power moving against her. Interesting.* "You must be terrified for your brother," Noel said.

"I do worry, but the Leopard Men are ever vigilant. They even stand guard next to the beds while we sleep. And we change our rooms every night."

"How wise. I'm reassured." *God damn it. Paranoia makes my job so difficult.* And then, as if he'd heard Niobe's voice, Noel corrected himself. *Not my job any longer.*

Alicia gave him a secretive little smile. "And we have other . . . resources. The PPA will soon be one of the great powers in the world."

Noel slipped an arm around Alicia's waist. It was a long reach. "Oh, you intrigue me. Might I know what constitutes these resources? I might find myself wanting to make a larger investment."

Alicia bestowed a flirting tap on the cheek. "Now, now, you mustn't be too nosy. Perhaps when we know each other . . . better."

The manager led them down to the vault. The massive steel doors were rolled back, but steel bars still separated Noel from the actual vault. The two walls that weren't covered with safety deposit boxes were discolored, and there were a few evidences of actual mold where the moisture from the surrounding soil had leached through the concrete. Noel made note of steel tracks beveled into the floor, cameras that had a depressingly wide angle of coverage, and tiny nozzles mounted up near the ceiling. There was a doorway into another room, and Noel could just see steel pallets stacked to a height of about four feet and covered with tarps. It could only be one thing: the treasury of the PPA.

And only twenty feet and a vast array of security devices lay between him and it. Noel looked over at the bank manager. "You have people watching those cameras?"

"But of course."

"Would you like to see the control room, dear Etienne?" Alicia cooed.

"Yes, please."

As they headed back up the stairs the manager asked, "And when might we expect monsieur's deposit to arrive?"

"It will take me several weeks to raise that much cash, and arrange to have it safely transported to Kongoville." *And by that time I hope to have recruited help, returned, and robbed you blind.*

Risen Savior Spiritual Center
Ashland, Oregon

THE RISEN SAVIOR SPIRITUAL Center looked like a cheap community college. A neatly kept "campus" with winter-yellow grass where dirty snow hadn't melted, flagstone paths, and concrete benches built to withstand Armageddon. Bugsy guessed that if the world ended in fire, there would probably still be something more comfortable to sit on. The residential buildings were in the back. They looked less like a cloister and more like dorms.

He asked a pleasant-faced woman in a conservatively cut blue dress where he could find Kimberly Joy and was directed to the back.

The meeting room looked less like college, and more like a preschool for adults. Soft couches and cheap linoleum tables. Inexpensive butter cookies and a cheap metal samovar squatting next to a stack of foam cups and a basket of herbal teas. Low bookshelves were filled with magazines featuring pictures of a white, big-eyed Jesus or his ecstatic white followers or else books with crosses on the spines. The woman by the window looked up as he walked in.

If he hadn't spent most of the plane ride out from New York reviewing his records, he wouldn't have recognized her. The long blond hair was gone, replaced by a shoulder-length soccer mom coif. The challenging grin was a tight, nervous smile with lines around it that made her mouth seem puckered, even when it wasn't. The free-breasted hippie chick had vanished. A thick-bodied grandmother in her not-so-great Sunday best remained.

And still, knowing who she had been, he could see her in the shape of her eyes, the angle of her nose. Kimberly Ann Cordayne, or the ghost of her.

"You must be Mr. Tipton," she said.

"Tipton-Clarke," Bugsy said, "but yes, that's me. Thank you for seeing me on such short notice."

"I had to sit with the Lord," Kimberly Joy said. Her inflection meant *I had to think about it.* Bugsy had a brief, uneasy image of Jesus Christ sitting on the cheap couch and talking the decision over with her like a cut-rate therapist.

"Well," he said. "Thanks. I'm working with the United Nations," he said, then regretted saying it. Her face went cold. "Not the black helicopter, new world order part. That's a whole different division. Real jerks. I'm with the feeding the starving African babies part."

"You don't have to condescend," she said.

"Sorry."

"I'm perfectly aware of what you think of me. You think I'm an emotional cripple who's spent her whole life bouncing from one cult to another."

"Mind if I have some tea?"

She nodded toward the samovar and the cups. He was a little surprised to find his hands were shaking. He'd fought in wars before. Having a Christian lunatic call him out shouldn't have meant anything.

"May I ask you a question, Mr. Tipton-Clarke?"

"Sure."

"Have you accepted Jesus Christ as your personal lord and savior?"

"Ah. Well, not as such, no. The big guy and I haven't ever really hung out, if you see what I mean."

"You will be condemned to hellfire and damnation," she said as if she were an insurance adjuster pointing out the fine print on a policy.

"If we can, let's table that just for a second," he said. "I was wondering if I could ask you about the Radical."

"Who?"

"The Radical. He goes by Tom Weathers now. You knew him back in sixty-nine. He was at the People's Park riot. I was led to understand that you and he were . . ."

It was like a caul had formed over her eyes. A grey film that wasn't really there. "I remember," she said. "I remember him. I never knew his name. I have been lost many times in my life. Yes, I know who you mean."

"The thing is, he's turned out to be kind of a . . . well . . . crazed, homicidal, political fanatic with the blood of hundreds if not thousands of people on his hands."

She closed her eyes for a moment and sighed. When she opened them, there seemed to be even less joy in them than before. "I am sorry to hear it, but I can't say I'm surprised. We were all enchanted by Satan. I am sorry he was called to do the devil's work."

"Lot of folks are sorry about that. Seriously. I was wondering if you could tell me more about your relationship with him, and how exactly he knew Mark Meadows?"

"Mark?" She laughed. "Oh, poor Mark. Mark didn't know the Radical. Neither did I. I had no relationship with him."

"But . . ."

"I spent one night with him, and I have not seen him again. I know you can't believe this, but I had sinful encounters with many, many men when I was young."

"Oh, I believe it," Bugsy said. "I've seen pictures."

Kimberly's face showed a flickering cascade of emotions—surprise, embarrassment, pleasure—and she looked out the window. He sipped his tea. It was too hot.

"What about Mark?"

"Mark was . . . Mark was my fault. I've accepted that. He was one of the many people I led away from the path of righteousness. We were in high school together. He was brilliant. Everybody knew that. He was going to be the next Einstein. Fascinated by chemistry and physics . . . all the sciences. I met him again in New York, and he hadn't changed. He was so . . . *square*."

With the last word, the Kimberly Joy Christopher mask seemed to slip, and Kimberly Ann Cordayne peeked out from behind it. Bugsy sat across from her, leaning forward to keep from sinking irretrievably into the couch.

"He wanted so badly to be part of the scene," she said. "He wanted to be free and unfettered by all the old morality that we'd been taught. He wanted to be political. And he just *wasn't*. He wanted . . ."

She paused, her head tilted as if she were listening to someone. Jesus, maybe. "That's not fair," she said. "That's not true. He didn't want any of those things. Not really. It was just that the men I was sleeping with back then were all like that. Not just the Radical. There was Jim and Teddy and Gabriel and . . . I couldn't make a list, Mr. Tipton. But they were all the same. Young, strong, political, sure of themselves. Mark wanted to be like them."

"Because he wanted to sleep with you?" Bugsy asked.

"He was a sweet boy," she said.

Ah, Mark, you poor little geek, Bugsy thought. *You wanted to get laid, and you wound up being her best girlfriend.* "What about Sprout?" he asked.

"I came back to Mark," she said. "It was later. I'd followed my chosen path. It led to . . . very dark places. I was very, very lost back then. I was looking for the light of Christ, and Mark was the nearest thing I knew. He was a good-hearted man. So when I needed a safe haven, I found him."

"You got married," Bugsy said. "Got pregnant. Had Sprout."

"I am a sinner," she said. "I have confessed myself to the Lord, and he has forgiven me. My sins have been washed from me." She sounded angry saying it. Like she was talking him into something. Or maybe herself. Kimberly Joy squared her shoulders, her jowly chin raised in defiance if not pride.

"Okay," Bugsy said. "Good. I mean, good on you with the sin washing and all. But . . . Sprout?"

"I hated it that I'd been afflicted with a retarded child," she said. "I found the thought alone repulsive. Do you understand how far I had fallen? God sent me a little girl made from purest love, and I rejected her in my heart."

"You sure fought like hell for her when it came time for the custody battle," he said.

"I was angry," she said. "I was weak, and I hated Mark because he was capable of loving her and I wasn't. So I made myself believe that I loved her, that I needed her, and I did everything I could to take her from him. And I suppose I succeeded. I wept when they made her a ward of the state, and put me away, too. And Mark. They called Mark an unfit parent because he was involved with the drug scene. And they took her away from him, too. This was all my doing, Mr. Tipton. The drugs, my daughter, Mark's so-called friends . . ."

"What about the Radical and Sprout? Why does *he* care so much about her?"

In the silence, the small wall-mounted heater clicked. The samovar let out a small hiss. Kimberly Joy Christopher looked into his eyes with distress and confusion that told him he had reached something deep within her. When she spoke, her voice was hoarse.

"What the fuck are you talking about?" she said.

◆

Wednesday,
December 9

The Lab at Nyunzu, Congo
People's Paradise of Africa

THE CHILD SOLDIER HAD told them the landmarks to watch for. The lab at Nyunzu, he'd said, was east of the town, so they'd encounter it first.

Wally cut the engine of the boat once they sighted the rocky island the kid had described; they let the boat drift downstream with the current, staying close to the southern shore and eventually tying up well before they were in sight of the compound. They plunged into the jungle as quietly as possible with Wally leading, his powerful arms clearing the way.

It might have been an idyllic march under other circumstances. Monkeys clambered overhead, calling and scattering; bright parrots and macaws flitted from branch to branch. There were calls: grunts and hoots and gurgles that Jerusha could not identify, and unseen forms that went crashing away as they approached. There were strange plants and flowers sprouting up from the ground at their feet. It would have been fascinating, had she been able to pay attention.

But . . . there was a smell, a horrible smell drifting through the jungle, and it grew worse as they approached the lab encampment.

Wally hunkered down suddenly, gesturing at Jerusha. Crouching, she crept forward. The smell was nearly overpowering. Through the cover of huge, paddle-shaped green leaves, she could see that the area in front of them had been cleared all the way down to the river. A backhoe, its bucket and wheels mud-encrusted, sat at their left not ten feet away. There were buildings erected there, most of them open-sided.

And there, in the humid shade . . .

They were caged in small boxes, stacked two high: children, none of them more than ten or eleven. They were emaciated and fly-blown. Thin fingers gripped the wire that wrapped their wooden cells, and they were guarded by children who were not much older than them and a few adults in military uniforms.

But it was what was closer to them that was truly horrifying. Near the backhoe, the earth had been dug up and disturbed. Black and bloated flies hovered over the clods; white maggots wriggled in the soil; white-headed vultures crowded there. Here and there, horrific forms thrust out of the earth in a mockery of life: an arm, a leg, a hand with splayed fingers, to be picked at by the vultures' hooked beaks. This was a mass grave, poorly covered, and the source of the stench. Jerusha felt her stomach heave, and she forced the bile back down.

Oh, God, this is worse than we imagined. . . .

Even as they watched, a door opened in a walled building with a rusting tin roof. Two Leopard Men emerged, a man in a doctor's white lab coat, and a boy of perhaps twelve accompanying them.

The boy looked frightened and uncertain. Jerusha felt Wally start as he saw them: one of the Leopard Men was the were-leopard they'd encountered on the river, with scabbed-over cuts on his face and arms. The doctor held a tray with several hypodermic needles on it. They went to the nearest of the structures holding the caged children.

"Let *him* do it," Jerusha heard one of the Leopard Men say to the doctor in French, gesturing at the boy. "Go on," he said to the boy. "Prove your loyalty. Prove you're a man."

The boy visibly gulped and plucked one of the hypodermics from the tray. He approached the nearest cage. One of the soldiers opened the lock, pulled at the rickety door, and reached toward the young girl inside, who was crouching as far away as possible. He grasped the girl's arm and pulled her halfway from the cage. "*Allez-y,*" the Leopard Man said. "Do it."

The boy plunged the hypodermic into the girl's arm. She screamed as he

pressed the plunger and yanked it out again. The soldier shoved her back in the cage and slammed the door shut again. And Wally . . .

Wally roared a wordless fury and sprang toward the Leopard Men. Vultures squawked and scattered out of his way. Jerusha didn't have time to stop his charge; in a few seconds, Wally was in the middle of a firefight and she could only respond.

Automatic weapons were chattering from all directions. She could hear bullets shrilling and tearing chunks from the leaves to either side of her; a green rain was falling all around her. Someone screamed—not Wally—and she heard the sinister, low growling of a leopard. Taking a breath, Jerusha pushed through the screen of greenery and into the clearing, trying to make sense of the chaos.

Everyone's attention seemed to be on Wally, who had closed on the Leopard Men. The doctor was running toward the lab building, his white coat flapping. The boy that had been with him was also retreating—toward the river. One of the Leopard Men was on the ground, his weapon gone to rust in his hands and his arms broken; the other had shifted to leopard form and was snarling at Wally, ready to leap. The guards were firing at him, and bullets were pinging and whining from his body, gouging shiny dings in the black iron.

Jerusha ran over the broken ground of the grave pit as the vultures scowled at her, not daring to look down and hoping that no one would see her. She plunged her hand into the seed belt, not caring what she brought out. She cast the seeds hard toward the soldiers. Green erupted around them—some were vines that she wrapped around the guards, tearing away their weapons from their grasp at the same time; a few were trees that she brought up thick between them and Wally, who had closed with the were-leopard. She half closed her eyes, trying to *be* the plants, to control as many of them at once as she could, as closely as she could. She heard the liquid snarl of a leopard.

Behind. *Behind.*

Jerusha turned even as the creature started its run toward her, lifting into the air with powerful legs, claws ready to rip and slice. She flung the seed in her hand toward it. It was a toss that would have made Curveball proud: into the beast's open mouth. She tore at the seed with her mind, with the power the wild card had given her, ripping the growth out faster than she'd ever done it before. In mid-leap, greenery erupted from the leopard's neck

and mouth: even as the creature slammed into her, even as she fell and the Leopard Man rolled past her. Roots grabbed the earth and held; the leopard yowled, a terrifying scream, and the cat was suddenly a man again, writhing and tearing at the branches still growing longer and thicker, rupturing his neck and finally tearing his head entirely loose from his body. Arterial blood fountained from the body as the tree shot upward.

A mango, Jerusha realized belatedly.

Two of the buildings were on fire. Jerusha didn't know why: perhaps stray bullets or ricochets had ignited the oil and gasoline cans scattered through the compound. Yards away, Wally slammed the other were-leopard to earth and stomped on it. The crack of its spine was audible even against the gunfire.

The nearest child soldier flung his weapon to the ground and ran screaming, and suddenly they were all fleeing. Strangely, she thought she saw blood running down Wally's left leg, a long line of it, and he limped as he took a step and spun around.

Wally shouted, *"Lucien! Where are you!"* Jerusha could hear the sinister crackling of the fire, and the plaintive, alarmed shouts of the kids in their cages. Wally had already moved toward them, putting his hand on the wires and dissolving them into ruddy powder. He was pulling kids out, calling for Lucien as he did so.

Jerusha shuddered. The were-leopard's head was staring at her, caught in the fork of a mango branch nearly at eye level. Mangoes were ripening around it, and Jerusha found herself shaking.

She went to help Wally.

Michelle Pond's Apartment
Manhattan, New York

"YOU NEED TO PAY these bills," Juliet said in a reproachful voice as she shuffled the piles of mail that covered Michelle's kitchen table.

"You know, I started going through them, and I just couldn't concentrate," Michelle said. "I mean, I don't really care right now. They aren't stuck in a pit of corpses. You know?"

She felt Juliet kiss her hair. "They'll still need to be paid," she said softly.

"After I find Adesina." Michelle glanced at Juliet and saw the pensive expression on her face. *I am being the bad girlfriend again.* And only a week out of her coma. It had to be a land-speed record.

"Sweetie," she said, touching Juliet's face. "You did more than anyone has ever done for me in my entire life. I'm sorry I didn't get around to doing all that grown-up stuff like naming you the executor for my estate, making a will, and us getting, well . . . anyway."

She pulled Juliet's face close, lingering as their mouths met and tongues danced. When they were both dizzy and needed air, she continued. "What I need to do is get to Adesina. And there's a way. It means asking Noel for a favor, which sucks. But beggars can't be choosers."

"What the hell is going on in here?" Joey said as she came into the room. Her hair was rumpled from sleep and there was a crease down one cheek where she'd slept on it. She flopped into Michelle's overstuffed armchair. "I don't s'ppose there's any coffee? Fuck."

"There's coffee and breakfast on the stove," Michelle said. "Eat fast because I'm calling Niobe in a few minutes to see if we can drop by." It was almost nine o'clock. She could call at nine. Nine was a perfectly reasonable hour to phone.

Michelle had had another dream the night before. This one was a little different. Adesina wasn't in the pit in this one. She was in a small room instead. The walls were painted a cold bluish white, and there were pictures pinned to the wall of storybook characters. Michelle didn't recognize most of them—and the ones she did know looked out of place. Someone had tried to make this room less antiseptic and scary, but all they'd done was accentuate that this was not a fun place for a child to be.

When Michelle tried to look around, she had slipped out of Adesina's memory and into one of her own dreams.

This was an old dream. She was alone in the house. It wasn't her parents' house. It was the strange, alien-feeling house that always appeared in this dream. She is inside it and lost. Then she sees the bunny. She starts to follow it. But it runs away. Finally, she comes to a door at the end of the hallway. The bunny must be inside. But when she opens the door, the room is bathed in blood.

Nine o'clock.

Michelle flipped open her phone. "Keep it quiet, I'm calling." A few minutes later she hung up. "Niobe says we can come over now."

"So, what do we need to take with us to the Congo?" Juliet asked.

"Well, you don't need to take anything," Michelle replied. "You're not going."

"You are *not* going to the PPA by yourself!"

"I'm not," Michelle replied. "Joey is coming with me."

That got Joey's attention. "What the fuck?"

"I need someone who's good in a fight," Michelle said. "Someone who can also blend in if she needs to."

"She's from *New Orleans*, not Africa." Juliet's voice had risen to a shout. "Have you lost your mind? And what are you going to tell them about her? She's your jungle princess?"

"Hey!" Joey said.

"She's going as my assistant," Michelle said.

"She can't be your assistant. She doesn't know the first thing about . . . about, *anything*! Arghhhh!"

Michelle was torn between frustration and guilt. She wanted to get to Niobe's place now, but she also needed Juliet to understand why she couldn't come to the Congo.

"Look, Juliet, I love you." She pulled up a chair next to Juliet and took her hand. "That's why I'm not going to take you into a banana republic where there's God-only-knows-what horrific shit going on. You're an ace. But, sweetie, your power, it's kinda deuce-y."

Juliet slumped in her chair. Her face crumbled, and Michelle felt sick to her stomach as Juliet began to cry.

"You are stupidly brave." Michelle kissed Ink's hand. "My God, you stood up to my parents. For that alone they should give a medal. I will not let you put yourself in harm's way unnecessarily."

Silently, Juliet wept.

"God damn it, Ink," Joey said. "This is fucking Africa, man. Lions and tigers and shit, guys with guns, and that Weathers buttwipe for lagniappe. You going to scare 'em off with your tats? Fuck that cheese."

"Yu . . . yu . . . you two dumbasses are completely inept when it comes to people!" Juliet hiccuped.

"It's true, we suck at that."

"Assistant? She won't fool anyone!" Juliet yanked her hand out of Michelle's and then grabbed a handful of Kleenex out of the box. "She'll screw it up the first time she opens her mouth. Look at her. She's a mess."

"That's why we have to make her over before we get Noel to take us there."

"Make me over?" Joey was outraged. "What the fuck."

"Nothing too elaborate. Just fix your hair and—"

"Hell, no. I like my hair the way it is."

"What *happened* to you in that coma?" Juliet asked between hiccupy sniffles. "When did you become so bossy?"

Michelle stared at her, perplexed by the question. "I'm doing what I always do. I take care of things."

Nyunzu, Congo
People's Paradise of Africa

"LUCIEN!" WALLY CUPPED HIS hands to his mouth. His voice reverberated across the smoking grounds of the laboratory. The whine of overtaxed boat engines receded into the distance, their own boat among them. *"Lucien!"*

Wally inhaled, swelling his chest with air like the bellows of a pipe organ. *"LUCIEN! Come on out, guy! It's me, Wally!"*

The corner of a tin roof *crash-clanged* to the ground when a mud-brick retaining wall collapsed. Jerusha's plants had damaged the wall; Wally's yelling shook it just enough to finish the job.

He paced through the ruins, forced to limp because of the jags of pain in his leg. Where a bullet had grazed a thick spot of rust . . . but he'd think about what that meant after he found Lucien.

Smoke stung his nose, burned his throat. He felt like he was choking. "You're—" His cough sounded like a stone knocking around inside a washing machine. He struggled to get the words out. "You're safe now."

His eyes watered. Was that the smoke?

Why hadn't Lucien come out yet? He must have been frightened by all the fighting. He must have been good at hiding, the little guy. Wally hadn't seen the barest trace of him. Not in the barracks. Not in the lab itself. Not in the cages, thank God.

And over there, at the edge of the clearing . . . No. Wally didn't want to look over there. Lucien wasn't there. He couldn't be.

"Lucien!"

"Wally."

"LUCIEN!"

"Wally!" Jerusha took his hand. "Let me help you."

Wally was so caught up with his search and his worry that he didn't no-tice right away that they were holding hands. But then he did, and his stom-ach did a somersault.

She pulled him toward a knot of children huddled together in the shadow of the ruined lab. The kids shrank back, clutched each other more tightly when the pair approached. They had tear-streaked faces and runny noses.

Jerusha knelt before the kids. She spoke to them gently, in French. She pointed at herself and Wally. Wally caught the name "Lucien."

The kids didn't say anything. They stared at Jerusha and Wally, wide-eyed. One little boy gave his head the tiniest shake. He said something to his companions, but it didn't sound like French.

"What did he say?"

"Not sure," said Jerusha. "But I think he's translating to Baluba for me."

"Hold on a sec," said Wally. He squeezed Jerusha's hand before releas-ing it. Freed children and emancipated staff members cowered when Wally limped across the clearing. The staff members looked even more frightened than the freed children; maybe they were right to do so.

Wally hurried to where he and Jerusha had stashed their packs, ignoring the pain in his leg. He dug out his photo of Lucien and brought it back to Jerusha.

She was talking with the little boy who translated for her. He had large, almond-shaped eyes. He looked to be nine or ten. His name was Cesar, she said.

Wally pointed at the photo. "Lucien?"

Cesar shook his head. So did the others.

Jerusha took Wally in one hand and Cesar in the other. She pulled them toward another, larger, group of kids. He held up the photo while she spoke in French and Cesar translated into Baluba. Nothing. Just confused glances.

They questioned everybody. A few of the former staff members trem-bled, or erupted into a torrent of French when Jerusha spoke to them. She translated their pleas for understanding, for mercy, for Wally and Jerusha not to hurt them. They'd been forced to do these terrible things against their will, she said. Jerusha's eyes watered, too.

Wally grew more anxious, his palm sweaty in Jerusha's hand, with every person they questioned. Every blank stare was another lost chance to find Lucien. Every shake of the head was another path to Lucien, closed.

Something tugged at his pant leg. He looked down. A little girl, not much older than eight or nine, looked up at Wally. Dozens of quivering fingers with gnarled, yellow nails protruded from her neck, arms, and legs; the poor thing was one of the dozens of jokers Wally had freed by disintegrating the cage doors. "Lucien?" she said quietly.

"Yes! Lucien!" He held up the photo. "Lucien?"

The little joker girl said something in French. Jerusha knelt beside her. They had a short conversation. It ended with the girl crying, and Jerusha turning pale.

"What? What did she say?"

Jerusha stood. She flung her arms around Wally, sniffling. "Oh, Wally . . . She says she was in a group of kids that received injections two days ago. She was the only survivor." Her voice broke. She hugged him more tightly. "I think Lucien was in that group."

"No. No, he wasn't. That's not true. She's wrong."

"She knew him, Wally. She's from Kalemie, too."

"No. Lucien's alive and I'm gonna find him."

"Lucien," said the girl. She raised her arm, pointing. The extra fingers all bent in the same direction, like stalks of wheat bowing before the wind. They pointed toward the edge of the clearing, toward that place where Wally didn't want to look.

Where the backhoe stood next to a wide mound of freshly turned soil. Where the jungle stank of death. Where vultures picked at the earth.

"No!" Wally limped to the mound. "No, no, no. Please, no." He grabbed the backhoe and heaved, ripping it free with the shrieking of tortured metal. The vultures squawked in protest, the wind from their wings buffeting Wally as they leaped for the sky.

Wally gripped the backhoe bucket with both hands and scooped a long, narrow trench out of the mound. He flung the dirt away. He did it again and again, each pass going a little bit deeper, each pass proving that Lucien wasn't here. Proving that Lucien was alive and safe. Somewhere.

Until he hit something soft. A tiny foot, caked in quicklime, curled toes sticking up through the mud.

"No!" Wally hurled away the broken backhoe arm; it whistled out over the jungle and disappeared. A distant *clang* echoed back a few seconds later, along with the screeching and shrieking of upset wildlife.

He fell to his knees. He dug with his hands. A shadow fell over him: Jerusha, weeping softly at grave's edge.

The grave held seventeen little boys and girls, their bodies all ruined by the wild card virus. Melted, crystallized, putrefied, skinless, boneless, faceless. Black queens, and jokers who had survived the transformation only to be shot in the head. Or what passed for the head.

Lucien was near the bottom.

His body had become a kite. Narrow bones like pencils formed ugly bulges in his waxy, translucent skin. They'd torn through in places, cracking his skin like fragile parchment. His face had become flat and two-dimensional, like a stained-glass portrait of a little boy. But he still had those ears, those ridiculously large ears . . .

Lucien had died in an *American Hero* T-shirt. It was part of a whole package of clothes that Wally had sent; it had his face on the front.

He lifted Lucien out of the grave. Jerusha held Wally while he cradled his dead friend. They stayed that way a long time. Wally's tears fell on Lucien's lifeless body, a rain of salt and rust.

Halifax
Nova Scotia, Canada

IT WAS A GENERIC cheap hotel room, old-fashioned enough to look that way even to Mark's eyes. Off-white wallpaper yellowed from decades of tobacco smoke before it was banned in even such out-of-the-way precincts as these, green pinstripes and *fleurs de lys,* a hunting print with dogs and guns and ducks on the wall. A little TV with bunny ears instead of a cable or satellite box. He smelled cleanser, heard the cicada drone of canned laughter on a TV set on the other side of a wall not strong enough. His alter ego didn't care much about comfort, far less luxury. All Tom cared about was security.

"Sun Hei-lian," he said. *I've got the mouth,* he thought, *and he doesn't know.* "Listen to me."

Sitting upright in bed beside him, combing that exquisite black hair threaded in fine silver, the naked woman froze. Her eyes alone moved toward where he lay on his side, fearing to move. "Your voice . . ."

". . . is different. Yeah. I'm not the Radical. Tom, you call him. I'm Mark."

Very deliberately she laid the brush down on the flimsy hotel nightstand. He knew very well that not far from it lay a compact black Makarov pistol.

Sun was an expert with a handgun. "Who are you? How did you take over Tom's body?"

"I'm the rightful owner," he said. "The man who calls himself Tom Weathers is a squatter." She didn't relax. But she brought her hand down to her lap. Good sign. "You look better firsthand," he said before he could stop himself. She furrowed her brow. "I've watched you, all along," he said, thinking, *Oh, Jesus, I sound like Earth's creepiest stalker.* "I see . . . pretty much everything Tom does. But for me it's all soft focus. Like a dream."

"Is this some kind of trap?"

"The Radical can make himself look and sound like anybody else on Earth. Why would he try talking with a funny voice out of his own mouth?"

It took her a moment to answer. "For a long time," she said, not looking at him, "I've felt there was something inside Tom. Something gentle. *Someone . . . kind.*"

She shook her head. "I was attracted from the first. He was a beautiful Western animal, stronger and more vital than any natural human being. And there was the *wildness* of him. Like an element of nature. Like wind and fire." Her hair swept across her face like soft banners as she turned to look at him. "Why am I telling you this?"

"Because I'm him," he said. "Only not really."

She frowned. "What do you want with me?"

Everything, he longed to say. But . . . what was he? What did he have to offer a woman like this? His own body was middle-aged and gawky, not prepossessing, not the body of a rebel Greek god. And he didn't even have it. And anyway, that wasn't the urgency that drove him like a dehydrated man's craving for cool water. "I wanted to thank you. For being kind to Sprout. But mostly to warn you. Somebody's got to stop him. Haven't you seen how he's getting shorter- and shorter-fused all the time, more violent in his outbreaks? He's losing his inhibitions."

"Stop him? How?" She seemed to be asking mainly from intellectual curiosity.

"I don't know," he said. *Maybe we can't.* He quelled the thought. Plenty of time to wallow in doubt later, when he was locked safely away back in the Radical's subconscious.

"How could you stop him?"

"Take back control."

"Can you?"

He grinned ruefully. His lips stretched in strange ways. As with seeing, *feeling* was different firsthand than at one remove. "No luck so far." He gave Tom's golden head a slight shake, the most he dared. "I won't tell you to trust me. Just trust your judgment. I think you know the truth already. Don't you? No one can control him. He can't control himself."

That perfect mouth thinned to a line. The thin network of lines that brought out only enhanced her beauty to his lost and lonely eyes. "Even if you are telling the truth—what can I do?"

"Help me. Try to find . . . something. *Anything.* If you can't let me out, you have to find some way to destroy us. Me. Him. Whoever . . . oh, shit. I'm losing it. . . ." He heard his voice grow vague, as if coming from ever-farther away. Her face flickered as his lids fluttered before his eyes. "Gotta go . . . he'll kill you if he knows I talked to you. I don't want anybody else getting hurt for this stupid-crazy dream of mine."

"Dream?"

"Peace, love, justice. All that good stuff. Turned out to be not that simple—no time. I can't stand hurting anybody else. Especially not you. But not anyone. Not ever again. If you can't let me out, you have to find some way to destroy us. Me. Him. Whoever. Please—"

Mark felt himself beginning to spin. "—destroy—"

And away he went.

"*Aaaahh!*" Tom Weathers sat up in bed and took his head in his hands.

She sat beside him, brush in hand, his Chinese angel. "The dreams . . ." she said.

"Yeah." His mouth was inexplicably dry. His tongue stung. "The dreams."

♥

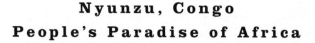

Thursday,
December 10

Nyunzu, Congo
People's Paradise of Africa

WALLY GAVE EVERY CHILD in the mass grave a proper burial. Especially Lucien.

It would have gone faster if he hadn't tossed the backhoe bucket halfway across the PPA. But he wouldn't have used it anyway. He wondered if Lucien had been alive to see the PPA men dig the trench with that backhoe, and if so, if Lucien had known he was seeing his own grave.

Wally used a shovel he found in the ruins of a supply shed. But the handle shattered under Wally's relentless drive to make things right. After that, he used his hands. All throughout, he refused Jerusha's repeated offers to help. This was Wally's job.

Hours and hours of digging. Wally's back ached, ferociously. Far worse pain came from kneeling on his injured shin, where the bullet had grazed a vulnerable spot thinned out by rust. It felt like a red-hot knitting needle had been rammed through his leg. But it was nothing compared to the pain in his chest, his heart. That was so intense he could hardly breathe.

The pain was a penance. He deserved it. His friend had been in trouble, and Wally had done nothing to help him. Nothing that made the tiniest difference, anyway.

Exhaustion claimed him the moment he finally took a rest. He woke with no diminishment in his pain. The burials were important, but they hadn't even begun to make things truly right. Could anything?

The freed children watched everything he did with a combination of fear and curiosity on their faces. They seemed to understand that he and Jerusha were their friends. But all the same they kept their distance. Wally wondered if they would ever be capable of trusting another adult. Even Cesar and the joker girl.

The kids needed breakfast. Together, Wally and Jerusha didn't have nearly enough food in their kit to feed so many.

Jerusha emerged from the only building that hadn't collapsed, crumbled, or burned down. Unlike the other structures, it was relatively sturdy: thick, reinforced concrete walls; a solid, pitched roof for keeping out seasonal rains; no windows. "Hey," she said. A thin, sad smile touched the corners of her eyes. "You're up."

"Yeah."

"How are you holding up?"

Wally shrugged. *Pretty bad*, he thought. *But better than Lucien and the others.* "The kids," he said, gesturing around the destroyed camp, "they need breakfast, but . . ."

"Don't worry. Let me handle it. You've done more than enough, Wally."

What would I do without you, Jerusha? "Thanks," he said glumly. She carried a folder, he noticed, like the kind that hangs in a filing cabinet. Tears had cleaned little paths from her eyes through the smudges of dirt and smoke on her face. "What's that?"

Jerusha sighed. She jerked a thumb over her shoulder, back toward the building. "That's where they kept their records. I found this," she said, shaking the folder. "Look, I hesitate to bring this up, but I thought you should know." She took his hand. "This isn't the only lab. The Nshombos have places like this hidden all over the PPA."

Wally's knees gave out. He sat heavily on a stack of bricks, the remainder of a corner support for one of the open structures. The bricks crumbled into a pile of rubble.

Jerusha showed him the folder. The lab here received its supplies of the wild card virus from a barge that traveled up and down the river. The barge, in turn, received its supplies from a central lab in Bunia, where they actually cultivated the virus. It was a huge program.

It had to be. For every hundred kids they killed, they might have created a single ace.

Changing them, Sister Julie had said. Wally had thought she meant the way they turned innocent kids into child soldiers. But that wasn't the half of it: they were trying to create an army of child *aces*.

Suddenly Wally saw a chance to make things right. Except—

What will *I do without you, Jerusha?*

"We have to get these kids somewhere safe," he said.

"I've been thinking about that," said Jerusha. "Since we don't have a boat anymore, and even if we did it wouldn't hold all of the kids, we'll have to start walking back east, toward Tanzania. Once we get somewhere with a working phone, we need to contact somebody on the Committee. They'll send help. Then we can go find the other labs."

Wally shook his head. "That'll take too long. Kids are dying every day." *Like Lucien.* "We have to split up."

Jerusha's mouth fell open. She gaped at him, as though he'd said something mean. She shook her head. "We can't."

"Them kids need a guide, somebody who can feed them, and somebody who can hide them in the jungle. I can't do any of that stuff, Jerusha. But you can do it all. You're exactly what they need." Wally shrugged. "Me? All I can do is break stuff. So I'll go to Bunia."

"But they'll know you're out here. They'll come looking for you."

"Heck, yeah. Every soldier or Leopard Man they send after me is one more that won't be chasing you. Even with the kids, your chances of hiding are way better than mine."

"I don't like this idea," she said. "I hate it."

"They can't hurt me." He looked down at his hands, flexing them into iron fists. "But I can hurt them."

"But your leg," she said, looking at the bandage taped over his bullet wound. The implication was clear: every day spent in the humid jungle made him less bulletproof. Made him vulnerable. But his iron skin didn't have to last forever. Just until he made it to the Bunia lab.

Once he tore that place apart brick by brick, the rest didn't matter.

He didn't tell her any of that. Instead, he said, "I'll be more careful. Now that I know about the danger, I won't let it sneak up on me."

He also didn't mention that he was running out of S.O.S pads. It didn't seem right to give Jerusha even more reasons to worry.

Michelle Pond's Apartment
Manhattan, New York

"ARE YOU READY?" NOEL asked.

He'd popped into Michelle's apartment in his new male form, and looking like he wanted nothing more than to leave as quickly as possible.

"Almost." Michelle zipped her small Louis Vuitton duffel closed. It had been part of a gift basket she'd been given at an awards show a few years ago. She hated the way it looked (and hated being a walking billboard for Vuitton), and she didn't care if it got lost or beat up.

"I need to see if Juliet is done with Joey." She went to the bathroom and knocked on the door. "Are you done in there? Noel's here and wants to get going."

There were muffled curses through the door. Then she heard, "Fuck me. That ain't half bad."

The bathroom door opened and Juliet stepped out. She gave Michelle a withering stare, and then went into the living room. Michelle could hear her offering Noel tea.

Joey was in front of the mirror staring at herself. "Fuck me!" she exclaimed. "Will you look at this shit?"

Juliet had managed to cover the Crayola red with a dark chocolate color. And she'd cut Joey's hair. For once Joey didn't look as if she was going out to panhandle. Juliet had even dressed her in a crisp white blouse and neatly pressed grey slacks.

"You look great," Michelle said. "Now stop talking. You're ruining the illusion."

"Fuck off, Bubbles." Joey brushed past Michelle and went into the living room. Michelle followed her. In the middle of the room, Noel was holding a mug that read: LESBIANS DO IT WITH GIRLS. A Lipton's tea-bag tag dangled over its edge. He had an expression on his face like a cat being given a bath.

Michelle smiled. "I think we're about ready," she said. "I know you're only doing this because of Niobe, but I want you to know how much I appreciate it."

"You shouldn't be doing this at all," Noel said, hastily putting the mug down on the coffee table. "Nothing good is coming out of the PPA right now."

This caught Michelle's attention. "You seem awfully well informed about what's going on there."

A smug expression flickered across his face.

"What are you up to, Noel?" Michelle asked softly.

"Nothing you need to be worried about. Are you ready?"

Michelle grabbed her duffel and turned to kiss Juliet good-bye, but Ink had already left the room. There was a brief stab of hurt, and then it was gone. What she was going to do was more important than a kiss good-bye.

"Yes," she said. "I guess we're ready to go."

"Good-bye, Ink," Joey yelled.

Noel stepped between them. Michelle felt a sudden jolt of cold as her apartment vanished. *Adesina*, she thought. *I'm coming.*

People's Palace
Kongoville, Congo
People's Paradise of Africa

"I WANT YOU TO make more use of the young volunteers," the President-for-Life said across his teacup in his most pedantic tone.

They sat at white wrought-iron tables in lush gardens surrounded by the high walls of the People's Palace. Nshombo wore his customary black suit. A trim, handsome man in his late fifties, with the polished and perfect and unyielding features of a statue of African blackwood, the President-for-Life was a certified genius, who spoke over half a dozen languages and dared share Tom's dream of world liberation. But he had no more tact than he did vanity. Nor charisma either.

"I don't need them," said Tom. "And they're *kids*. They don't belong in a war."

"Yet they have served us so well," Dr. Nshombo said. The four tiny Dandie Dinmont terriers lying at his feet raised cotton-ball heads and glared at Tom with eyes like suspicious obsidian buttons. "Khartoum was a great success, Field Marshal. As was the Sudd. With more seasoning, our young volunteers may soon be the equal of any foreign aces. Even Ra."

The mention of Ra made Tom bristle. Old Egypt's resident protector was the only wild card in the world who might be his equal. "Are you listening to a word I'm saying?"

"Boys, boys." Alicia Nshombo clucked and shook her head. She was packed into a flamboyantly flower-printed dress and a sunbonnet. "You know you're best of friends. Let's have peace between us. Pretty please?" Despite her appearance and her Harlequin-romance tastes, Alicia was scarcely less intelligent than her brother. She was also Tom's staunch ally in the increasingly fucked-up politics at the center of the PPA.

Tom Weathers frowned at her for a handful of pounding heartbeats. Then he stood up. "I'll get back to you on that," he said, and stalked back into the palace. But before he even pushed through the French doors he knew he'd give in. It was for the Revolution, and the Revolution was bigger than he was. *Just don't get to thinking* you're *bigger than the Revolution, Comrade Kitengi,* he thought bitterly.

United Nations
Manhattan, New York

"COULD SHE HAVE BEEN lying?" Lohengrin asked. *COOhd she haf beehn lAHying.*

Bugsy lay back on the office couch, the UN-approved fair-trade leather creaking under him. "I don't know," he said. "I mean, sure, maybe. She could have. But she'd just told me about how she was a big ol' ho who'd boffed anything that moved and didn't love her own kid. We weren't really in withhold personal information mode, if you see what I mean."

Lohengrin frowned and looked out over Manhattan. The winter light made the city look cleaner than it was. The German tapped his hands together in something between impatience and confusion. "That is very odd."

"That's what I thought," Bugsy said. "But just because our first guess was off doesn't mean we're screwed. Okay, so Sprout isn't Tom Weathers's kid. The Radical and Cap'n Trips didn't know each other because they'd slept with the same woman."

"Captain Trips?"

"Mark Meadows. He went by Cap'n Trips back when he was trying to be the kind of guy he thought Kim would be into. Selling drugs, running a head shop, hanging out with aces. But that's the point, isn't it? Meadows was part of that scene during the two and a half decades that Weathers spent underground. Sixty-nine to ninety-three is a pretty long time. Lots of things could have happened."

Lohengrin sat. His time on the Committee had aged him. Bugsy remembered when he'd come on, guest ace on *American Hero*. There hadn't been the weariness around his eyes back then, or the sense of crushing responsibility. Maybe he'd lost it in Egypt. Maybe since then. Making the world a better place turned out to be a shitty job.

"Very well," Lohengrin said.

"You doing all right, big guy?"

Lohengrin shrugged. With shoulders like that, it was a more tectonic motion than it would have been for Bugsy. "There are problems. You cannot know, Jonathan. The politics, the budget . . ."

"You know, it's funny you should mention that. The next step on the whole Tom Weathers thing kind of depends on the expense account," Bugsy said.

Lohengrin's brows rose.

"There's still got to be a connection between Meadows and Weathers," Bugsy continued. "And the next most likely one is that something happened between them back when Meadows was chancellor of South Vietnam. Sprout was there. The Radical showed up in the same general part of the world not long after."

"Yes," Lohengrin agreed, but pulling the word out several syllables to make it clear he was waiting for the expensive part.

"Well," Bugsy said. "It seems like we ought to talk with Meadows about it, and since he's all blowed up . . ."

"You want to send Cameo," Lohengrin said.

"Well, both of us. Me and her."

Lohengrin smiled. "You're sure you aren't just trying to get a free vacation with your girlfriend?"

"She's not my girlfriend," Bugsy said. "She's channeling my girlfriend. And her boyfriend, for that matter."

"Simoon has a dead boyfriend?"

"No, Cameo does. It's complicated."

A hint of amusement seemed to touch Lohengrin's eyes, but it might have just been the angle his head was at.

Bugsy yawned. "Look," he said. "Cameo is a professional and an ace. She's on the Committee. She's the obvious choice. If you want me to follow up on the connection between the Radical and Sprout, it's going to mean paying market price."

"Fine," Lohengrin said. "I will discuss it with the others as soon as possible."

"You bet," Bugsy said. "And can we get tickets on the company card? The airlines are giving me shit about the discount again, and if . . ."

"*Ja, ja,*" Lohengrin said.

"Or you could see if Lilith's in town, save us time and money both."

Bugsy hadn't meant it as a dig, but Lohengrin bristled.

"Sorry," Bugsy said.

"Nothing to be sorry for," Lohengrin said.

"No, really. If I'd known Lil was really Noel, the British hermaphrodite in really good drag, I would totally have waved you off that night."

"I appreciate that."

"And, you know, she's an ace. Or, that's to say he is. Or . . . y'know, Noel's an ace. It's a full-on transformation. It's not like you got a hummer and just didn't notice her Adam's apple."

"Jonathan?"

"And it was Vegas. You know, weird things just happen in Vegas. I knew one guy I would swear wasn't into midgets when he went there for his honeymoon. Three days later, he and his new wife are—"

"*Jonathan.*"

"Yes, boss?"

"If I approve the expenses, will you leave?"

Grand Hotel
Kongoville, Congo
People's Paradise of Africa

"WHAT DO YOU *MEAN* you don't have a reservation for me?" Michelle asked indignantly. She had been a supermodel once, and she did indignation very well.

The young clerk behind the reception desk looked very unhappy. "Miss," he replied. "I do not see any reservation for a Michelle Pond."

"This is your fault," Michelle snapped at Joey. "I ask you to do one thing.

One thing! And you can't even manage that." She turned back to the clerk. "I don't suppose you could find us something? Anything. We've come such a long way and we're both exhausted." She gave him her very best oh-goodness-please-help-me look.

It worked.

"I think we might be able to arrange something," he said.

Michelle breathed a sigh of relief. There was no way to make a reservation and then pop into the hotel a few hours later without arousing suspicion. She had hoped pretending that they had lost the reservation would cover her showing up out of the blue.

"I have a suite available," he said after typing into his terminal for a few minutes.

That's gonna be pricey. The interest rate on the big cash advance she had taken to finance this trip was going to be hell to pay, too. But it didn't really matter to Michelle. What mattered was getting to Adesina.

"The suite would be perfect. Thank you so much for accommodating us this way." Michelle gave him her very best you're-just-the-nicest-person-in-the-world smile.

He beamed back at her and slid two room cards across the desk. "You know, you look very familiar to me."

Michelle smiled at him. "Oh, I used to model," she said. "I'm here on business now. I've decided to start my own clothing line. I've been told that the PPA has the best garment workers in the world."

"That is true. The hotel has a wonderful tour of Kongoville. Would you like me to book you two seats? It will give you a very good feel for our city."

"Oh, mostly I want to see the Congo River. I hear it's beautiful. Can I get a taxi there?"

He gave her a shiny smile. "Certainly, but the bus tour also takes you to the river. And you will see many other wonderful places along the way."

Michelle wanted to drag him across the desk and explain to him that a little girl was suffering in a goddamn pit of corpses and she really didn't have the time to go sightseeing.

"My brother-in-law drives the bus," the clerk continued. "He's a very good driver."

She nodded politely. His persistence about the tour became clear. But, in a group of tourists, perhaps she and Joey wouldn't stand out quite as much. And she needed to figure out where to go next. "How long does it take?"

"Only two hours."

"Two tickets," she said.

Nyunzu, Congo
People's Paradise of Africa

WALLY WAS SITTING ON a pile of rubble near the smoldering lab, scrubbing fiercely at his body with steel wool, as if he could scrub away the memories as easily as the blood, soot, and rust. "Here," Jerusha told him, picking up one of the S.O.S pads and crouching down behind him. The few pads left in his pack had all been well used and were starting to fall apart and rust themselves. The piece she held was tearing loose in her fingers even as she started scouring his back, cleaning away the rust spots there that he couldn't reach.

The rust was deep there—not just on the surface of his skin. She worried about that. She worried about the bandage tied around his leg. "Feels good," Wally grunted. "Thanks, Jerusha."

"I'm scared, Wally," she said. "How's the leg?"

He shrugged. "Fine," he said. "Just a scratch where the skin was thin. It'll grow back quick."

"I'm sorry we didn't get here in time to help Lucien. I'm going to miss you. I'm going to miss you terribly, and I'm going to worry every second until I know you're safe."

"Me, too," he said after a moment. "You're gonna have your hands full with those kids. They ready? We can't stay here; they'll be coming back soon."

Jerusha looked at the children. There were fifty-two of them; she counted. Twenty-nine had yet to be injected; eight had been given the virus but hadn't yet turned their card. Fifteen were jokers who hadn't yet been culled: the little girl whose body was studded with hundreds of fingers, complete with fingernails, like a porcupine made of severed hands; a boy whose lower half was a gigantic fish tail that needed to be kept constantly wet; a boy whose face was missing eyes, sockets, and nose, nothing but unbroken skin from his forehead to his mouth as if he were an unfinished sculpture; a girl whose skin pulsed and glowed a bright yellow . . .

Cesar had told her that sometimes they waited to make sure that the jokers didn't have some power they'd missed. The children were all hungry,

all abused, all frightened. They huddled in a group near a jungle trail leading away from the clearing, eating the breakfast she'd created for them, an
amalgam of fruits from her seeds and some of the food in their kit. They'd
stripped the mangoes from the were-leopard's tree, all except those on the
branch that held the Leopard Man's head.

The children were watching the two of them uncertainly, as if they
weren't certain if they could trust their rescuers or if they might be led to
something worse. She could hardly blame them. "Are we doing the right
thing, Wally? Maybe . . . maybe we should stay together . . ."

Wally's steam-shovel jaw clanged shut. "No," he said. "I gotta do this,
Jerusha. For Lucien."

"Okay." Jerusha put down the S.O.S pad and came around in front of
him. She put her hands on either side of his face. Leaning in, she kissed
him. The kiss was awkward, his mouth all cold iron under hers. His hands
first went around her, then fell away, then came back again. "You stay alive
for me, Wally," she said. She had to stop, sniffing and wiping angrily at her
eyes. She took his hand, pressing her small fingers against his. "And I'll stay
alive for you. Deal?"

"Okay," he answered. He was staring down at her hand. "Jerusha,
cripes, I . . ."

"Don't say anything," she told him. "It'll just make this harder." She
leaned in toward him again. She kissed his forehead, then—again—his mouth.
This time he responded, his arms going around her and hugging her. She held
the embrace for several breaths, then pushed away from him. "It's time," she
said.

Wally groaned to his feet. Jerusha looked at the kids. They were watching, but whatever they were thinking was hidden behind expressionless,
hollow faces. She pulled the strap of the automatic weapon around her
shoulder—one of the several abandoned by the child guards as they'd fled. A
few of the older children had armed themselves as well. She wondered if she
or any of the kids could actually use the weapons.

"It's time to go," she told the children in French. "We've got to get you
out of here." Cesar translated the French into Baluba. The children stood as
Jerusha sighed. "This way," she told them, and began walking toward the
head of the trail leading east, toward Lake Tanganyika and—she hoped—
Tanzania. As they passed the head of the trail, she tossed a handful of seeds
onto the ground, bringing the new growth high enough to cover their tracks.
Wally was watching her. She waved to him as the fronds lifted; he waved

back to her as the lush greenery rose between them. When she could no longer see him, she turned eastward. The kids had gathered around her. She put her arms around the nearest of them.

"Come on," she said. "We have a long walk ahead of us."

♣

Friday,
December 11

Kongoville, Congo
People's Paradise of Africa

THE BUS TOUR TOOK them to the Kongoville University. Michelle hadn't expected it to be so large, or so pretty. There were new buildings going up, and the older buildings were settled into beautiful tropical landscaping.

"KU is the premier university in the PPA," the guide said in French-accented English. "The Nshombos believe that education is the most powerful tool against the repressive regime that once ruled here and against the tribal wars that once marred the unity of our nation."

As the bus rolled by, book-toting students dressed in brightly colored patterned shirts and khaki pants smiled and waved at the tourists.

Michelle waved back. "Would it kill you to wave at them?" she asked Joey.

"I don't give a shit about those fuckers," said Joey. "Why the fuck would I wave at them?"

"Because it's a nice thing to do."

"Fuck that. I didn't come to be nice to some fuckers I don't even know. If I wanted to be *nice* I could have stayed in New Orleans."

"We need to find a way upriver," Michelle said suddenly. "That's where we'll find Adesina."

"Yeah," Joey said with a sigh. "This is the fifth fucking time you've told me."

By the fourth stop, Michelle was beginning to regret going on the bus tour. They'd seen the renowned farmer's market, the hospital, and the central sports complex. Everywhere they went, people smiled and waved at them. It was as if the entire population of Kongoville was eternally happy. It was downright weird.

And she was feeling oddly jet-lagged, even though they'd skipped the jet. Maybe it was just the muggy afternoon. When they climbed back into the bus, she slumped down into her seat. She would close her eyes for just a minute . . .

It's dark in the pit. Nighttime again. She knows that Adesina is near, but she doesn't want to crawl across the bodies to find her.

"I'm coming," she says, but she doesn't know if Adesina can understand her.

"Bubbles."

How does Adesina know her other name?

"Bubbles."

She's confused, and then Adesina is grabbing her arm.

"Jesus, Bubbles, wake the fuck up." Joey was shaking her. "We're here."

She sat up groggily. "Where?"

"How would I know? Some fucking place or another."

It was a tomb.

"This is Our Lady of Pain, the people's martyr," said the tour guide, once he'd led the group inside. "She is considered a saint by Dr. Nshombo. As you can see, she's wearing the highest honor our country can bestow: the Golden Hero of the PPA. Sadly, she was murdered by the war criminal Butcher Dagon just a few short hours after receiving the commendation."

Our Lady of Pain was laid out in a glass coffin. She was dressed in virginal white and there was a large gold medallion around her neck. Her body rested on red satin.

Michelle glanced at the corpse and suspected that it wasn't an actual body, but a wax figure. But then Our Lady of Pain's hand moved, and she had to keep herself from jerking backward. She heard a snicker behind her.

"Joey," she hissed. "Cut that out."

"No can do, boss. This is too much fun."

The corpse shot Michelle the finger, and then Our Lady of Pain's hand dropped back to the crimson satin pallet. Luckily, the rest of the tour was on the other side of the glass casket.

"Don't do that again," Michelle whispered. *"Ever."*

"You're no fucking fun at all," said Joey.

Somewhere over the Pacific Ocean

THE AIRPLANE HUMMED AND shook. Out the window, the ocean was a featureless darkness below them. The flight attendant—a Vietnamese woman who looked about twelve—passed by trying not to stare at the severed human head in the window seat on its cushion of bright green wasps. Bugsy felt the urge to yawn, but with his torso broken down, there was no breath behind it.

Nick, beside him, slapped at Ellen's arm, pushed up the brim of the nasty swamp-water fedora, and scowled. Bugsy smiled apologetically and drew the stray wasp back into the pile. "Do you have to do that?" Nick asked.

Bugsy re-formed his chest enough to speak, pulling the button-down blue shirt up as he did. Arms, legs, anything below his diaphragm, he left as insects. "It's way more comfortable," he said. "These really long flights I get a kink in my back."

Nick shook his head. "You really don't care about anybody else, do you?" he said.

"What?"

"Do you know how uncomfortable it makes people when you do that?"

"Jeez, sorry. But do you know how uncomfortable it makes me when I don't?" Bugsy crossed his arms, bands of wasps making a rough approximation of normal anatomy. "Look, Nick, whatever it is, why don't you say it, okay?"

"I am saying it. You treat being an ace like it gives you permission to ignore other people. When I drew my ace—"

"No, Nick. No, this isn't about great power coming with great responsibility, all right? Let's get down to it. You're jealous."

Now Nick crossed his arms. The airplane dropped like an express elevator, then steadied. The fasten seat belts light went on with a chime. "And what exactly is it that I have to be jealous about?"

"Hey, I feel for you," Bugsy said. "It's not really like it's Ellen I'm with when Aliyah and I hook up, but Ellen's in there someplace. It's her body, and I know she feels what we're doing. She's thinking about you, but whatever. Of the four of us, you're the only one who never gets any action, and I'm really sorry about that. But I didn't kill you or Aliyah. I didn't make the rules about how Ellen's powers work. And I don't think—"

"This is crap," Nick said. "I'm not the jealous one. You are. You hate it that she brought me along and not just your girlfriend's earring."

Bugsy felt his annoyance bump up toward anger. The conversation about which artifacts—if either—to bring on the trip to Saigon had been between him and Ellen. That Nick was talking about the details of it meant that once again the two of them had been having internal conversations about him. "All I said was that Aliyah's earring wouldn't look out of place, and your hat might."

"You mean my 'sad-ass lump of felt and weeds'?" Nick asked, quoting the fight verbatim.

"I just meant that the hat's been through a lot," Bugsy said. Some of the wasps started moving around, making little hopping flights, growing agitated. "Ellen's a very attractive woman, and we're going to stand out here anyway."

"And you didn't want her bringing me back every time you were in the hotel," Nick said.

"Well, no, actually I didn't," Bugsy said. "Matter of fact, I like being with Aliyah. I enjoy her company. I enjoy sex with her on those occasions when Ellen isn't plopping you on her head the second she walks through the door."

Nick smiled. Bugsy thought the expression was nastier than usual. "So why don't you tell me some more about how you're not jealous."

Bugsy chuckled because the alternative was to start yelling. He pulled the remaining wasps back in, filling out the arms of his shirt, the legs of his pants. His anger was starting to send them a little too far afield, and unintentionally stinging some poor bastard three rows up wasn't going to make the trip any better.

"Look—" he began.

"You have a lot to learn about women," Nick said. "You have a lot to learn about people, for that matter."

Bugsy didn't precisely mean to do what he did next. It was like it just happened, his arm moving of its own accord, his fingers closing on the ruined fedora. Nick's eyes had a moment to widen, and then they were Ellen's. The storm in her expression was full-on category five.

"Look," he said, before she could speak, "this isn't the place for me and him to work out our shit, okay? This is a really unpleasant, complicated set of relationships, and we're heading for Vietnam with about an inch and a half of legroom each. If you want to kick my ass, wait until we're on the ground."

Ellen snatched the fedora back from his hand, but she didn't put it on. "We *will* have this conversation again," she said.

And you will *take his side*, Bugsy thought. He didn't say anything, only nodded. Ellen turned away, putting the tiny airline pillow onto her shoulder, her back toward Jonathan.

"You know," he said, "space is really tight. If you put the earring in, we could stretch out together, and—"

"In your dreams," Ellen said.

Congo River
Kongoville, Congo
People's Paradise of Africa

THE BRAKES HISSED AS the bus slowed to a stop at the end of a long pier leading to a murky green-brown expanse of water. There were vendors set up along the edge of the pier with jewelry, baskets, T-shirts, and hand-carved doodads. Filing off the bus with the rest of the tourists, Michelle and Joey were immediately hit with the earthy smell of the Congo.

The guide started talking, but Michelle tuned him out. She was feeling an incredible urge to get on the river and head north. It itched across her mind. She turned around to talk to Joey, but Joey had vanished.

Michelle skirted several piers, looking for Joey as she went. Plenty of people stared at her, but no one stopped her, so she kept going. She'd tried to dress nondescriptly in khakis, a white button-down shirt, and tennis shoes. But being a six-foot-tall platinum blonde made her stand out no matter what.

"Joey," she hissed. "You miserable brat!"

"*Bubbles.*" A hand landed on her shoulder. She swung around—hands up—ready to bubble.

"Jesus! Joey, you little shit."

"It's time to rock and roll. I found a way upriver. Boat's close by."

Michelle considered for a moment. "Joey, the Committee really screwed the pooch when they passed on you."

"Yeah," Joey said bitterly. "I'm fucking handy."

Impulsively, Michelle hugged her. "You're *extremely* handy." But then she remembered the night she and Joey had spent together, and pulled away. "So where's this boat?"

"Follow me."

The man appeared out of nowhere. Michelle would have bubbled him if Joey had not caught her arm. He smiled at Joey in a way that creeped Michelle out, and motioned for them to follow.

Tied to a short pier was a beat-up twenty-five-foot boat. It had a large motor on the back. Two men with guns emerged from the small cabin. They eyed Michelle and Joey.

"Which one is her?" asked one in French.

Michelle understood him. But doing runway in Paris had given her more of an ability to understand French than to speak it.

Their guide pointed to Michelle.

"Let's see it then," the shorter of the two said.

The guide repeated what the man on the boat had said.

"She's not your fucking dog," Joey snarled. "She don't perform on command."

Their guide translated. The man in the boat shrugged and turned to go back into the cabin.

"I'll show them," Michelle said.

"Fuck that, Bubbles," Joey replied. "We're paying them an assload of money. They don't need a show."

"Christ." Michelle opened her hand and created a bubble. It was soft and rubbery. His partner stared gape-mouthed as the bubble formed, and he hit the deck when she let it fly. Then she sent it flying into the back of the man who wanted to see her power. There was a loud "oof" as the bubble hit. The man pitched forward, and his gun flew out of his hand and clattered to the deck.

Michelle started another bubble. This one was for show. When the man she'd hit turned around and saw her, he held up his hands. In her very rough French she said, "I would rather be friends. This is business, yes? We want to go upriver." She closed her hand, popping the bubble, and felt a rush as she absorbed its energy. "I'm Michelle."

"Gaetan," he said, jabbing a thumb into his own chest. Then he pointed to his partner. "Kengo."

"Can we come aboard now?"

Gaetan nodded. Michelle turned to Joey. "Are we good to go?" Joey brushed past her and climbed into the boat.

<h1 style="text-align:center">Ministry of Joy
Kongoville, Congo
People's Paradise of Africa</h1>

"TOM," ALICIA NSHOMBO SAID, settling her bulk in its stressed white-and-blue floral-print dress in her chair behind her tiny white desk with its ormolu trim after an embrace of greeting. "We need you."

He dropped into a chair across from her and rubbed his jaw. Stubble rasped. The insides of his eyeballs felt *just* like that. He hadn't been sleeping well. "What?" he asked. He bobbed back and forth in the chair.

Alicia's office was in an old colonial-era building downtown on the Kinshasa side, Belgian-built in the time when King Leopold was treating the natives in a way that'd get an antebellum southern plantation owner prosecuted for treating his slaves. Doc Prez wanted her to have her digs in the new compound but she wanted to assert independence. And what Sis wanted, Sis got. The decor was froufrou to the max: all white and flowers and swirly gold. The walls teemed with pictures. One stuck out: a photo of Alicia in polo outfit, straddling a clearly dubious horse that looked as if it would be more at home pulling a beer wagon. The thought of Alicia playing polo blew Tom's mind, but he'd bet she never lost.

"Enemies have violated the People's Paradise," Alicia was saying. "Near Nyunzu. Terrorists attacked one of our special facilities. They've murdered my *babies*."

"Shit," Tom said. That Alicia didn't chide Tom for his language showed how freaked-out she was. "Who?"

"That is one of the things we need to find out. Tom, it would be very bad if these terrorists were to escape with any of my babies. Such lies they would tell. The world would never understand."

You'd have a shitstorm on your hands, you mean, Tom thought. "I can take care of it."

"Oh, I'm sure you could," Alicia said, "but this is such a wonderful op-portunity to see what our young volunteers can do. I want you to take a few of them to Nyunzu, Tom. This will be another test for them, a chance for them to show us how brave they are, and loyal. Let them avenge their mur-dered brothers and sisters!"

Sofiensaal Concert Hall
Vienna, Austria

"YOU WERE WONDERFUL," NIOBE said as Noel emptied the hid-den pockets in his coat. There was still some applause from the audience that remained in the Sofiensaal concert hall.

Noel kissed her. "Thank you, my dear, but you are biased."

"The critics will agree. You'll see when you read the reviews tomorrow." She sat down to wait while he changed.

Unlike more old-fashioned magicians, Noel didn't perform in the tailcoat. He wore a black leather jacket, black silk shirt, black slacks, and black boots. It was actually his usual mode of dress, but tonight he opted for a hand-knitted Nordic sweater and an overcoat. Vienna was gripped in the icy claws of a wind raging out of the Russian steppes, across the Hungarian plain, and screaming, bansheelike, through the city.

Despite the cold there was a knot of woman gathered at the stage door. Niobe hung back while Noel signed program books and kept up his flirta-tious, practiced banter. Finally they were gone. The limo driver held open the back door of the car.

"Darling, I'm restless, I'd like to walk back to the hotel. It's not that far," Noel said.

Niobe tucked her gloved hand beneath his arms. "Then I'll walk with you."

"Are you sure that's wise?"

"Exercise is good for me. Dr. Finn says so." She poked him in the ribs. "And he told you not to coddle me."

"My prerogative." But he gave in and waved away the driver.

Their route took them past the twisting columns of the Karlskirche, modeled on Trajan's column in the Roman Forum. An old man pushed a chestnut-roasting cart down the sidewalk on the other side of the street. The rich, loamy scent of chestnuts and the sharp bite of charcoal had Noel suddenly ravenous. He ran across the street to see if the man had anything left.

He had only a few, cooked until the shells were black, but he was happy to pluck the chestnuts out with gnarled fingers and load them in a paper cone. Noel ran back to Niobe and thrust the cone into her hands. "You'll like these. And not just to eat, they're better than mittens."

They shelled and ate chestnuts, watched their breaths steam, and just before the wind became too brutal they reached the hotel. They had a suite, and a room-service dinner was waiting for them. Niobe settled onto the couch, sighed, laid a hand over her belly. "I still can't believe this is my life."

Noel leaned down and kissed her. "Happy?"

"Very."

On the Lukuga River, Congo
People's Paradise of Africa

WALLY DIDN'T REALIZE JUST how much he'd come to depend on Jerusha until she was gone. Somehow, she'd made it possible to endure the sorrow that threatened to crumple up his heart like so much tin foil. But now Wally had only his thoughts for company. He didn't know how to bear the guilt and grief over Lucien's death all by himself.

After Jerusha left with the kids back toward Tanzania, Wally started working his way west, farther up the Lukuga. She erased their tracks with new plants, while Wally went out of his way to leave the most obvious trail he could. He ripped down everything in his path; he tore branches and leaves; he stomped his feet, pounding perfect footprints into the soft earth; he littered his trail with banana peels, mango rinds, granola-bar wrappers, and even the occasional smear of peanut butter. He did his best to make it look like he was a whole bunch of people.

His clues wouldn't last long in the jungle, especially the food. But they didn't have to. Just until folks came to investigate the sudden destruction of the Nyunzu lab. They'd follow his path because it was the only path to find. He wondered, too, how long it would take Jerusha and the kids to get to Lake Tanganyika.

Twin pangs of worry and loneliness fueled another surge through the thick growth along the river. He kept as close to the river's edge as he could manage. That way he could be spotted from a passing boat. And he kept an eye open for the barge that carried supplies of the wild card virus.

Dusk fell. As it did every evening, the sounds of the jungle—what little he could hear over the constant *crash, crack, crunch* of his passage—changed. The noise of life, raucous and loud, birdcalls and primate vocalizations and other things he couldn't begin to identify, gave way to more subtle things: the buzz of insects, the gurgle of a stream, the whisper of a breeze through the foliage, the rustle of leaves as something slinked past. With practice, he'd be able to tell the time entirely from the jungle noises.

Though he didn't need it, he built a fire that evening. The biggest he could manage. It took a lot of work, because everything was so damp. But it was visible, he hoped, from quite a ways. He got the idea by trying to think like Jerusha. She was smart, and always had good ideas.

She would've been proud of him.

She'd kissed him.

Another pang. *Oh, nuts, Jerusha. Please take care of yourself. 'Cause I gotta see you again, when this is over.*

The Grinzing
Vienna, Austria

THE GRINZING WAS A pretty, old-fashioned, and rather rural section of town situated in the foothills. It was like a welcome mat for the Vienna Woods, and with its array of small weinstubes, Biergartens, and restaurants it was a perfect place to end a ramble through those woods. It was very late, but the small green lamps still glowed at several restaurants, indicating they were open.

Noel's contact had named a particular Weinstuben. It wasn't the most savory-looking establishment, but then, Noel reflected, his contact wasn't all that savory. After dinner Noel begged off coming right to bed and instead taken a shower. As he'd hoped, the combination of a late night, late dinner, and pregnancy had Niobe sleeping deeply. She hadn't even stirred when he let himself out of the room.

One customer, an older man, sat at a corner table. A carafe of white wine was in front of him, and a Wiener schnitzel the size of a place mat hung off the sides of a plate. Potatoes and a basket of heavy brown farmer's bread completed the carb-loaded meal. It took a minute for Noel's eyes to adjust to the gloom. Once they had he studied the man's features—thin face with a network of wrinkles around the eyes and mouth, a ropy neck, and swollen knuckles, a symptom of creeping rheumatoid arthritis—yes, it was definitely Ffodor Mathias, aka Karolus Kowach, aka Nicolao Tholdy, aka Blackhole.

He was wanted by Interpol, known to the Silver Helix, he'd been convicted five times, but he was a hard man to keep locked up, given his ability to bend light waves and make himself invisible. He bent them using gravity. Which meant he could also make heavy objects light and light objects heavy.

When you were planning on stealing a crapload of gold he would be a useful man to have along.

"So, what's the job?" Mathias asked without preamble as Noel slid into the chair across from him.

"Liberating the state treasury of the PPA."

"I want ten million dollars," Mathias said.

Noel threw the Wiener schnitzel in the Hungarian's face.

Once Mathias clawed away breading and grease he found himself looking down the barrel of Noel's .40 caliber Browning. "Okay. Now that we've established what you want, let's discuss what you'll actually get."

"I'm old," Mathias whined. "I need to get out of this game."

"Three million, and you can pretend you'll actually retire," Noel said as he stood up.

"You ruined my dinner," Mathias complained.

Noel threw a handful of bills onto the table. "Buy another. I'll be in touch."

♠

Saturday,
December 12

Noel Matthews's Hotel
Vienna, Austria

"WHERE HAVE YOU BEEN?" Niobe's arms were folded across her chest and her expression was thunderous.

"I couldn't sleep, I took a walk—"

"Do *not* lie to me, Noel Matthews! Are you back working for the Silver Helix?"

"No, God no, you know I'd never do that after . . . after . . ." He had a sudden image of the tiny smears on the floor of his parents' house, all that remained of the tiny ace children he had sired with Niobe.

Niobe sank down on the couch, and her arms were lowered to clasp her belly. Alarmed, Noel stepped forward. "Are you—"

"I'm fine," she snapped. "I just can't stand it when you lie to me. What are you doing?" He hesitated. She stood up abruptly and grabbed her suitcase out of the closet. "Either we're partners and you trust me, or we're not and you don't, and I'm not going to raise a child in that kind of atmosphere."

"I'm trying to protect you."

"Well, *don't*."

They stared at each other for a long time.

So he told her. Not everything, but enough to give her the shape of his thoughts and plans about the PPA and the Nshombos.

He found himself pacing as he talked. "The truth is, this is going to be a bitch. I have some idea of the security measures, but by no means all. It has to look like the Nshombos looted the treasury or they'll just blame Siraj or Britain or the U.S." He threw his hands in the air. "It would be a good deal easier if I could just kill them."

"The way you killed the Nur?" Niobe asked. Noel nodded. "And look what that led to. Thousands of dead jokers, thousands of dead soldiers, a bunch of young kids playing hero with a river of blood on their hands. Please, don't fix things by killing people anymore. You're not the bad guy. Let the bad guys do the killing."

And an idea began to grow. It would be tricky, but when had tricky ever bothered him? If he could pull this off there was no chance of the Nshombos becoming martyrs, or the West or Siraj being blamed for their deaths. He grabbed Niobe by the shoulders and pulled her into a long, deep kiss.

"What?" she gasped when he finally released her.

"You, my darling, are a genius."

He loved it when she blushed.

On the Lukuga River, Congo
People's Paradise of Africa

WALLY WOKE TO FIND the fire still smoldering. The damp wood sent up a roiling column of smoke. It drifted over the jungle like an ash-grey arrow on the bright blue sky, pointing straight at Wally. He couldn't think of a better way to announce his location, so he took his time with breakfast.

It worked. The whine of a distant motorboat echoed up the river. Wally screwed the lid back on a plastic jar of peanut butter and dropped it into his backpack alongside the bananas and mangoes Jerusha had grown as a parting gift. Then he hunkered down in the brush and waited.

Soon enough, a small PPA patrol boat zipped around the bend. No kids on this one; Wally breathed a sigh of relief. The soldiers followed the smoke straight to the edge of his makeshift campsite. They landed their boat on the riverbank not far away.

Five minutes later, it was Wally's boat.

As much as he hated to, he left a couple guys still standing, so that they could report what they'd seen: a metal man, heading deeper into the PPA in a stolen boat.

Nyunzu
Tanganyika Province, Congo
People's Paradise of Africa

NYUNZU STANK OF ROTTING bodies and shit. The foulness overwhelmed even the stench of burning and the river Lukuga's primitive smell. Leopard Men and soldiers moved among smashed cages of wood and mesh. Mud-brick walls and tin roof panels fallen in on themselves and smoldering. A small forlorn-looking tractor, from which a powerful arm, probably a backhoe, had been wrenched—recently, because the steel at the break gleamed bright, rather than being crusted with rust like dried blood. And everywhere twined and stood and sprouted an inexplicable profusion of plants, as if the secret ace lab had been built by a mad gardener.

"Well," said Tom, arms akimbo, staring eye to eye at a man's head wedged into the fork of a branch of a mango tree that stood unaccountably in the middle of the ruined compound, "these counterrevolutionary motherfuckers are into beheading. Might be Muslims. Forty or fifty."

"There were only two, sir," the commando said.

Tom scowled. "Shit." *Aces.* "That's a bummer."

At Tom's feet Leucrotta crouched on spindle shanks, making whining sounds low in his throat. He was developing a tendency to show doglike behavior even in human form. Beside him the two spookiest little kids on Earth, Ghost and the Hunger, stood gazing at the devastation with big blank eyes. Their presence amid all this horror didn't bug Tom. He was starting to get behind the *beauty* of the kid-ace trip. Terrible beauty, yeah. But beauty.

Two men in brown-and-green Simba Brigade camouflage approached, pulling a third between them. He was unarmed, bareheaded, his blouse torn open, his trousers stained. He stank of piss and shit, presumably his own. His escorts spoke to him in the local lingo.

"They say this one survived the attack, *Mokèlé-mbèmbé*," one said. "He speaks of a woman who killed with plants, and a metal man that nothing could hurt."

"Sounds like aces, all right," Tom said. They even sounded familiar somehow. He could call Hei-lian; he carried a satellite phone, for which only she and the Nshombos had the number. A different phone and number every day. Otherwise the imperialist NSA could track him and some CIA pencil-neck in Virginia could fire a tank-busting Hellfire missile at his head from a remote-controlled drone.

The Leopard Man went on. "He says the metal man went north along the river. The woman took the young volunteers and headed east toward Tanzania. She made the jungle grow up suddenly to cover their trail."

Nice try, thought Tom. "Ghost, you can track a fart through a feedlot. You go get the metal man."

She looked at him with her saucer eyes and nodded, slowly, once. Tom turned to the Leopard Man. "You get hyena-boy and the Hunger. Take some soldiers along."

"What shall I do with the patriotic volunteers?"

Tom shrugged. "They're of no further use to the People's Paradise, Lieutenant." He turned to the survivor. "Oh, and as for you, numbnuts . . ." He looked to the Hunger and jerked his head at the man. The soldier howled as the boy sank sharp teeth into his leg. "You have the honor of performing one last service for the Revolution: you get to show your comrades the penalty for letting it down."

Somewhere in the Jungle
Vietnam

BILLY WAS A JOKER. He looked like a desiccated monkey, thin strips of dark flesh still clinging to old bone. His eyes seemed almost deflated, and he smelled like a bowl of chicken soup someone had left out for a week.

He drove like a man on fire. "This your first time in Vietnam?" he said as the jungle whipped past their Hummer.

"Yes," Bugsy said, his hands digging into his knees as Billy whipped around a corner Bugsy hadn't known was there.

"Great country. Had some hard times. That what you here for? Something about Moonchild?"

"More about a friend of hers. Mark Meadows."

"The nat," Billy said. "I never met him. Heard about him, though."

"He was an ace."

"Really? What could he do?"

"I don't know."

"Ace with no powers, eh?" Billy said. "Sounds like a nat to me." The dead monkey spun the wheel again. The Hummer groaned and screamed like a dying animal. Bugsy closed his eyes, then opened them again. If they were clearly going to hit a tree, he could bug out. A few dozen wasps getting crushed would be a lot easier to recover from than his brainpan sailing through the windshield.

"Yeah, I was Joker Brigade right up until I was in the resistance against it," Billy said. "That was a fucked-up scene. We all came here because we bought into the whole line about Vietnam being a haven for victims of the wild card."

"Lot of aces?"

"Some, I guess. Mostly it was jokers and joker-aces. Place got really fucked up. Bad shit happened out there, man. Really bad shit. It was the Rox that did it. Jokers saw the Rox get wiped out, figured that was what the whole world was going to be like. Lot of angry freaks out here in the jungle with guns. No one said it, but we all kind of understood it was about revenge. All except Moonchild."

"You knew her?" Bugsy said.

Something the size of an orange hit the windshield with a soft thump and an inhuman shriek. When it bounced off, it left a streak of blood. Billy turned on the wipers as he drove. "Saw her a few times, that's all. She turned it all around." Billy's voice was almost reverent. "She was the one that pulled all the good guys together. She was the soul of this fucking country."

"What about other aces?"

"What about 'em?"

"When Moonchild was fighting the good fight, didn't she have any help?"

"Oh, yeah. We had some powers working for the good guys. There was a little asshole called Cosmic Traveler. Total douche, but he got a lot of prisoners free. There was this fire guy took out a bunch of enemy airfields. Some kind of were-dolphin called itself Aquarius fucked up the river patrols real good. And here we go."

The Hummer broke out of the underbrush and skidded to a halt, gobbets of mud and weeds flying from under its spinning wheels. Two men on motor scooters shouted at them. Billy leaned out the window and jabbered back, gesturing with one skeletal hand. The men made gestures that Bugsy assumed were rude and continued on their way.

In the backseat, Ellen yawned and stretched. "Are we there?" she asked sleepily.

"End of the road for today. I'll get the archives to you tomorrow morning," Billy said. He was either grinning at her or his mouth was trapped in the death's-head rictus. Either way, Ellen smiled back at him.

"Thank you very much," she said as Bugsy stepped shakily out of the car.

"The rooms are ready," Billy said. "Just go on in, turn right, and go up the stairs. I'll get the bags taken care of. No troubles."

Bugsy walked into the little wayhouse, his legs feeling weak as spaghetti. The great battles of Vietnam had been fought throughout the country, but the final one that broke the New Joker Brigade and put Moonchild in position to reconstitute South Vietnam had been here. And so when the archives had been crated to honor the fallen leader, this was where the government had decided to build the academic and cultural temple.

It was also the best guess for where to find something—a pen, a chair, a ceremonial robe—belonging to her chancellor, the late Mark Meadows.

Bugsy went into the room and lay on the bed, staring up at the faux-bamboo roof. The mattress felt wonderful. Ellen came in behind him, but went straight back for the bathroom.

The more he looked at it, the more plausible it was to Bugsy that the Radical had figured into the events in Vietnam. He was beginning to think Weathers might even have had connections to the Rox War. It was pretty clear that Weathers had been employing the powers of the aces that surrounded Moonchild. And then the notably, vocally pacific Moonchild got taken out, and the Radical came onto the world stage.

It was too convenient to be coincidence. The question was whether the Radical had been stealing the powers, or if there had always been a cabal of aces working with him behind the scenes like a sort of Committee of Evil Wild Cards. He had to agree with Billy that Meadows seemed more like a deuce or a nat than the ace he claimed to be, but he could very plausibly have been the mascot and front man. Once Ellen channeled him, they'd know a lot more.

The shower went on in the bathroom, and a moment later he heard the rush and splatter of water against skin. A beetle the size of a hummingbird buzzed in through the open door, and Bugsy chased it out again with a few hundred wasps.

Billy appeared in the doorway, three suitcases bumping along behind him. He looked at Bugsy, at the bathroom door, and shook his head. "Here's the stuff. You kids rest up, and I'll be back in a couple hours, get you some dinner."

"Thanks," Bugsy said. He wondered whether it was appropriate to tip one's UN-provided translator, or if that would just be condescending.

"I got to tell you, man, the world has changed since I was your age," the zombie chimp said. "Makes me think I was born too early."

"Yeah?"

"In my day, a hot-looking woman like that with a joker? Would never have happened."

Bugsy frowned, trying to think of any jokers Ellen had dated. The penny dropped. "Wait a minute," he said, sitting up. "You think *I'm* a joker?"

The chimp nodded to the green insects swarming in and out of Bugsy's skin.

"What would you call it?" Billy asked.

The Santa Cruz Islands
Solomon Islands

"*YOU CALL YOURSELF A* father?" the pinched, reproachful voice asked in his dream. Tonight Mark Meadows wore faded bell-bottom jeans and a sunburst tie-dye T-shirt with a picture of Jerry-fucking-Garcia on it. "*You're putting children in danger. You're helping turn them into killers. What the hell is wrong with you?*"

"They are warriors," Tom said. "Warriors for the Revolution. They stand for something. I stand for something. You're just a drug-soaked old hippie."

"*But I did stand for something. Peace and justice and freedom. And you—you're losing it. You used to not make war on kids. Now you make war with them. You cared for Sprout. It was your only contact point with humanity. The only thing close to a redeeming feature. How can you look her in the eye now, man?*"

Tom swung a fist with all the armor-shattering power of Starshine. Mark's image shattered like a stained-glass window into an infinity of brightly colored shards.

And each laughed at Tom as they faded into darkness.

◆

Sunday,
December 13

In the Jungle, Congo
People's Paradise of Africa

JERUSHA MISSED RUSTY MOST of all.

The kids were both less and more of a problem than she'd expected. They were frightened, they were abused, and they tended to stay clustered around her as they moved through the jungle. A few of them, like Cesar, spoke French well enough to act as translators for her; a few were old enough and mature enough to serve as leaders for the ragged troop. Their names rattled in her head—Cesar, Abagbe (the finger-studded girl), Waikili (the nearly faceless boy), Eason (the fish-tailed joker), Naadir (the glowing skin child), Gamila, Dahia, Machelle, Rac, Saadi, Efia, Pendo, Pili, Wakiuri, Dajan, Idihi, Hafiz, Kafil, Chaga, and on and on . . . Jerusha despaired of ever matching all the names to faces.

None of them were aces as far as she knew, though the jokers were obvi-ous enough, the ones that the PPA and Leopard Men of Ngobe had evi-dently decided to evaluate for possible uses before disposing of them as they had the rest. Since she'd left Rusty behind, she'd been shepherding the group steadily eastward—she'd made sure that Wally had the GPS unit, hop-ing that a compass would be sufficient for her needs.

All she needed to do was find a telephone and call Babs: the Committee

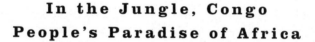

could get her out. Jayewardene could send a fleet of UN helicopters, or meet them at the shore of Lake Tanganyika with boats, or . . . well, they would have a way. She only needed to head east. Head toward the lake and Tanzania.

And avoid being caught.

Simple.

A good half dozen of the children could not walk on their own, or barely so. Eason had to have his fish tail constantly moistened or he'd cry out in pain as the scales dried and cracked. Jerusha and the older children took turns carrying those who could not walk. Some of the older ones wielded machetes to cut down the worst of the brush. They spread out in a ragged hundred-yard line through the jungle, a line that without her constant attention would have grown so long that the children at the end would have been lost. She had to constantly urge the youngest and weakest to keep moving, had to constantly switch out those carrying the infirm, had to stop those at the front just as frequently so the stragglers could catch up.

She tried counting them frequently to make certain they were all there, but most of the time lost track of the count. Eventually, she abandoned that entirely, hoping that the kids would let her know if one of their own was missing. When they stopped to rest, the children would huddle around her as if they all wanted to press next to her, as if they craved the reassurance of her touch or her voice. For many years, Jerusha had wondered whether she'd ever be in a relationship stable enough that she would feel safe having her own children. Now she'd acquired over fifty of them—and she was alone.

Occasionally on those frequent rest breaks, Jerusha would use her wild card ability to restore the jungle growth along their trail in hopes that it would make them more difficult to follow. Hopefully, they *weren't* being followed; hopefully, Rusty's tactic would work and the Leopard Men would follow him instead.

It was the blind joker Waikili who made Jerusha wonder. He came up to her hours after they'd begun their march, tugging on her safari jacket. "They coming, Bibbi Jerusha," he said to her in imperfect French, seeming almost to stare at her with the blank, dark skin of his face. "They coming after us."

She could see the fear radiating out into the group at his words, all of them whispering to each other, a few breaking out into terrified wails and tears. "Shh . . ." she told them. "Cesar, tell them they must be quiet. Waikili, how can you know this?"

"I *know*," he said. "I don't have eyes, but I *feel* them here." He tapped his forehead. "They find the camp. They following the steel man, but some of them follow us, too."

"You're just guessing, Waikili," Jerusha said desperately. "You can't know. It's not possible." Even as she said it, she worried that she was wrong, that the joker Waikili might have also been a hidden ace.

Waikili shook his head into her denial. "I *know*," he repeated. "I am not wrong."

Jerusha bit at her lower lip. They were all staring at her now. "All right," she said. "If they're following us, then we just need to move faster than they do. They won't catch us. Come on, we've rested enough. Let's go."

The Santa Cruz Islands
Solomon Islands

"WHAT'S THAT?" SPROUT ASKED.

They had come to a high point: a dinosaur-back hump of volcanic ash bedded on sandstone that showed through down by the beach. The island was forested and densely undergrown. Its nearest neighbor lay over sixty miles away and, key, it was uninhabited except for monkeys, tropical birds that were equally loud to ears and eyes, and a colony of wiry skittish goats. Nobody ever came here.

That was a vaguely cruciform mound grown over with tough native grass. Only the double-vaned tail betrayed its real nature. "A B-25 bomber, honey," Tom said. The son of a successful, hard-charging Air Force general, his . . . predecessor . . . had been an avid warplane buff as a kid. And Tom had access to some of his memories, though not all. Especially the early ones.

"What's that?" his daughter asked him.

My *daughter*, he thought, defying his tormentor of the night before. "A warplane for dropping bombs. They fought a lot of battles around here during World War II. This plane was probably based at Henderson Field on Guadalcanal, a few hundred miles from here. Must've been shot down."

He hadn't come here just to give the lie to the old hippie's reproach. Sending those kids after the aces who had smashed Nyunzu had given him a pang. They were aces themselves, sure, and some of them were scary as shit, but they were still kids.

He needed to hear Sprout's voice, feel her hand in his, see the pure and innocent love in her clear blue eyes.

"Will they bomb us?"

He laughed and led her away. "I don't think so, sweetie. They better not, or Daddy'll teach 'em better!"

"Which Daddy?" she asked, her eyes huge and solemn beneath the sun hat Mrs. Clark insisted she wear.

It took him a moment to register the question. Then it hit him like a punch in the nuts. "What do you mean, honey? I'm your daddy."

Mulishly she shook her head, making her ponytail flap from shoulder to shoulder of her blue-and-white sundress. "My real daddy. I miss him. Why can't I see him?"

"I'm your real daddy. The only daddy you got."

"I want my real daddy! You made him go away! You're mean. Ow—you're hurting me!"

From orbit the island was invisible amid the ocean's endless blue. The Radical screamed. No one could hear. He launched a sunbeam at a random angle into the atmosphere, saw it flare briefly as air turned incandescent.

Feeling the prickle of capillaries bursting under the skin and a tickle in his eyeballs he flashed down, drew a deep breath, and back. Then west, against the Earth's rotation, crossing the terminator into darkness.

Hanging above North Africa he found the pale green blotch of the Sudd. He flashed to twenty thousand feet, scanning the Earth like a hungry eagle.

He found a Caliphate Multiple Launch Rocket System battery isolated from its main force. Bad move. Like Judgment he appeared among them, spread screams and fire and death and left fireworks lighting the sky behind him.

He felt *much* better then.

Somewhere in the Jungle
Vietnam

ALIYAH LAY BESIDE HIM in the bed, tracing Ellen's fingers across his bare chest. They were both naked, apart from the earring. The sun was pressing in at the window. Her body was warm and soft and comforting, curled against him. Ellen's right breast lay exposed by the folds of blanket, the nipple reacting to the cold now instead of their play. He popped a wasp free, sent it looping through the still air, and then back down onto his belly and into the flesh. Up, loop, back. Up, loop, back.

"What are you thinking?" Aliyah asked.

"Nothing," he said. "Just grooving on the postcoital bliss."

"Did you have a fight?"

"You mean ever in my life?"

"I mean since we were together last."

"Ah," Bugsy said. "Well, yes. On the plane, Nick and I had a little slap-fight. I talked it over with Ellen last night."

It was the nice way to put it. Talked it over sounded so much better than had a knock-down, drag-out, emotional dramafest. And still, Ellen had woken up this morning, put in the earring, and Aliyah had come to bed. And they'd fucked. Which was part of the problem.

I don't have a girlfriend, he'd said at the height of the argument. *A girlfriend is someone you spend time with. Me? I have a sex toy that you take out of the closet when you want to pretend you're with Nick.*

He didn't remember now exactly what Ellen had said back. Something about Bugsy thinking with his dick. But now this. Aliyah. Maybe he should have gotten up, gotten dressed, shown her the bug-and-bicycle sights of rural Vietnam. The impulse had been there, but then she'd put her hand on his cock, and there had been a bunch of other impulses instead.

Or maybe Ellen had just wanted some time to pretend she was with Nick. And who the hell was he to tell her that was a bad thing?

"You're angry with her," Aliyah said.

"Nah. I'm just tired. Long plane rides always fuck me up for a couple days. And . . ."

"Is it me?"

He shifted to look at her. Ellen's face took on a softness when Aliyah was wearing it. He tried to remember whether she'd been that vulnerable when she was alive. He didn't think so. Something about being dead must make a girl less secure about herself.

"It's not you," he said. "You're great. You've just got some lousy room-mates."

The knock on the door was gentle. Aliyah pulled the blankets up just as Billy's skinned head poked through. Bugsy could feel the tension in her body and remembered that she'd never met the joker. That had been Ellen.

"Sorry, man. We're running a little late. We'll be down in a minute," Bugsy said.

"No trouble," Billy said. "But if we're going to get there before the curator gets pissed off, we'd better get it swinging."

"Five minutes," Bugsy said, and the corpse monkey withdrew. Bugsy's fellow joker. Aliyah leaned forward and kissed him slow. "I know I have to go,"
she said. "But listen. Whatever's bothering you? Don't let it get you down,
okay?"

"I'll be fine," he said.

"I love you," Aliyah said.

Bugsy felt a presentiment of regret in his breast. Not the actual emotion,
but its echo, bouncing back down to him from someplace still in the future.
*Would you have said that when you were alive? Or are you making do with me,
because I'm the best you can do, what with being dead and all?* "I love you,
too," he said. She smiled and took out the earring.

Ellen came back to her body and hitched the blanket tighter around herself. Bugsy looked away. "Billy is, ah, downstairs . . ." he began.

"I heard. Five minutes," Ellen said, and walked to the bathroom. With
the shower running again and him not invited, Bugsy did the quick-and-
dirty alternative of bugging out, letting each wasp groom its neighbors, and
re-forming. It wasn't quite as good as a real bath, but it beat doing nothing.

It was closer to twenty minutes later, but they got on the road. An hour
after that, they arrived at the archives. It was a squat concrete building with
a sloped roof that looked more like a strip-mall restaurant than an official
government museum. Billy loped up to the door and held it open for them.

Inside, the atmosphere was equal parts bureaucratic office and cheap
roadside attraction. Gold foil surrounded maps and displays written in Vietnamese chronicled something, but Bugsy was damned if he could say what.
Most out of place was a framed still from some kind of cheap horror-porn
film. A huge, misshapen thing loomed over the jungle, lightning arcing from
its improbably clawed hands to an exploding Vietnamese tank. Pure creature-
feature schlock, except that this particular beast also had a disproportionately
huge penis, fully erect and easily as threatening as its claws.

As the curator—a grey-haired man with thin lips and a surprising smile—
carried on a fast, incomprehensible conversation with Billy, Ellen came up to
Bugsy's side and considered the movie still. "Cute," she said.

"Vietnamese *hentai*," Bugsy said. "Who knew?"

The curator went through a wide double door, talking seriously over his
shoulder all the way. Billy said something in a high chitter that Bugsy guessed

had more to do with playing up his simian looks than with the language it-self. The joker ambled over. "Ah, yeah. The big fight," he said. "That was back when Moonchild got taken captive. Vietnamese army sent an armored divi-sion to kill us all. Joker Brigade, Moonchild's dissident faction. Fucking every-one. They didn't care. Then that big son of a bitch showed up, trashed the whole place."

"You mean, that's *real?*" Ellen said, leaning in toward the image.

"That's what this place is celebrating." Billy sounded a little offended at their ignorance.

Bugsy considered the monster and tried to make it fit in with the theories about the Radical and Mark Meadows. If Moonchild had had something like that on the leash, she might have been able to stand up to Tom Weathers. Bugsy had the creeping sensation of looking at a clue that he just couldn't quite interpret.

The curator came back with a robe and a framed picture. He spoke rap-idly to Billy. Billy nodded back, saying something in turn. The curator made a satisfied sound and stood back, waiting.

The picture was Mark Meadows. He looked older, more tired, less care-free. But it was unmistakably the same guy Bugsy had seen in the pictures from the seventies back in New York. Only now, instead of the purple and yellow Uncle Sam outfit, he was wearing a robe of gold and green. The same one Billy was handing to Ellen. To Cameo.

"Okay," Bugsy said. "Here we go."

Ellen settled the robe on her shoulders, took a deep breath, and closed her eyes.

A moment later they opened, and Ellen was still looking out of them. Bugsy put down the picture of Meadows next to the still frame of the penis monster.

"What's the matter?" he asked.

"I don't . . . it's not working."

"Have we got the wrong robe?"

Billy turned to the curator, pointing and screeching. The curator took the question poorly and started screeching back. The two men gestured wildly, talking over each other. Ellen stepped up next to Bugsy. Her face was unread-able. "I think it's the right robe," she said.

"Then what?"

"Then Mark Meadows is alive."

Khartoum, Sudan
The Caliphate of Arabia

ALL HOSPITALS SMELL THE same—alcohol, blood, feces, fading flowers, disinfectant, and sickness.

Prince Siraj held a handkerchief—liberally sprinkled with aftershave—to his nose. Noel had smelled worse. Since this hospital was in Khartoum, you had the added charm of cots lining the dingy concrete walls. Each cot held a moaning, crying patient. Some held two. "You know, we could have held this meeting in Paris again," Noel said.

"I want you to see something." Siraj's tone was terse, despite being muffled by the square of linen. He pushed open the door to a room. There were only four beds inside. Whoever they were here to see clearly rated.

Noel followed Siraj to a bed near an open window. A desultory breeze filled with heat and the reek of camel dung floated through. A skeletal figure lay in the bed. His skin stretched over the bones in his face, and his eyes were so sunken that Noel thought they had been removed. His long beard looked like moss hanging from an ancient dead tree. The single sheet rose and fell as the man sucked in air in short, shallow gasps. An IV hung next to the bed. The man's arms were purple and black from the needles. Noel tilted the IV bag toward the light and read, *D5 half normal saline KCL20meq/multivits.*

"This is how he looked ten days ago," Siraj said.

Noel took the iPhone and inspected the image. The white robe strained over a vast belly and the cheeks above the beard were ruddy and fat, as if Santa had decided to holiday in warmer climes. He glanced again at the figure in the bed. There was enough in the shape of the brow and jaw for him to recognize it as the same man.

"You know what this means?"

"I won't deny you the pleasure of telling me."

Siraj shot him a venomous glance. "He's starving to death. *Starving!* He's lost 209 pounds in a week. Nothing helps. At first he stuffed himself, but then he became too weak to lift the food to his mouth. Now this." The prince flicked the bag with a forefinger. "And it's having no effect." Siraj paced back and forth at the foot of the man's bed. The sunken eyes flicked back and forth following his movements. Desperation gave some life to the dark irises. "When he could still talk he said he was bitten by a little boy. There were three of these monstrous children present at Khartoum. One of them could take down a building. The other reduced people to shriveled husks. Where are they coming from? How many more of these monsters does Weathers have?"

"I'll be going back to the PPA in a day or two. I'll see what I can discover."

"In a day or two?" Siraj's voice rose in outrage. "What the hell have you been doing?"

Noel tried to hang on to his own fraying temper. "Assembling my team. I'll be putting them in place in Kongoville."

"If you locate these monsters, kill them," Siraj ordered.

"That will make the PPA even more paranoid, and make it that much harder for me to accomplish my goal. Also, I don't kill children."

"Scruples? From you? What a joke." Siraj read the fury in Noel's eyes. "You'd best keep your temper. Remember my little love notes."

"Right now I have both you and Weathers threatening me. I kill you, I have only one threat."

That logic seemed to back Siraj down. He looked away.

Noel let him mull on that, then asked, "And how are you coming on arranging a cease-fire?"

"Jayewardene is making arrangements. But once I land in Paris my location will be known. What's to keep Weathers from just killing me? Or sending one of these child aces after me?"

"Request that the Committee provide security. Weathers is crazy, but he's not a fool. He didn't try to fight in New Orleans. He's powerful, but numbers will always win out."

"Remember, you only have to the end of the year."

Noel tuned out the boring loop of threats and demands. He wondered how Niobe was feeling. How she was doing. Fourteen and a half weeks. A week and a half—ten days and they would be at that magic sixteen-week mark. Out of danger. On their way to a child.

"I may change the date. I need this done quickly—"

Noel interrupted. "Look, we can do this right or we can do this fast. You don't get both. Oh, and we also can't do it cheap. I need money. Enough to look like a credible first deposit at the bank."

"I want it back."

Noel just gave him a look. "Isn't it a small price to pay for the Caliphate?"

On the Lukuga River, Congo
People's Paradise of Africa

IT WASN'T LONG AFTER Wally stole the PPA patrol boat that he first noticed the itchy feeling between his shoulders, like he was being watched. He reminded himself that this was a good thing. That he *wanted* the PPA to watch him, keep tabs on him. Because more people following Wally meant fewer people following Jerusha and the rescued kids. The more the PPA watched him, the less it could watch her. Its soldiers couldn't be everywhere at once.

All true. But it was a creepy feeling, all the same.

He paused for a lunch break only when he couldn't ignore the growling of his stomach any longer. His canteen was empty, too, so it was time to pull aside. Wally went ashore in a shaded cove hidden by a bend in the river. He hauled his gear a few dozen yards into the jungle. After fishing out two more chlorination tablets, he returned to the river with his canteen. Chlorine made the water taste terrible—like he'd fallen into a swimming pool and accidentally taken a gulp—but he'd insisted that Jerusha and the kids take both biological filtration bottles. Wally was distracted, still thinking about Jerusha, when he returned to the spot where he'd stashed his gear.

A flash of something pale caught the corner of his eye while he packed his canteen away. He looked up, expecting to see a bird or maybe even a monkey.

And that was when he saw the ghostly little girl. She emerged from the jungle without making a sound.

"Holy cripes!" Wally dropped the canteen and scrambled backward on his hands and feet.

She looked to be eight or nine years old. She wore a pristine white dress, like something a little kid would wear to church. Incongruously, Wally wondered how she kept it so clean in the jungle. But then he noticed that her passage didn't disturb the underbrush. She passed right through it, and she didn't cast a shadow. Like a ghost.

The girl stared at him with wide eyes dark as a moonless night. She held her hands behind her back. The only sound was the gurgling of water from the canteen.

Wally's heart hammered away at the bars of its iron cage. It felt like forever before the tightness in his throat receded enough for him to speak. He struggled to form a coherent thought. "Where the heck did you come from?" he managed.

The girl didn't answer. If she heard him at all she showed no sign of it. All she did was stare at him with those cold, cold eyes. She didn't even blink.

"Holy cow, kid. You scared the stuffing out of me." Wally regained his feet. He took a step forward. She backed up. "Are you lost?" Another step. The girl backed up again, receding into the jungle. "Hungry?"

The last thing he noticed before she disappeared completely was that her feet didn't touch the ground.

Wally's appetite had fled. Like the rest of him wanted to do. He abandoned thoughts of lunch. Instead he picked up his gear and forced himself to walk back to the boat rather than run. The itch between his shoulder blades was painful now, like a hot nail in the back.

He put miles and miles between himself and the little girl before nightfall made it impossible to go any farther. And even though he knew it was silly, he was careful to pitch his tent on the opposite side of the river from where he'd stopped for lunch. He forced himself to eat, even though his appetite hadn't returned.

Wally tossed and turned in his sleeping bag for what felt like hours. When he did manage to drift off, dark and disturbing dreams haunted him. He slept fitfully.

He snapped wide awake just before dawn, after a particularly vivid dream about somebody trying to slit his throat. But he was all alone in the jungle.

Mackenzie District
Northwest Territory, Canada

"YOU'RE LOSING IT, MAN," the hippie asshole said. Behind the thick round lenses of his specs his eyes wavered like blue drops of ink refusing to quite dissolve in water. Tom longed to punch in that weak face, oddly ascetic as it was, with the gaunt cheeks and wispy goatee and an air of general sadness that infuriated him the more. "You can't hide from it much longer."

He and the *other* floated in a sort of fluffy Void in which only they had color and form. "So what? So fucking what? You think you can take your body back? That shit's gone forever, Meadows. If I lose it we all die."

"If that's so," his enemy—the only thing he feared—said calmly, "that wouldn't be so bad. Because you're losing control of your power, too."

He laughed. "I'm the most powerful ace on fucking Earth. Who's going to do anything to me?"

"It's not what others do to you. It's what you do to the world. The whole human race. You're turning into an extinction-level threat."

He laughed again, a bit more wildly. "If I wipe out humanity, who the fuck'll miss us? All your hippie friends these days say humanity's a plague."

"What about the oppressed?" his gentle inquisitor said doggedly. "What about your Revolution?"

"Hey, maybe I fulfill the historic process by ending history. Shit *happens*, man."

"But if people make shit happen," Meadows said, "others can stop them doing it."

"Ha! You and what army?"

Tom became aware of shapes seeming to swim around them. His eyes couldn't resolve them as anything more than vaguely human-shaped blurs of color: grey; an orange that flickered like the reflections of flames; a disc half moon-silver and half black, with S-curved demarcation; a black infinitely deep, shot through with tiny parti-color points of light that did not illuminate the darkness.

"You forget whose friends they were to start with," Mark said.

"They're mine now. You got nothing, you weak, lame puke. You *are* nothing. And I'm tired of your shit." With a force of will Tom drove himself upward and out.

Abruptly he was sitting upright in a bed, cold air pricking his skin where sheets and layers of heavy blankets had fallen away. A faint smoke smell and heat of banked coals emanated from the fireplace. Big snowflakes beat like giant moths against the window of the cabin in the Arctic pine forests of Mackenzie District in Canada's Northwest Territory, almost as remote as the mid-Pacific.

He had come alone. He needed to try to get his head straight. Sun Heilian was starting to look at him funny. She was too damned smart, that woman. *She's just a woman*, a voice told him. *The world's half full of them.*

Tom shook his head and rubbed his face, where for some reason beard bristles never grew. "She loves Sprout," he said, "she loves *me*." And he thought, *Who's laughing? Who's that I hear?* And inside him was colder than outside the log walls of the cabin.

♥

Monday, December 14

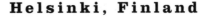

Helsinki, Finland

"I DON'T REALLY WANT to be crawling through a computer screen in the security office," Jaako Kuusi, aka Broadcast, mumbled around a mouthful of creamed herring.

Noel placed a spoonful of caviar, some chopped egg, and chopped onion on a cracker. "Well, how else can we do it?" He took a bite and the sharp taste of fish and salt brought an explosion of saliva to the back of his mouth.

"There's a guy in the States. I kept track of computer aces for our service."

Noel nodded. Jaako did occasional freelance work for the Finnish secret service, and he and Noel had crossed paths a few times. "And what does he do?"

A gull appeared out of the fog and snow, and dove past the window of the Helsinki restaurant. Its raucous cries grated like rusty hinges. "The Signal on Port 950."

"That's nice, what the hell does that mean?"

Jaako shook his head. "That's his name, his handle, not his power. But it suggests his power."

"Would you get to the point?"

"You sound just like Niemi," Jaako complained, referring to the head of the Finnish secret service.

"You don't have to be insulting. Niemi is a nasty piece of work." Noel dished up more caviar.

"And Flint was such an angel?" Jaako asked. "I think you have to be a perfect shit to run one of these agencies."

"I'd agree with that," Noel said.

"So, why pull this heist on the Nshombos? Why not get them hauled up in front of the Hague? Rumor has it you put Flint there." Noel just smiled, and Jaako looked disappointed. "Oh, come on, give me something?"

"No." Noel paused for a sip of vodka. "Now tell me about the Signal. What's his power and why do we need it?"

"The guy can project his consciousness into any computer on the Internet that is listening on Port 950. When he's inhabiting a computer, he can use it like any user—copy files, send jobs to a printer, connect to another computer. But here's what's useful for us. He can also use any peripheral devices as if he were the interface software."

Noel slowly set down his glass. "He can control the security devices in the vault."

Jaako formed a gun with his fingers, pointed it at Noel, and pretended to pull the trigger. "Bingo."

"Yes, we definitely need him," Noel said.

"Which brings us back to me avoiding that whole security office issue. If you can find the guy—he's a total recluse—you need to convince him to let me into his space so I can enter the vault from his computer screen in the United States."

"And if I can't find him or convince him?"

"I won't join your party."

"I'll find him." Noel paused for a moment, then added softly, "Do I need to remind you not to mention this little endeavor to anyone?"

"I won't. A chance for a couple of mil. Mum's the word." He made a zipping motion across his lips.

"Yes, and just to assure your silence . . ." Noel slid an eight-by-ten envelope across the table.

Jaako opened it, pulled out the photos, blanched, and quickly shoved them back into the envelope.

Noel knew what they contained. A particularly horrible variety of child pornography, and he'd downloaded them from Jaako's computer.

"How did you get these?" Jaako demanded. He tried to sound threatening, but it came out breathless.

"I stole your computer. And I'll deliver it to Niemi if you don't play nice."

"You're a bastard. Talk about Niemi or Flint. *You* could be running one of these agencies."

"And you're a pervert, but I'm going to make you a rich pervert." Noel stood, threw down money, and walked out into the Finnish blizzard.

Saigon, Vietnam

BUGSY PRESSED THE CELL phone against his ear. The rumble of traffic was almost enough to drown out Barbara Baden's voice.

"No," Bugsy said. "I'm in the middle of this thing for Lohengrin."

"You'll need to take a break from it," Babel said. "Jayewardene wants as many members of the Committee as possible to be at the conference for security detail. I've arranged a private flight for you. How soon can you be at Ho Chi Minh Airport?"

Bugsy pressed the phone to his chest, leaned forward, and asked Billy the same question. Around them, the highway was buzzing with traffic following no recognizable traffic laws Bugsy had ever seen. Semis screamed past them at a hundred kilometers an hour. Granted that wasn't so bad when you put it in miles per hour, but three digits still made him nervous.

"Five hours," the joker said with a shrug of his desiccated shoulders. "Shouldn't be a problem."

Babel must have heard, because as soon as Bugsy put the phone back to his ear, she was speaking.

"I'll have the flight ready for you. It will be official UN business, so you can skip all the customs and airport security."

The line went dead. Bugsy closed the phone. Nick, sitting beside him, raised Cameo's eyebrows. The guy still hadn't forgiven Bugsy for knocking the hat off on the plane into Vietnam. "Change of plans?" Nick said.

"How would you feel about a lovely few days in Paris watching the Caliphate stall for time? Turns out there's a peace conference that they want us to be at."

Billy shouted something that sounded obscene and swerved violently.

The tires squealed, and the car fishtailed for a few heart-stopping seconds before shifting back into a recognizable lane. Nick looked a little pale.

"Sounds fine, assuming we get there."

Coeur d'Alene, Idaho

THERE WAS ANOTHER BLIZZARD in Coeur d'Alene, Idaho. Noel peered through the windshield of the rented car. The wipers were in a losing battle with the snow. He'd tried to teleport to the Steunenberg farm, but Google Earth had failed him. This place was so remote and the shot from the satellites so cursory that Noel had found himself standing in ankle-deep mud with a bitter wind slicing through his topcoat, surrounded by fallow fields.

So he'd teleported to Barcelona and warmer climes, used an Internet café to check a location for a Hertz in Coeur d'Alene. He then teleported back to Idaho and rented a car. While he waited for a young pimple-plagued boy to bring up the car he perused through the file on his iPhone about Mollie Steunenberg, aka Tesseract.

He skipped past the downloads of season two of *American Hero*. It had been painful to watch. Mollie hadn't had a good run. Her power was formidable. Her tolerance for backstabbing limited. She'd been voted off in the fifth week, and her final confessional had been filled with anger, confusion, and a desire to get even with "the Heathers." Noel had to do a bit of research to understand that reference, but once he did, it was just another angle to use with Ms. Steunenberg. That and her age. At seventeen she'd either be idealistic or a completely self-absorbed teenager.

Noel made the last turn through an open gate in a long white fence, and then the house appeared out of the storm. It looked like a Norman Rockwell painting, complete with a Christmas tree twinkling in a front window and smoke pouring from the stone chimney. A big barn lay off to the left, and as Noel stepped out of the car he heard the lowing of cattle.

Since he wanted to test her power in a real world setting rather than the artifice of American television, he locked his keys in the car.

The brass knocker on the front door was etched with the words "Bless This House." It was All Americana perfection. Noel considered the file he'd compiled—nuclear family, mom, dad, nine kids, eight boys and one girl, grandma and grandpa living in the house, and all of them farming the family land. Noel began to despair of ever attracting this young woman into a life of crime.

There was the sound of many running feet, and the door was flung open to reveal a long hallway filled with a sea of young boys ranging in age from seven to seventeen. "I'm looking for Ms. Mollie Steunenberg," Noel said. "Is she in?"

"MOLLIE! THERE'S SOME GUY HERE FOR YOU!" one of the boys shouted.

"HE SOUNDS LIKE A FAG!" another yelled.

"Mollie's got a boyfriend, and he's a fag," the smallest boy lisped in a singsong.

There was a clatter of boots on the stairs at the far end of the hall. Mollie Steunenberg was short, plump, and cute, with curling red hair and a sprinkle of freckles across her nose. She had dark brown eyes and they were brimming with anger. "Shut up, you *jerks*." She pushed through the gaggle of boys. Now Noel could see the family resemblance, and his flagging hopes soared. "I'm Mollie," she said, and stood, arms akimbo, and stared challengingly up at him.

"I'm Mr. Fontes with the Brookline Agency." He handed over one of his fake cards. "We're in the business of developing and utilizing wild card talents in a variety of industrial settings." Noel had a feeling that a hardheaded farm girl from Idaho wouldn't buy the idea a movie agent was interested in her so he'd invented Mr. Fontes and the Brookline Agency. "Your fourth-dimensional powers have some interesting applications, and we'd like to talk with you about employment."

"Great. Let me get my coat."

"Don't you want to talk here?"

Mollie looked horrified. "Oh, God, no. There's no *privacy* here." She bestowed a glare on her brothers.

"But your parents . . ." Noel began.

"They're watching *Wheel of Fortune* and they hate to be interrupted."

Wheel of Fortune. It couldn't be more perfect.

Once outside Noel made a production of having locked his keys in the car. "If we could get a coat hanger from the house," he said.

Mollie made a face. "My brothers will think you're lame, and I'll get even more shit from them. I can get the keys."

Noel watched as she focused on the car door. A small opening appeared in the metal. Mollie reached through and her hand vanished, and appeared out of the dashboard of the car. It was disturbing and rather creepy, as if her arm had bent into strange, twisted angles. But of course she was reaching through a fourth-dimensional gate. It wouldn't be normal.

She snagged the keys and tossed them to Noel. He allowed himself to biff the catch, and had to fish them out of the snow and mud.

Special Camp Mulele
Guit District, South Sudan
The Caliphate of Arabia

MID-AFTERNOON IN THE SUDD was the hottest part of the day. Some hippos drowsed in the nearest arm of the river with just their ears and bulbous eyes and road-humped backs showing above the brown water. Even the little birds that groomed their thick hides for ticks and parasites had given up and sought shelter until the heat of day passed.

Tom touched down on white dirt packed firm by small feet. Special Camp Mulele drowsed under open-sided tents and awnings that did little more than cut the sun's sting. Some of the child aces sobbed quietly to themselves. A pair of the younger kids sat cross-legged playing patty-cake, one with child hands, the other with the blunt furry tips of giant spider legs. Ayiyi was an Ewe kid from Ghana's Togo River region, west along the coast from Nigeria. His folks had moved to Lagos looking for work a year before its liberation. Only ten, he had a kid's head sticking out of the body of a black-and-white spider with a yard-long body and an eight-foot span on his eight fuzzy legs. Like any spider, Ayiyi had humongous fangs and creepy little jointed leg-things to bring food to his maw. But he ate with his human mouth. It was a process Tom could never bear to watch. Those nasty fangs injected a venom that immobilized its victims with sheer pain, as it liquefied them inside their own skin.

"Listen up, kids," Tom called in French, then repeated it in English. "We got things to do."

They stopped and turned to him. Some faces were sad, some horrifying. In all of them he saw a kind of hunger, avid as that of any starving man peering through the window at a plutocrat's feast. *They're looking at me*, he thought. *They know I have something to give them. A purpose to their poor twisted lives. Purpose to their suffering. Is that really such a bad thing?*

"It's time to step up and fight for the Revolution," he said, and grinned. "We're gonna have us some *fun*."

International House of Pancakes
Coeur d'Alene, Idaho

THEY FOUND A TWENTY-FOUR-HOUR IHOP. Noel, fearing what would pass for cuisine, satisfied himself with a cup of coffee. Mollie was tucking into Stuffed French Toast drenched with strawberry syrup and piled high with strawberries and whipped cream.

"You know that came out of a can," Noel said with a nod toward the whipped cream. "It has never come within even waving distance of an actual cow."

"It's good."

Noel suddenly felt far older than thirty. He was preparing his opening statement when Mollie took it away from him. "So, is there really a Brookline Agency? 'Cause I've never heard of it, and I've been looking for some way out of here, and away from farming."

Noel leaned in confidentially. "No. But I'm going to found it right after the holidays. It seems to me the most logical and frankly brilliant idea."

"So, why did you come asking after me?"

"Because I do want to utilize your powers. Just not as a means of securing spent nuclear fuel."

"Hey, now *that's* a cool idea." She took another huge bite of toast and mumbled, "Okay, but what is it you really want me to do?"

"Help me liberate some ill-gotten gains from some very bad people."

Mollie frowned. "That doesn't sound legal."

"It's not . . . technically . . . but morally it's very pure."

"I don't want to go to jail."

"The funds are in Africa."

He watched the frown vanish, and he could even follow the thought process. *Outside of the United States it's anything goes. If you steal from foreigners it's not really stealing.*

"And I'd get paid for this?"

"Three million dollars."

"Sign me up."

In the Jungle, Congo
People's Paradise of Africa

THE JUNGLE WAS THEIR enemy, as much as any pursuers.

The jungle didn't want them to walk straight east. It forced them to jog north or south to find a good place to ford the frequent streams, or to avoid pools where crocodiles lurked in the rushes. It made them bypass hills that were too steep for the children and the burden of the jokers like Eason who they carried. It laid tree roots and ravines across their path. It send hordes of mosquitoes and huge black flies to torment them. It yammered at them with a thousand eerie and strange sounds that made the children shudder and cry in return. It plagued them with heat and humidity; it wrapped them in a claustrophobic world of green and brown that smelled of wet earth and rot.

Despite Waikili's continued insistence, they'd yet to have any visible indication of pursuit. Jerusha didn't have time to worry about that. The environment itself was trial enough.

They were moving down a long slope to where—well below—Jerusha could see the glimmer of yet another stream. She was trying to help the kids carry the improvised stretcher with Eason, so that they didn't spill the joker child onto the ground. That had already happened too many times. The sight of Eason flopping on the ground with his fish tail reminded Jerusha uncomfortably of her childhood when her goldfish had leaped from their bowl onto the table. "Careful, Saadi," she said to one of the children. "Watch where you're stepping."

From behind her, upslope, there was a cry, then a shout of "Bibbi Jerusha!"

She left Eason and went running up to where several of the children were gathered around someone. "It's Efia," Cesar said as she approached. "She's been bitten. A snake . . ."

Jerusha crouched down alongside Efia, who was sniffing and holding her right leg. At the girl's ankle, there were beads of blood and the joint itself was puffy, the skin blotchy and dark. She was speaking in Baluba, her voice choked with sobs. "What's she saying?" Jerusha asked Cesar.

"It bit her twice—on the ankle, then on the hand when she reached down." Efia held out the hand. Like the ankle, it was already visibly swollen, the skin darkening around the puncture wounds.

Jerusha had already swung her pack from her shoulders, digging in it for the snakebite first-aid kit. "Did she see the snake? Does she know what it was?"

Cesar asked Efia, who shook her head and spoke a quick few words. She was panting, her breath too fast.

"It was brown and yellow, about as long as her arm. It's not one she knows. It went back into the brush after it bit her."

"All right," Jerusha said. "Everyone be careful, that snake is still around here. Tell Efia it will be okay. Just lay back and relax. Here . . ." She handed Cesar a roll of bandages. "Tie a strip of this around her leg and arm right above the wounds—tight, but not too tight." There was cobra antivenom in the kit, but without knowing if the snake was a cobra or not, Jerusha didn't know whether it might do more harm than good. The instructions in the kit were of little help.

Efia was crying. Jerusha stroked her head. The girl was sweating. "Kafil— get some water and a cloth. Put it on her head." Jerusha opened the suction device in the kit and placed it over the wound, pulling on the plunger. An ugly mixture of pus and blood came out. The children gathered around made noises of disgust, and Efia's cries became louder. "Hush!" she told them. "Let me work. . . ."

She knew from her experience in the parks and the occasional snakebites there that suction usually did little to remove the venom, nor could it stop the necrosis of the tissue. She also knew that victims needed to be seen by a doctor as soon as possible after a bite. Here, there was only Jerusha and whatever was in the kit.

The swelling was worsening, and Efia's breath was shallowing. Her eyes were closed. Jerusha could feel panic rising in her own chest. She quickly filled a syringe with the antivenom and injected it into Efia's arm.

She resumed using the suction device on the bite sites. "Come on," she breathed toward Efia, who had slipped into unconsciousness. "Come on, girl . . ."

She worked on the girl, as the jungle howled derision at her, as the children watched, as monkeys chattered and chased each other through the tree branches overhead, as the shafts of sun slid through the gaps in the canopy overhead. Efia's breathing continued to worsen. Sweat poured from her, then ominously stopped. The skin around the wounds putrefied sickeningly.

Jerusha suddenly realized that she hadn't heard Efia take a breath in far too long. "No!" she shouted. To the jungle, to the children around her. "No! Efia . . ."

There was no answer. Only the still and silent body in front of her.

Damascus, Syria
The Caliphate of Arabia

DAMASCUS LAY ON ITS plateau gleaming like scattered self-luminous jewels in the night.

Tom Weathers touched down in the old town on a plaza in front of a giant white building whose dome and minaret, lit respectively gold and blue, marked it as a major mosque. Under his arms he carried Ayiyi and the Mummy. The Darkness rode his back, her arms around his neck and her pipe-stem legs wrapped around his waist.

There wasn't much traffic here this late. Tom let them down to the pavement. "Okay, this time you're on your own," he told them. "The Darkness will give you cover; you other two wander around and, y'know, spread the love." He looked closely at the Darkness. She had her arms crossed and a dubious expression on her dark pixie face. "Candace, you sure you'll be okay by yourself?"

"Of course I will, silly fool," she said. "No one can see me. No one find me."

Solemnly she touched the eyes of both other children. Venom dripped from Ayiyi's spider jaws and fell hissing on the pavement. The Mummy only nodded, her face unreadable beneath the bandages that covered her.

Candace raised her arms, and Darkness issued from her mouth, ears, eyes. Rolled away from her like smoke. In a heartbeat she was gone, shrouded in black fog.

Before the cold black tentacles closed around him Tom Weathers was in orbit.

♣

Tuesday, December 15

On the Lualaba River, Congo People's Paradise of Africa

THE LUKUGA RIVER JAGGED sharply to the north just before joining the Lualaba. Wally studied a map in his guidebook. The Lualaba was itself a tributary of the famous Congo River.

He passed a village nestled where the two rivers met. Kongolo, according to the guidebook. He slowed down, so that the villagers could get a clear look at the metal man driving a PPA boat. Most fled. But a few folks saw him and pointed. He sped up again when Kongolo was behind him.

A barge floated somewhere on this tangle of waterways. A barge that had supplied the Nyunzu lab with the virus that had killed Lucien. Wally kept reminding himself to leave a few survivors when he finally found the barge. Survivors who could report his whereabouts. Which, he hoped, would keep people off Jerusha's trail.

The files from Nyunzu said the central lab, the centerpiece of the PPA's project to create an army of child aces, was in Bunia. He found the village on the map, tucked up in the northeastern corner of the PPA. After taking care of the barge, he'd go as far upriver as he could, then strike out over land toward Bunia.

Wally was so preoccupied with the map, glancing up only occasionally to keep the boat on course, that he didn't notice when the river widened and slowed. *Thud.* The boat ran aground on a sandbar at the edge of a marshy stretch of river. The impact jarred the guidebook from Wally's hands; the pilot's chair creaked under his shifting weight.

"Awww, heck." Wally slammed the throttle into reverse, but the boat didn't budge. Its sleek prow had sliced into the sand like a knife, but now it was wedged in there good and snug. "Nuts." He killed the throttle and climbed out. Muck squelched underfoot. It oozed up to his ankles. "Well, that's just great."

The marsh was an expanse of chest-high river grass dotted with a smattering of wispy, droopy trees. Jerusha could have told him exactly what kind of trees they were.

Jeez, do I ever miss you, Jerusha. Stay safe, okay?

Here and there, rivulets of brackish water cut channels through the stands of grass. Wally thought about this. The barge had to come through here on the way to and from Nyunzu; he'd traveled the entire length of the Lukuga River without seeing it. So there had to be a way through.

Twenty minutes of searching revealed a circuitous channel just wide enough for a barge. It was almost invisible until he was right on top of it, hidden by the river grass. But entering the channel at its outlet would have meant turning around, heading back up the river, and searching for the entrance. That would take a couple of hours. On the other hand, it wasn't all that far from his boat to the channel. Wally decided to portage.

The important part was getting a good grip. He lifted the prow out of the muck, then walked his way under the boat, hands overhead, until he reached the center of balance. Another heave freed the stern. He sank to his knees, but he managed to heft the boat overhead. *So much for my bandages*, he thought.

As strong as Wally was, carrying a boat through a swamp took a lot of work, even for him. Each step was a struggle to free his legs of the sucking mud without losing his balance. Rivulets of sweat ran down his face. Water and marsh slime pattered from the hull onto Wally's pith helmet. The occasional portage during canoe trips up in the boundary waters had never been this tough. But slowly, carefully, he made his way.

Wally gave one final heave. The patrol boat splashed back into the navigable portion of the river, ready to resume its pursuit of the barge.

He hunkered down for a breather at the water's edge, panting like he'd just run a marathon. This was the river, all right. The water rippled where the current picked up again. He unwrapped a granola bar.

Something launched out of the water, clamped on his leg, and yanked him into the river.

The next thing Wally knew, he was facedown on the river bottom with what felt like a hydraulic press squeezing the heck out of his leg. It flipped him over. Wally caught a glimpse of green amid the bubbles and froth in the murky brown water.

His lungs ached. He couldn't see. Something rough smacked him in the face.

Wally aimed a fist, blindly, at the crushing pressure just below his knee. He poured everything he had into it. The blow landed on something scaly with a muffled *crunch*. The dazed crocodile loosened its grip.

Wally pulled free. He flailed for the surface, desperate to pull air into his burning lungs, but he wasn't much of a swimmer. The iron skin didn't do much for his buoyancy. His field of view receded into a narrow tunnel.

His fingers brushed a bundle of tree roots. Wally wrapped both hands around the roots and pulled for all he was worth. His head broke the surface. His chest creaked like old bedsprings as he sucked down a lungful of air.

The croc grabbed his leg and pulled him under again.

"Crip—" *Splash.*

They hit bottom again. It felt like the lousy thing was biting right through the iron. He'd have dents for sure. The croc outweighed him; using its tail for leverage, it flipped Wally like a pancake. His hip erupted in wrenching pain.

The death roll. That's what Jerusha had called it.

Wally doubled over when the croc rolled under him. He reached the jaws clamped around his shin. Wally grabbed the croc's snout, one hand on each jaw, and pulled.

Wally felt a tremor as he pried apart the croc's jaws. But it fought him for every inch. *Judas Priest, this thing is strong.*

Its forelegs scrabbled at his chest. The massive tail hammered at his arms and legs.

Wally pulled his leg free, then launched himself back to the surface with a kick to the croc's gut. The croc surfaced a split second after he did. Gasping for air, he finally got a good look at the thing. It had to be twelve feet long.

The croc lunged again. For something so large, it was surprisingly fast. Wally clamped his hands around the tip of its snout again. This time, he squeezed until he could lace his fingers together. The croc couldn't open its mouth.

But it could still use its tail to pound at Wally. Which it did. Furiously.

Wally raised his arms overhead, pulling the croc's head and forelegs clear of the water. It thrashed, sending Wally toppling over backward. But as the croc landed on him, he threw his legs around its midriff and his arms around its throat. He squeezed.

They went under again, wrestling at the bottom of the river. The croc writhed in his grasp. It couldn't twist around far enough to bite him; Wally's shoulder was pressed into its throat. It tried to smash him, using its weight to pin Wally to the mud. The blow expelled the remainder of the breath Wally had been holding. That loosened his grip just enough for the croc to spin around until Wally held it from behind, but he didn't release it. The ridges along its back scratched his chest. Wally's field of view receded into the tunnel again. He locked his ankles together, squeezing until he felt the creak of reptile bones.

The croc coiled its free half like a spring, then launched them both with one colossal thrashing of its tail. They broke the surface, Wally's arms and legs still clamped around the croc. They crashed on the riverbank. Pain shot up and down Wally's back.

Crack. Something snapped under his grip. Then another, and another. Ribs.

Crimson froth issued from the corners of the crocodile's mouth. It struggled, weakly, to free itself. Wally let go. It dove back in the river.

Wally staggered back, shaking. His entire body trembled with the last vestiges of adrenaline and the first twinges of, *Holy cow, that thing could have killed me.*

He slumped against a tree. Part of him knew he had to dig out a towel and start drying himself as quickly as possible. But he couldn't catch his breath. His arms and legs throbbed with bruises from the battering they'd received. It felt like every joint in his body had been stretched apart, especially his hip. His ribs burned.

Slowly, the panicky feeling ebbed, leaving only aches and pains in its place. He watched the retreating crocodile. The post-adrenaline crash left him giddy.

Well, gosh, get a load of that, he thought. *Just like Tarzan!*

Wally pounded his chest with both fists. The jungle echoed with his best imitation of Johnny Weissmuller.

But the post-adrenaline crash hit him hard. Almost before the last echoes of his triumphant yell had faded away, his eyelids became too heavy for him to lift. Heavier than the boat, heavier even than the crocodile. The need for sleep defeated him before he could towel off.

Something bumped his neck. A loud *clink* snapped him out of a deep nap some time later. The ghostly little girl stood over him, a ten-inch knife clutched in her tiny fist.

Bahr al-Ghazal Region
The Sudd, South Sudan
The Caliphate of Arabia

THE GHAZI COMMANDO SHRIEKED wildly as Ayiyi, clinging to his back, plunged his fangs into his shoulder through the tail of his green-and-white checked *keffiyeh*. The boy face above the spider body gleamed with Christmas glee.

"That's the way, man!" Tom shouted. The camp grew flames, whipping like pale yellow and orange banners in the merciless sun. A Ghazi jumped from behind a blazing BMP-3, aiming a stubby AKSU carbine at Tom's face. Tom plucked it from his hands and tied the barrel in a knot, shattering the synthetic forestock. Then he handed it back. "I know it's trite, man, but sometimes the old ways are best."

The dude had balls, Tom had to give him that. Rather than accept the useless steel pretzel back he batted it away and fired a brutal sidekick into Tom's solar plexus.

Tom had already bent his body at the center to bring the rim of his rib cage protectively over the vulnerable nerve junction. He took a step back. "Tae kwon do, huh? Nice shot. Try this on for size." He drove a palm-heel strike into the center of the man's chest. The commando's eyeballs popped clear of their sockets. Juice squirted from his nose and mouth and ears as his rib cage flexed clear to his spine, squishing heart and lungs and liver and other incidentals. The Ghazi flew up and away, flopping like a rag doll, to slam against the radar dish of the armored barge that had dropped the elite mechanized recon squadron here on the west flank of the Simba Brigades.

Tom's kid aces, augmented by two were-leopards and a squad of non-shape-shifting Leopard Man commandos, were raising adequate hell among the cars and crews. Tom wanted the barge. Blowing up and sinking it would look *really cool* for the cameras. Hei-lian and her crew were squatting ass-deep in a nasty stagnant pool a quarter mile away, capturing the action through the papyrus shoots.

It would've been easier, of course, to zap the barge before it off-loaded the squadron, but Doc Prez wanted his new aces showcased in action, show-ing the world how not just every ethnic group but every age group of the People's Paradise was stepping up to fight imperialism.

Tom raced toward the papyrus screen at the water's edge. Without pause he dove in. Drawing in a deep breath he willed himself to *change* even before his outstretched fingertips touched the roiled brown syrupy surface.

Then he floundered, his belly scraping bottom. *What the fuck?* he won-dered in amazement. *I'm supposed to be a fucking super-dolphin now!*

Another voice, deep and sonorous, said clearly in his mind: *You are unwor-thy. I care nothing for these land dwellers. Your madness endangers the creatures of the sea as well. I go, and wish you only failure.*

The words were French, with a Québécois accent. He had never heard that cold, contemptuous voice before. As the Radical. But in memories from his hated hippie predecessor he recalled hearing it from his own altered mouth . . .

In his befuddlement Tom ran out of air and broke through gasping ten yards from shore. A gunner on the barge's superstructure spotted him. A 12.7-millimeter heavy machine gun opened up like Doom with a stutter, throwing up really enormous jets of water around him.

He sucked deep breath and dove. The water deepened rapidly. Despite its weight of armor, the Caliphate barge had a shallow draught for river work, especially relieved of a hundred tons of armored car. Tom had plenty of clearance to swim beneath to the other beam. He may not have a dolphin's torpedo speed, but he still swam with more than human strength in arms and chest.

When he broke the surface of the water there wasn't a face in sight on the barge's starboard side. Everybody's attention was fixed on the battle the other way, no doubt looking for the shattered body of the PPA's un-mistakable field marshal and general rock star of World Revolution, the Radical.

He laughed. Laughing, he rose. He could have scuttled the vessel with a single blinding lance of white light. Instead he stretched out his hand. "Burn, baby, burn!" he shouted, and rained down fire from the sky.

Noel Matthews's Apartment
Manhattan, New York

Don't get me wrong. I'm not looking to start a revolution. But somebody's got to step up to the plate because governments have failed. We live in the freakin' twenty-first century, and here we are with people starving, and armies fighting in the Sudan, and for what? Oil? National pride? We could achieve wonders, hell, make that miracles—end hunger, travel to the stars, have perfect privacy and total freedom, but we've got to get out of the trees. We've got to tamp down the monkey brain. . . .

Noel leaned back from the computer screen. The rant continued for several more pages, but he had read enough to have a sense of the writer. *An idealist, but angry and cynical. I can work with that.*

Working from the handle provided by Broadcast, Noel had determined that the Signal on Port 950 was really Robert Cumming, age twenty-three. He lived in Chicago, Illinois, and he was a joker. He avoided almost all human contact, but he still had to eat.

Noel checked his watch. The groceries were about to be delivered to 865 Lake Shore Drive, apartment 723.

People's Palace
Kongoville, Congo
People's Paradise of Africa

HE WAS STILL FREAKED out when he stalked into the war room of the Nshombos' new vanity palace in K-ville, a great gleaming concrete iceberg, a true city within a city, if still a bit raw. The air-conditioning inside was like a frigid river flowing outward. Tom still welcomed it after the stinking sauna heat of the Sudd, and the diesel-reeking heat of K-ville. But it raised goosebumps on his arms.

That fucker, he raged. *He stole Aquarius from me. He lessened me.* Long ago, when his enemy ran around in a purple Uncle Sam suit calling himself "Captain Trips," he invoked his "friends" by taking unique decoctions of psychoactive chemicals, each and every one devised by Meadows in hopes of invoking *him*. The man who called himself Tom Weathers now. The *Radical*.

At last Mark Meadows got his way. And Tom had had things *his* way ever since. But it had come at a cost: Tom didn't dare use any kind of drug more mind-warping than coffee or chocolate. No pot. No booze. Not even antihistamines. Because anything that altered Tom's consciousness risked snapping his mind and body back into the long dark prison of Meadows's subconscious.

But the only way of reclaiming the surly shape-shifting Canuck who called himself Cetus Dauphine was to re-create the drugs that Meadows used to invoke him. Tom felt sick certainty that wouldn't work, either: no formulation his enemy had ever tried had sufficed to bring back Starshine after he "died," or martial-arts goddess Moonchild once she retired from the world in horror at taking a human life. And while Tom had access to many of his predecessor's memories, he lacked Mark's biochemical genius. He couldn't even *try*.

"Oh, Tom," Alicia Nshombo said, rising as he came through the automatic sliding door. Video screens covered the walls of the room beyond, showing moving scenes of battle in the Sudd, of Congo-basin forest, of everyday life in K-ville. "I am so glad you are back."

Dr. Nshombo sat behind a vast gleaming black African blackwood desk. As usual the President-for-Life's face showed no more reaction than the desktop.

"The United Nations has offered to broker a peace conference between ourselves and the Caliphate of Arabia," Nshombo said gravely. If he was capable of talking any other way Tom had never heard.

"So? Fuck 'em."

Alicia uttered a little gasp and pressed fingers to her mouth. She'd reacted the same way the thousand other times she'd heard Tom use such language. "Tom, *cher*," she said. "Please don't take such a tone with my brother. You need each other so much."

Dr. Nshombo wasn't one to mouth meaningless phrases. He went on as if Tom had not spoken. "I have decided it is in our best interests to participate. I mean to send our foremost jurist, Dr. Apollinaire Okimba, as our representative. He enjoys an impeccable reputation on the world stage. His participation will play well, as our clever young friend the Chinese colonel would say."

"You're shitting me," said Tom. "You're not actually gonna *negotiate* with this fat imperialist Allah freak?"

"Our representative will deliver to Siraj our ultimatum: either he withdraws his support from the genocidal aggressors in South Sudan and pulls back his armies, or we shall destroy those armies, depose him, and liberate the suffering people of the Middle East from the chains of a brutal superstition. There will be no negotiation."

Tom could only stare at his old comrade. "Yeah, well, that will play well, I'm sure."

Dr. Nshombo's brows twitched a millimeter closer together. It was the equivalent of a normal man throwing a rage fit. But Alicia's mouth crumpled, pursed between plump cheeks, and her eyes got dewy behind her batwing glasses at Tom's rudeness. "But Tom," she said, "if the Arab gives in, the war will end."

"Siraj *won't* give in. It'd mean crawling home on his belly. And the U-fucking-N? Those Committee fuckers helped protect Bahir when he kidnapped my daughter!" He was half standing and all shouting.

Nshombo faced him impassively. "The Revolution must come before your petty desires for vengeance, Tom, but I am not unmindful of the wrong you suffered." Then he actually smiled. "It is not my intention to send Dr. Okimba to the Paris peace conference at all."

"No?" Tom goggled.

Dr. Nshombo began to laugh.

Robert Cumming's Apartment
Chicago, Illinois

ONE HUNDRED DOLLARS SIMPLIFIED the negotiation with the delivery boy. Noel stood in front of the apartment door, set down one sack, and rang the bell. He idly noticed that the sacks contained mostly pasta Meals in a Sack, bags of potato and tortilla chips, and several different kinds of cookies.

He expected a behemoth to answer the door. What actually stood framed in the doorway once it was opened was an incredibly tall and incredibly thin monochrome joker. Despite his youth, his hair was grey, his eyes were grey, and his skin was greyer. "You're not Chuck," Cumming said.

"No."

"What do you want?"

Noel was pleased. He hated people who didn't get to the heart of a matter, and instead wasted time asking, *"Who are you?"* and *"How did you get here?"* or *"How did you get the groceries?"*

"I'm the man who's going to give you the opportunity to change the world," Noel said.

Wednesday, December 16

In the Jungle, Congo
People's Paradise of Africa

RUSTY, I NEED YOU. We should never have split up. I can't do this. I can't.

But there was no choice. She'd already lost one of her charges to the jungle, and she worried about Rusty, about where he was and who might be after him. The despair threatened to overwhelm her: they might both be dead soon, Wally lost in the jungle somewhere, and her with these children who clung to her as if she were their only hope.

She kept the kids crawling forward as long as they could during the daylight hours, and huddled together with them around a small fire at night, when the sounds of the jungle surrounded them and their imaginations jumped at every noise. She fed them from the food her seed pouch could produce—strangely, to Jerusha, it seemed the jungle wasn't the best place to forage and find food. *You are their only hope.* She could nearly hear Rusty saying it. *Cripes, Jerusha, you're all they have. You gotta do this.*

So she would: without much hope, without much optimism. Because going forward was the only path she had. Because they would all die if she gave up now.

They came across a village one day. With some trepidation, Jerusha sent

Cesar into the village to inquire about a telephone. She had the children wait well away while she crept closer in case Cesar ran into trouble. She carried one of the automatic weapons with her, though she knew it would be her last choice—her hand stayed near the seed pouch.

But Cesar came back safely, shaking his head. "No telephone," he said. "They say the lines are all cut down around here. There are no phones. You have to go all the way to Kalemi, they told me. There maybe they have phones." He shrugged. "It's a long walk to Kalemi. But we can get there." She almost laughed at his confidence, wishing she were as sure as he was.

Late that afternoon, they came to a river. Jerusha wasn't certain whether this was the Lukuga looping across their path, or some other stream, but there it was: a slow-moving brown ribbon in the green landscape, a hundred yards across.

Jerusha muttered under her breath, checking the compass. Yes, east was *that* way, across the river; yes, the current was moving north. She looked to her right. Upstream, the river curved ominously to the west before becoming lost in the trees and brush and the high understory of the jungle. She could turn south and follow the river, hoping it would curve east again soon and allow them to continue toward the lake.

Or they could try to cross. Here.

She hesitated. She wanted to cry, to break down and let the fears run their course, but she couldn't. The children crowded around her as they always did when they stopped. She could feel their hands clutching at her, their voices calling.

"Let's all rest for a bit," she told them, and the kids dropped gratefully to the ground. They pressed next to her and each other as she sat, snuggling up to her in a mass of dusky skin and ragged clothes.

Waikili did not sit. On the outside of the rough circle around her, he turned slowly with his blind eyes as if seeing a vision. "Bibbi Jerusha," he said. "They *awful* close."

Jerusha sighed. She turned, looking back over her shoulder into the green expanse behind them, imagining she could see motion there in the green twilight. "All right," she said, "then we have to go across."

"But Bibbi Jerusha," Naadir said, her skin pulsing bright even in the sunlight. "I can't swim!"

Others echoed the cry: Abagbe, Gamila, Chaga, Hafiz . . .

"We're going to walk across," she told them. "You just have to trust me."

The seeds in her pouch were dwindling, but there were still several kudzu seeds, and she'd stripped the seed pods from some of the local vines she'd found as they'd walked. She walked to where the banks of the river seemed to be closest together, dropping several seeds there a few feet apart from each other. The vines erupted from the ground, and she directed their growth as if it were a symphony, weaving the tendrils in and out from themselves so that they formed a tight mat that slid down the shallow bank and out into the water, the tendrils writhing and curling as they grew, the roots digging deeper into the earth and the base of the vines thickening. The children watched, shouting and laughing as the mat—three or four feet wide now—slid across the river pushed by the growth behind it, the current tugging it downstream.

Gardener shot quick tendrils out from the front of the improvised bridge, letting them shoot forward until they reached ground on the other side and wrapped themselves tightly to the trees there, lifting the bridge out of the water so that it rained droplets down into the river. She sent more tendrils out to strengthen the structure, to stabilize it with forearm-thick vines. It took minutes and it tired her tremendously. "Go on," she said to Cesar when it was finished. "Start getting them across."

Cesar gulped audibly, but he stepped onto the vines. They gave way under his weight, creaking and sagging. He took another step. Another—and then he was out over the water. He bent his knees, pushing at the bridge; bouncing. It nearly reached the river's surface at the middle of the span but it held, and Cesar grinned at Jerusha. *Très bon,* he said. He gestured to the children, and they started across, four of them carrying the stretcher with Eason.

"Waikili?" Jerusha asked. He was still staring with his featureless face back the way they'd come.

"Soon," he answered. "Not long now." He shivered, visibly, and his hands went to his head. "It hurts to hear them," he said. "It hurts."

Jerusha went to him, crouching down to cradle the boy in her arms. She glanced back over her shoulder to watch the children crossing the river. Cesar was already across and Eason's stretcher were almost there, the rest following, some helping those who couldn't walk over easily themselves or were too frightened to step onto the vines. "Hurry!" Jerusha called to them. *"Rapidement!"* She picked up Waikili and ushered the remaining children onto the bridge.

Holding Waikili, she started across the span herself. The vines gave more than she expected under her weight, and she slowed her pace so that the children ahead could reach the other side before she dragged the vines down too much, handing Waikili to Cesar, who had come back to help her. "Get him across," she said. "Now!"

She heard the warning shouts even as she reached the three-quarter mark, even as Cesar and Waikili reached the other side. "Bibbi Jerusha! Behind you!"

Carefully, watching her feet on the tapestry of vines, she half turned. A group of perhaps a half-dozen people had emerged from the jungle on the far bank: PPA soldiers, accompanied by a man in a leopard fez and two small boys. One of the children was taller and more muscular, with large eyes; the other was smaller and emaciated, ribs showing starkly under stretched skin. They were no older than the children she was shepherding.

As she watched, the larger boy's form seemed to shift and change, and a strange beast dropped to all fours on the bank where he'd stood: huge and hunched, a hyena larger than any lion, misshapen, monstrous, with gigantic black jaws. It opened them and roared challenge across the river.

Leopard Men. Child aces. Jerusha's stomach churned.

The man in the leopard fez held up his hand in front of the were-monster. He started across the bridge, smiling. "You!" he called to Jerusha in heavily accented English. "It will do you no good to run."

Jerusha closed her eyes. Her plants . . .

She imagined those roots on the western bank withering, dying, turning brittle and releasing their hold on the earth. As the Leopard Man shifted form, as the snarling, feral creature faced her on the bridge, Jerusha dropped, hugging the vines. There was a loud *snap* as the support for the improvised bridge gave way, and Jerusha was suddenly in the water, still clinging to the vines as the current took her downstream.

She heard a feline yowl of distress behind her. As she desperately clawed her way forward, she felt the children pulling at the vines also. As soon as her feet could touch the mud at the bottom of the river, she had the supporting tendrils wrapped around the trees on the other side release as well. "Let it go!" she shouted to the children as she clambered up the muddy slope. They tossed the remnant of the bridge into the river. "Run!" She gestured at the children. "Into the trees!"

She could hear the shouts from the opposite bank, and the click of weapons being readied. She didn't dare look behind. She threw herself into the underbrush as automatic weapons cut loose, the bullets tearing chunks from the trunks and leaves all around her. She crawled forward. The firing stopped abruptly.

Gasping for breath, she chanced a look behind her. On the far side of the river, three of the soldiers were dragging a wet and furious Leopard Man from the water. The monstrous hyena thing was only a boy again, and the emaciated child simply stared across to where they'd vanished. They'd cross the river in pursuit, Jerusha was certain, but they'd have to find another way across. She'd bought herself time, but nothing else. If they could find help . . . Make that telephone call . . .

A hand touched hers: Cesar. "Follow me, Bibbi Jerusha. They're all waiting for you."

Kongoville, Congo
People's Paradise of Africa

SIRAJ'S MONEY WAS DEPOSITED in the bank. Monsieur Pelletier was very popular. Mathias had been introduced as the location scout for Monsieur Pelletier, and was set up in a Hilton in downtown Kongoville. Noel had checked the room for bugs and found a boatload. The Leopard Men and the Chinese and Indians were definitely listening. Good.

A portion of Prince Siraj's money went to buy a house on the outskirts of the city. Noel settled Mollie there, well supplied with food, Cokes, and a stack of romantic comedy DVDs. Jaako was with Cumming in Chicago. Noel didn't want to think about how they would amuse themselves.

Noel had gone into the center of the city to monitor the traffic and security around the bank during the night. Tomorrow he would show Mollie the yacht. He hoped he wouldn't have to actually get her into the hold of the boat. All she had to do was open a doorway.

On the way he'd checked in on Mathias and found him eating a room-service meal and reading Proust. *Whatever floats your boat*, Noel thought, and he realized that what floated his boat was just what he was doing. Pitting himself against implacable foes, and finding the victory.

He loved the game. It had been hard to leave it. But he loved Niobe more. And their son to come.

On the Lualaba River, Congo
People's Paradise of Africa

WALLY TOOK TO CALLING the little girl Ghost. She haunted him.

Every waking moment of the day, she stalked him. Patiently. Relentlessly. And, like rubbing a lamp to summon a genie, merely closing his eyes for a few minutes brought her out of hiding. Always with that big knife.

It didn't matter how far he traveled, nor how fast. Pushing the throttle of his stolen boat as far as it could go made no difference. Ghost kept up with him.

Sometimes, if he turned his head just right, and strained to see the riverbank through the corners of his eyes, he'd catch a brief glimpse of something pale drifting through the trees. Pacing the boat. Waiting for him to nod off again.

He'd tried sleeping in the boat, in the middle of the river. It made no difference. She floated across water as easily as she floated through the thickest jungle. In the end he gave up on that, because the boat didn't have an anchor, so sleeping there presented additional risks beyond getting stabbed in his sleep.

And that was the problem. If he wasn't traveling through the jungle—during rainy season, patches of skin crumbling away, new rust spots appearing daily, and with a dwindling supply of S.O.S pads—Ghost's knife wouldn't have been much of a problem against his iron skin. But he was. And sooner or later Ghost would figure it out; she was too persistent not to.

This far he'd been lucky. She kept aiming for the neck. Trying to slit his throat. How long before she found the holes in his shoulder, his arm, his legs?

Wally did the only thing he could: he didn't sleep. Jerusha would have told him it was pointless. That nobody could go without sleep forever. And she would have been right. It was impossible not to sleep.

The cottony fog of exhaustion filling his head made the simplest tasks—reading a map, steering the boat, pitching a tent—almost insurmountable challenges. It felt like he was doing everything underwater, or that there was a layer of glass between him and the world. Two sleepless nights had turned him into a zombie. How far to Bunia?

But he pushed on. Because the longer he stayed at it, the farther he drew Ghost away from Jerusha and the kids. Ghost was a problem for Wally, but Jerusha wouldn't have a chance against her.

He traveled the river from sunrise to sunset, from the first light of morning until the last glow of sunset faded in the west. And during the long, dark nights, he huddled by his campfire, fighting an exhaustion more powerful than any crocodile.

◆

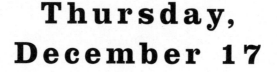

Thursday,
December 17

Paris, France

SIMOON SMILED, LEANING AGAINST Bugsy's arm. The soft Parisian fog was bitterly cold, but it looked gorgeous. The Eiffel Tower loomed in the distance, the thick air making it seem ghostly. The steam rising from his cup of coffee vanished into the air, but the smell of roasted beans and the lingering taste of butter pastry and powdered sugar were immediate and oddly comforting. They walked slowly as dawn gradually turned up the dimmer on the whole world. The low clouds effectively hid east.

"It's beautiful," Simoon said. "I mean, oh, my God, I'm in Paris! I always wanted to come here, but I never . . . I mean . . ."

You thought there would be time, Bugsy thought. *You didn't figure on getting slaughtered before you could hit college. Who does?* "It's nice," he said out loud.

She looked up at him, concern in her expression. The earring dangled. In the Paris morning, the one earring looked like the walk of shame. Someone seeing them together would think they'd been up all night talking and drinking and fucking and singing soft songs to each other. All the things you were supposed to do in Paris.

"Are you okay?" she asked.

"Hmm? Oh, yeah. Sure. I just get a little nervous when it's too cold to really bug out."

"Why's it too cold?"

"This?" he said, nodding to the fog, the frost, the pavement gone slick and dark. "When I'm swarming, I've got a lot of surface area. I'd go hypothermic in about a minute. There was this one Christmas when I was eighteen, I thought it would be funny to sneak into the neighbor's house?"

"Let me guess," Simoon said. "There was a girl."

"And a lot of eggnog," he said. "It wasn't a good decision. Anyway, by the time I had enough of me back together that I was more or less human again, they had to take me to the hospital."

"And that's really what you were thinking about?"

Ellen's face looked young with Simoon in it. Would she understand? Could someone who'd barely started her life and died see how sad it was to walk through a Paris morning and know she'd never be able to do it all for real? "Yeah," he said. "That's what I'm thinking about."

She didn't push the issue. Maybe she was talking with Ellen in the weird back-of-the-head way they did. Here was a fucked-up thing. Romantic morning in Paris, coffee and fog, a beautiful woman on his arm. Possibly two beautiful women on his arm, depending how you counted it. And he felt lonely.

They made their way back toward the Louvre in relative silence. A cat scampered across the street before them. A boy on a moped skimmed through the growing traffic, laughing and earning a volley of honks and shaken fists from the people in cars. By the time they reached the museum, Bugsy's coffee had gone tepid.

On the Congo River, Congo
People's Paradise of Africa

THE PIT IS WARM from the decaying bodies. The smell makes Michelle cough and gag. She crawls to Adesina. But when she tries to embrace her, she finds herself holding a wormy creature. Repelled, Michelle pushes the creature away.

"Adesina," she says. But she doesn't really want to see her. The smell and the decay and the rotting flesh make her want to throw up.

Michelle jerked awake. She was lying on one of the short bunks in the boat cabin. The light coming through the windows was grey. It was still raining. She got up, raked a hand through her hair, and quickly braided it. Joey would be ready to get some sleep.

As she came topside, she saw Joey huddled under a tarp. She looked very frail, and there were dark circles under her eyes. Whatever had been bothering her clearly hadn't stopped when they left Kongoville.

Michelle grabbed one of the ponchos hanging next to the cabin doorway. It was already wet and she shivered a bit as she pulled it on. She pulled the hood up, then carefully made her way across the slippery deck to Joey.

"You should go belowdecks and get some sleep."

Joey didn't even blink as the rain hit her face. "I can't sleep."

Michelle sat down next to her. "Of course you can sleep. Go lie down. You'll be fine."

Joey stared out at the jungle that was slipping by. "You know what's out there?" Her voice was cold.

"No," Michelle replied.

"Death. If you walked out there, the fucking ground would bleed." Joey grabbed her hand. "Can't you feel it? Not even a little bit? Fuck, Bubbles, it *smells*. Decay and rot." Joey squeezed her hand. Anyone else it might have hurt. She was strong for such a little thing. But Michelle was at a loss for how to help her.

Juliet would know what to do. But she wasn't here, and for that, Michelle was very glad. If the number of bodies Joey was sensing was any indication, there had been massacres here.

Michelle looked into the jungle, hoping to see anything of the destruction that Joey was feeling. And silently, the jungle looked back.

In the Jungle, Congo
People's Paradise of Africa

IT WAS LATE AFTERNOON, and they stood on a ridge overlooking a deep valley. They were trying to determine the best route down the face of the slope when Waikili touched her arm. She only needed the look on his blind face to know.

"Are they . . . ?" she asked Waikili. The boy nodded. "They're close?" she asked. He nodded again, silently, and her stomach knotted in fear. Cesar was standing alongside her, and she saw the muscles twist along his jawline. "Cesar, take the children and get them down into the valley. Make them hurry. I'll . . . I'll try to stop them here."

Cesar swung the weapon he carried from his shoulders. "I am staying here with you, Bibbi Jerusha."

"So am I," another of the older girls—Gamila—echoed, and suddenly they were all saying it, gathering close around her.

"No," she said firmly. "You can't. At least, not all of you. We have three weapons: Cesar, Gamila, and you, Naadir, all right, you three stay. But the rest of you must go. Quickly, now! You don't have time, and I don't want any argument from anyone. *Go!* Someone take Waikili's hand; make sure that the young ones don't get lost, don't spill Eason on the ground . . ."

They obeyed, if reluctantly, and she watched the knot of children slip away into the foliage downslope as she wondered if she would see them again. Cesar, Gamila, and Naadir gathered around her, looking fierce and brave . . . though she could see the fear in their eyes and in the way their muscles tensed as they wrestled the heavy weapons in their arms.

"Spread out here at the ridgetop," she told them. "Make sure you have a good view of our trail up the slope, they'll be following it. And get yourselves behind the big trees. I'm going to stand here at the top, where they can see me. If they attack me, or if you see me attack them, then I want you to open fire. Now, listen to me—make it a short burst, just one, and then I want you to *leave*. Do you hear me? I want you to go find the others. Don't look back, don't worry about me. Just run. Promise me you'll do that."

They responded with solemn nods of their heads. "All right, then," she said. "Let's get each of you set."

The first sign she had of their pursuers was a flitting glance of a leopard fez downslope from her, the man's form rising from the fronds of the undergrowth. He ran a hand over his mouth, staring at Jerusha, standing at the top of the ridge in the end of the trampled path left by a hundred feet.

He ducked back down again. She heard him call to someone.

A few minutes later, others appeared: three teenaged soldiers behind him armed with automatic weapons, the muzzles pointed at her. Jerusha was acutely aware that she was not Rusty, that if those weapons fired, she would likely be dead. The Leopard Man smiled up at Jerusha, his eyes masked behind aviator sunglasses, the fez bright in a shaft of sunlight piercing the canopy of the trees. "Ah, the plant lady," he said in his accented English.

"We meet once more, with no river to protect you this time." The smile vanished. "I want the children you have stolen from us," he said. "Give them to me, and I will let you go."

"No, you won't. That's a lie," Jerusha told him.

The smile touched his lips again. "The truth then. Give them to me, and I will make your death a quick and painless one."

"You can't have them," Jerusha told him, and with that she opened her mind to Gardener's wild card power.

She'd placed the seeds carefully, scattered along their trail. She'd touched each of them so that she could feel them in her mind, could caress the coiled power within. Now she wrenched them open: angrily, coldly. Vines sprang up from the floor of the jungle as Cesar's, Gamila's, and Naadir's guns fired. Two of the soldiers went down; Jerusha wrapped a vine around the Leopard Man, feeling the vines slip as he shape-shifted. She tightened them harder, directing the growth of the plant: it whipped violently to the left, slamming the were-leopard against the massive trunk of an umbrella tree. She heard the ugly sound of its skull hitting wood, and suddenly there was only an unconscious man snared in her vines.

The gunfire had stopped; she hoped the children had obeyed her, but she didn't dare look back to see if they were fleeing. Two more soldiers had appeared—she caught the duo in more vines before they could fire, snatching their weapons away, wrapping them so that they couldn't move, and lashing them to the ground.

A grey-yellow shape bounded toward her from the left: the monstrous hyena thing. She chased the creature with the vines, but they were too slow. It roared as it came, its terrible mouth a snaggle of ivory teeth. A tree erupted from the ground in front of it, but the beast dodged to the side, and the branches that snatched at the creature slid harmlessly along its flank.

Jerusha plunged a hand into her seed belt, but she knew she was dead, that it would be on her in a moment.

More gunfire rattled from the ridge behind her, tearing the ground directly in front of the creature. The were-beast snarled in defiance, a roar that made the hair stand on the back of Jerusha's neck, but the creature turned and leaped away back down the slope, vanishing into the undergrowth.

Far down the slope, she saw the second child for an instant: with his gaunt, haunted face. Then he turned and followed the other boy down the hill.

It seemed to be over. The forest was hushed, even the birds silent after the clamor of the guns. Jerusha went to the Leopard Man, snagged in his cage of vines. She heard Cesar scrambling down toward her and she waved him back. "Go to the others."

"You need me." He hefted the gun. "For this."

She knew he would do it, that he was more than willing to kill the man, that he knew as well as she did that there was no option here. She also knew that Cesar was still only a child—a child who had seen too much death and violence already. He didn't need to be part of this. He didn't need this memory to color all the others. She shook her head. "No."

"If you leave them alive, they will come after us again," he told her, his dark eyes stern. His lips pressed tightly together into a dark line.

"Go to the others," she told him again. "Make certain that they're all right, that there aren't more soldiers after them. That creature may come after them next."

Cesar stared at her for several seconds. Finally, he shrugged and went back up to the ridge; she heard him call to the other two.

"Let me go, plant lady, and I promise you I will leave," the Leopard Man said. Jerusha turned to him. He was gazing at her. Blood drooled from a cut on his forehead and one eye was swelling shut. "I will take my men with me. Let me go. I swear this. The truth."

"How do I know you will keep your promise?"

The man licked bloodied lips. "I give you my word. I swear to God. I swear on the lives of my wife and children, who will weep if I die."

"You have children?"

The man nodded. "Yes. In my pocket, there are pictures. I could show you."

"You have children," she repeated, "and yet you could do what you have done to these other children?" Jerusha said it softly, and the man's eyes narrowed. He shifted abruptly back to leopard form, snarling and roaring; she tightened the vines around him, around the soldiers. She was crying as she manipulated the plants: in frustration, in fear, in rage. She heard them scream, heard the screams fade to moans as the vines clenched tighter, sliding up to wrap around throats, to slide into open mouths to choke them. The were-leopard at her feet clawed futilely at the ground, and again he shifted back to human form. He was staring at her, but the eyes were now dead and unblinking.

She watched for a long time, until she was certain that he was no longer breathing.

On the Lualaba River, Congo
People's Paradise of Africa

GHOST MATERIALIZED OUT OF the darkness at the edge of his campfire, silently watching him. Her toes dangled an inch from the ground. Light from the coals glimmered on her dark eyes. She looked diaphanous in the silvery moonlight.

Wally's eyelids slid lower . . . lower . . . The muscles in his neck relaxed. His head dropped. The effort not to fall into a dead sleep made his eyes water.

Ghost's feet drifted into his narrow, blurry field of view. She reared back, winding up for another whack with the knife. Wally jumped up and lunged at her.

His body passed clean through her. Ghost's body had no more substance than a wisp of smoke. He landed beside the dwindling campfire with a *clang* and a *thud*. "Ouch." He looked up. Ghost stared down at him, expressionless as always. "What's your name?" he asked.

She drifted back into the jungle. Silent. Unreadable.

He stood, brushed himself off. But Wally knew she was out there, waiting and watching. So he sat cross-legged beside the dying fire and called out, "My name's Wally."

The answer was a silence punctuated only by the chirping of nocturnal wildlife.

♥

Friday,
December 18

The Louvre
Paris, France

THE SECURITY DETAIL FOR the peace conference was an unholy mélange of mercenary commando and hotel concierge. The hotels for blocks around the museum were booked. Negotiators for the Caliphate, emissaries from the People's Paradise of Africa, UN experts and security, the press of fifty different nations. The perimeter was a greatest hits album of the Committee. Walking in toward the Louvre, Bugsy saw three different flyers floating menacingly in the cool Parisian air. Snipers dotted the rooftops like postmodern gargoyles. In the courtyard, milling around the famous I. M. Pei glass pyramid, were groups of men and women in suits and soldiers in urban camouflage.

When they came close enough to see the familiar forms of Lohengrin and Babel, Simoon released his arm. As if by a common understanding, Simoon reached up and plucked out the earring, and Ellen was walking at his side. Not two lovers in Paris, but two colleagues working for the Committee. And Lohengrin didn't have to figure out the right etiquette for talking to a dead girl.

Klaus had the lockjawed look that Bugsy associated with the Teutonic God-Man feeling like someone had stepped on his dick. The fog was burning off, the first blue of the sky peeking through. Babel and Ellen were speaking in French. Apparently Ellen spoke French. *The things you learn.* "So how's the war?" Bugsy asked.

Lohengrin shook his head, the jaw clamping tighter. "We were putting together an exploratory subcommittee on sanctions against the Nshombos," he said, the round, full vowels cut almost short with frustration. "Only word got out. Now I have eight memos condemning the existence of the subcommittee and a second subcommittee forming to explore better methods of creating exploratory subcommittees."

Bugsy chuckled. Lohengrin frowned deeply, then smiled, then laughed and shook his head. "There was a time when we were effective. Now, it's all become bureaucrats talking to bureaucrats over drinks at the Louvre while people suffer."

"Isn't that always what it comes to?" Bugsy said. "I mean, look at what we're doing. A peace conference. What exactly is that but a place for the kids with the most toys to get together and have a gentlemanly conversation about who's going to kill the most innocent people? We wouldn't be doing this at all if hauling out tanks and missiles and battle-ready aces wasn't actually more destructive, right?"

"I know," Lohengrin said with disgust. "And yet those days in the desert, marching from the Necropolis to Aswan with the army of the Caliphate slaughtering people and biting at our heels? Then at least we could do something."

Aswan. Where Simoon had died.

"Yeah," Bugsy said bitterly. "The good old days. So what's my line?"

Lohengrin tilted his head. In all fairness, it was a pretty obscure way to ask the question.

"Where do you want me?" Bugsy said. "I'm here being all secure and detailed. I figure . . ."

Lohengrin nodded and took Bugsy's elbow, leading him a few steps away from Babel and Cameo. "We need you for coordination. A few dozen wasps here and there throughout the perimeter, but not so many that you would seem . . . out of place in the reception hall."

"So no dropping a leg or anything."

"No."

"Okay, but I'm going to need warm spots. Sluggish, half-dead wasps aren't going to fit your bill."

Lohengrin frowned.

"Cleavage works," Bugsy said. "If you've got anyone with cleavage. Hey! Joking. Just joking. But seriously, it does work."

"I'll do what I can. But if trouble comes, I want you to warn us. I do not like the mix of people here. Too many armed men, and it stops being security."

"Who do we have on the inside?"

Lohengrin nodded across the courtyard to where Burrowing Owl was making polite talk with Tricolor, the local ace host and face of all things French and vaguely trite. Snowblind was just behind them.

"That all?"

"You, me. Babel. Cameo. She did bring . . ."

"Simoon and Will-o'-Wisp," Bugsy said. "We'll have firepower if we need it."

Lohengrin nodded, but he still didn't look happy.

"Toad Man as well, provided we can convince him to stop the frog's legs jokes. And you know Garou?"

"Don't think we've met," Bugsy said.

"*Garou!*" Lohengrin called. A decent-looking man came over, eyebrows raised in question. "This is my old friend, Jonathan Hive."

"Good to meet you," Bugsy said, holding out a hand. "I've heard a lot about you."

Garou looked nonplussed, but shook Bugsy's hand all the same. "We've met," he said.

"We have?" Bugsy said.

"Twice."

"Ah."

Garou nodded to Lohengrin and walked away, looking less than amused.

"Apparently, I have met him," Bugsy said.

"Yes."

"Well, at least I got the big faux pas of the night out of the way early."

♣

"Ah, Paris again."

"And the weather couldn't be worse," Siraj grumbled from where he sat next to Noel in the backseat of a Mercedes limo.

Noel looked out at the falling rain and couldn't disagree. Through the murk and fog the Louvre loomed. The stones were stained grey from dirt, soot, and exhaust. In the dim light it looked like what it was—a fortress.

His was not a fanciful nature, but Noel found himself looking away. "Now remember. Talk, talk, talk," he said.

"Yes, yes, I know, I'm not an idiot or a child," Siraj snapped. The big limo breasted the honking, darting minis and citrons like a shark through minnows. Siraj kept his tone offhanded, but the anxiety showed through. "Do you think Weathers will be here?"

"I doubt it. He's not the negotiating kind. If Nshombo is here it won't take much effort to drag this out endlessly. Punch the right buttons and he'll go on about dialectic materialism for fucking hours."

"Lovely," Siraj said sourly.

Noel laughed. "Remember, we're playing the tune here. Enjoy it."

The car slowed and rolled to a stop at a security checkpoint. Noel, in his role as Prince Siraj's attaché, offered over their identification. The French soldier peered at the papers, then peered into the car, nodded in satisfaction, handed back the documents, and waved them through.

The car joined the line of vehicles disgorging passengers in front of the I. M. Pei glass pyramid. In the west the setting sun managed to struggle out from beneath the hem of the clouds. The glass facets of the building grabbed the fire and glowed red and gold.

Noel checked his watch. It was still seventeen minutes until he could have access to Lilith. He didn't think he would need her, but he would have preferred to have this party either in full day or full night.

Another soldier, this one in more antique, comic-opera uniform, opened the back passenger door. Siraj stepped out and Noel followed. He shot the cuffs of his shirt until he had the perfect rim of white beneath the cuffs of his tuxedo coat. Noel had opted for the traditional white tie. He didn't want to stand out in this gathering.

They entered the pyramid.

♠

"Dr. Okimba?" a sleek UN gopher said. "I'd like to introduce some of the Committee members who are providing security for the peace talks."

Tom Weathers nodded his head. It was still his head. It still *felt* like his head. But to the glittering crowd beneath the smoked-glass and steel pyramid it was the big, shaven, plump-featured head of Dr. Apollinaire Okimba.

"Your Honor, Simone Duplaix from Canada, whose ace name is Snowblind. And Nikolaas Buxtehude from Brussels. He's called Burrowing Owl."

"Enchanted," Okimba said, cupping the soft hand of the girl in a tight black T-shirt and black jeans and raising it to his lips. Her bobbed hair was electric blue, with a gold stripe dyed in her bangs. Okimba didn't know her from Grace Slick, but Tom Weathers had met her in Kongoville, before the Committee turned on the PPA—and Tom. "It is always a great pleasure," he murmured, "to meet a young woman as formidable as she is lovely."

He turned to the second ace. Burrowing Owl was a short shit about as wide as tall, wearing an odd pointy brass cap, goggles, and old-time leather flying clothes under what was either a feathered cape or folded wings. He clicked his heels and nodded as Okimba shook his hand. The hands were big and red and massively calloused, as if he used them to burrow with. "Deeply honored, sir," he said.

"Likewise." This was a groovy power, though one Tom didn't use much. Which was too bad; he was a pretty good actor, if he did say so himself. He looked and sounded and even smelled exactly like the jurist: a large, fat, heartily affable black man in his early sixties.

The real Dr. Okimba was a major legal eagle. He was also a counterrevolutionary pain in the ass who made a lot of noise about civil rights for the citizens of the People's Paradise. Right now the good doctor was enjoying captivity deluxe and incommunicado in a suite in the Nshombos' vast new palace.

The gopher was burbling about how historical this all was. Tom tuned him out. He was scoping the crowd, checking out the opposition. Several of the Committee members who'd been in Africa last year were there: big Buford Calhoun looking as out of place in his human skin as he would as a toad the size of a Volkswagen; the Lama, snickering at what Tom suspected was a most unsagelike dirty joke; Brave Hawk, visible through the glass of the pyramid overhead as he soared the pink and pale green sunset sky on combat air patrol. No one he couldn't handle, if it came to that.

Tom excused himself and moved off as if to find a waiter serving champagne. He wouldn't dare drink it. He didn't trust himself to keep from showing sudden fury on his borrowed face. He'd just spotted a tall, handsome dude with white-blond hair hanging to the broad shoulders of his Savile Row suit. Men and women crowded around him like groupies at a rock concert. He was the German ace Lohengrin, current chairman of the Committee and global superstar. But Tom knew that broad-jawed smiling face from another setting. Jackson Square in New Orleans. Where Tom had gone to rescue his kidnapped daughter.

"*Keep it cool, lover,*" Hei-lian whispered in his ear. She and her Guoanbu nerd-gnomes were ensconced in a *pension* just across the Seine, keeping track of the proceedings via a shitload of little audiovisual pickups studded literally all over him and siphoning feeds from the innumerable media cameras present. "*You've got a job to do.*"

Tom made himself nod. *Smile while you can, you square-headed Nazi puke,* he told himself. *Payback's a motherfucker.*

Then by a trick of acoustics he heard Simone burble to her companions, "Oh, my *God*, did you *see* that? That fat geezer totally came on to me!"

Tom allowed himself a grin. *I guess I'm glad Doc Prez hasn't let Alicia feed this fat fuck to her pets after all,* he thought. *Shit, this is* fun.

◆

Siraj opted for the escalator rather than the winding staircase. As they glided down Noel noted the white linen-draped buffet table, the white-coated waiters slipping through the crowds with trays of drinks and canapés for those too lazy to walk to the buffet. The glass above them, the white marble underfoot turned the usual drone of conversation into a sound like clashing cymbals. The setting was fantastic, but as a place for diplomatic conversation it left much to be desired.

Noel noticed Lohengrin's golden head looming above the crowd. Here and there a leopard-print fez thrust above the crowd, marking the presence of Leopard Men. Secretary-General Jayewardene, with Babel at his side, moved through the crowd looking plump, smug, and serene. Or perhaps that was just him showing a *what, me worry?* diplomat's face to the world.

Personally, Noel was worried. There was a level of free-floating tension that was almost like a metallic scent beneath the smell of perfume and canapés.

Siraj walked away to greet Jayewardene. Noel snagged a glass of champagne and started moving toward the buffet. He noticed Lohengrin skittering off in the other direction.

Wondering if it was just coincidence, Noel changed course and moved toward Lohengrin. The young German ace looked around wildly, spotted Jayewardene and Babel, and started heading for them. *Tallyho,* Noel thought, and ducked into a clump of people. He moved through the crowd, staying out of Lohengrin's sight until he stepped out of another knot of people directly in front of the younger man.

Klaus reared back like a startled horse. "Didn't you and I have a weekend in Paris?" Noel asked.

Blood washed up Lohengrin's neck and suffused his face. "Don't talk about such things," he said in a low whisper.

Noel thought back on those times when, as Lilith, he had seduced and pumped (so to speak) the big German ace for information about Jayewardene and the Committee.

"I cared for you. I told you my deepest dreams. I planned for a life together—"

"I used you. Get over it," Noel said.

Lohengrin's expression registered both hurt and shock at the blunt reply. "Have you ever cared about anything?"

"Don't go there, Klaus. I have many things I care about. You just don't happen to be one of them."

"Would you ever consider coming back to the Committee?" Lohengrin asked. "We could use you."

"No, thank you."

"So, the good work of the Committee means nothing to you?"

"No. I think you're a bunch of idealist idiots."

"Then why are you here?"

"Because there are things I do care about."

"I think you are a coward. I think you got scared in Jackson Square, and now you leave others to fight your battles."

"And I think you haven't gotten over discovering your Lili Marlene was a boy." Noel clinked his glass against Lohengrin's and sauntered away.

♥

The conference began with the reception; the Louvre closed for a private party, and how classy was that? Tables laid out with the most expensive snack food known to man. Soft music supplied by a string quartet in somber attire. And milling around like guests at a party, the representatives of the bloodiest war on the planet. Over there by the stairs Prince Siraj, who now commanded the same people who had been trying to kill Bugsy in Egypt. On the far side of the space, Dr. Okimba radiated charm and goodwill on behalf of the PPA. And all around them, spreading out for miles, the greatest works of human art, as if by rubbing Okimba and Siraj against civilization, maybe some of the chrome would stick to them.

The whole thing appealed to Bugsy's sense of the absurd. He slouched over to the bar—because what better symbol of peace than an open bar—and got another rum and Coke. The Committee was out in force. Lohengrin, smiling and preening in front of the cameras for an international news network. Garou still smirking at him coolly. Toad Man filling up on free prawns.

Cameo folded her arm in Bugsy's, smiling the way she did when she didn't mean it. "I just talked to Babel."

"Uh-huh. Um. You're wearing the earring. Are you . . . ?"

"Ali's here, but she's letting me drive. Jayewardene's had one of his hunches. There is going to be trouble. He thinks something may happen with Dr. Okimba."

"Ah. Right. Who's that?"

He felt her go stiff. "You're joking, right?"

"Yes, totally joking," Bugsy said. "Okimba. Doctor. Jurist. Big name in the PPA, chief negotiator, hasn't killed anyone we know of. So what's the word? Do we think someone's going to go for him? Or is he going to turn all ninja assassin in the middle of the talks?"

"I don't know. But Lohengrin needs people near him and ready without seeming like they are."

"I'm on the case, boss," Bugsy said, giving a snappy salute only slightly marred by the lack of two fingers. "Don't worry about it too much though. Hunches. Gut feelings. Jayewardene's just nervous, right?"

"Not really," Cameo said.

"Where is the object of all concern?"

Cameo nodded toward the center of the room.

And there, standing alongside the bad guys' head good guy, was Noel Matthews, looking slightly less smug than usual. The little Brit had changed a lot since the days when he'd used his skills at sleight of hand to flummox the aces of *American Hero*. He'd even changed in the time since their adventures in Texas and New Orleans with the nuclear kid. If it was possible for a man to look relieved and hunted at the same time, that was Noel Matthews.

"Hey," Bugsy said. "Want to go kill two birds with one stone?"

"It depends," she said. "What exactly do you plan to kill?"

"Trust me. We've got the perfect excuse to go hang close to Okimba. Let's go talk some shop." Bugsy tipped the bartender and walked across the most elegant, civilized room in Western civilization.

Noel didn't see him coming until he was too close to ignore. "Mr. Tipton-Clarke," Matthews said with a half smile. "Or do you prefer Hive?"

"I answer to any of them. You know Cameo?"

Noel nodded politely. Dr. Okimba smiled like he was hoping they'd both go away.

No chance of that.

"I was hoping I'd run into you," Bugsy said. "We're doing some work for the Committee, and I needed to ask you something. Maybe you can help out too, Doc."

"I'm pleased to be of service," Noel said in a tone that suggested he might not actually be pleased, "but—"

"It's a little thing. All history and background stuff. Nothing important. I've been finding out some more about our partners in peace over in the PPA. It's been a trip. Have you ever been to Vietnam, Doc?"

Okimba's eyes went a degree wider. "No," he said carefully. "I don't believe I have."

"We just got back," Bugsy said with a smile. "Nice place. Lousy traffic. Anyway. I've been looking at the early life of our man Tom Weathers, and especially the nice retarded lady Sprout?"

"I am sure," Noel said, "that Dr. Okimba isn't—"

"No, please," Okimba said. "Continue."

"Bugs," Cameo said, and the tone of her voice was a warning.

"Well, we all kind of know the Radical's not the world's most stable guy. No offense, Doc. But it turns out this one girl, Sprout, is like the only person on the planet he's not willing to sacrifice. So I was wondering how you knew to grab her in particular."

"I do not understand," Dr. Okimba said. "It was *Bahir* who took Sprout."

"Well, sure," Bugsy said, "but that's Noel. Bahir, Lilith, and . . . Oh. Shit. That was still a secret, wasn't it? Look, Doc. Forget I said anything, okay?"

♣

It took all of Tom's self-control to keep from frying both men where they stood on general principles. "How *dare* this man show his face at a peace conference!" he boomed, volume rising. His bull-hippo bellow echoed from the pyramidal roof; everyone else had stopped talking at once. Heads turned to stare. "I demand that this man be arrested immediately! He is a spy, an assassin, an international war criminal! I demand *justice*."

Jonathan Hive's eyes had gone wide in a suddenly pale face. "I didn't mean to pee on anybody's parade—"

Around them voices broke the silence like so many falling crystal goblets, some brittle with confusion, others sharp with anger. Tom's fury had welled up like lava as his own voice rose. It was the look in the Englishman's indigo eyes—half stricken, half calculating—that convinced Tom of his guilt. "You *ratfucker*," he screamed, making no pretense of hiding his own voice. "*You kidnapped my daughter!*"

He raised his arms as if reaching for Noel Matthews's throat. Flame billowed red from his palms.

♠

"Oh, *shit*," Bugsy said, and his body literally exploded into a cloud of green wasps. His clothing puddled on the white marble floor.

Noel threw himself to the side, and the blast of flame roared past him. He felt its searing heat upon his cheeks, smelled burning hair, and felt the bite of fire on his shoulder.

Dr. Okimba's round fat face was shimmering, running, changing. Into Tom Weathers.

And Noel was on fire. A quick glance revealed the flames dancing across his tuxedo jacket. He needed to get the fuck out of here, but he didn't want to transform into Lilith in front of half the world's media. Ripping off his jacket, he grabbed a glass of bourbon from a man's hand and tossed it on the flames. They roared up greedily, consuming the alcohol. Noel whipped the coat into the face of an oncoming Leopard Man.

All around him people were shouting and guns were appearing, the muzzles like small dark mouths ready to spit death. Weathers was coming after him. Apparently incinerating Noel was not going to be enough. Weathers wanted his hands on him.

Noel seized a champagne bottle out of an ice bucket. He placed his finger over the top, shook it hard, and sent the resulting fountain of bubbly into Weathers's face. As the Radical roared and cursed, Noel danced away from him, grabbed Prince Siraj by the back of his tuxedo jacket, and pulled him off his feet, out of the line of fire. Siraj landed hard on his back on the marble floor. The fire alarms were howling, and the sprinklers sprang to life. Water pattered onto Noel's body. He kicked off his shoes. The force of the fall had driven the breath from Siraj's lungs. He lay gasping in the center of the floor.

Fortunately, in addition to being hard, the marble was slick. More so now that it was wet. Noel tangled his fingers in Siraj's collar and dragged the winded leader behind him beneath a banqueting table. "Stay down," he hissed.

◆

"Fuck!" Tom yelled in pain and anger. His eyes stung from the champagne, and the green insects were all over him. Each sting felt as if a hot needle had been plunged into his flesh.

He wreathed a hand in fire and slapped himself where he felt the insects crawling, then loosed another blast of flame at those buzzing around his head. Wasps fell to the floor like crisp black snowflakes, along with a few hapless bystanders. It didn't help. The wasps kept coming. Tom went insubstantial, moved from the green cloud of pain. Then he phased back in and flamed them.

He became aware of his Leopard Man detail fighting to keep his back clear. Alicia's pets had shape-shifted; those who couldn't scythed bullets from Micro UZI and Beretta 93 machine pistols. Screams erupted from the crowd.

Pivoting widdershins, Tom jetted flame from his left palm. An operator from the home-team *Service de Protection des Hautes Personnalités* had jammed a hand inside his suit coat. The man shrieked as a plasma burst lit him up. He fell to the shiny floor, dead on the instant. The cartridges in whatever handgun he'd been going for cooked off like a string of fireworks.

Something heavy hit Tom on the back. His chin cracked against the polished concrete floor. White sparks shot through his brain. Pain ripped into his left shoulder, accompanied by rank animal smell and guttural growling. Rough fur rasped his left ear.

Tom got palms on smooth concrete and thrust upward hard. Although whatever the hell was gnawing on him weighed as much as a big man, Tom's superhuman strength snapped him upright. Reaching back with his right hand he grabbed a handful of coarse fur and muscle like wound steel wire. The jaws clamping his trapezius slackened. The beast squealed as Tom dug fingers in.

He found himself holding a huge black wolf by the scruff like a naughty puppy. It twisted in his grip, snarling, trying to bite. Bloody drool trailed from its jaws. Shreds of Tom's muscle dangled from its teeth.

"*Fuck* you." Turning quickly, he flung the wolf up and away with all his ace strength. The creature shot up and hit one of the metal braces that made up the pyramidal roof. It howled as head and hindquarters shattered the tough glass-laminate panels on either side of the strut. Limp, the beast plummeted. What hit the floor with a sodden thump was a naked dude.

"*Garou!*" he heard somebody shout.

"I fucking *hate* shape-shifters," Tom said.

SPHP types hustled screaming attendees out the door. Others aimed guns at him. He took flight and laughed as they ripped each other with full-auto bursts. A couple went down. Another staggered backward, screaming into the mouth of a leopard that was biting his face and raking his guts out onto his Armani shoes with black hind legs.

The Radical torched a couple more pigs, then touched down as their buddies booked. Even brave men weren't eager to tangle with somebody who could fly, toss you like a Frisbee, and set your ass on fire. He swiveled his head, searching chaos for Noel. The sneaky little shit needed badly to be burning.

♥

Bullets flew overhead. A woman screamed in agony, and flames splashed across a stone pillar.

The long drape of the tablecloth hid them. But there was an itch between Noel's shoulder blades. The flatware and the mahogany table were not going to stop one of Tom Weathers's plasma blasts.

And indeed a second table, about three feet to their right, blew to pieces. A long splinter flew into Siraj's leg. The prince shrieked, grabbed his calf. His hands turned red as blood pumped between his fingers.

There was no time for first aid. The room reeked of smoke and blood. Noel was nearly deafened. The screams and shouts that filled the room seemed to be coming through cotton batting. Noel needed Lilith. Needed her now.

He put the fear in a little box and set it aside. He did the same with his thoughts of Niobe. Noel concentrated, and felt his body begin to shift. Then the table was flung over revealing them like bugs under a rock. China, crystal, and flatware ware clattered all around them.

It was one of the Leopard Men, grinning, enjoying the moment. The closest thing to hand was a fish fork. Noel snatched it up, rolled, and came to his feet. Only inches separated them. Noel could feel the man's breath, warm and liquor-laden, on his face. He drove the small fork deep into the man's eye, and gave it one final slap that left it lodged in his cerebral cortex.

Never gloat, he thought . . . and heeding his own advice he finished the transition to Lilith, grabbed the writhing Prince Siraj, and got the hell out of Paris.

♣

The woman with Prince Siraj was pale as ice, with raven hair cascading down her back. Her eyes were silver. *Lilith.* Hot sweaty nights in Africa flashed through Tom's memory.

All the time I was fucking her, she was fucking me. Well, now I'm going to fuck her up. Payback's a bitch, bitch.

But no sooner had he seen her than she was gone, and Siraj with her. Tom roared and loosed a sunburst at the place where they'd been standing. The heat bubbled paint on the walls and made the lights explode. Connections clicked in place in his mind: *The golden-eyed man—the silver-eyed woman—they're both Matthews!*

"Why don't you pick on someone your own size?" a voice said in a German accent you could spread mustard on.

Lohengrin. Tom whirled, and showed him teeth.

And suddenly the big guy was encased in plate armor that glowed a soft white. On his arm a shield, in his hand a broadsword, on his breastplate the Grail. A winged helmet covered his entire head.

"If it isn't Heinrich Himmler's wet dream," said Tom. "Well, you're broiled bratwurst now." He raised his hand and gave the German a blast of flame. It hit the shining shield. And splashed.

Even Tom's faster-than-normal speed wasn't enough to get him fully clear of the whistling sword stroke as Lohengrin stepped forward. He winced as the glowing blade laid his left cheek open, and came back with a full-power palm-heel shot to the middle of the shield.

The knight flew back, bowling over aces, nat security, and Leopard Men in human and leopard form. Lohengrin hit a wall. The wall lost. He slumped down from a sort of vertical crater. Tom saw a leopard snatched off the floor and into the air by what looked suspiciously like a long, pink tongue. *Fucking Buford*, he thought. Then something erupted through the floor right beneath his feet, knocking him up and over. He hit hard on his ass, jarring his whole spine. A dark form hovered over Tom. *Burrowing Owl.* Those were wings, outspread now, though they didn't flap. The Belgian ace folded them and dove helmet-first at Tom.

Tom rolled right. A grinding whine rattled his teeth in their sockets. Tiny cement bits stung his face. He threw up an arm to protect his eyes. When he dropped it the flying man had vanished. He'd left a hole drilled right into the dark cement of the Louvre entry floor. "How the hell did he do that?"

Lohengrin answered with his longsword. Tom rolled right. The blade bit into the cement for half its three-foot length. Tom rolled back, swinging his right foot across him in a fierce crescent kick. He caught the blade's flat. He expected the blade to snap. Instead it ripped a big divot out of the cement as it snapped from the knight's gauntleted hand. Then it vanished.

Neither surprised Tom enough to put him back. But the glowing fist-sized spiked ball whistling down toward his face did. He threw up an arm, managed to block the morningstar's stubby handle. It didn't stop the ball on its chain. It whipped around and slammed into the side of Tom's head, just behind his left eye.

Once more superhuman reflexes saved him; he yanked his head sideways far enough to keep from having a spike driven into his brain. But the ghost steel bit painfully into his temple. He felt his left cheekbone break, shoot pain back through his brain like white lightning, tasted blood as a spike pierced his cheek.

Tom kicked. His sole caught the spectral tasset that protected the top of Lohengrin's right thigh. The knight's feet shot out from under him. His faceplate shattered cement beneath him as the morningstar disappeared.

Head pounding, Tom jumped to his feet. Lohengrin popped up just as quickly. A spike-backed battle-ax appeared in his hand. "Shit, where do you *get* those?" Tom asked, and loosed a sunbeam. It struck the center of Lohengrin's breastplate. It seemed to shatter into a hundred backscatter shafts of blinding light. Tom heard screams as bystanders got scorched.

He launched an overhead right at Lohengrin. If he didn't knock the knight into something hard enough to jelly his bones, he'd at least stun the fuck enough to finish him. But the German learned fast. Rather than blocking with his shield he swung it up like a tailgate. Its edge jammed painfully into Tom's biceps, jamming the punch midflight. Its freight-train momentum still blasted Lohengrin back, skidding across the floor with a shriek of ghost-steel digging furrows in concrete. But he caught Tom a glancing shot under the arm with his ax.

Tom gasped and dropped to one knee. The blow had either busted several ribs or chopped them right through. And Lohengrin had kept both his feet and his grip on his weapon. His ice-blue eyes glaring over the top of his shield from behind narrow eye slits, he charged.

But Tom learned quick, too. He flung his left palm up toward the ghost steel-masked face. Lohengrin read the threat within the gesture. He tried to throw himself aside. He was almost fast enough to defeat Tom's movement. But not faster than *light*. The sunbeam clipped the left side of the winged helmet, enveloping his eye slit. Tom saw hell-glare flare within.

When Lohengrin hit the floor and rolled onto his back he was once more a studly German dude in a suit, with arms outflung and the left side of his face a smoking mess.

♠

Bugsy saw the room from ten thousand angles, each one of them moving, spinning, trying not to get killed. He'd lost too many wasps already. If too many more went down, he wouldn't be able to re-form. Endgame. Over. Dead unless Cameo used some little tchotchke of his to haul him back out of the grave. He swirled around, going in for fast stings on the PPA Leopard Men, distracting the guys with just guns, and trying to stay clear of Tom Weathers.

Then Lohengrin went down, ghost steel armor blinking out like it had never been there, and Tom Weathers towering over him for the kill.

Ah fuck it, Bugsy thought, and dove in.

From all across the Louvre, the wasps dove in toward a single target: Tom Weathers. The Radical turned at the sound of wings, flame dancing out. Bugsy split, shifted, tried to avoid the fire. He felt wasps cooking off like a deep, unspecific ache. Lohengrin was moving, moaning. He had his hands up, cupping his seared face.

Not letting you kill him, Bugsy thought and pressed in. A dozen wasps got through, stinging Weathers on the back of the neck and curling around toward his eyes.

Ellen's voice came out of nowhere. "Bugsy! *Drop!*"

No. Not Ellen's.

Simoon's.

Bugsy retreated, pulling his wasps together in a corner near the men's room. The wind picked up, grit in the air. Bugsy shifted his insect bodies into the more familiar flesh. There weren't enough. He could feel his breath rattling in his lungs. The tendrils of sand in the air bit at his skin.

Which meant it was shredding Weathers.

Simoon's wind shrieked like a banshee, the sand looking more like a fog. The glass pyramid was already pocked and white where she'd brushed against it. Weathers, in the worst of it, lifted off his feet, arms and legs swinging, and crashed against the wall.

"That's my girl," Bugsy said weakly. "Get him."

Baghdad, Iraq
The Caliphate of Arabia

THEY LANDED HARD ON the red-and-black Persian rug. Noel left Siraj whimpering on the floor, ran, and yanked an embroidered runner off a table. He couldn't help but notice in one of those odd dislocating thoughts that always float past when a person was in a crisis that he hadn't disturbed a single item of bric-a-brac on the table.

Returning to Siraj, he pulled out the splinter and wrapped the leg tightly in the runner. He stood and wiped his bloody hands down his pants. "I'll let them know you're here. They'll get you to a hospital."

"Never mind me," Siraj gritted, through teeth clenched against the pain. "Get a gun. You have to go back. Go back and kill him. Make certain of it this time."

"You seem to be under the misapprehension that you can still give me orders. Quite wrong. You just lost your hold on me. The secret is out. Weathers knows, and there's nothing you can do to me. Now my wife is a target, and I'm more concerned about her than I am about you. Here's some free advice. Never sleep in the same place twice, and get yourself some good doubles. Good luck."

And he teleported away.

The Louvre
Paris, France

"FUCK!" TOM EXCLAIMED AS the wind slammed him into a wall upside down. He felt like a character in a fucking cartoon. The fire blasts he'd desperately launched in all directions had fatally flamed several people, including at least one Leopard Man. But he didn't know who the hell was doing this to him.

The wounds Lohengrin had dealt him were weakening him fast from blood loss. Tom willed himself insubstantial and dropped to the floor as the miniature twister spun him back out in the middle of the room. By now most of his escorts were down. They'd been able to do little more than keep the enemy aces off Tom's back. Now they converged on him with a vengeance.

A blow to his kidney made him gasp with pain. He turned into a right hook that busted his jaw and spun him back, and caught a glimpse of a big handsome woman in a suit, with black shiny braids flying about her dark face. She'd been introduced to Dr. Okimba as Wilma Mankiller, a Canadian strongwoman ace from the Blood branch of the Blackfoot Nation.

Tom prepared to flame her. Again the floor surged beneath him. He hit hard and rolled across the floor. Burrowing Owl flashed right through the spot where he'd been and ground his way into the floor without seeming to slow. *That dude's starting to piss me off.*

Tom saw another figure flying beneath the pyramid. It launched a beam at him: red, white, blue. The fallen Kraut knight wasn't the only one who knew the danger of an aimed palm. Tom hurled himself away. The French ace Tricolor's signature beam seared Tom's right side as its main energy blasted the floor. Gritting his teeth against the pain, Tom shot back a fire blast. Three-toned light flared around the slim figure. *Fuck. Force screen.*

He was plucked off the floor and caught in a bear hug from behind. He thrashed his legs and snapped his head back, but the Blackfoot ace was a canny enough grappler to keep her face away from his attempts to pulp it with the back of his skull.

Tom knew he was stronger than she was. He could've broken free. If he hadn't already been weakened by all the battering and bleeding. It was all he could do to keep from passing out from the pain her embrace caused to his seared and busted body.

Through agony-slitted eyes he saw the flying Frog aim his hand again. He phased out. Wilma Mankiller bellowed in surprise as the tricolored beam hit her.

Almost at once Tom rematerialized. Going insubstantial took more out of him than any other power. He dropped to his knees and was instantly bowled over as Burrowing Owl erupted through the floor beneath him again.

In midair Tom flung out an arm. White light lanced from his palm. The beam transfixed the flying man's torso. He dropped straight down smoldering without making a sound.

Other aces were all around him, crowding in, pummeling him, but they couldn't use beam weapons for fear of toasting each other the way Tricolor had toasted Mankiller. But they hurt him. He felt his left arm break. Something else lanced through his guts from behind, almost buckling his knees. He lashed out in all directions. He managed to knock down a guy who looked like he was made of some transparent semiliquid crystal but felt like metal, won free of the scrum, if not the fucking hateful bugs.

Something wrapped itself around his waist. It clung as if covered with glue. He felt himself yanked off his feet, saw he was being pulled toward a car-sized toad squatting to one side of the melee. "Oh, fuck *me*," he moaned. He had no choice but to go insubstantial again. The bulbous eyes seemed to bulge more than usual as his captive passed clean through him. Tom stopped behind Toad Man, spun, grabbed him by a hind leg. Then a flashbulb went off in Tom's skull. White dazzle filled his eyes as migraine pain blasted his brain.

Snowblind. He'd never experienced her power firsthand but he knew what it did. The blindness would last for minutes; if he stayed here he was well and truly fucked.

But the pain also shocked enough adrenaline into his system for one final surge of superstrength. He flung Toad Man up at the pyramidal roof. Then he launched himself in normal flight, steering toward the crash.

Agony bathed his legs as some sort of energy beam brushed them. For a split second he expected to implode his skull on an intact strut. At this point he could give a fuck. Instead he felt cold high-altitude air on his face, smelled diesel fumes and fireplaces. He was clear.

With no perceptible interval he was in orbit, feeling vacuum tugging at his skin and the cold of space sucking warmth from his bones.

But alive. And free.

For now.

◆

Ellen was kneeling at Lohengrin's side. She was naked, except for the cameo at her neck. Bugsy was naked. The Louvre was really a hilariously stupid place to be hanging around naked.

The sirens were all around. Men and women in paramedic's uniforms. Police. At least one SWAT team.

Bugsy knelt beside Ellen. "M'okay," he said.

"You're not," she said.

The gurneys were coming out. Garou's body covered in a blanket, blood soaking through the cloth. Snowblind was on her feet, but only with the assistance of two medics. She was crying. Buford was walking around, apparently unhurt, but with a stunned expression. Burrowing Owl was dead, too. And there, along the wall, a dozen nat soldiers and security men. And as many of the PPA's Leopard Men. All of them incapacitated or dead.

Bugsy coughed. His lungs felt fragile. His body felt too thin, like if you held him up to a flashlight, his bones would show. He'd never lost that many wasps at once. He wasn't sure he could. "Klaus," he said. "You okay?" Lohengrin did not answer. He turned to Cameo. "He's going to be okay, right?"

Ellen's face was the answer. He wouldn't be okay. Nothing would. "Come on," she said. "Let's go."

"I need clothes."

"I'll find you some," she said. "Come on. Give me your arm."

She found him a security jumpsuit, black and slick but warm. Bugsy let her dress him, let her put her arm under his. Together, they walked slowly back to their hotel, just a couple of blocks away.

"Aliyah?" Bugsy said as they reached the revolving glass door.

"She's fine. I put the earring away."

"Okay."

"I need you to walk a little farther."

"I'm on it," Bugsy said, but it took a long moment to get his legs to move.

Back in the room, he collapsed on the bed. The mattress sighed under him. Ellen sat on the little love seat, sipping coffee and looking bleak.

"My fault," Bugsy said to the ceiling as much as to Ellen. "My fucking fault."

"You didn't kill anyone," she said.

"I pissed him off. My bullshit crap about Bahir and Noel Matthews. If I had just . . ."

"If you just hadn't made him angry?" Ellen said. Her voice was soft and sad and amused. It was a voice that knew too much about loss and death and pain. "How many women in the shelter say the same thing, Bugs? It wasn't you. You were in the wrong place at the wrong time, and you said the wrong thing."

"I'm always saying the wrong thing."

"Well, yes, but that's why we love you," she said. It didn't occur to him to ask who *we* was in this context until later, and by then he was too tired to speak. He heard the shower running. The bed shifted as Ellen climbed in, her arm across his chest, her legs pressing against his.

"I don't think I can . . ." Bugsy said. "I mean, you're beautiful but I'm just kind of . . ."

"Go to sleep," she whispered.

"Yeah," Bugsy said. "Okay."

He dreamed about fire.

Noel Matthews's Apartment
Manhattan, New York

SHE WAS DOZING ON the couch with a crocheted comforter covering her. The *pop* of displaced air as Noel teleported into the flat didn't disturb her. A book had fallen from sleep-slack fingers and lay on the floor beside the couch. The tail was thrown over the back of the sofa like the body of a heavy python. For an instant it felt almost like a fist had closed on his heart. Noel pressed a hand to his chest, and felt Lilith's breasts flatten. *Nothing must happen to her.*

He allowed the muscles and bones to shift, restoring him to his natural form, then knelt down at the side of the couch. Niobe's lashes trembled on her cheeks, and a small murmur passed her lips. Noel bent even closer to see if he could hear, but it was just a breath of sound.

The skin of her cheek was soft against his lips, and she smelled like Shalimar. He loved the oriental quality of that perfume. She stirred and mumbled.

"My heart," Noel whispered.

"Oh, it's you. You're home," and her arms snaked around his neck.

"Dearest, I'm here to take you"—he hesitated, remembering her fury in Vienna when he'd tried to lie and hide from her—"someplace safe."

Niobe sat up. "Safe? What's happened?"

"Weathers knows that Noel Matthews is Bahir and Lilith."

She kicked away the comforter. "We can go back to the island. We were safe there."

Noel shook his head. "No, I'm going to take you to Drake. He can protect you."

"He could protect us both."

"Weathers would come after me. A lot of people will get hurt in the cross fire. Maybe even you. I'll play the merry fox to his hound while I—" He broke off abruptly.

"While you what?" Suspicion sharpened Niobe's words. "Will people die?"

"Hopefully very few."

"Weathers?"

"Probably. Hopefully. He seems like a man who holds a grudge." Noel forced a smile.

"And then it's over, right? Forever." She folded her arms protectively over her stomach. Noel nodded. "Promise!"

He pulled her into a tight embrace. "I promise. I will be completely, totally, and forever out of that life."

♥

Saturday, December 19

On the Lualaba River, Congo
People's Paradise of Africa

SLEEP HAD BECOME AN ephemeral, abstract concept to Wally. Sleep was the thing his body tried to do to pass the time between attacks from Ghost. His exhaustion was so complete that he could nod off almost instantly, but Ghost woke him too frequently for the sleep to do any good. He never got more than an hour or two before she returned.

She's just a little kid, he reminded himself. Wally wouldn't let himself be angry. Not with Ghost. Somebody had made her this way. She was just a little girl.

But that was little consolation, when their interaction unfolded the same way every time: Ghost hit him with the knife. He woke up. He tried and failed to catch her. She receded into the jungle.

Over and over and over again. All night long.

When morning finally came, Wally woke to find the sun shining in his eyes. He moaned and rolled over, trying vainly to fend off the headache. But it was the perfect recipe for a migraine: massive sleep deprivation capped off with a burst of sunlight straight into his tired eyes.

Sunlight? Wally sat up. Rays of light streamed through the tatters of his shredded tent.

Ghost, it seemed, was just as frustrated as Wally.

Ellen Allworth's Apartment
Manhattan, New York

BUGSY SWAM SLOWLY UP toward consciousness. The ceiling was familiar. He was at Ellen's place. *New York, thank God.* His body felt thick and sluggish. The general sense of illness might have been jet lag or the weird systemic rebellion of having lost too many wasps at once. The sheets and pillow were crisp and cool and deeply comfortable, except that was desperately hungry.

He levered himself up out of bed and stumbled to the living room. The pajama legs were too long, folding up under his feet and trying to trip him. Ellen, alone on the couch, was gently stroking the ruined fedora. Will-o'-Wisp. Nick.

"Hey," Bugsy said. "You okay?"

Ellen looked up at him, the corners of her mouth turned down. "Sure," she said. "It's just . . . I'm still a little messed up after Paris. I didn't know Garou, but I had coffee with Burrowing Owl before things got bad. He was a nice guy. He was going to Marseilles after the conference. Now he won't."

"Yeah. I mean, you could take him, I guess. If it's important."

"I could," she said. Her voice was tired and thin. "They're all like that. My Nick. Mom. Aliyah. All of them. I'm always the last chance. The one hope of doing whatever it was that wasn't done before they had to go."

"You don't have to, you know," Bugsy said.

"Of course I have to." She held up Nick's hat, as if it was a counterargument. "I'm one of them myself, right? The queen of holding on after it's too late."

How long had it been? he wondered. How many years exactly had the real Nick been gone, and Cameo holding on to the memory of him. Keeping the reminder of his absence fresh every time she put the hat on, pulled him into her body again, talked with him. How many times in that private internal conversation had she told him how much she loved him? How many times had he said it back to her?

He was looking at a wound that was never going to heal, bleeding again. "Hey," he said gently. "I know this is hard. Seriously. At some point, you've got to let him go—"

"No, I don't. I can't. I can't let any of them go, Bugsy, because if I do, then they're dead. Really dead. Finally dead. Permanently. As long as I can bring them back. Talk to them. *Be* them . . ."

As long as you can do that, nothing ever ends, Bugsy thought. *As long as you can do that, you're going to be carrying everything and everyone forever. Your mom. Your boyfriend. My girlfriend. You're responsible for keeping all of them alive, because they're already dead. You poor bastard.*

"Yeah," Bugsy said. "Okay."

On the Congo River, Congo
People's Paradise of Africa

THE PIT. AGAIN. MICHELLE is sick of the pit. She is sick of the smell, and the dark, and the bodies.

"Adesina?" she sighs. "Where are you?"

A hand drops onto her shoulder and she jumps. When she turns, no one is there. The pile in the pit shifts. It moves as if possessed.

"Adesina!"

"Miss! Wake up, miss."

Michelle jerked awake.

"Your friend," Kengo said. "I'm worried about her."

She pushed her hair back from her face and sat up in the bunk. "Did she sleep?"

Kengo shook his head. "I don't think so. Maybe a little. She just keeps staring into the jungle. And she says things. Is she crazy?"

"You mean more so than usual?" Michelle poured herself a cup of water from the container on the small galley counter. It was warm and brackish, but given how crappy her mouth tasted she figured it could only help. "I'll go talk to her."

She went topside. It wasn't raining, but the humidity was so high it might as well have been. The sky was overcast and there was a preternatural quiet.

Joey was still sitting on the back bench of the boat, huddled in the poncho.

"You should take that off," Michelle said. "It's not raining anymore."

Joey glanced up at her and Michelle was shocked to see how bad she looked.

"I'm cold, Bubbles. Really fucking cold."

Michelle squatted down and took her hand. It was icy and she wanted to sympathize, but she didn't have time for Joey to fall apart. She needed her to be Hoodoo Mama.

"You're going to get sick if you don't rest," Michelle said. "At some point we're going to be walking, and you need to be stronger."

"Walking through blood?"

"Whatever it takes."

Joey leaned in closer to Michelle and started stroking her arm.

"I'm cold, Bubbles," she said again. Her voice was thick with Cajun honey. "I'm so cold. We could warm each other up. You remember, like we did back home. It was cold then, too."

"It wasn't cold," Michelle said, pulling away. "It was in the middle of a hurricane and it was a mistake. I'm not making the same mistake again."

"You're a hard-ass, Bubbles," Joey said sadly. "I always thought you were so nice, so fucking sweet with your blond hair and your green eyes. Not anymore. You'd walk over corpses to do what you needed to, wouldn't you?"

"Maybe," Michelle said. "But I don't want to be walking over yours. Go get some sleep."

Joey pulled the poncho over her head and then handed it to Michelle. "They're all so fucking little," Joey said. "Do all the kids die here?"

"I don't know. I'm just trying to save one."

Joey stumbled past her and went inside the cabin.

And as Michelle watched the jungle slip by on the river, it began to rain. She pulled on the poncho and lifted the hood over her head.

Then, over the rain, she could hear something that made her want to cry. It was the sound of Joey and Kengo fucking. Joey was using Kengo to fuck away whatever was preying on her out there in the jungle.

On the Lualaba River, Congo
People's Paradise of Africa

SOMETHING HAD TO GIVE. It did, finally, around midday.

Wally guided his boat into a shaded cove along the river when the rain came. The patter of raindrops on his head felt like somebody had taken a jackhammer to his skull. Even the tiniest ripples on the water vibrated the boat enough to make Wally moan in agony. He'd given Jerusha all of their painkillers, so he had to ride out the migraine.

He wondered if he shouldn't just give himself over to the PPA. Anything had to be better than this.

Wally lay down in the boat. What point was there in going ashore? His tent was useless. He closed his eyes. Sleep claimed him instantly.

Until his leg erupted in searing pain. Wally yelped. He sat up, fast enough to rock the boat.

Ghost huddled over his shin, jabbing at a rust spot with her knife. She pivoted the knife, digging at a rivet. Wally realized she was trying to pry his rivets out, to open up his leg and get a better target. It hurt like heck.

"Hey, knock it off," he said. He reached for her.

Ghost saw him, and dematerialized again. But her preoccupation with the rivets in his leg delayed her just a fraction of second, which was enough time for Wally to dart forward and touch the blade with a fingertip.

It became a ghost knife in her hands. Then it became a ghost knife with a rusty blade. And then it was a ghost knife handle and a pile of rust.

Yep. Steel.

Ghost looked at her ruined knife, then at Wally, then at the remains of the blade. For the first time, the expression on her face changed. Her little eyebrows squeezed together, the corners of her mouth turned down. Anger? Fear? Irritation? Wally couldn't read her.

She lifted the wooden knife handle threateningly, but she looked a little confused. It might have been cute, if she wasn't trying to figure out how to stab him. Was she planning to hit him with it?

"Awww, come on." Wally shook his aching head. "Give it a rest, would ya?" He lay down in the boat again. "Try to get some sleep," he slurred. "You're still growing."

Sleep claimed him. And it held him for many, many hours.

On the Congo River, Congo People's Paradise of Africa

KENGO CAME UP FROM the cabin. Michelle expected him to have a smile on his face, or to be swaggering, but instead he just looked frightened. He moved stiffly, like an old man. He gingerly sat down next to her.

"There is something wrong with your friend," he said.

"Really? It didn't stop you from screwing her."

"She is pretty." His hands shook as he lit a cigarette. "And I thought, well . . . it doesn't matter. Yes, I slept with her. But she is so violent." He put the cigarette into the corner of his mouth, rolled up the sleeves of his shirt, and showed Michelle the scratches along his arms. "My back is worse. I don't know what is chasing her, but I think it rides somewhere inside her."

Part of Michelle wanted to sympathize with Kengo. After all, Joey had scared him and hurt him. But part of her just wanted him to shut up. She couldn't worry about both Joey and Adesina.

"Is there a place called Kisan, along the river?" Michelle asked.

Kengo shook his head. "No, no place called Kisan. Do you mean Kisangani?"

Something about the name rang inside Michelle. She knew she'd never heard it before, but it sounded right.

"Yes, that's it," she replied. "Kisangani. I need to find the Kisangani Children's Hospital." When Kengo said "Kisangani," a memory of her dream about Adesina became sharper. The details were suddenly more in focus.

"You do not want to go there," Kengo said, holding his hands up in front of him. "That's a very bad place."

"There's something important I have to do there."

He stared at her for a moment. "You are both madwomen. Possessed."

Michelle opened her hand and let a bubble form. "The demons fled this world on September 15, 1946," she said as she let the bubble loose into the murky river. Water spewed up from the small explosion that followed.

"Do you think any demon would dare come here now?" She got up. "Now stop screwing around and get me to Kisangani."

People's Palace
Kongoville, Congo
People's Paradise of Africa

"HEI-LIAN?" HE SAID SOFTLY from the doorway.

She sat in the living room of the apartment on the People's Palace's third floor watching satellite television. She jumped at his voice. Her green silk robe fell open, letting her bare left breast peek out. "Tom?" she said ten-tatively. "What are you doing out of bed?"

"Mark. I talked to you before. Please say you remember?"

"Yes," she said warily. "I'm still not sure if it's a trick. You claim to be Tom's alter ego. Mark Meadows."

"He's *my* alter ego. Never mind. The answer is, I don't *know* what I'm doing up."

She frowned. She didn't bother closing the robe. Her beauty cut him like the blade of Lohengrin's glowing sword. Whose kiss he remembered, sadly, as well as hers.

Feeling as if he were wrapped in cotton batting, he teetered to the arm of the sofa and sat near her. She lowered herself to perch on the edge of the cushion like a finch ready to fly away at the first hint of danger.

"I know it's night, and the moon's up. I can feel myself healing, even if I'm not feeling the pain I should be. That's weird. When he's gone through this before it hurt like hell. Anyway, why is he even here? He won't spend the night the same place twice running, and he's here in the palace? After trashing the whole peace conference?"

"When Tom got here he was raving, in obvious agony," she said. "I could hardly believe he was even alive. The medics gave him sedatives and put him on a morphine drip. When his injuries began to heal visibly, I suggested they bring you—*him*—here." She shrugged. "Hard to get better in hospital. It's bet-ter in a familiar bed."

"Yeah." Mark nodded slowly. "So that's it. He doesn't take pain well. Ironic, huh? He's tried so hard to stay off any kind of drugs for fear I'd take back over."

"Have you?"

Did she sound eager, or was he wishful-thinking again? "No way. Sorry."

"What do you want?"

He drew a deep breath to nerve himself. "This is harder than I thought. First, to get it over with: I love you, Sun Hei-lian. I've fallen for you hard."

Her expression didn't flicker. "Very well."

"Yeah. I know. Pretty bizarre, right? And what I feel doesn't put you un-der any obligation. Which is good, because you need to get away."

"What do you mean?"

"Away. From here. From Tom. Sooner or later he'll turn on you. The way he turned on Dolores. She was his lover, too. She worshipped him. And he killed her."

"That was Butcher Dagon."

"It was Tom. Dolores was going to tell the world that Dagon was working for Alicia, staging phony atrocities to justify the PPA invasion of Nigeria."

Hei-lian did not seem too surprised. She studied him. "You say you care about me? About *me*, not just what I can do for you, with my pussy or my skills or my contacts?"

"Yeah."

"But nobody's cared about just me. Not since—since my father disowned me for joining the intelligence service to get him out of prison."

"You deserve it, Hei-lian. But the truth is, it's not only about you. Tom's losing it."

Her breath caught. "I've begun to suspect that, too."

"You're scared of him. I've seen it in your eyes. Even if Tom can't."

"He's good at not seeing things he doesn't want to." She slumped forward, resting arms on thighs. "I've tried to warn Beijing. They won't listen. They can't see beyond the oil and the coltan and all the other resources they need to try to keep their economic boom alive."

"He'll turn on them, too."

"But I've seen another side of him. That's what's so strange. He can be so gentle, even kind. To Sprout. Sometimes to me. That's you, isn't it?"

He shrugged. "You could kill him, couldn't you?"

She blinked and drew her head back on her slender neck. "What?"

"You're a highly trained agent. You could kill him while he slept. You could to it tonight. All I have to do is go back in, lie down, and let go." Mark shook his head. "I don't have much longer anyway. He's starting to come out of it. I can feel him stirring . . ."

She got up and walked a few paces from him with the green silk tail over her robe brushing the pale backs of her thighs. The television nattered mindlessly on low volume. "You'd let me kill you?"

"I'm *asking* you to kill me." He sucked in breath through his teeth. "I know you've got a gun. I don't want to live with what he's done. What he's doing. And I *really* don't want to ride along for what he's going to do. The murder, the destruction. And this child ace thing—the utter rape of innocence, man." He shook his head. "Death's got to be better than watching it all happen, knowing I was the one who set it all in motion. It's not like it's much of a life to lose, anyway. You've got a gun and you're good with it. End it now."

Sun walked toward him. "I've thought of killing him. But I haven't. I loved him. I thought. I've been trying to figure out if there was some way to get him help." She stopped just short of him. Her body almost touched his. He could feel her warmth and smell her personal scent. It always reminded him of green tea. "And now I *know* there's something worth preserving inside him. For Sprout's sake, if nothing else. I won't kill him or you. Until I know there's no other choice."

He started to say something. She stretched up on tiptoe and kissed his cheek. "You're a good man, Mark. I haven't known many of those. Go back to bed. And relax: if I can't find some way to help you, then I will find a way to kill you. And that's a promise."

♣

Sunday, December 20

Kongoville, Congo
People's Paradise of Africa

"TOM, NO!"

Hopping furiously, he tried to pull on a pair of jeans. Outside, it was still night in K-ville.

That bastard Meadows, Tom thought. *He actually stole my body for a joyride.* His memory was a blank for what the hippie puke had done. But he knew it had happened.

"You're not strong enough," she said. "You're still healing. I saw you when you came in. You looked . . . you looked as if you couldn't possibly survive."

And the fuckers dosed me with drugs. I told them never to do that! "Yeah, well, I'm better now," he said. "I found out who shot me and kidnapped my daughter. And now I'm going to make the motherfucker pay."

"What about the Nshombos?" she asked. "They weren't happy about what happened in Paris. They won't want you setting out on your own selfish vendetta."

"The little bastard's their enemy, too," he said. "He committed crimes against the People's Paradise. If they can't see that, fuck 'em."

On the Lualaba River, Congo
People's Paradise of Africa

AFTER CATCHING UP ON his sleep, Wally spent a lot of time checking himself for rust spots. He'd let the problem slide while he was too exhausted to do anything about it. He managed to get the worst of it, but there
were places he couldn't reach. And he only had the single damp towel to
work with. It never dried out.

He'd been completely submerged during his fight with the crocodile, and
had been out in the rain a few times since then, but until now he hadn't
had much chance to do anything about it on account of Ghost. She still followed him. But without her knife, that was pretty much all she could do. He
tried talking to her every time he caught a glimpse, but inevitably she backed
off.

He landed his boat at river's edge after a particularly hard rain. Rainwa-
ter sloshed around the bottom of the boat, soaking his pack, not to mention his feet. He hoped to find suitable leaves in the jungle, something that
would help him wipe everything down. Also, he had to pee.

Everything reminded him of Jerusha. She would have been able to tell him
which plants to look for, which leaves to use. Right off the bat. She wouldn't
have laughed at his clumsy attempt to build a rain shield for the boat out of
leaves and limbs. Well, she might have laughed, but not unkindly. She had a
nice laugh.

Wally lost track of the time. He spent more time than he had intended
on his ultimately unsuccessful side trip.

On the way back to his boat, he heard voices coming from the river.

He crept back to his landing site. Leaves rustled. Undergrowth crackled.
And his joints—still sore from the fight with the croc—groaned like the hinges
of an old door. Wally wasn't built for stealth.

But the newcomers didn't seem to notice. Whatever they were talking
about (another pang of loneliness, another memory of Jerusha), their conversation indicated no sign of alarm. He peeked through the long leaves of
a bushy fern.

"Wow," he whispered.

A hospital barge had moored itself at the center of the river. It looked to
be thirty or forty feet long, perhaps a little more than half as wide, with a
flat hull. Most of the deck was taken up with a narrow cabin, built of sturdy

timber with a pitched roof of corrugated aluminum. Clean white paint blazed in the sun, bright enough to make Wally squint. The walls and roof were marked with red crosses.

A long, sleek whip antenna arced over the roof; it bobbed gently when the barge swayed on its anchor line. The space inside was probably divided into multiple rooms; Wally counted two doors on the near side. The guy on the roof wore the uniform of a Leopard Man. Regular soldiers patrolled a narrow walkway around the cabin. A handful stood on the side facing the riverbank, where Wally had gone. It seemed pretty obvious they were discussing the stolen PPA boat.

These were the men who'd delivered the virus to Nyunzu. The virus that had killed Lucien, and all the other kids Wally had buried with his bare hands.

He clenched his fists. *Well, I've found it. Now what?*

The barge towed a small rowboat. Three soldiers climbed in, threw off the ropes, and rowed over for a closer look at Wally's stolen boat. One shouted something to his colleagues. He pointed at the rusted orange stump where the forward gun mount had been.

In response, the men on the rowboat unslung their rifles and started peering nervously into the jungle. So did those watching from the safety of the barge. It seemed they'd heard about Wally. *Good.*

The easy part was that he didn't have to take them by surprise. Better if he didn't, in fact: the barge had a radio. If the barge reported an attack here, that could only help Jerusha's chances of escaping with the children.

The hard part was figuring out how to get to the barge without getting soaked again. He also didn't want to lose his own boat. *What would Tarzan do?* Wally thought for a few seconds. *Heck, yeah! He'd swing onto the barge.*

Wally craned his neck, looking for overhead vines. There weren't any. *Nuts.* Wally sighed. The vine thing would have been neat. He watched the rowboat, the barge, the ripples on the water . . . *Huh?*

Wally looked again: ripples on the river. Tiny inverted "V"s, glistening chevrons pointing at a barely visible snout, two eyes, and the back ridges of a river croc. The PPA men hadn't seen it.

If he waited for the men to come ashore, he could take care of them pretty quickly. But others might take his motorboat while he was busy. He'd lose his chance to destroy the barge, plus he'd have to walk all the way to Bunia.

Wally resigned himself to getting wet again. *Rats.*

He leaped out of his hiding spot, ululating like Johnny Weissmuller. Ignoring the pain in his legs and hips, he charged down to the river, pulping the underbrush beneath his feet. With the running start, he cleared the final twenty feet with a single jump. He cannonballed into the river, a few feet behind the crocodile, before the landing party had time to react. Their colleagues on the barge shouted warnings. Somebody managed to squeeze off a burst from his rifle. The rounds pattered harmlessly into the river.

Wally grabbed the croc's tail with both hands. It twisted around, angry as it was ugly. It tried to snap at him. But he heaved, swung the hissing reptile in a few wide circles overhead until it made a nice whistling sound, and released it.

The croc's snout hit the middle guy right in the gut, knocking him clear off the boat. Its thrashing tail clotheslined the guy on the left. The rowboat flipped, tossing soldier number three into the river.

Heh. Bet Kate's never done that.

The barge men opened fire while he slogged his way to the rowboat. A hail of bullets *pinged* and *whanged* from Wally's chest, sliced into the water on either side of him, and tore through the jungle behind him. A row of bullet holes perforated the rowboat, but they were too small to sink it before he paddled over to the barge.

Over the crackle of gunfire, Wally heard the whir of machinery. A soldier on the barge cranked a hand winch, nervously winding up the anchor line while peering over his shoulder at Wally's advance.

"Oh, no you don't, pal." Wally reached the barge. Two soldiers stood over him. They fired on his head, shoulders, and arms from a few feet away.

It hurt. In spite of his best efforts, rust had pitted his skin everywhere. He felt new trickles of warm blood on his back and neck.

Wally snapped off a length of wooden guardrail. He swung it like a bat, sweeping the soldier's legs out from under them. They thudded to the deck. Wally heaved himself onto the barge, then stomped them both. They didn't get up.

That's for Lucien.

A low snarl sounded above and behind him. Before Wally could turn, the leopard tackled him. It landed on his back, raking its claws through vulnerable rust spots.

Wally screamed in pain. He reached backward, grabbed the giant cat by the scruff of the neck, and tore chucks out of his own back when he pulled it off him. He swung the leopard through a full two-seventy, smashing it upside down on the deck with tooth-rattling impact. Wally brought the segment of rail down on its throat, hard enough to puncture the deck, fixing the transformed Leopard Man in place.

That's for everyone else.

Time to end this, before the PPA folks realized they could hurt him. He needed to clean his wounds. Wally hoped they'd had enough time to send an SOS.

The rest of the crew abandoned ship when he tore his way into the cabin. He smashed everything that looked even vaguely scientific, especially all the glassware.

Then he punched through the planking and dropped into the hold beneath the deck. The hull itself was wood, but a series of riblike spars ran the length of the barge to give the hull its shape. And those were metal. Wally disintegrated them two at a time, one in each hand.

The hull pulled apart. Water gushed up through the seams. The barge listed to port, then crumpled, then sank. But not before Wally salvaged two fuel canisters.

When he lugged them back to his motorboat, he found Ghost standing on the riverbank. Openly staring at him with a strange expression on her face. She didn't back away as he approached, and she didn't threaten him with the knife handle. Wally paused. They stared at each other.

"My name's Wally," he said.

Ghost hesitated before she receded into the jungle.

On the Congo River, Congo
People's Paradise of Africa

"WE COULD TAKE YOU all the way there," Gaetan said. "But it will take much more time. And the closer we get to Kisangani the more dangerous the river is."

"You were paid a ridiculous amount of money for our passage," Michelle said.

It was raining and she, Kengo, and Gaetan were hunkered down in the cabin. Joey was huddled under the poncho on the back bench of the boat.

"It would take many more days to reach Kisangani on the river," Gaetan replied. "I have a friend who is a pilot. He flies out of a small airstrip not far from here. He owes me a favor and I am certain he will give you a good price to take you there."

Faster was better. Her dreams were now filled only with the urgent need to get to Adesina. And the feeling didn't fade when she woke up. It itched and burned in her mind. It was almost as bad as the fire in her veins after her coma. The farther upriver north they went, the worse the sensation. They were going in the right direction.

"Fine," she said. "But we better get a decent deal."

In the Jungle, Congo
People's Paradise of Africa

THE LANDSCAPE WAS STEEP and furrowed; Jerusha often felt they were making more progress vertically than horizontally. It rained at least once a day, but the rain never seemed to reach them. The canopy of the jungle merely dripped continuously, and the air below was ferociously hot, humid, and still. They forded a few more creeks and small rivers rushing through the valleys, though thankfully none of them were as wide or deep as the one they'd crossed before. The rest breaks became more frequent—the exhaustion of scrambling up the verdant slopes and helping the children who couldn't help themselves took much from all of them. The children were increasingly hungry and the fruit and vegetable seeds in her pouch were nearly exhausted.

She worried that the pursuit of them might mean that Rusty . . . no. She wouldn't think that. She wouldn't.

Waikili seemed nervous. His blind, blank face seemed to survey the jungle around them. "Those two children?" Jerusha whispered to him, so that none of the others would hear.

Waikili nodded. "They're out there," he whispered back. "And the one moves so fast . . . *Leucrotta* is his name."

"How can you know that?"

"I know. He wants to eat us."

Jerusha kept them moving all through the day, and pushed them even through the twilight. The sun was already down, the trees little more than darker lines in a grey murk. The kids were strung out in a long column as they clambered along a ridge. Jerusha was already looking for a spot to halt for the night, some small shelter.

A wailing cry came from the rear of the line, a shrill of terror too abruptly cut off and followed by shrieks and shouts from the other children. "Cesar!" Jerusha shouted and the boy unshouldered his weapon as they ran back toward the sound, Jerusha unsnapping the covers of her seed-belt pouches.

Naadir, the child with glowing skin, was there as well, the shadows of the other children streaming away from her, near the stretcher that carried Eason. But it wasn't Eason that was the problem. He gaped like the others from the stretcher, pointing with a trembling finger. "Bibbi Jerusha," he said. "It was awful . . ."

She pushed through the children. In the greenish illumination of Naadir's skin, she could see one of the older boys, Hafiz, lying on the ground in spatters of blood blacker than the twilight. Jerusha's breath hissed in. Something had torn away the boy's face, ripped it from his skull so that all that was left were black-red furrows through which bone gleamed sickeningly. Another quadruple line of furrows had been carved over his chest; more across his abdomen, so deep that his intestines had spilled out.

"Go up to the others," she shouted to the children. "Go on. Did someone see this?"

"I did," Eason said in halting French. "I heard a growl, then something . . . I think it was that creature at the river . . . it came from the bushes, and leaped on Hafiz. It was only a moment, and then it was gone into the bushes over there, and Hafiz . . ."

"Leucrotta," Waikili whispered. Eason was staring at the body from his stretcher, his tail thrashing wetly.

Jerusha glanced at the undergrowth around them. She could see nothing, not in the gloom. The noises and calls of the night denizens mocked her. "All right," she said. "All of you, go to the others. Two of you get Eason's stretcher. Tell them to make a fire—now. Cesar, go with them."

"What about you, Bibbi Jerusha?"

"I'll be along in a moment. Go—quickly. I'll keep you safe. I promise." She hoped it was a promise she could keep.

They obeyed, hurrying away in Naadir's glow as Jerusha crouched down next to the body of Hafiz. She shivered. "You can't do this," she said in French to the darkness. "I won't let you do this. I'll stop you."

She heard laughter answer her from the gathering darkness: a boy's laughter, a child's. Jerusha shivered again.

Standing, she scattered seeds around the body, and covered Hafiz in a blanket of cool green before hurrying to join her charges.

Sofiensaal Concert Hall
Vienna, Austria

A SECTION OF THE pitched roof of the Sofiensaal collapsed with a rumble as Tom showed himself on the rounded top of the old concert hall's facade. He felt the heat of flames at his back. They silhouetted him nicely against the night sky. But the whole thing was liable to cave at any minute. *Better make this quick*, he thought.

"Listen up," he shouted down to the media crowding the surprisingly narrow street, east of Vienna's center. He knew they had shotgun mikes trained on him.

The Vienna cops in riot armor who competed with the journalists for space were pointing things at him, too. Most of those weren't microphones, though. The street pulsated with red and blue lights. "I'm the Radical. I'm here to bring an international assassin and war criminal to justice." Somebody started bellowing German at him through a bullhorn. He ignored it. "I want Noel Matthews. This was the last place he performed. From here on I'm going to lay waste to any place that limey bastard does his fake magic. And that's just the beginning."

He gave that no time to sink in: thanks to decadent capitalist-consumerist technology the whole world could watch the speech to its black heart's content. Instead he raised a hand to torch the most obvious SWAT-type van, just for punctuation.

Nothing happened.

What seemed like a hundred cops opened up from below. The muzzle flares were like photoflashes at a Superbowl halftime. Tom went to light speed, emerged in orbit.

On one side, infinite night chilled him. On the other he felt the searing heat of the sun, which had already brought dawn to Western Europe.

He flashed back down, emerging a couple thousand feet above the blazing hall, intending to hover while he worked out what happened.

But he didn't hover. He dropped like a brick.

"Tough luck, schmuck," a voice said in his head in a distinct New York accent. *"You won't use me to do your dirty work anymore, you genocidal commie creep. I'm outta here."*

As the heat rose and roared at him Tom spotted a patch of darkness to the east, just this side of the Danube.

To orbit, down.

It was a park. He collapsed on a cast-bench. He panted with reaction. A few blocks away flames danced in the sky. *"That was JJ Flash, man,"* said the hated voice in his head. *"You just lost him. For good. Why don't you save your-self some grief and pack it in?"*

"Fuck you, you hippie piece of shit. You think you've won? Do you?" A geyser of yellow flame shot up as the Sofiensaal roof went. "I was gonna give people a chance to give up that shit Matthews. But now I'm going straight to Plan B." Without even rising from the bench Tom held out a hand. Bricks exploded from the row house across the street as the glare of a sunbeam played across it.

So it began.

♠

Monday,
December 21

Ellen Allworth's Apartment
Manhattan, New York

BUGSY PUT SOME BACON on to fry, and started the coffeemaker. The little kitchen radio was turned to an NPR station and he turned it on to drown out the sighs from the living room.

". . . Simon and this is NPR's Morning Edition. Vienna is in flames this morning, victim of an attack by an ace believed to be Tom Weathers, also known as the Radical. Reports say that the destruction has resulted in at lest twenty dead and over two hundred injured."

Bugsy leaned against the counter, listening with a sense of profound dread in his gut. This was getting out of control.

"The Radical is also believed responsible for the destruction at the Louvre Museum in Paris, where a peace conference between the Caliphate and the People's Paradise of Africa ended in a bloodbath . . ."

He turned off the radio. The bacon popped and splattered. The coffee machine gurgled like someone strangling a cat. The telephone shrilled. This was just not starting off to be a good day.

When, after the fourth ring, it became clear that Ellen didn't care if the telephone rotted in hell, Bugsy found one of the handsets by the toaster and answered.

"Is this Bugsy?"

"Most days. Who's this?"

"It's Billy."

"Billy?"

"Your translator? From Saigon?"

The dead chimp.

"Oh, yeah. Hey. Billy. What's . . . what's up?"

"I'm going to be in New York next month. I was thinking you could show me where a joker could see a little action, you know what I mean?"

Yes, Bugsy thought, *you mean that you still think I'm a joker. Prick.* "Hey, yeah. Well, we should check on my schedule. I can maybe . . ."

"And I got something to trade."

"Trade?"

"You help me out, introduce me to the local girls like your woman? You know, who don't mind that a guy's got a few differences? And I can tell you who your guy was hanging with before he came to 'Nam."

"My guy?"

"Meadows. I've been rooting through the archives, you know. Just to see? And turns out, he was buddies with a guy right there in New York."

"You got a name?"

"I do."

There was a long silence.

"Do we have a deal?" Billy asked.

"Of course we do, man," Bugsy said. "Us jokers have to stick together, right?"

At the far end of the line, Billy laughed like someone kicking an accordion to death. Bugsy found a pen and copied down everything the translator said. He thanked him. They hung up.

Ellen looked up as he walked back in the room. "Yeah?" she said.

"Yeah. I need to find someone who'll sleep with a zombie chimp."

"Anything else?" Ellen asked. "Cure for cancer? Ten million tax-free American dollars?"

"An address for a guy named Jay Ackroyd," Bugsy said.

Ellen frowned. "You mean Popinjay?" she asked.

In the Jungle, Congo
People's Paradise of Africa

JERUSHA HAD NO IDEA how far they'd come or how far they had yet
to go. She had no way to gauge that. She kept hoping that over the next
ridge she'd see the blue line of Lake Tanganyika, but it never appeared. There
was only the next ridge, and the next, and the one after that, an eternity of
them growing increasingly hazy and blue with distance.

Rusty, why did we do this? Why aren't you here with me?

There was no answer to that, either. She looked back westward, deep
into the heart of the PPA, and she wondered where he was and what was
happening to him. She prayed that he was still alive, still safe. She prayed
that one day they would see each other again. That was all that kept her
feet moving.

That, and fear.

Waikili, when she asked if they were still being hunted, nodded fiercely.
"He's out there, Bibbi. Leucrotta. He thinks it's a game. He laughs, him and
the other one, the hungry one. They think it's funny how scared you are."

Leucrotta struck again during the day's march, as they pushed slowly
through a thicket of thornbushes with long, black needles. Naadir, the girl
with glowing skin, was snatched away suddenly at midday, a trail of blood
leading off into the thornbushes. She'd been one of the four children carrying Eason's stretcher, lagging behind the main group with their burden.
"There was a blur and roar, and she was gone . . ." the other three children
said. They were sobbing and crying, and no one wanted to pick up Eason's
stretcher again. "We need to leave him, Bibbi Jerusha," Idihi, one of the
boys, said. "To carry him is too dangerous now." He glanced at the other
joker children who were being carried. "Maybe them, too. We could all move
faster."

There were murmurs of agreement from within the crowd of children.
Eason began to wail, thrashing in the moist canvas, but Jerusha hushed them.
"We're not leaving *anyone*," she told them. "No one. We'll moved slower if
we must; we'll stay together. Those with weapons will stay in front and behind and to the sides. But *no one's* being abandoned. That's not going to happen. Now, I need four of you to pick up Eason's stretcher."

Only Cesar moved. She looked around at the frightened faces. *"Now!"*

she barked. Finally, Abagbe and two more of the older children took the other ends of the stretcher. "Good," Jerusha said. "Let's go."

She stayed at the rear alongside the stretcher as they moved, looking behind frequently and fearing what she'd see there, knowing that she'd have to face their pursuer again—not a monster, but a child doing monstrous things.

She looked at the thornbushes, at the seed pods they carried.

She took several.

People's Palace
Kongoville, Congo
People's Paradise of Africa

"AND I SAY IT must stop." President-for-Life Dr. Kitengi Nshombo didn't raise his voice, but it seemed to crack like a rifle shot. "This personal indulgence of yours has thrown away years of the goodwill we have worked so hard to build."

"The French fashion magazine even canceled its photo shoot after Paris." Alicia sniffled into a handkerchief. "I was so looking forward to that."

Her brother gave her a grumpy look, then turned his ire back to Tom. "It was bad enough when you disrupted the peace conference with no apparent provocation: the world media now treats Siraj as a victim. But now, with you doing more damage to Vienna than World War II—"

"I'm taking the battle to the imperialists. In a way they've never felt it before."

Nshombo shook his large, shiny, close-cropped head. The hair had begun to turn the color of iron. "The media have begun to paint you as a madman. And that brush stains our revolution!"

His anger turbocharged Tom's, which already didn't need it. *"Fuck that, man!"* he shouted. "Who cares what the running-dog media say? That's a load of uptight bourgeois bullshit and you know it."

Slowly, Nshombo blinked. "Concern for our global reputation is not bourgeois propriety. It is practicality. Purely practical! You are indulging your personal passions to the detriment of the Revolution."

The president's office was big and grand, with a desk as huge as his sister's was tiny, in jet-black African ironwood with potted palms at either end. Huge gaudy African nativist paintings jostled for space with important-looking photos on the paneled walls. The Spartan Nshombo, whose only real weakness in life was the Dandie Dinmont terriers he raised, looked more out of place here than his sister would've in chubby leopard mode. But Alicia had insisted in taking a hand in the interior design. The office of the President-for-Life of the People's Paradise had to *look* like one, she claimed.

"Now, boys," said Alicia herself. She sat in a precariously dainty chair by one of the palms. "Please, boys. Be nice. Everyone wants to be nice, now."

Tom didn't want to hear it. "You're going soft, man," he told Nshombo. "You've been away from the frontline struggle too long."

Nshombo slammed a hand down on his desk with a gunshot noise. "*This is the forefront of the real struggle, right here. I direct the Revolution. It is up to you to carry out my designs.*"

"Then stand back and let me carry them out, man. You can't make an omelet without breaking eggs."

"*Boys,*" Alicia sobbed, wringing her hands. Her eyes, huge and soft and brown and swimming with tears behind the lenses of her bat-wing glasses, implored him. "Brother, our Tom has a real grievance against this arch-colonialist assassin, *non?* We should not hinder him." The handkerchief came out and dabbed her eye.

Dr. Nshombo's brow furrowed.

Though his eyelids rasped his eyes like files and the blood ran through his veins as if it had broken-glass edges, Tom didn't forget what a good ally Alicia was. Quite. He turned and paced a couple of steps away from the gleaming black mass of the desk.

"Very well," Dr. Nshombo said with a little exhalatory gust. "But you must bring this campaign to a close very soon. Or else let it go."

"Let it *go?*" Tom's eyes flashed.

Alicia stood up to lay a soft damp hand on his arm. "Tom, please."

He nodded spastically. "All right."

He left.

Has it all started to go to your head, Kitengi? All this loot and luxury? he asked himself as he stalked tall, echoing corridors. *Or—wait. You've got Alicia's Precious Moments ace babies now. Is it possible you think you no longer need* me?

He stepped outside, gazed up at the stinging tropical sun, and cracked his knuckles. *Don't make that mistake, Comrade Nshombo. Or a hard rain is gonna fall.*

Lucerne, Switzerland

"... OUTFITTING QUITE AN EXPEDITION," the clerk said in that strangely guttural yet singsongy German that was unique to Switzerland as he ran the reader across the tag on another climbing harness.

"*Ya, genau,*" Noel said shortly. He didn't really want to get into a discussion of mountains he'd climbed with a garrulous rock climber. His cell phone vibrated in his coat pocket. "*Entschuldigen,*" he murmured to the clerk, and stepped off to the side. It was his theatrical agent, Frank Figge. "Whoever it is, tell them no," Noel said as Frank was drawing breath for his first word, "unless they want their audience massacred when Tom Weathers shows up."

"She said that would likely be your response," came Frank's strident cockney tones. "But she said to offer you greetings from one practitioner of the trade to another."

Noel sucked in a quick breath. "Did she leave a name and number?"

"Yes. Sun Hei-lian." Noel memorized the number as Frank rattled it off. "Thanks, I'll call her."

"How does she rate, and I don't?" Frank complained, but Noel hung up on him and dialed Sun's number.

"What do you want? And make it quick, because I'm not giving you time to trace this call," Noel said when she answered.

It was the mark of a professional that she didn't demur. "I need your help dealing with Weathers." There was no hint that she remembered or even cared that one time they had indulged a three-way with Tom Weathers while Noel was in his female form.

"You know how I *deal* with things," Noel said.

"And that I will not permit," was the cold reply. "Everyone wants him to die, but I've discovered something—"

"He's not such a bad guy," Noel said sarcastically.

"He's mentally ill. I'm pretty sure he's schizophrenic. There's another personality inside him—gentle, kind—I've been talking to that personality. If we can bring him out—"

"Getting Weathers on a couch is going to be a little tough."

"Yes, it offers challenges. The best place to treat him would be the Joker-town Clinic. Your ace powers will enable me to get him there in an eyeblink. Before he can waken and . . . and . . ."

"Crush us like bugs?" Noel asked sweetly.

"It's in your interest, too," Sun said defensively.

"Why doesn't your own service incapacitate Weathers and try to bring out this other personality?"

"We are rapidly approaching the point where they will decide he is too dangerous to live."

Now *that* was alarming. Noel didn't want Weathers killed yet. Not until the insane ace had taken care of the Nshombos for him. "And I take it you'd be the person to execute that order?" Noel asked.

There was a long silence, then Sun said, "And I won't do it." Her voice was low, passionate.

"Why not? God knows he deserves it."

"Not if he's sick. He should have the chance for redemption," Sun said.

It was the last response he had expected, and he suddenly had Niobe's voice echoing in his memory. *Thousands of dead jokers, thousands of dead soldiers, a bunch of young kids with a river of blood on their hands.*

But I didn't kill them. I just killed one man. For the best of reasons. I couldn't foresee what would happen, Noel thought.

The brutally honest part of his nature took up the debate. *Some would argue that the only difference between you and Weathers is one of scale.*

"Do you think that's possible?" Noel asked, and suddenly it was terribly important to him what she said.

"Yes, yes I do."

"You're putting yourself at odds with your country and government," Noel said softly.

"Yes."

"Why?"

There was again a long silence, finally she said, "I love the man he may yet become."

Noel pulled on his lip and considered the Chinese woman. She was one of the few people Tom Weathers trusted. He realized he had solved the transfer of information problem. "I'll help you, but I want something in return." And he told her what he needed.

"So, yet more killing before he's free?" Sun said bitterly.

"At least he'll be killing people who richly deserve it, and it's my price," Noel answered.

She sighed. "All right. I will contact you when I'm ready." She sounded unbelievably sad, and then Noel realized she had hung up.

He slowly put away his phone and considered. Of course he wasn't going to trust Niobe's safety to the questionable science of psychiatry. Weathers needed to die.

The question was, who did it?

◆

Tuesday, December 22

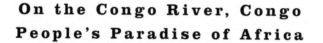

On the Congo River, Congo
People's Paradise of Africa

THE PILOT'S NAME WAS Japhet. His face was crisscrossed with pink scars that shone against his dark skin. There was a rifle slung across his shoulder and he had a pistol holstered under his left armpit. Before Michelle's card turned, he would have scared the shit out of her.

Joey had found a dead chimpanzee near the airstrip and raised it up. Japhet called it a bonobo. He didn't seem surprised in the least by the zombie bonobo, not even when Joey carried it around like a baby.

"Stop playing with that zombie," Michelle snapped. It gave her the willies. "It's not helping. And it grosses me out."

"Jesus, Bubbles, you are such a fucking pussy when it comes to slightly moldy flesh." Joey made a kissy face at the bonobo. The bonobo made the same face back at Joey.

Japhet looked quizzically between them. "I still need one thousand U.S. to take you to Kisangani."

"I can give you five hundred," Michelle said. "And this watch." Michelle pulled off her Bulova. It wasn't very expensive, but it was pretty. Maybe Japhet would go for it.

Japhet gave the watch a skeptical look. "It's not that valuable."

"You can tell people it belonged to the Amazing Bubbles." She held her hand out, palm up, and let a small bubble form in it. Then she targeted a can lying in the dirt about twenty-five feet away and let it fly. The can jumped and pinged as if it had been shot.

That made him smile. "You give me an autograph, too?"

"As many as you want."

Ackroyd & Creighton Investigations
Manhattan, New York

JAY ACKROYD—POPINJAY—LEANED against his desk, arms crossed, a sense of world-weary amusement radiating off him in a way Bugsy had only dreamed possible. *This*, Bugsy thought as he finished his explanation, *is what I want to be when I grow up.*

The office wasn't pristine. An old coffee cup was sitting on the desk, a pile of folders rose up on the desk. But there was a comfort in the man as he moved through the room, a sense of professionalism that said, *Hey, I didn't start the most powerful ace in the world on a killing rampage. That was you.*

"Okay," Popinjay said slowly, like he was eating something he really liked the taste of. "So you want to figure out what the relationship is between the Radical and Mark Meadows?" He seemed to think the question was funny.

"The Radical's on kind of a killing spree, you may have noticed. If Meadows is still alive, he may have the key to stopping Tom Weathers," Bugsy said.

"You could look at it that way," Popinjay said. "Here's the thing, Mark Meadows and I were on Takis together, and—"

"Takis? Like the other planet, Takis? With the aliens that made the wild card?"

"That would be the Takis," Popinjay said. "I was there. With Mark. That whole cadre of aces that hung out with Cap'n Trips? Jumping Jack Flash. Moonchild. Cosmic Traveler. They're all him."

Bugsy blinked. "I don't get it," he said. "Mark Meadows was Moonchild?"

"And Starshine. And all the rest."

"And the Radical . . ."

"And the Radical. Mark is a pharmaceutical genius. Depending on which drugs he took, he became different people."

"Yeah, okay," Bugsy said, his hundred different bits of information falling into place at once. "That's usually just a metaphor, you know."

"Not for Mark. The Radical was the holy grail for him. He'd managed to get there once. The first time, as a matter of fact. Way back in the sixties."

"People's Park," Bugsy said. "I got that."

"It wasn't really the same guy, though. Tom Weathers came later. That one was just the Radical. Ever since then, he's been trying to get that particular high back. All the others were . . . well, I wouldn't say failed attempts. But less than successful."

Bugsy stood up, pacing slowly back and forth. "Aquarius. The were-dolphin guy?"

"Mark Meadows."

"Starshine?"

"Mark. And Monster."

"Jesus! The Radical was the Cock That Ate Chicago?"

Popinjay nodded, then grew somber. "They were all him. Or parts of him or things that he took out of the world and became. I was never really sure. But they were all named for songs, you know."

"Songs?"

"Sure. Jumping Jack Flash?"

"It's a song? I knew it was a Whoopi Goldberg movie."

Jay Ackroyd shook his head. "All of them are songs. Listen to a good oldies station. You'll find all of them there. Aquarius. Starshine."

"Moonchild?"

"By King Crimson," Jay said, "released in sixty-nine. Same year Mark became the Radical for the first time."

"Vietnam was brought out of civil war by a pop song?"

"You could look at it that way," Jay Ackroyd said. "The thing you have to understand about Mark Meadows is he's a really good person. Yes, he saved Vietnam. He saved more than that. You remember the Card Sharks?"

"Was that the show on Cinemax with the girl in Vegas and the chimpanzee?"

"I was thinking more the conspiracy to kill every wild card in the world. They were holding Mark prisoner in China back in ninety-four. Guy named Layton was beating Mark to death. Mark swallowed a bunch of drugs. Who really knows what? And then . . . the Radical returned. I know what he's become, but before all this happened, the Radical saved your life."

"He seems to regret it now."

"Yeah, I know. Whatever's going on with Mark, it's . . . complex. Seems like his 'friends' are aspects of his personality. Maybe they started out being external—part of the drugs, part of the world, whatever—or maybe they were always inside him. But the Radical was all of them together. Like a multiple personality disorder where there's one persona who knows everything? Tom Weathers was the perfected image of Mark Meadows. He had all the powers of all the others. He was . . . he was what Mark wanted to be, but never was."

"Well," Bugsy said. "Holy shit."

He left in a daze, taking the subway back to Ellen's. He couldn't get his head around Mark Meadows, sad sack icon of the summer of love, being not just Tom Weathers but all those other aces, too. Or the idea that the Radical—the same one from Paris—had saved the world once. Saved him, personally, and every other ace and joker in the world from the Black Trump. It changed things, but he wasn't sure how yet.

He missed his stop and had to walk back five blocks through the cold December wind. When he got in, Ellen was sitting at the kitchen counter, the slightest frown showing between her eyebrows. He put down his coat.

"What did you find out?"

He told her all of it. Takis. Vietnam. The 1960s. Sprout and Kimberly Ann Cordayne and Mark Meadows, really nice guy. Monster and Jumping Jack Flash. And with every word, he found himself talking louder, gesturing wider, getting angry. "We've been fighting a hippie's wet dream about Che Guevara! All of it, *all* of it, is the one guy's psychodrama about not being . . . I don't even know. Radical enough in nineteen fucking sixty-eight! Do you have any idea how many people have died because Mark Meadows wasn't sufficiently cool?"

"Hundreds," Cameo said. "Thousands."

"And a couple dozen more last week. And next week, who the fuck knows?"

"And," she said, "how does that help you stop him?"

Bugsy paused and raised his hands in a gesture that meant *No clue.* "And you know what," he said, "it isn't even that. It isn't even that he wanted to be this bronzed Adonis. Do you know *why* he wanted that? To impress a girl.

To get into Kimberly Ann Cordayne's jeans. *That's* what all of this is about. Back in sixty-I-don't-even-know-what, little teenage Mark Meadows got a perfectly understandable boner for Kimberly in his French class, and now that same erection is blowing people up in Vienna. It's the past, Ellen. The past is killing us.

"And that girl? The one with the funny laugh and the enchanting tits that got Mark's hopes up? She's gone. She doesn't even exist anymore. I've seen her, and she looks like somebody's grandma who just got out of a methadone clinic. Even if he was exactly the guy who would have rocked her back in sixty-eight, it doesn't matter. That girl's gone. She's dead. And people are *still* dying in order to fucking impress who she used to be."

"Bugsy—"

"It's sick, Ellen! It's sick, and it's wrong, and it's straight-out pathetic. He's holding on to this idea of who he's supposed to be. This idealized image of who he thinks she would have wanted, even though she doesn't want that, and he can't ever really be more than Mark Meadows's psychological failures in a fucking Halloween mask. And so he's turned into this twisted, empty, evil, sad-ass version of himself and hurting a bunch of people who had nothing to do with it."

"Hey—"

"It's like a poison. It's like he drank too much of the past, and now it's poisoning us."

He stopped. Somewhere in the rant, he'd started crying. He leaned against the wall, wiping the tears with the palms of his hands.

When Ellen spoke, her voice was soft. "We aren't still talking about the Radical, are we?"

"I don't know," he said. "I don't think so."

On the Congo River, Congo
People's Paradise of Africa

WHERE THE HELL IS Japhet?

He said he needed to go to the village and pick up some supplies, but Michelle thought he was taking too long.

She'd had another dream about Adesina while she dozed off waiting for their pilot. Another pit dream, more vivid than before. The smell was even worse, something Michelle hadn't thought possible, and the compulsion to get to Adesina was becoming overwhelming. It was like a radio station coming in clearer the closer you got to the signal.

Joey was cradling the chimp on her lap, while it stared up at her with its dead eyes. Michelle thought she might hurl. The bonobo was beginning to stink. The heat wasn't helping things.

"I need to get bigger," Michelle said suddenly. "We don't know what's waiting for us at Kisangani. Could you raise a couple of zombies and have them pound on me?"

Joey made a circle in the dirt with the toe of her shoe. "There's always dead bodies, Bubbles. How many do you want? There are hundreds here." Her voice started to have a singsong quality, and that was worse than the nonstop swearing.

"Just a couple."

It took a few minutes, but soon a couple of decrepit zombies came shambling up the dirt road.

"I don't know," Michelle said. "They don't look like they'll do much."

"They'll be fine," Joey replied.

The zombies began to hit Michelle. She'd taken much worse pummelings, but they did make her plump up like yeasty dough.

"Okay," Michelle said. "I'm good for now. I don't want to add a lot more weight to the plane."

Michelle was going to say more, but she'd just seen Japhet coming up the road, carrying two string bags loaded with fruit and brown paper-wrapped packages.

When he got closer she said, "Did you get everything you need?"

He nodded. His mouth was pulled into a tight line. "We must leave quickly. When I told a friend at the store that I was taking some people to Kisangani, he got a funny look on his face. It seems there have been men looking for strangers—American strangers."

"What did he say?" Joey asked her. When Michelle translated the conversation into English she said, "This could be a world of hurt coming."

"You're probably right," Michelle replied. Then she spoke again to Japhet. "Can we leave now?"

"Yes," he said. "But I'm going to need more money. I won't be able to come back here for a while."

"Fine," Michelle said. It would wipe out the rest of her cash, but there was no other choice. "Can we help you load?" He nodded and pointed to several boxes sitting near the single-engine prop plane. When he climbed into the plane and started the engine, it sputtered to life in a way that didn't fill Michelle with confidence.

Michelle and Joey were loading the last of small cargo boxes when Japhet jumped from the plane, yelling something Michelle couldn't quite make out over the engine noise. Then he pulled the pistol from his holster and started firing. Michelle turned around. Bounding up the dirt road, kicking up dust, came seven huge leopards.

"Shit! *Go!*" Michelle yelled at Joey. She pushed her toward the plane, then spun and let a barrage of bubbles fly at the leopards. These were rubbery, nothing lethal about them. But they would hurt like hell. She didn't want to kill the leopards, but animals didn't normally behave this way. *What the hell was going on?*

The bubbles hit two of the cats, one in the shoulder, the other in the leg. They went down and rolled over and over in the dusty road. But the other five kept running toward the plane.

Michelle saw that Joey was still outside. Japhet grabbed her arm and yanked her toward the open plane door. Michelle felt claws sinking into her back and she was slammed into the side of the fuselage. She bounced off the plane, spun around, and saw another leopard leaping at Joey as she scrambled into the plane. Its claws raked down the back of her leg. The zombie bonobo leaped up and grabbed the leopard's head, then started gouging out its eyes.

The other leopards were on Michelle. They clawed and bit her, but that only made her fatter. She created bubbles the size of soccer balls and sent them into each cat's chest. The leopards popped up into the air. As the first one hit the ground, she heard Japhet's pistol. The leopard screamed and then turned into a naked man.

Michelle scrambled, grabbed Japhet, and yelled into his ear, "Stop shooting. They're people."

"No. They are Leopard Men." He spat. "They're not getting my plane!"

"Let's get the hell out of here." Michelle released rubbery bubbles at the remaining leopards. He nodded, jammed his gun into his holster, and climbed into the plane. Michelle followed, yanking the door shut behind her.

Joey sat on one hip on the far seat. Her leg was bleeding and stained her pants brownish red. There were four deep gashes in her flesh and blood was welling up in them. Japhet climbed into the pilot's seat and started the plane down the dirt runway.

"Do you have a first-aid kit in here?" Michelle asked. She glanced out the windshield and saw the end of the runway—and the jungle where it stopped—coming up way too fast. "Christ, we're not going to make it."

Japhet just laughed and pulled back hard on the throttle. The plane shuddered, bounced up and down a couple of times, then rose in the air. Michelle could hear jungle foliage whapping the underside of the plane.

"No first-aid kit," he said. "There's a bottle of water you can use to clean the wound and I have a clean T-shirt in one of those packages." He pointed to the string bags he'd brought from the village earlier that were now on the floor in front of Michelle's feet. "You can use it for a bandage. It's one of those wrapped up in brown paper."

She pulled the first twine-tied parcel out and held it up. "Is it in here?" she asked. He nodded. She undid the twine and discovered a couple of T-shirts, underwear, and socks. "That's what you were doing in the village? Your laundry?"

"No," he said defensively. "Laundry is woman's work. There's a widow who does it for me. I give her money and bring medicine for her boy from Kisangani and she washes for me."

Michelle rolled her eyes, grabbed one of the T-shirts, and retied the package. "You got a knife?" He nodded and fished one out of his pants pocket and handed it to her. "Thanks." She crawled back to Joey. "This is going to hurt."

"Just do something, you fucker," Joey said. Her voice trembled and Michelle knew she was crying.

Michelle got to work tearing up the T-shirt. The jungle slid by below them, every mile bringing her closer and closer to Adesina.

In the Jungle, Congo
People's Paradise of Africa

THROUGH THE GAP BETWEEN the hills ahead of them, there was a line of darker blue. *Lake Tanganyika.*

The sight filled Jerusha with hope. Maybe, maybe she could do this . . .

They had moved into less fractured ground. The hills were lower now, the jungle beginning to give way to more open ground. They were moving across a wide field of tall grass, making good time, following a half-hidden trail. People obviously came this way occasionally. The sun beat down on them, but after the half gloom of the jungle, it felt good to see unbroken sky overhead. She was hoping to find another village, perhaps a phone . . .

Waikili was walking alongside her, his hand grasping hers. She felt his fingers tighten. "Bibbi . . ." he said. "He comes again . . ."

"Cesar! Everyone!" Jerusha shouted as she dropped Waikili's hand. "Watch—"

There was no time to say more. She saw the grass rippling to the right of the path they followed. She heard the roar of the monster. She heard the children shrill in alarm and someone's gun firing widly. She saw the ruff of tan hide as the hyena-lion leapt and heard the terrible clashing of its jaws.

She saw it toss a child's torn body aside even as she ran toward it. Cesar and Gamila were firing into the grass, the chatter of the gunfire causing birds to erupt from the trees bordering the field and tearing the frond of grass. "Stop!" she told them, panting. "Wait until you can see him . . ."

The silence was deafening, the roar of the weapons still echoing. Three of the children were badly injured, claw-raked as the were-creature had passed through the line, and there were two still bodies with other children around them: Pili and Chaga. "Are they . . . ?" The children didn't need to answer. She knew. "Waikili," she said. "Is he still there?"

"Yes, Bibbi Jerusha. He has decided it's time to end the game."

Jerusha nodded. "Cesar, Gamila," she said. She was staring into the field, at the faint path of trampled grass where the boy had gone. "Take the children and keep moving."

"Bibbi . . ."

"Do it," she snapped, not looking at him.

She heard him call out to the children both in French and Baluba. She heard them pick up Eason's stretcher, heard them half run down the path away from the bodies. She rummaged in her seed pouch, cast seeds in a close circle around her.

"I know you're there," she called out in French. "I'm here. I'm alone. You want to end this? Then take me first."

Laughter answered her from the grass.

"Come on," she told him. "I'm waiting for you."

There was more laughter, moving now, sliding to her left. She turned toward the sound.

He came almost too fast for her, a blur of motion. Jerusha tore at the seeds she'd scattered with her mind, and a mass of thornbushes lifted toward the sky, the black knives of the bushes snagging and tearing at the hyena body of the child ace, lifting him in midleap. Even so, the claws of his right paw ripped along her arm and Jerusha cried out in pain and shock. She could smell his foul breath, and her face was spattered with his saliva as he roared. As the thornbushes lifted him, the beast struggled in their grasp and she stabbed him a thousand times with the long black thorns. Branches broke and tore, scattering black snow as he tore at them furiously. The claws raked at the thorns, at her, at air; she retreated, still trying to wrap him in her dark, deadly cage. She could feel him slipping loose.

Too strong. She could not hold him. He was too strong.

He roared. The branches holding him creaked and splintered even as she tried to strengthen them.

Then she heard Cesar shout, heard his weapon fire. The were-thing screamed as the bullets tore into its tan hide, as Jerusha wrapped yet more thorn limbs around the beast to hold it, to slow it. And suddenly, it was no longer a beast but a naked child snagged in thorns and dying, his own face shattered and broken. Cesar was still firing, and the child's body shuddered and writhed from the impact of the bullets. *"Stop!"* Jerusha screamed at Cesar. *"Stop. It's over."*

The gunfire ended. Blood dripped to the ground from the still, broken form. Jerusha turned away from the sight, unable to look. Cesar was grinning, and she hated the look of triumph and satisfaction on his face.

The grass swayed near the path, and another boy emerged: the emaciated child, just a hand's reach from her. He had a waif's face, with eyes too large and too sad in his sunken face, his belly drawn tightly in, his arms and legs no more than sticks. His mouth was open, as if he were trying to speak.

"Bibbi!" She heard Cesar calling to her in alarm. "No!"

The child glanced from the body in the tree to Jerusha, his eyes shimmering with tears. "You can come with us," she told him. "You don't have to be with them anymore. You can be free of all this. I can help you. I'll get you to people who can help you."

He cocked his head toward her as she spoke. Jerusha didn't know if he understood her French, but she hoped he could understand the tone. She held out her hand toward him, and he took it in his. She could feel the trembling in his fingers, could feel bones under the thin wrapping of skin and tendons.

His hand tightened on hers. He pulled her arm forward, and as she stumbled to catch her balance, his mouth yawned open and he bit down hard on her forearm.

"No!" She didn't know if the shout came from her or Cesar. The boy grinned at her, licking lips dark with her blood. The wound burned, as if his saliva were acid. Cesar's gun stuttered and the child ran, plunging back into the high grass. "Stop!" Jerusha shouted: at the child, at Cesar. She cradled her injured arm to her belly. *"Stop! Come back!"*

Cesar came running to her. He looked at her arm, and she saw his eyes fill with tears. "It's okay," she told him. "I'm fine. It's just a bite. He's gone. We've won here. It's over. Come on, let's go get the others."

"Bibbi Jerusha . . ."

"I'm fine," she told him sternly. "Let's go. I'm fine."

She hoped that she was right.

Ubundu, Congo
People's Paradise of Africa

"THIS CAN'T BE KISANGANI," Michelle said. The landing strip was cracked mud and ruts, surrounded by thick jungle. Not a building was in sight. "Kisangani is a city."

"Kisangani was a city," Japhet said. "Now?" He shrugged. "There's an airport in Kisangani, yes, but they aren't fond of independent contractors like me. The cut they want of my merchandise is outrageous. There are police at the Kisangani airport, too. And soldiers, and Leopard Men, and men in suits who ask inconvenient questions about flight plans and passengers. It is better here in the jungle. The people living here keep a runway clear and I bring them what they need."

"Capitalism at its best," Michelle murmured.

"And the two of you have already been more trouble than I bargained for."

Michelle smiled at him. "It looks like you know your way around trouble."

He gave her a toothy grin. "That I do."

"Where are we, then?"

"Outside Ubundu. Kisangani is that way." He pointed. "From here you must walk. If you lose your way, find the Congo and follow it downstream. It was a pleasure to meet you, Bubbles." He took her hand and shook it. "Get your friend to a doctor. Wounds go bad fast in the jungle."

"I'll do my best," she replied. By the time they heard his engine roar past overhead, she and Joey were already deep in the green, making their way through thick underbrush.

Japhet had left them a machete, and that was certainly a help. But Joey was not happy. "Fucking asshole," she complained. "Look at this shit. Walk, he says. There's no fucking *road*. And where are the elephants? I thought Africa was full of fucking elephants. Their own graveyards and everything. One dead elephant, that's all I need, we could fucking *ride* to Kisangani."

With every step they took toward Kisangani, Joey grew more and more agitated. By late afternoon, she was furious. "You don't fucking know, Bubbles," she muttered. "You can't feel it. There's dead shit all around. Kids, dead kids. So many dead kids. I can *feel* the little fuckers rotting in the ground."

Michelle gave her a shake. "Okay, I got it. Dead kids. A lot of them." *And one who is still alive.*

Joey looked up with a furious expression on her face. "You're the coldest bitch I've ever known, Bubbles. I'm telling you about fuck only knows how many dead children, and you don't give two brown shits. Ink would *never* have acted this way."

Michelle released her. "I'm not Ink. Thanks for the insight. But those children are dead. We can't do a damn thing about them. Adesina is still alive."

Joey glared at her, but there was a weird glassy-eyed quality to it. Michelle put her wrist to Joey's forehead.

"Christ," she said. "You're burning up." She squatted down and pulled the bandage up to look at Joey's leg wound. It was bright red and swollen. "We need to get this looked at. Soon. Look, when we find Adesina, we'll find out who killed those other kids. If there are as many dead as you say, there has to be some sort of record. We'll do something."

Joey grabbed her arm. "You fucking promise, Michelle? Do you swear?" She swayed a little. Michelle suddenly felt horrible for bringing her along. Yeah, Joey could raise zombies, but she was as fragile as any nat herself and still a kid herself in many ways.

"I promise," she said.

The Red House
Outside Bunia, Congo
People's Paradise of Africa

THE SUN HAD LEFT the sky, leaving only a lavender glow with a hint of blood to silhouette the trees on the ridge west of the huge and complicated old red-brick colonial mansion. Bugs called from the chopped-back trees and brush. Something big and dark—either a bat or a really humongous moth—flew past Tom's head to vanish over the steeply pitched slate roof.

In the grey-velvet twilight stood Alicia Nshombo, stuffed not quite successfully into a dark tunic and jodhpurs. *Her secret-police boss suit*, Tom thought as he hovered briefly before the white-roofed portico. A slight man in a doctor's coat fairly hopped from foot to foot at her side.

As Tom touched down on the grass Alicia trundled forward to catch him in her usual moist embrace. "Dear Tom," she said, kissing him on the cheek, "welcome to the Red House. This is Dr. Washikala. He's the director of our facility here."

Washikala swallowed before saying, "It's an honor to meet you, Field Marshal *Mokèlé-mbèmbé*." At Alicia's gesture the little doctor turned and trotted up the steps to open the door. Tom started to follow.

From somewhere out of sight around the house to his left he heard children wailing and crying. There was a big frame annex there. He stopped with one foot up on a step.

The noise quit. An engine revved. A moment later a panel truck rumbled past. A beat later a black Land Cruiser followed. The man in the passenger seat wore unmistakable Leopard Man drag: a brimless leopard-skin hat and sunglasses at night. The others wore the cammies of PPA regulars—second line infantry, not Simbas.

Tom stood frowning after them until the guards at the brick house to the north had opened the wrought-iron gates with the spiky tops. The truck headed off toward the west, its yellow beams bouncing like an insect's feelers before it, up the flank of a ridge scraped bare for a hundred yards beyond the wire. The Cruiser followed.

Dr. Washikala cleared his throat. "Comrade Field Marshal. If you please—"

Alicia seemed to be studying Tom intently. Without a word Tom mounted the steps and went inside.

A strong chemical smell filled the air. It must be some kind of cleaning agent. Washikala trotted past as if afraid he'd burst into flames if the sleeve of his coat so much as brushed Tom. Alicia walked by his side. "So you come at last to the heart of the matter," she said.

"Who am I here to see?"

"Two most promising products," Dr. Washikala said. "*Moto.* The name is self-explanatory: it means *fire* in Lingala. You should exercise caution. He doesn't have perfect control of his abilities yet. The second we call Martial Eagle. For our largest African eagle. She's"—he glanced nervously at Alicia—"she's a joker-ace, really. She has the head and wings of the eagle; the rest is a normal if undernourished eleven-year-old female."

"And why did you accept her?" Alicia sounded as if she was on the verge of being disappointed.

"Oh, Eldest Sister," the doctor squeaked. "We thought—surely she can serve the Revolution. She flies." He looked imploringly at Tom with liquid-brown eyes.

"Could she carry a kid?" Tom asked.

"Oh, yes. I—I'm sure of it."

"We can use her. If that's true."

"*Bon,*" Alicia said, beaming. "The doctor guarantees it." She gave the doctor a meaningful look. Before she could continue a sound reached their ears. Tom recognized the snarl of distant machine-gun fire. Neither the sturdy brick walls nor the bulk of a ridge sufficed to mute the unmistakable sound.

Tom narrowed eyes at Alicia. "You must understand, Tom," she said. "We get so many black queens and jokers."

"And of course there are the deuces," said Dr. Washikala. He seemed eager to establish his bona fides as a hard-ass after the near faux pas with Martial Eagle.

"What do you think?" Alicia said, sounding half worried and half, strangely, sympathetic.

"I think," Tom said, "you got to break eggs to make omelets. Now, show me to my two new recruits."

♥

Wednesday, December 23

Lake Tanganyika, Congo
People's Paradise of Africa

THE LAKE SEEMED AS vast as the country they had already traversed. It lay in front of them, endless, the horizon fading into sky.

Jerusha sat on the lakeshore with her children gathered around her. They had come out of the jungle north of Kalemie. Since the attack by the two child aces, Jerusha had found herself driven to the edge of exhaustion. Her body burned. Her clothes fit too loosely.

And the hunger . . .

She was eternally famished, but it wasn't a hunger that food could assuage. She had grown banana trees and mangos for the children, given them brief gardens of vegetables so they could eat, and she had taken her meals with them, but they didn't fill her. Nothing filled her. Her body seemed a vast emptiness, scorched by whatever the child's bite had injected into her. Her body was eating itself, slowly, burning away fat and muscle and tissue to keep itself going.

And she was tired. So tired.

She fumbled with the seeds left in her pouch and stared at the lake. There were thirty miles or more of deep water between them and Tanzania—

she could not bridge that, not even if she had thousands of seeds. They could try to run back into the jungle again, but they would be found. There was no help for them, not here in the PPA.

Through the heated fog in her head, she tried to think of a solution, her fingers fumbling with the seeds. The last time she'd tried to cross the lake, with Wally, the patrol boat, leaving them clinging to the dying baobab . . .

A tree. A tree would float.

There were three baobab seeds left in her pouch. She plucked out one of them, tossing it as far as she could into the lake, opening the seed as it flew through the air: a massive trunk, but yes, bend the branches upward so that it made the skeleton of a hull, big enough that all of them could cling to the branches. A few of the branches she spread out flat and thick like pontoons, so that the strongest swimmers could hold on there and kick with their legs to move them. The roots and top she fanned out high and large, so that perhaps it would catch the east-flowing wind and help them.

It was an awkward boat, a terribly slow ark. But it would suffice. It would *have* to suffice.

The children watched, calling excitedly as she formed the baobab vessel for them. Some of them were even laughing, as if this were a new game. They seemed to sense how close they were to safety. "Okay," she told Cesar. "Tell them to get aboard. Anyone who can swim, get on those longer branches so you can kick and push us. Hurry!"

She waded into the water—colder than she remembered, as if there was nothing on her body to keep away the chill—and helped them as much as she could with her injured and crudely bandaged arm, watching each of them clamber into the water-slick trunk, helping those who the wild card had rendered less mobile.

Finally, she pushed with what little strength she had left and pulled herself up. Cesar and several of the children were kicking, white water splashing around their legs, but their improvised craft was making little headway, and the water was now too deep for Jerusha to stand in.

"Bibbi Jerusha." She heard the call: Eason, still in his stretcher. His fish tail flapped on the canvas. "You carried me," he said in halting French, "now it's my turn. . . ."

Jerusha nodded to Cesar, to Gamila. They lifted the stretcher, let Eason tumble into the water.

Eason swam, his tail churning the water white behind him. He went to the rear of the baobab, grabbing the largest root with his hand, and his tail kicked.

Their baobab raft began to move steadily out into the deeper water.

Kisangani, Congo
People's Paradise of Africa

"THOSE FUCKERS," JOEY MUTTERED. "Those fuckers."

Michelle didn't reply. She'd stopped talking to Joey earlier in the day. Nothing she said helped. The closer they got to Kisangani, the angrier Hoodoo Mama became.

It had started with the first grave.

"They're here," Joey said. "They're down there in the dark. The fuckers just left them there."

"Show me where."

Joey plunged through the forest. Michelle followed. They came upon a small clearing. To one side there was a large boxy trailer. In the center of the clearing was a large mound of newly turned dirt. Michelle stared at it, her stomach doing nauseated flip-flops. Then a strange coldness came over her. "Are they in there?"

"Yes."

"How many?"

"A lot. I want whoever did this," Joey said in a calm, soft voice.

"I do, too," Michelle replied.

"I'm going to raise them."

"No," Michelle said. "Do you want to find whoever did this? Fast? We have to keep going."

"God damn it!" Joey screamed, spittle flying from her mouth. "You're just going to leave them down there in the dark? You fucking bitch."

Michelle didn't answer, but went to the trailer and carefully opened the door. She poked her head in, but the trailer was empty except for an old desk and a couple of stainless-steel medical tables. There was a medicinal odor inside. In the trash can in the corner she found empty bottles of disinfectant and rubbing alcohol.

Frustrated, she threw the empties back into the can. The disinfectant would have helped some with Joey's leg, which was swollen and angry-looking. She looked around again, and noticed for the first time the colorful cutout pictures on the walls. *Pictures from children's books.* They were full of smiling happy animals and smiling happy children.

Slowly, she made her way around the trailer. With the exception of the bottles in the trash and the pictures on the walls, it seemed to have been stripped clean. She sat at the desk and started opening drawers. They were empty except for paper clips. She felt under the desk, but there was nothing there.

Then she pulled the desk away from the wall, and she heard a *snick* as a file slid down to the floor. She reached behind the desk and grabbed it.

Unfortunately, it was written in French. Michelle's French wasn't good enough for her to translate it all, but she did see Alicia Nshombo's name more than once as she paged through the paperwork. But in the bottom of the file there were photos.

The pictures were of dead children, each with a series of notes clipped to the photo. Most looked like jokers and had been shot in the head. The rest were black queens. Some hardly looked human anymore. Michelle thought she might throw up.

"What's that?"

Michelle looked up. Joey was standing in the doorway. "I'm not sure. I don't read French."

"You talked to Gaetan and Kengo just fine."

"That was simple conversation. This is reading. And it has all sorts of stuff that I just don't understand."

"Let me see."

Michelle closed the file. "There's nothing here."

"Let me see the cocksucking file, Bubbles." Her voice was smaller than usual.

Reluctantly, Michelle handed the file over. Joey opened it and glanced at the papers inside. She looked puzzled, then she saw the photos.

"I'll kill them all," she said, but there was little strength in her voice.

"I'll help you," Michelle said. "But first we need to find them."

"I can do that. We'll just follow the trail of dead." Joey glowered at Michelle; her eyes were glassy and she was swaying a little. "Hoodoo Mama is *handy*."

Lake Tanganyika
Tanzania

THE BAOBAB RAFT WAS spotted when they were halfway across, and
Denys Finch was on the Tanzanian patrol boat that responded. "Hey!" The
rhinoceros horn on his snouted face gleamed in the sun. He looked at the
baobab boat, at the children filling its branches like dark human fruit. His
eyebrows raised. "Need a ride?"

Jerusha hugged the joker as the crew brought her and the children
aboard. "How . . . ?" she asked, too exhausted to say more, her belly rumbling
with hunger. She was famished; she burned with it.

"Been taking the plane up looking for you two since you left, couple
times a day. Was about to give up on it, too, if you didn't show in a day or
two. I saw the baobab and radioed to these blokes. Where's your metal fellow?"

"He's not here."

"Oh." Finch looked as if he wanted to ask more, then evidently changed
his mind. "You look like you haven't slept in a week or eaten anything in a
month."

"We could all use food," she told him. "It seems like so long since . . ."
She stopped. Shook her head to rid it of the images of food rising in her. "Is
there a satellite phone on this boat? One that works?"

Finch called out to one of the uniformed men. A few moments later, he
was handing her a largish rectangle of black plastic. "All yours," he said.

Jerusha peered at the phone. She entered in the number she'd wanted to
call for days now. There was a crackle of static, a hiss, then a distant, clear
ring she could hear through the steady churning of the patrol boat's twin
engines.

"United Nations," someone said on the other end. "Committee for Extraordinary Interventions."

"This is Jerusha Carter," she said. "Gardener. I need to speak to either
Lohengrin or Babel. It's extremely urgent. No, I'm sorry, it *can't* take hours.
I don't *have* hours. . . ."

Bahr al-Ghazal Base
The Sudd, South Sudan
The Caliphate of Arabia

TOM STOOD BESIDE THE mess tent and watched as the sun fell into the endless sea of washed-out green reeds, turning them to dark thin shadows that made intricate patterns as they slow-danced to the music of a sluggish breeze. Somewhere to the north a battle murmured, rattled, occasionally boomed with a flash that lit the orange and indigo sky a startling yellow-white.

He squeezed his eyes shut against the swollen red sun. It felt as if the inside of his eyelids were lined with sandpaper. His arms and legs felt like cloth bags filled with powdered lead. His brain felt as if his skull were stuffed with cotton balls. He couldn't remember when he'd had his last decent night's sleep.

Do I even fucking dare *to sleep now?* he wondered. *That prick Meadows almost got me for good last time. He actually managed to steal control of my fucking body.*

All over Tom felt the sick rush of violation. It wasn't theft. It was soul-rape. *And* he'd stolen some of Tom's most potent powers.

Tom feared no one on Earth. But he lived in increasing terror of the hippie in his own head.

Despite feeling the fatigue thicker than the heat and heavier than the humid turgid swamp air; despite being so tired he felt as sick as if he'd been caught by some awful tropical disease himself, the very thought of sleep filled him with a terror that almost blanked his mind.

"*Fuck* it," he said. He turned about on one Converse knock-off tennis shoe and walked back into the dimness of the tent. It was time to load up on coffee.

I just won't sleep, he decided. *Until I'm strong enough not even Meadows can challenge me anymore.*

It was coming. He *felt* it.

Soon I'll be invincible.

Robert Cumming's Apartment
Chicago, Illinois

CHICAGO DID HAVE GOOD pizza. Cumming's apartment reeked of pepperoni, garlic, and tomato sauce. The tall joker sucked down Coke after Coke. Jaako and Mollie drank beer. Noel and Mathias sipped a heavy, rich Chianti.

The pictures that Noel had snapped with the tiny cuff-link camera were strewn across the coffee table. Red fingerprints dotted more than a few of them. "What do we think those might be?" Noel pointed at the grooves in the floor and ceiling.

"In a world where people can teleport and walk through walls you want a nasty surprise inside," Mathias said with a shrug. "I'm betting metal walls run back and forth across the vault. Cut you in half if they hit you."

"So, can you figure out the pattern?"

Cumming shook his head. "They wouldn't be that stupid. They'd let the computer randomize the movement of the walls. I think we just need to turn them off. Otherwise you guys going in are going to be hopping around like fleas moving from dog to dog. I'll control the cameras so everything in the room will look normal. But you'll need to work fast because my movement of the walls will start to look like a pattern. If the guards are sharp they'll spot it."

"And you can do all that?" Noel asked.

"Yeah, if the security computer at the bank gets set to port 950 I can control everything in those rooms that's controlled by a computer."

"And how do we do that?" Mathias asked.

Cumming shrugged. "Somebody's got to go into the security office and reset the computers."

"And who does that?" Mathias asked, his tone pugnacious.

"*Moi,*" said Jaako, and pointed to his chest.

"And won't the security guards notice when this guy comes crawling out of the computer screen?" Mollie asked.

"The guards are going to be occupied elsewhere," Noel said. "There might be one left behind, but I'm confident Jaako can handle him."

"So let me give you the information you need to make the switch," Cumming said. "I've poked around, and the bank's firewall is running Redhat. We still need the root password, but every office I've ever seen has it written down and Scotch-taped inside a drawer. So here's what you do. First go to / etc/sisconfig su to root. Once you're at root . . . vi space IP-tables and add this line . . . minus A space RH-firewall F-1-INPUT space. . . ." Cumming was writing while Jaako pulled his lower lip and frowned at the ever-expanding lines of gobbledygook.

Mathias pulled Noel's attention away when his blunt finger thrust down on one of the embedded nozzles high in the wall. "I want a respirator just in case those fire off. And we must expect that the floor is rigged to sense an increase in weight. That will not be controlled by a computer."

"How do we get around that?" Mollie asked rather shrilly.

"As you teleport, Mathias is going to have to make you weightless." Noel looked over at the little man. "Please don't cock up the timing." The Hungarian nodded and lit another cigarette. Noel hoped he sounded unperturbed and confident, but the level of complexity was daunting, even for him.

Well, at least he knew he could get out fast if the whole thing went pear-shaped. His biggest worry was making sure Weathers somehow made the connection between the missing gold and the Nshombos. He didn't have that one figured out just yet.

Jaako's rather nasal voice pulled him back to the conversation. "You're going to look a pretty bunch of fools floating around and bouncing off the safety deposit boxes."

"Hey!" Cumming said. "Pay attention. You got the 950 space minus J, ACCEPT, right?"

"You know I don't have any fucking idea what you're talking about," Jaako said.

"You don't have to. You just have to follow instructions and not have a typo. You have a cell phone. If you get confused you can call me."

"How are we going to maneuver in there?" Mollie asked.

"There's equipment for that," Noel said. "And Jaako, you understand that you're going to be part of this party in the vault, right? Mathias can make the gold weightless, but it will still have mass. It will take all four of you to control the pallets and guide them through the door that Mollie will open."

This time the use of the word "you" elicited a response. "What do you mean *you*, kemosabe?" Mollie asked. "Aren't you going to be with us?"

"You better fucking be with us," Jaako said.

"I'm going to be getting guards out of the bank. I have an . . . associate who will handle the teleport."

"Wait just a damn minute. This is the first time we've heard about another person," Mathias said. "I'm not sharing with another person."

"You won't need to." Noel took his time lighting up a cigarette. Cumming made a big point of waving his hand in front of his face and coughing. Both Noel and Mathias ignored him. "She's my girlfriend. She'll share in my share . . . so to speak."

"And we can trust her . . . why?" Jaako asked.

"Because I say you can."

"This isn't cool," Cumming said. "We should at least meet her. Make up our own minds."

"And do what? You can't pull off this heist without a teleport. She is a teleport. We either abort or you accept my judgment."

There was a long silence while the other four looked at each other. "Yeah, well, okay," Jaako finally said. "He's got a reputation for pulling off the impossible."

"And you know this, how?" Cumming asked.

"We've crossed paths in our other lives."

Mathias grunted, and ground out his cigarette in a piece of cold pizza. "Since none of us seem to be ready to quit—what happens then?"

"The gold goes to the warehouse you rented. Shares will be allocated, then Mollie will open another doorway into the yacht and you'll shove it through."

"Seems a shame to go through all of this and not keep it all," Jaako sighed.

"And that wasn't the deal and you knew it going in," Noel said, his voice low and a little dangerous.

"There are four of us and one of you. We could change the terms," Mathias said.

"And his girlfriend," Jaako added.

"Yes, but she's not here," Mathias said, and the deep wrinkles in his face made him look like an angry old turtle.

"Hey!" Cumming blurted out. "I'm doing this because the Nshombos are dictators. And this thing about the kids is . . . is . . . monstrous." He paused, his jaw worked, and he added lamely, "And I'm not a crook."

Noel looked over at Mollie. She was bright red and looked distressed. "Mollie?" he said softly.

She stepped closer to him. Noel gave Jaako and Mathias a teeth-baring smile. "Jaako. You know who I am and what I was. You might want to let Mathias know."

Cumming tugged at Jaako's sleeve. "Let's finish this. Once you've typed in all that you save the file and exit and then at the command line type service space IPtables space restart."

Restart. That's what I'd like. Restart my life once and for all so I never have to do this kind of thing again.

His cell phone vibrated. Noel stepped aside to answer while the nerdish whine continued as Cumming went over everything with Jaako one more time. It was Lohengrin.

He didn't mince words. "Gardener has escaped from the People's Paradise with a group of children. They're starving, some of them are sick. Many of them are jokers. We need to get them to a hospital. Preferably the Jokertown Clinic."

"And you're calling me because . . . ?"

"Because the UN cannot be formally involved, so I cannot send a plane. And you're much faster than a plane anyway. And because I hoped there might be a human being hiding in you somewhere."

Oddly enough it hurt, an actual physical grip in the gut. "All right. I'll see what I can do. E-mail me their location so I can bring up a satellite image."

A few moments later his iPhone chimed.

Katimba, Tanzania.

♣

Thursday,
December 24

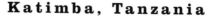

Katimba, Tanzania

LOHENGRIN HADN'T KNOWN HOW many children were with Gardener. It turned out to be a lot. Noel counted more than forty.

They lay in the shade provided by a large tree and the overhang of a corrugated tin hut. Gardener had her back against the tree. The girl looked terrible, wasted, gaunt.

A cold fist closed down on his gut. Noel had seen this before—in a hospital in Khartoum.

Five kids slept around her, their heads resting on her lap and thighs. Using a large leaf as a fan, Gardener kept the flies from their faces. Some of those faces weren't very human. As Lohengrin had reported most of the children were jokers.

Gardener's eyes widened as he appeared, and she reached a clawlike hand into her seed pouch.

She didn't know him in his Etienne form. He quickly shifted back to Noel. The children who were awake cried out in terror as his body reshaped itself. Their cries woke the others, and the air was filled with wails, sobs, and cries.

Gardener relaxed when she realized who he was. "Hush, hush," she soothed. "He's a friend. He's here to help us. In the blink of an eye he can have us in a city where there's food and beds. Hush, hush." Her voice had the quality of a song.

But Noel did the calculation, and didn't like the tally. Assuming he could carry four at a time it would take him twelve trips. Thirteen to bring Gardener.

He dropped down on his knees next to her. "What's your most pressing need?" he asked.

"Food. The kids are hungry. I had been growing food for them, but I've been too"—she made a gesture that indicated her emaciated body—"too weak to do much."

"Look, I can't carry . . ." Her eyes filled with tears, and Noel hurried to add, "It's all right. It's all right. I've got another way to get them out. A better way, but it's going to take me a bit of time to arrange things. I'll bring back food and some docs from the Jokertown Clinic to hold them until we can get transport here."

"The roads are terrible. There's no way—"

"Trust me." It gave him an odd jolt when he said the words. He rushed on. "The girl I'm thinking of will make roads unnecessary."

Kisangani, Congo
People's Paradise of Africa

"FUCK ME," JOEY SAID on the outskirts of the city. "This place is crazy."

Michelle agreed. The jungle was moving back into the city, reclaiming it. The roads had been blown up. Trees were growing up through some of the houses. A few had been completely taken over by vines. Chimpanzees jumped from rooftop to treetop and back again. The city was silent except for the calls of birds and chimps. Occasionally, in the distance, they heard the popping of gunfire.

Adesina was closer now, and it was hard for Michelle to stay focused on what she was doing. They kept working their way through the torn-up streets, trying to keep their bearings. There were several groups of buildings visible in the distance. The pilot had told them one of these would most likely be the place they were looking for.

They pushed on. At the end of one devastated street, they found themselves at a small hospital. It didn't look like the buildings Michelle had seen in her dreams, but she decided to go inside anyway. Joey's leg needed to be looked at. The need to get to Adesina was raging in her. But if Joey collapsed, Michelle might never reach Adesina. And if she did, there would be no Hoodoo Mama to help her fight for the child.

The hospital's walls were painted a pretty terra-cotta color. THE ALICIA NSHOMBO HOSPITAL FOR WOMEN was stenciled on the unbroken front doors in French. Through the glass Michelle could see an overgrown courtyard in the center of the building. "How did this stay intact?" she asked.

"I got no cocksucking idea," Joey said. Then she giggled. This was so odd Michelle stopped and looked at her. Joey gave her a sweet smile for an instant, before her angry Hoodoo Mama face popped back up.

Michelle pulled the door open and Joey followed her inside. The reception area was tiny, a couple of chairs and a desk. There wasn't anyone at the desk.

"Hello?" Michelle tried to make her French singsongy, the way Kengo's accent sounded, but it mostly sounded stupid to her. There was no answer, so they went into the hallway. Sunlight filtered through the windows. There were monkeys in the trees in the courtyard.

They walked down the quiet corridor, passing in and out of patches of sunlight cast across the floor. The walls here weren't painted an antiseptic green or white color. They were azure, cornflower yellow, and brick.

To the left was a large open ward. There were two rows of beds facing each other. Mosquito netting was draped over each bed. One of the patients saw them, and waved at them with her left hand. Her right hand was missing. Neither Joey nor Michelle waved back.

A nurse came over to them. "May I help?" she said in French. "Do you know one of our patients?"

"My friend needs a doctor to look at her leg," Michelle said.

"This isn't a clinic," the nurse said, switching to English. "It's a survivor hospital. The doctors have already done their rounds and have gone to another hospital for the afternoon. We don't have many of them."

"Well, can *you* look at her leg?" Michelle was getting pissed. Adesina was so close, and all they needed was to get Joey's damn leg looked at. How hard was that?

"Lie down on that bed and I'll be right back," the nurse said, pointing to the only empty bed in the ward.

Joey collapsed onto the bed. The woman in the next pushed herself up, then pulled her netting away. She was young, no more than a few years older than Michelle. There were scars on her face. It looked as if she'd been slashed by a knife.

"Hello," she said in heavily accented English. "You are a long way from home."

"Yes, we are," Michelle replied. *Where the hell was that damn nurse?* "My friend's leg is hurt."

"I see that. May I touch your hair?"

The request was so odd it snapped Michelle out of thinking about Adesina. "Uhm, well, I guess so." She walked over to the woman's bed and bent down. The woman stroked the top of Michelle's head, then ran her hand down Michelle's braid. "Oh, it's very soft. I've never seen hair like this before."

Jesus, Michelle thought, *I cannot believe I'm having hair chitchat right now.*

"I use to braid my daughter's hair." Tears welled in the woman's eyes. "Your braid has come loose. I could fix it for you." The nurse hadn't come back yet and even though the request was odd, it wouldn't take long.

"Sure."

The woman undid Michelle's braid, and then combed her fingers through Michelle's hair before she started plaiting it. "I'm Makemba," she said. "Will you be here long? Kinsangani is an odd place for you to be."

"I'm looking for a friend," Michelle said. It was close enough to the truth.

The nurse came back carrying a metal tray with disinfectant, gauze, bandages, a curved needle, a packet of suturing material, and a syringe. She told Joey to roll onto her stomach. Joey jerked when the nurse started cleaning the wound. "These look like claw marks," the nurse said. "How did you get these?"

"We got attacked by some leopards."

"It's dangerous in the jungle," the nurse said. "And these wounds will need stitches."

"It's fucking dangerous everywhere now," Joey said. "Ow! You fucker! That hurts!"

"Shut up and take it." Michelle expected Joey to glower at her, but Joey just closed her eyes.

"What happened to your daughter?" Michelle asked Makemba as the woman finished Michelle's braid.

"She died," Makemba said softly. "They came from Uganda and they killed the men in our village. Then they raped the women. All of the women were raped, even my daughter. She was six. They slashed some of our faces. Some of them raped us with their guns after they were finished raping us with their . . ." Makemba fell silent.

"Those fuckers did that?" Joey asked quietly as she opened her eyes. She began to shake.

"Oh, yes," the nurse said, "but the Nshombos put an end to it. They punished as many men as could be caught. Then they put out bounties on the heads of the ones who'd escaped." She paused. "All the women here have been raped."

"*All* of them?" Michelle felt sick. "Every one in this ward?"

"In the entire hospital. And this is just one of the hospitals for the survivors. It has been going on for years. They can't go home. They're outcasts now. But the Nshombos are taking care of them. It is Alicia Nshombo's great work. She is the Mother of the Country."

Michelle looked around the room. The women closest to them were all leaning forward in their beds. And they smiled at her. *God, how can they smile at all?*

Makemba pointed at the woman directly across from her. "She was raped by ten men. After they finished, they killed her sister and her mother. She had a baby from it and left it at an orphanage." She pointed at the woman in the bed to her right. "They made her watch as they raped her eleven-year-old daughter. Then six men held her down and raped her. Then they used their guns to rape her. She no longer has control of her bladder or her bowels. The doctors have done four surgeries on her."

Michelle held up her hands. "Please. No more."

Makemba grabbed Michelle's wrist. "You have to let your people know that the Nshombos are helping us. They are making our lives better. Without Alicia Nshombo we would all be dead or trying to live in the forest."

Michelle pulled her hand away. The Nshombos ran everything in the PPA with an iron glove. They had to know about the experiments on children. But how to reconcile that with this hospital? Maybe she was wrong. Maybe the Nshombos knew nothing about the children in the pit.

"Your leg will be fine," the nurse said. "I'm going to give you a shot of antibiotics." She reached into her pocket and gave Joey a small bottle. "Here are some more to take. One a day for seven days. Those stitches will dissolve on their own."

Joey shoved the pills into her pants pocket. "Thanks," she said gruffly.

"What do we owe you?" Michelle asked.

"Oh, nothing," the nurse said cheerfully. "There is free health care since Dr. Nshombo came to power. I hope when you go home you will tell everyone how the Nshombos have made a real paradise of our country."

The Red House
Outside Bunia, Congo
People's Paradise of Africa

"GATHER ROUND," TOM TOLD the child aces assembled in the dining hall of the big Red House, whose eye-watering smell of carbolic cleansers seemed barely to mask a scent of decay. Dr. Washikala hovered in the background, scrubbing gaunt brown hands against each other. The major commanding the security contingent stood listening keenly at military brace in his tan uniform, shades, and leopard-skin fez. He was middling tall and wiry, like all Leopard Men. The only fatso in the Leopard Society seemed to be its Mama Alicia.

The child aces turned apprehensive expressions toward Tom. "We got problems. Major problems," he told them, his voice rasping. "The imperialists who attacked Nyunzu have now destroyed a medical barge and smuggled the children they stole across the border into Tanzania. We've lost Leucrotta, the Hunger, and Ghost. They failed to stop the imperialists. It's up to us now, you dig?"

He stood a moment, surveying their small faces, unmarked human and joker alike. They shuffled nervously in their chairs or on the floor. Ayiyi scratched behind one ear with one of his mouth parts.

"Mummy and the Darkness are helping the Mother of the Nation now. Ayiyi, I'll hyperflight you to Kongoville to guard the President-for-Life. Wrecker, Moto—you stay here and help defend your brothers and sisters. The rest of you . . . do what you can. Any questions?"

No questions. In fact, they were pretty quiet for a bunch of kids. Tom figured, vaguely, he'd dazzled them with his revolutionary eloquence.

Blythe van Renssaeler
Memorial Clinic, Jokertown
Manhattan, New York

"WOW, NEW YORK CITY," Mollie said in tones of reverence. "It's really . . . noisy."

Noel was both amused and irritated by her simplicity. But that wasn't fair. How could he expect eloquence about steel canyons and symphonies of taxi horns from a girl whose life experience consisted of Coeur d'Alene, Idaho, and that strip mall surrounded by freeways that was Los Angeles?

"Maybe we can go to Macy's when we're finished? And I'd like to see Central Park, and Tiffany's, and the observation deck on the Empire State Building."

Noel knew all the movies that had produced the list: *Miracle on 34th Street, Barefoot in the Park*, and *Aces High*, with its romantic version of Peregrine and Fortunato's "affair." "First let's bring those children back to civilization," he said.

He had taken Mollie to Katimba so she had a sense of the place. A joker nurse had gripped him by the collar with her twig fingers, and said a single word—"Hurry." Now he and Mollie stood in an alley next to the Jokertown Clinic. Finn and an army of nurses and orderlies were mustered at the sliding-glass doors. He had alerted the centaur doctor to Gardener's condition and given him a brief description of the steps that had been taken in the Khartoum hospital, to no avail.

He hated that so many people were going to witness Mollie's power, but comforted himself with the knowledge that Americans never paid attention to news outside of the United States. And he had to do this. He had expended so much effort—emotional, financial, and physical—on having a child with Niobe, and now he found he reacted to every crying child. But not with the irritation that had been the reaction of an earlier self, but with a fierce need to *react, protect, comfort*.

He nodded to Mollie, and one of her doorways appeared in the grimy bricks of the neighboring building. A gust of hot, moist air blew through, and immediately became a cloud of fog when it met New York's December chill. The doctors and nurses came through carrying children.

Noel dodged them in the doorway, and went to Gardener's side. He picked her up. It was like holding a bundle of twigs. "You're a miracle worker," she whispered weakly. "Thank you."

"I'm a practical man with a lot of contacts. And you're welcome." And Noel carried her back through to New York, and delivered her into Finn's care.

Kisangani, Congo
People's Paradise of Africa

"**I WANT TO KILL** those fuckers," Joey said. "The ones that did that to those women." She was limping, but she seemed to be doing a little better.

"It sounds like the Nshombos have already punished most of them," Michelle replied.

Joey glared at her. "You don't understand."

Michelle stopped. "Yeah, I do understand. You were raped, too. And every one of those women hurts just like you. Only worse. You can't undo what happened to them, and you can't undo what happened to you. I'm sorry. But right now, we can save one little girl."

"It ain't enough." Joey's voice was almost a wail and there was fury in her eyes.

"No," Michelle replied with her mouth set in a grim line. "It never is."

♠

Friday, December 25
CHRISTMAS DAY

The Pampas
Western Uruguay

"YOU NEED TO LET well enough alone now, Mr. L.," Mrs. Clark said sternly. "It's not right to be moving the girl every few days hither and yon across the globe. By whatever unholy means you're using to move us."

The wind boomed and hissed and made the long green grass lie down by ranks and then pop up again as it shifted. It was a warm, fair spring day here in the Pampas, in western Uruguay. A crappy little country nobody up in *el Norte* knew about . . .

"I trust we'll be able to leave the girl be for a spell, to find herself a place in this land, forsaken by the good Lord as it is," Mrs. Clark said pointedly.

Tom shook his head. He realized his thoughts had wandered down a side path—and into a standing microsleep her voice had jarred him out of. It was the only kind of sleep he allowed himself these days. And mostly because he didn't have a choice: it just snuck up on him.

"*Mr. L.* Are you *quite* certain you're listening to me?"

"Huh? Yeah. Sure. I—I just nodded off for a moment there. Been working late . . . in the office."

She sniffed a sniff that plainly said, *If you don't want to tell me the truth, I'm sure it's your business.*

"Very well," she said, taking in his red, sunken eyes and three-day stubble. "You can go in and see the girl."

Nodding obediently, Tom stooped to pick up the big package he'd set before the doorstep. Its weight posed him no problem; it was big enough to be tricky to hold on to, though. It was wrapped in paper where fucking teddy bears cavorted with candy canes, and tied up with gold ribbon and a vast gold bow.

The girl of course was not much more than a decade the redheaded old dragon's junior. But Sprout was, and would always be, a girl. *The* girl, to Mark.

"Tom!" he said aloud, snapping his head upright and clocking the top of it painfully on the doorjamb into the sheepherder's hut he'd had refurbished as another bolt-hole months before. "I'm Tom, God damn it. Not fucking Mark."

Behind him Mrs. Clark sniffed loudest of all. No need to wonder what *that* one meant.

"Sprout?" he called tentatively. "Sprout, honey?"

"I'm in here," she called.

The place was dimly lit by electric lights powered off a generator fueled from huge buried liquid propane tanks—some of Tom's makeover. All his efforts couldn't stop it smelling of lanolin and ancient cigarette smoke. Some elderly wool rugs, their once-bold patterns faded by age and various accretions, didn't help much with either smell.

He knelt and set down the gift-wrapped box. Straightening and turning, he hit his head on the frame of the door at the end of the low hallway. "Fuck, fuck, fuck!"

"*Mr. L.!*" came Mrs. Clark's reproving bark.

"Sorry. Fuck." He ducked low and stepped in.

Sprout lay on her belly on a futon with a red and black flannel spread, her stockinged feet in the air. His heart turned over. The half-assed light of a bare forty-watt bulb hanging from the ceiling made her look for an instant as if she really was the age she acted. She was just turning, plucking an iPod earbud from beneath a sweep of grey-threaded blond hair.

"Daddy!" she said. Her face lit with a smile. She jumped off the bed, leaving a big hardcover book open to show color paintings of dinosaurs. She caught Tom in a fierce hug and buried her face against his chest. "You're coming home."

He blinked. He wasn't thinking too clearly. But he'd be okay. He always was. "Uh—yeah. Yeah, sweetie. I'll be coming home to stay. Like, soon. Once I take care of some . . . uh, business."

A great sense of peace flowed through him. It was as if the warmth of her body suffused his soul. He sagged. His eyes sagged with foolish tears. *Knock off the bourgeois sentimentality*, he ordered himself sternly.

But it was just—just such a relief. To feel safe. Accepted. *Loved.*

I don't want to leave, he thought.

His daughter pulled away. She looked into his blue eyes with clearer ones the same hue. Tears ran down her smooth cheeks. She smiled. It seemed a touch sad, somehow. "You're going away," she said.

He shrugged. "Well, sweetie, a man's gotta do what he's gotta do. It's my duty. Like, destiny."

She reached up and took his face in both hands. He blinked in surprise. She'd never done that before. Sprout pulled his face toward hers. Uncomprehending, he yielded.

She kissed his forehead.

"Good-bye," she said, speaking more carefully than usual. "You tried your very bestest to make everything all right for me. Thank you."

She let him go. He smiled at her. "Sure, Sprout. Anything for you, honey."

He turned back to the low dim hallway. "Here," he said, turning back with the huge box cradled dubiously in his arms. "Merry Christmas."

She squealed with delight. "Oh, what is it? What, what, what?"

"Open it and find out."

As she dropped to her knees and began to tug at the bow he crooked a grin and nodded at the open book on her bed. "I hope you like dinosaurs."

Blythe van Renssaeler
Memorial Clinic, Jokertown
Manhattan, New York

THE THIRD SEASON OF *American Hero* was playing on the static-ridden television mounted in the corner of her room.

Jerusha watched it mostly because it was easier than turning her head. Peregrine was interviewing someone called Adamantine, whose disturbingly smooth body looked like it was computer-generated rather than real. Their words sounded like so much mush in Jerusha's ear. "I'm very proud to have been chosen for this show," Adamantine droned in a voice pitched heroically low. "I'm ready to prove myself here, and to prove to America that I deserve to be the next American Hero, like the great heroes who have been here before me."

Do you know how stupid you all sound? she wanted to rail at Peregrine, at Adamantine. It was all so petty, so unimportant. That was the one lesson she'd taken away from her own stint on the program: none of it mattered at all.

Dr. Finn cantered into the room, his hooves bagged in sterile slippers, muffling the clatter against the linoleum floors. The centaur snagged the chart from the wall holder, glancing over it. His blond head—the hair touched with grey at the temples—shook as he made a note and placed it back. He placed his pen back in the pocket of the lab coat he wore.

"Take two aspirin and call you in the morning?" Jerusha said.

He favored her with a wry smile. "I wish it were that simple."

"Pretty much anything would be simpler than this." Jerusha lifted an arm, stabbed with a double set of IVs. She was surrounded by a metal forest of poles with plastic fluid bags hanging from them. A tray piled with plastic-domed plates sat on one side of the bed, from which wafted the smell of cafeteria food.

Finn's tail flicked, almost angrily. "Your body's locked in overdrive, Jerusha. You're burning up calories at an impossible rate. But your digestive system isn't absorbing nutrients very well at all. That's why you're constantly famished. Your body's devouring itself because that's all it has to feed on."

"So tell me that you can fix it." She saw the answer before he spoke, and fear stabbed her. "You can't, can you?"

"Not yet. We're still running tests, and we have a few ideas to try. We'll figure this out."

"You do a good job of sounding confident, Doc. And if you *don't* figure it out?"

"We will," he said firmly. "Now, get some rest, and let me get back to my lab work. I'd hate for you to think that we've been taking all that blood for nothing." He checked her IV levels, patted her shoulder, and left the room. She smiled at him, because she thought it was what he would want to see. The brave patient, suffering in silence.

When the door closed, she let the smile collapse. *Dying. You're dying.* She could feel it, a certainty in the pit of her stomach. She was going to leave this all. Soon.

She wanted to cry, but she wouldn't let herself. She shouldn't feel pity for herself, not when so many others were suffering and had suffered worse. She thought of New Orleans, of Bubbles, Ink, and Hoodoo Mama. She thought of her parents—on their way here from Yosemite, Dr. Finn had told her.

She would miss them all.

She thought of Wally, wandering somewhere in the People's Paradise, intent on his quest. *He* was still alive. She was certain of that. He had promised her . . . and she had made the same promise for him, a promise she was going to break. *You stay alive for me, Wally. And I'll stay alive for you . . .*

She would miss him most of all.

Jerusha clenched her hands in the bedsheets. Her arms were brown, dry sticks on the white bedsheet. She let the sobs come then. She could not hold them back.

Ellen Allworth's Apartment
Manhattan, New York

BUGSY SAT IN CAMEO'S bed. Ellen was in the living room, humming to herself. The last couple of days, she'd been in a pretty good mood, or if she hadn't, she'd faked it well enough that he couldn't tell the difference. She'd even put the earring in, giving Bugsy and Simoon the night and most of the morning together.

He didn't know why she'd done that. He'd been on the edge of calling the whole thing off and going back to his own much-neglected place, but she'd become Simoon. She'd pulled him back. And that was what he didn't understand.

He thought about Popinjay's description of the Radical. The one face of a multiple personality who knew what all the others were up to. Was that Cameo, too? Was it really Simoon he was kissing, or was that echo of her just another facet of Cameo? Was Nick really Nick, or the embodied memory? Were there four of them sharing this apartment, or really only two?

The fact was Ellen's wild card didn't bring people back from the dead. The objects she used to channel people only held the memories from the last time the thing and the person had been together. Simoon—the real Simoon—had experienced that last fight, had known she was dying at the hands of the Righteous Djinn. The one he'd been sleeping with had never had that experience.

So what did that tell you?

The phone rang, and Ellen picked it up. Bugsy rolled over onto the pillow. He had to do it. He had to call this whole thing off, go start hanging out at the bars around entomology conferences. Get a normal girlfriend. Just before he did it, he had to finish talking himself into the belief that breaking up wouldn't mean killing Aliyah all over again. He had to believe that she'd never really been there, and he hadn't managed that yet.

"Hi, Babs. What's up? What? Jerusha's in town!" Ellen said from the other room. "No, I didn't know. How is she?"

A silence. When Ellen's voice came again, it was as harsh as sandpaper. "What do you mean *dying?*"

Somewhere North of Kindu, Congo
People's Paradise of Africa

IT WAS THE STRANGEST thing.

Wally slowed again when he passed the village of Kindu, a few days after destroying the floating laboratory. He wanted folks to get a good look at him. He expected much the same reaction he'd received in Kongolo, where the sight and sound of a PPA boat had caused most folks to flee.

But they didn't.

It began with just a handful of folks out on the docks. They pointed at Wally, jumped up and down, shouted to one another. More people came outside, and more still, until they lined the docks and shoreline. He couldn't tell what they were saying.

But it sounded, for all the world, like cheering.

Huh. Wonder what that's all about. Holiday, maybe.

Past Kindu, he sped downriver as fast as possible, leading what he hoped would become a concerted effort to chase and catch him. Anything to give Jerusha an edge.

He also felt a great urgency to get to the Bunia lab while he could still fight. Before all of his skin rusted and rotted apart. Because that was getting worse every day.

By the time he passed Kindu, Wally had burned through both of the fuel canisters he'd salvaged from the barge. He turned for the riverbank around sunset, the engine coughing and sputtering. He coasted the last few feet, saving a few splashes of gasoline for the morning, when he'd set the boat on fire. With luck, the smoke would draw more pursuers. It had worked before.

At some point he had to leave the river anyway. According to the GPS, he'd traveled a few hundred miles since splitting off from Jerusha. Eventually the Lualaba would turn west and become the Congo River; following it all the way to a tributary that flowed down from around Bunia would take him hundreds of miles out of his way. And *that* was ignoring the little problem of Boyoma Falls: six miles of waterfalls at the transition from Lualaba to Congo.

Striking out overland was the only choice.

The evening's first stars glimmered overhead in a clear sky with no threat of overnight rain. Which was a nice break, since his tent was ruined. He whistled. A guy sure could see the stars here, out in the middle of nowhere. Better than he'd ever seen them anywhere else, even better than from the middle of the Persian Gulf.

He wondered if Lucien had known many constellations. It would have been fun to ask him about that.

Ghost hovered nearby while Wally succeeded, with much difficulty, to clean the leopard scratches on his back. He treated them with disinfectant lotion, and even managed to place clean new bandages on them. It would have been a lot easier with Jerusha's help. It would have felt better, too. The lotion felt hot and itchy when Wally did it, but Jerusha had a soothing touch.

She'd kissed him.

"Good night," he said to Ghost. She didn't respond. But she didn't run away, either.

Sleep came easily that night. But his dreams pelted him with nonsensical images all night long. Images of Lucien, and baobab trees, and Ghost, and crocodiles, and Jerusha.

Kisangani, Congo
People's Paradise of Africa

NIGHT HAD FALLEN. JOEY and Michelle were walking through a part of Kisangani that the jungle had taken over. Occasionally, a chunk of road appeared under their feet and they could still make out the shapes of houses even though some were falling down or covered in foliage.

Michelle was beginning to think the nurse had given them bad directions when she saw a collection of red roofs on the next hill. They were the same roofs as the ones in her dreams about Adesina.

Joey fell against Michelle. Michelle grabbed her arm and steadied her. Joey's flesh was still hot. "Hold on." Michelle touched Joey's forehead and it was burning. *She's in no shape to go into a fight.* "I'm going to take you back to the hospital."

"Fuck you are!" Joey yanked her arm out of Michelle's grasp. "We have to help the kids. They're just little fuckers and they're close. So close. I can help. Look." A zombie staggered out of a crumbling house. Hoodoo Mama's zombies were never what might be called graceful, but this one looked drunk. It tried to hit Michelle, but it missed her and Michelle didn't even move.

"We need to go back to the hospital."

"No! No!" Joey grabbed Michelle's hand. "The kids really aren't very far away. I'll stay here. You go on. Find that little fucker you're looking for."

"I don't want to leave you . . ."

"Bubbles," Joey said. Her voice was softer. "You'll come back for me. I can sleep here. I just need to sleep awhile." She limped to one of the overgrown houses, pulled aside the vines covering the door, and went inside. Michelle followed.

Inside was a table, some wooden chairs, and a small bed. Joey pulled the tattered cover off the bed. The mattress was moldy, so she slid that off as well. There was a sheet of plywood underneath. Joey lay down on it.

"Look, just go find that little girl. I'll come after I sleep. I'll meet you in the morning. I can follow the trail of dead." She closed her eyes.

Michelle was torn. She desperately needed to get to Adesina, but she didn't want to leave Joey.

But the compound was so close.

Adesina was so close.

Blythe van Renssaeler
Memorial Clinic, Jokertown
Manhattan, New York

JERUSHA CARTER LOOKED LIKE hell.

The woman he'd known had been vibrant, alive, rich and funny and vital. The woman in the hospital bed before them now could have been in the final stages of AIDS or cancer or starvation. Her muscles were atrophied, the protein all cannibalized for the energy stored there. Her eyes had sunken back into her skull, the pads of fat thinned and gone away. Her smile was painful to watch.

Ellen sat on the edge of the bed, holding Jerusha's withered hand. Lohengrin was at the foot of the bed in a wheelchair, his own hospital gown looking cold and insufficient. Half his head was wrapped in gauze, his one remaining eye staring out like something equal parts ice and rage.

Slowly, her voice catching on itself, Jerusha made things worse. The Nshombos, Rustbelt and his missing sponsored kid, the Radical and the child aces. Bugsy listened to the whole ugly story, and found himself shocked but not surprised. The crazed bastards in the PPA had remembered what they'd all let themselves forget: the wild card was first and foremost a weapon.

When Lohengrin spun his chair and pushed himself out into the hallway, Bugsy followed. "I am calling the Committee," Klaus said. "I am calling Jayewardene. This is an *abomination*."

"Yeah," Bugsy said.

"We will arrange an action," Lohengrin said, pushing his wheels harder at every second syllable. "A strike force."

"Lohengrin, hey, hold up. *Lohengrin!*"

The German spun, blocking a nurse, and held up a finger as if scolding Bugsy. "If this is not what the Committee is for, then it is for nothing. If we are not to prevent things such as this, we have no reason to be. I no longer care what the Chinese ambassador or the Indian consulate say! If any stand against us, then they are in the wrong!"

"Yeah, but that aside," Bugsy said, "we're in a hospital. *You're* in a wheelchair."

Lohengrin frowned. The nurse went around them, making impatient noises under his breath.

"I'm just saying, we went up against the Radical without an army of wereleopards and the Kindergarten Kill Klub to back him up, and he handed us our collective ass," Bugsy said. "You get Jayewardene to sign off on it, we can all go off to Africa, and that's great. But what the hell are we going to do once we get there?"

◆

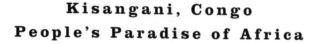

Saturday,
December 26

Kisangani, Congo
People's Paradise of Africa

IT WAS STRANGE TO see the pretty little buildings with their red roofs and the neat pathways. It all looked so friendly and innocent, except for the heavily armed soldiers patrolling through the compound. A few of them wore the leopard-skin fezzes she'd seen in her dreams.

When the wind shifted, the stench of the pit floated to her. Michelle walked into the compound. It took a moment before she was noticed, but when they saw her all hell broke loose. The soldiers began to shout, and pointing their guns. Michelle hoped they would shoot her.

One of the soldiers began barking questions at her. At least she assumed they were questions. He was speaking in some local dialect. She smiled at him and held her palm up. A bubble appeared and he stopped talking. Then she let the bubble fly. It hit him full in the chest. He flew backward, gun tumbling in the air with him.

It got the reaction she'd hoped for. The other soldiers started firing on her and she started to expand as she absorbed the kinetic energy of their bullets.

By the time the soldiers had emptied their clips to no effect, the Leopard Men had transformed into cats. They sprang at her, and Michelle fell backward, buried under a pile of leopards. They ripped at her flesh with their teeth and claws, and she laughed. Each bite, each slash left her bigger and more powerful than before.

Just when she was about to blast them off, she heard a sharp command. *"Stop it! Stop it right now!"*

The leopards jumped away from her and slunk over to where a short, fat woman was standing. She was dressed in a bright, geometric print dress with an equally bright kerchief in her hair. Michelle hauled herself up, palms up, ready to bubble.

"I know who you are," the woman said. "You are the girl who saved that city in America."

"And who are you?"

The fat woman chuckled good-naturedly. "I am the sun, the moon, and the stars here. I am the Mother of the Nation. I am Alicia Nshombo. And I have your friend." She gestured, and a soldier came forward, carrying Joey in his arms. She was unconscious and limp.

"We've been tracking you two since you got off the river," Alicia Nshombo said cheerfully. Her English had a lilting accent. "We lost you after you went with that pilot, but then you went to one of my hospitals. Wasn't that wonderful? The nurses there love me."

"What do you want?" Michelle asked.

Alicia snapped her fingers, and two guards appeared with a chair. "I don't know. Why are you here?"

"Sightseeing," Michelle said. She was furious at herself for leaving Joey behind. It was an amateur move.

"In Kisangani?"

"We got a little lost."

Alicia laughed. "My dear, you *are* amusing. And quite pretty. Has anyone ever told you you're very pretty?"

Michelle just stared. She wanted to say, *Seriously? I've been a model my whole goddamn life. Yeah, you could say I've been told that.* Instead she said, dryly, "Thank you, what a nice thing to say." And she tried not to notice the way Alicia was eyeing her.

"I like you," Alicia said. "Perhaps you and I can come to an arrangement. We have doctors here. They can help your little friend." She snapped her fingers again, and the guards carried Joey off to one of the pretty little buildings. "If you give me any trouble, I will have her killed. We don't want that, do we? You'll come and have dinner with me. We will talk." She got up from her chair and started walking away. The leopards followed her.

So did Michelle.

Southwest of Bunia, Congo
People's Paradise of Africa

"GEEZ," SAID WALLY. "WHAT kind of kid doesn't like peanut butter?"

Rain drizzled through the canopy of old-growth trees, pattering softly on Wally's poncho. Off in the distance, far to the east, across a wide valley, the rain merged with the grey mist shrouding the craggy foothills of the Ruwenzori Mountains. The sickly sweet odor of mud and decaying vegetation, combined with the pall of charcoal smoke from upwind villages, threatened to put Wally off his lunch. Not that he smelled much better; he knew that when he finally removed his poncho, it would carry the musk scent of sweaty iron.

He held a jar of peanut butter in one hand, a banana in the other, both extended toward Ghost. He sat just inside the tree line at the edge of a grassy plain, getting a little shelter from the downpour. The trees also hid him from the helicopters; he'd been hearing those more and more frequently the past few days. The girl floated silently at the center of the meadow, where the rain fell hardest.

But the raindrops never fell on her; never touched her. Just as her feet never *quite* touched the ground.

She'd been drawing closer. He caught glimpses of her all day long now. No longer did she only come out at night, when he went to sleep. She floated after him through the forest without making a sound.

Wally said, "I bet you've never had peanut butter before. It's real good, I promise. I practically grew up on this stuff."

If Ghost understood his offer, she showed no sign of it. All she did was stare at him: motionless, unblinking, broken knife in hand. Unaffected by the drizzle that passed through her insubstantial body.

"Suit yourself," he sighed. "But you don't know what you're missing." He tossed the food in his pack, zipped it, pulled the straps over his shoulders, and limped off across the misty meadow. Ghost followed, always trailing at a discreet distance.

Even when he'd run to catch the tail end of a passing train. She kept up with the train, floating through the jungle just off the tracks. They'd covered a lot of ground that way.

Talking seemed to help. He acted like she was a normal little girl, like she wasn't a child soldier sent to kill him. He talked about Jerusha, his home in Minnesota, Jerusha, his family, his friends, Jerusha, places he'd visited, Jerusha . . . He didn't mention Lucien, or what had happened to him.

It was a one-sided conversation, of course. For all he knew, she couldn't understand a word of it. But that wasn't the point. He was friendly. Unthreatening. An adult that wouldn't hurt her.

But the more he talked, the more she hesitated before backing away. And sometimes, if he pretended not to watch, he could see from the corners of his eyes how she'd cock her head, turning an ear toward him as he spoke.

Ghost was listening.

A guy didn't have to be John Fortune to figure out that she was a product of the Nshombos' secret laboratories. She was one in a hundred, one of the lucky few who drew an ace rather than a joker or the black queen. If lucky was the right word. Because the way Wally figured it, once her card turned, that's when the worst part started. He wondered how much time had been spent brainwashing her, desensitizing her to violence, teaching her to kill, forcing her to practice. Just as they would have done to Lucien, back in Nyunzu.

Wally didn't know a ton about kids, but he refused to believe the damage was permanent. He refused to believe that such a little girl could be forever broken, like Humpty Dumpty.

So he talked to Ghost. He figured that was as good a start as anything.

He kept to the meadow; good cover was getting hard to find in this part of the PPA, which was largely open grassland. But the mist and rain meant a helicopter would have to get pretty low to see him. Low enough that he'd hear it long before it saw him. And walking across open ground was something of a relief, after days and days thrashing through the jungle. His leg still hurt, where a bullet had grazed through the rust and where Ghost had tried to pry out a rivet; it wasn't healing. The bandages came away stained with greyish yellow seepage when he cleaned the wound every evening.

As long as he got to Bunia while he could still do some damage. He had to find somebody to care for Ghost, too.

Kongoville, Congo
People's Paradise of Africa

NOEL DROVE THE RATTLING old tow truck through the darkened streets while Mollie sat nervously beside him. They both wore black balaclavas to cover their faces. He was in his Lilith form, and dressed in Lilith's trademark black—slacks, boots, silk shirt, and a light jacket to cover his shoulder rig. It was hotter than hell but he wanted to be well armed, and didn't necessarily want his compatriots to know just how well armed. One boot had a small built-in holster for a tiny ankle gun. The other had two sheaths for knives. He had another gun in a holster clipped onto the waistband of her pants.

He took the final turn without braking. The bank was directly ahead of them. The goal was the ATM that had been retrofitted onto the white marble exterior. It had all the beauty of a wart on a beauty queen.

Noel swung the truck around and backed in close to the ATM. Mollie jumped out, and using her power thrust a chain and a hook through the marble and hooked them around the ATM.

She jumped back into the cab, and he gunned the engine. The ATM tore out of the wall with a sound like a bridge collapsing. They drove down the street with the ATM box bouncing along behind them like a hog-tied calf. It threw up sparks each time it hit the pavement.

A glance in the rearview mirror showed security guards boiling through the front doors of the bank. Noel laughed and was briefly disconcerted by Lilith's icy, lilting tones. He was once again losing track of who he was at any given moment.

"What now?" Mollie asked through lips narrowed by tension.

"We pull out the last guard."

"How—" Mollie broke off when Noel suddenly stopped the truck. "What?"

"Out," Noel ordered.

As he jumped out Noel reached beneath the seat and extracted the final element of his plan—a big bag of money. Once in the street he threw it hard. It hit the pavement and burst open, sending dollar bills flying in every direction.

The guards who were pelting down the street like hounds after a fox checked at the sight of the money.

The other cars on the street jerked to a stop. People jumped out and began grabbing up money. More people emerged from the apartments over the shops. The guards joined in the melee, trying to grab money, keeping people from grabbing money. A final guard came barreling through the front doors of the bank.

Noel grabbed Mollie around the waist and teleported them both into Mathias's hotel room in the Hilton. He then pulled out his phone and called Jaako, waiting in Cumming's apartment. "Go," he ordered.

He snatched up a small mountaineering rifle. It had been retrofitted with powerful magnets rather than spikes. It would carry the climbing rope to the walls, and they would use the rope to maneuver in the vault. He handed the rifle to Mollie. "Don't drop it."

Mathias stubbed out his ever-present cigarette and came into the circle of Noel's arms. He drew in a sharp breath when he was pressed against Lilith's bosom, but Noel suspected he was reacting to the feel of the gun more than the flesh.

Noel took them *between*.

It was disconcerting as hell, and Noel felt his stomach trying to climb past the back of his tongue as they appeared in the center of the vault, spinning in the air about seven feet above the floor. He swallowed hard.

Mollie squeaked, and dropped the rifle.

"*Scheisse!*" Mathias yelled.

Noel managed to get his toe under the rifle and kick it toward the ceiling. Mathias pointed at it, and it began to float. Mollie made another funny noise. Noel followed her gaze to a wall-mounted camera. The lens seemed to be vomiting flesh. Noel had a visceral memory of watching his grandmother grinding pork for sausage. "Be ready," Noel said to Mathias.

The flesh stream began to expand and take on human features. Only Jaako's lower legs remained in the camera lens. The Finnish ace had magnets strapped to his hands. He twisted sideways and slapped a hand against the steel of the safety deposit boxes. It was like watching taffy being pulled as he flexed and squirmed and pulled his legs out of the camera. The magnets gave him some purchase for the final tugs, and then Mathias took over making Jaako weightless.

"Okay. Good," Noel said. He fired the grappling line toward the doorway to the gold room. The first magnet hit on its side and didn't catch. Noel reeled it in before it hit the floor. He tried again. This time the magnet held.

Everyone held hands, and Noel hauled them along the rope to the doorway. The pallets bulked like the backs of prehistoric beasts in the room. Mollie stared wide-eyed at the gold ingots. "Wow," she breathed.

"Good-bye, North Dakota, eh?" Noel said with a smile. "Mollie, do your thing."

She stared hard at the back wall of the inner vault. A wide doorway appeared. It was dark beyond the threshold.

"I thought you set up work lights?" Noel said to Mathias.

"I did—"

Jaako said, "Oh, crap." There was a metallic shrieking and one of the interior walls slid from its pocket cavity. It was heading straight at them as they hung helpless in midair.

Several things happened at once. The pallets of gold lifted a few feet off the floor, and Noel hit the floor of the vault with a jar. The others rained down around him. They all went frantically scrambling out of the way of the oncoming wall of metal. At the same moment alarms began to whoop, an earsplitting sound inside the metal vault.

Then they were in the room with the gold. They formed a line. Jaako, who was the youngest and the strongest, started the first pallet floating toward the yawning opening. It was like a bizarre bucket brigade as each member of the team gave each pallet an adjustment and a shove, sending them through the fourth-dimensional opening.

They sent sixteen pallets through before Noel's phone rang. "Get out! Get out! They're opening the time lock on the vault!" came Cumming's voice.

"That's it, we're done," Noel yelled.

"But there are still seven pallets," Mollie yelled from her position at the edge of the door.

"Tough. We're done." Noel made a swooping gesture like a woman herding geese, and they all tumbled through the doorway. It irised closed behind them.

And Noel realized he was cold. His breath steamed. They were not in the Congo any longer.

Kisangani, Congo
People's Paradise of Africa

"DO YOU LIKE THE food?" asked Alicia Nshombo.

"It's fine." Actually, it was pretty disgusting. Michelle wasn't even certain what she was eating.

A table had been placed in the center of the compound, and Alicia and Michelle were seated side by side. A big fire had been built in the middle of the open area. The guards kept adding wood to it, though it was already hot as hell.

"Oooo, entertainment," Alicia said, clapping her hands like a child. Several of the guards came into the clearing leading a group of men, naked but for small loincloths. Their bodies had been painted with leopard spots.

Across the fire, Michelle saw other men carrying large drums. They sat down and started playing. Then leopards came into the clearing. There were at least twenty. They batted and clawed at each other, roaring and hissing.

"Isn't this fun?" Alicia said, smiling.

"Well, it's something," Michelle replied. *One bubble is all it would take.*

"I have been doing some thinking," Alicia said. "In New Orleans, you absorbed a nuclear explosion."

"You know how rumors are." Michelle poked at a mysterious piece of meat on her plate. The leopards rolled in the dirt. The men in loincloths began swaying to the beat of the drums.

"Hmmmmm, and our Tom was the cause of that, wasn't he, Miss Pond?"

Michelle dropped her fork. "What do you want?"

Alicia pouted. "You aren't being any fun. Did you enjoy your visit to my hospital? The one for the survivors. I am very proud of those. The animals who prey on our women deserve to be punished. It's women who do all the real work." She started gesturing with her knife. "Men are very stupid about sex. They use it as a weapon. They use it as punishment."

"And what about the children?" Michelle asked. "Are they being punished, too?"

"Oh, there must be sacrifices when you're building a nation." Alicia put her knife down and wiped her mouth with her napkin. "May I call you Michelle? Michelle, you are a very powerful woman. Oh, yes, I know these things. Even here we see the CNN. Our Tom is very powerful too, but it may be you are his equal. He tried to kill many people in New Orleans, and yet you saved the city." She popped a morsel of food into her mouth. "Tom Weathers is unpredictable and dangerous. He has been a great help to my brother, but now he is turning the world against us. My proposal is simple. Kill Tom Weathers, and I will not kill your pretty little friend."

"Maybe I don't care if she gets killed," Michelle said. "Maybe I have reasons for being here that have nothing to do with her."

Alicia rose from the table. "Don't be silly, my dear. If you did not care about her you would have killed me already."

She walked close to the fire. Nine of the leopards stopped biting each other and began mewling and purring. They wove themselves around her, and she reached up and undid her kerchief. Her hips swayed to the drums as she undid her dress and let it drop to the ground. Her breasts were pendulous and hung down to her waist. One of the leopards came close. Alicia let it nuzzle and lick her nipples until they hardened, then she pushed it away.

The men in loincloths moaned. They crawled toward Alicia. She proceeded to lick and bite them across their chests and backs until they bled. Each time a man was bitten, he started shaking and convulsing.

The drums beat in time. The leopards started mounting each other. Alicia snapped her fingers, and the men she'd just bitten rolled on their backs and ripped their loincloths away. They were tumescent. One by one, Alicia straddled them. She fucked each one until he came. When she was done, she sauntered back to where Michelle sat. Her thighs glistened.

Behind her, naked men and women crawled into the firelight. The drums beat louder, and the cats ripped and clawed anyone in reach. Bodies slid against each other, hands groping breasts and buttocks. Mouths licked and sucked.

"Do you like our entertainment?" Alicia asked. "It will go on all night. You should stay and watch. You can give me your answer about Tom Weathers in the morning."

Steunenberg Barn
Coeur d'Alene, Idaho

NOEL FELT HIS BODY morphing back to his normal form. Wherever he was it was daylight outside. He smelled animals and manure. Instinct replaced conscious thought. He threw himself sideways, hit the floor (it was dirt and straw), rolled to his feet, and drew the gun from his shoulder rig and the gun from behind his back. There was the roar of a shotgun blast but it was muffled because his ears were still ringing from the alarms.

The muzzle flash showed him Jaako being blown backward, erupting blood as the pellets took him full in the chest. Noel quickly narrowed his eyes and sought for the shadowy form behind the shotgun. *There.* He doubletapped. The figure folded over, gave a grunt, and fell to the ground.

Mathias went scrambling into a stall. The cow and calf inside began lowing in alarm. The wooden side boomed as the cow kicked at the intruder.

"Shit! Somebody's got a gun!" someone else yelled.

Noel whirled and fired two shots at him. From the grunt Noel knew at least one bullet had found a target.

Off to his right Mollie screamed and cried out, "Daddy!"

Noel sprinted toward her. Someone reached out and grabbed the back of his jacket, bringing him up short.

"Got her . . . uh him!" one of the brothers caroled in triumph. His captor was behind him. It was a bad angle for a gun. Noel went limp. The sudden loss of resistance took the young man off guard, and he nearly dropped Noel. It allowed him to bend over enough to reach the sheath in his boot. He dropped the Browning Hi Power, pulled the knife from the sheath, flipped it until the blade was pointing straight back, and drove it deep into the boy's belly.

The boy added his screams to Mollie's; there were curses coming from the father. . . .

Guess I didn't kill him. Pity. Noel reached Mollie, flung his arm around her throat, and pulled her tight against him. Her screams became a gurgle as he laid pressure on her windpipe.

"Mollie? Mollie, honey?" Mr. Steunenberg called out, panicked.

"I have her and I will blow her brains out unless you throw down your guns and turn on a goddamn light." There was the sound of things hitting the straw. Halting steps moved to the side of the barn, and suddenly fluorescent lights sprang to life.

"Mathias, secure their weapons," Noel ordered.

The Hungarian emerged from the stall. Now Noel could see the carnage. Jaako was well and truly dead. His chest looked like raw hamburger. One brother lay on the straw with a sucking chest wound, victim of Noel's first shots. The Steunenberg paterfamilias clutched at his thigh, blood seeping from between his fingers. Another brother lay on the straw, hands clutching at his stomach. He alternated whimpers with calls for *mama*. Still another brother, this one maybe fourteen or so, cowered against a giant bale of hay.

Noel ground the muzzle of his pistol into Mollie's temple. "Now, Mollie, you're going to open a doorway to the warehouse in Kongoville. And you, Mr. Steunenberg, you and your uninjured son are going to move these pallets through that doorway because if you don't I'm going to kill Mollie. Then I'm going to hunt you down and kill you too, and that means your other two sons will die because you won't be able to call for an ambulance."

"My wife . . . my wife will be calling the police. They'll be here real soon."

"Oh, I doubt that. Because the last thing you would want is the police coming around, and you having to explain how you have all these pallets of gold ingots." Another twist of the gun brought a whimper from Mollie. "Now make up your mind. I'm not a patient person, and you're interfering with my plans."

The man looked from his suffering sons to his daughter trapped in the curve of Noel's arm. Noel loosened his grip on her throat. "Mollie, help your daddy make up his mind."

"Daddy, we need to do what he says."

"Good girl," Noel said, and patted her cheek with the barrel of the gun.

Steunenberg gave a short, curt nod. One of Mollie's fourth-dimensional doors opened in the center of the barn. Steunenberg and his son pushed the still-floating pallets through the doorway. This time Noel saw the familiar outline of the warehouse they had rented lit by work lights. Once all the gold was back in Africa Noel pulled Mollie through. Mathias followed.

"You gotta let her go," her father called out desperately.

"In time."

Central Park
Manhattan, New York

IT WAS SNOWING. NOT hard, but steady. Dots of white no bigger than a pinhead drifting down from the occluded New York sky. Bugsy and Simoon walked along the twisting pathways of Central Park, the world white and grey around them. He was trying not to touch her. Snuggling up right now would have been a lie.

"So no word yet," Simoon said.

"No. Not yet. Jayewardene's fighting it out with the bigwigs of the global internationalist conspiracy or, you know, whoever. He'll get an answer pretty soon."

"I wish there was a way to get past the Radical and talk to Mark Meadows, you know?" Simoon said.

"I wish there was a way to kick his fucking ass," Bugsy said, his tone light and conversational. "It freaks me out how everything we do in this country is about what happened in 1968. It's not just Meadows, it's everyone. It's the Vietnam war and the Summer of Love. It's Jimi Hendrix and Janis Joplin and Thomas Marion Douglas, who was, by the way, an arrogant dick. I met him."

"I know you did," Simoon said. A dog bounded through the snow, barked at them once, and bounded away.

"I look at all the shit that's going on now. The Nshombos. Kid aces, I mean holy shit, that's creepy. And the Sudd. And New Orleans. And Egypt and the Nur before that. That seems like plenty enough without hauling along three decades of old business. It just . . . it pisses me off. It just pisses me off."

"You don't have to do this," Simoon said. "I mean, if you don't want to." She stopped and sat on a stone bench. Her breath was a mist. A fog. A ghost.

"Do what?" Bugsy said.

"Get all worked up and angry," she said, looking up from under Ellen's lashes. "I get it. I do. You're breaking up with me, right?"

Bugsy's heart stilled and sank into his belly. He looked at his shoes. He sat. She was crying.

"It's not going to work," he said. "You're great. And Ellen's good folks. Nick . . . well, given that I'm sorta kinda sleeping with his girlfriend, I guess he's taken it all pretty well. But this . . . Aliyah, this is nuts."

"I don't know," she said between sobs. "Did I . . . do something wrong? Was I . . ."

Jonathan took a deep breath. Oh, this sucked. "You *died*. Years ago. In Egypt."

"I don't even remember that," Simoon said.

"I do. And here's the thing, if we were just fuck buddies, hanging out, having that post-AIDS hookup culture casual it-is-what-it-is thing? To begin with, you would never have gone for me. You traded down when you found me, and I love you for it, but we both know that's true. And another thing, you'd have ditched me by now. Or I'd have ditched you. We'd have had coffee some night, agreed that we'd be in touch about next weekend, only really weekend after next, and we'd both never follow up."

"That isn't true," Simoon said in a voice that meant she knew it was.

"So why are we together?" Bugsy went on. "Because you're dead and don't think you can do any better. And because I feel like I'm killing you if we break up."

"Aren't you?" she whispered.

"No. I'm not. Because you died years ago."

"Convenient," Simoon said bitterly. "Really nice and simple and convenient for you, isn't it?"

"Actually, it really sucks. But look. It was talk to you about it like this or else just tell Ellen to never put the earring back in. And I did it this way."

"Why?" she said. "So you could hurt the girl a little more before you killed her?" She was talking about herself as if she were someone else. As if Ellen were speaking and not Simoon.

"So I could say good-bye before I let you go," he said.

"You're a fucking monster," Simoon said softly. There were tears steaming on her cheeks. The snow around them was grey.

"Okay," he said.

"This is really what you want?" Simoon said.

"Yeah."

For a long moment, neither of them moved, and then with sudden violence, Simoon plucked out the earring and slammed it into his palm. By the time the metal touched him, Ellen was sitting beside him. Simoon was gone.

"Hey," Bugsy said.

"I'm sorry," Ellen said gently. "For what it's worth, you were right. It couldn't have gone any other way."

"Thanks," he said.

"Its not like that for me and Nick, you know," she said. "I couldn't do what you did. I can't walk away from him."

"Okay," Bugsy said.

They were quiet. The dog barked again, its voice muffled by distance and the fallen snow. Ellen patted him on the shoulder and stood. Simoon's last tears had dried on her face, but Ellen only looked a little weary.

"Come by and pick up your things anytime you want, okay?"

"Yeah. I'll do that," Bugsy said.

Cameo nodded and turned away. He watched her walk, the thickening snow moving her away faster than mere distance could. She stopped, looked back. He could see the frown on her lips. When she called out, it was like a voice coming from a different world.

"You aren't a monster," she yelled. Bugsy raised a hand in thanks, and Cameo nodded and went back to her walk. To her apartment. To Nick the Hat and wherever that weird little psychodrama was leading. But without him.

He sat for a while, letting the chill sink deep into his bones. A jogger huffed by, wrapped in a turquoise track suit, white iPod cords dangling from his ears. A siren rose and fell and faded in the distance. Bugsy opened his hand.

It was a nice enough earring. Not spectacular, not cheap. Inoffensive. He tossed it up and down a couple times, measuring its weight by the impact against his palm, then stood, walked to the edge of the path, and launched it out into the snow. He didn't see where it fell.

Afterward, he treated himself to a bookstore and some coffee.

Kongoville, Congo
People's Paradise of Africa

"I KNOW HE'S IN the Sudd, but get the word to Weathers somehow," Noel instructed Sun. "The gold will be in place in a few minutes." He hung up his phone.

"What do we do about Jaako's share?" Mathias asked as he loaded his share of the gold into suitcases.

Noel shrugged. "Well, it's not like he had a widow or orphans to care for. Divide it equally between us."

"And what about me?" Mollie muttered. Noel had tied her to a support pillar in the warehouse.

He squatted down in front of her. "Mollie, my dear, you have the necessary instincts for a life of crime, but you have to learn one key lesson. Never betray your associates. Unless you're clever or lucky enough to kill them all you will find yourself . . . well, in your current situation."

"You're probably just going to kill me," she said, and she couldn't quite hide the quaver.

"No, your power is too useful, and I may need it again. I'm very annoyed about Jaako because his power was quite unique, but I'm not going to trash another power on something as pointless as vengeance." He stood and felt his knees crack. "Now let's finish this."

Mollie opened a doorway into Cumming's apartment. His gold was delivered. Noel's was sent through to the abandoned farmhouse in the Hebrides. Mathias was pushed through into the winestube in the Grinzing. He shrugged at Noel's raised eyebrow. "I own it," he said.

"What about mine?" Mollie asked again.

Noel took an ingot off the remaining stacks, and laid it in her lap. "Here. A little grubstake."

"That's not fair!"

"I'm not killing you or your hillbilly family. You should be grateful. Now open the door to the yacht."

"No," Mollie said. Silence stretched between them as they matched stares. She broke first, unable to hold his gaze. "You . . . you won't kill me. Not in cold blood."

Before Noel could disabuse her of this notion, Mathias intervened. He came between Noel and Mollie, and knelt down next to her. "You're a little girl. Very young. Very foolish, but you could have a big career. I would help teach you if you wanted to work with me. I've been a criminal for forty years. I've met many criminals. This man . . ." He gestured at Noel. "He's a killer. They aren't common. He'll do what he says."

Mollie audibly gulped. The doorway into the hold of the yacht appeared. Noel was relieved. He hadn't really wanted to reformulate the plan, but Mathias's words echoed in his head, and felt like a weight on his chest.

But I've changed. I'm not that person any longer.

And he looked down at the gun in his hand. He didn't remember drawing it.

Bahr al-Ghazal Base
The Sudd, South Sudan
The Caliphate of Arabia

THE PAINTED CHILDREN'S CHANTING raised the hairs on the back of Tom Weathers's neck. The bonfire capered high, throwing yellow flames and brown smoke spires into the face of the dense Sudd night. His eyes watered to the smoke of the pungent dried acacia he'd hyperflown in for the ritual. The fire cackled as if it had a life of its own.

He imagined Noel Matthews inside that fire. Twisting. Screaming. Charring. *Melting.* But he knew that couldn't be. Matthews was a fucking teleport. Tom would have to finish him fast. *Yeah, you think you're so smart, Meadows, you fuck,* he thought. *But I got your number. Sleep is for the weak anyway.*

He surveyed the circle of small faces, human and otherwise, all shades turned orange by firelight, eagerly watching him. He could feel their hunger: to strike out at the world that threatened them. That made them *hurt.* Could see it in the feral glitter of their eyes, hear it in their chanting: *Death, death, death to imperialists! Death, death, death!*

The same rage and desire burned in his own chest, bared and painted in violent smears and jags and drenched in glittering Sudd sweat. "Yes, death," he cried out, throwing his arms up over his head, baying like a wolf at the moon. "It's time for justice. Time for righteous payback! Down with the oppressors. Bring them death!"

The twisted children howled in reply.

His cell phone rang.

Tom's ring tone came from Jefferson Airplane's "Volunteers of America." Grace Slick screaming, *"Up against the wall, motherfucker!"* Appropriate as the sentiment was, the interruption *pissed him off.*

He dug in the hip pocket of his faded blue jeans, pulled out the phone, and flipped it open. When he saw the caller's name he waved his hand at the circle of chanting children. "Wait one. Got to take this." Turning away from the bonfire, he hunched over and pressed the phone to his ear. "Heilian? This isn't a good time—"

"No," she said in her best clipped secret-cop colonel voice. *"You must listen* now. *The Nshombos' private yacht. Get there at once."*

Dr. Nshombo's Yacht
Kongoville, Congo
People's Paradise of Africa

A FEW LIGHTS STRETCHED wavering yellow fingers across dark water. The big yacht itself showed few lights, though its white hull gleamed like sun-bleached bone.

With a loud thump Tom landed on the hand-polished hardwood deck a few yards aft of the superstructure. *Damn*, he thought, *misjudged a bit.* As he straightened a voice shouted in angry French from his left.

Thrusting a hand into his pants pocket, Tom turned. A Leopard Man in mufti—slacks, a dark T-shirt with a *Miami Vice* sports coat over it, the inevitable blackout shades, and leopard-skin fez—was hauling a Micro UZI machine pistol out of a shoulder holster. "No one is allowed aboard," the Leopard Man shouted, aiming his handgun-sized piece. "Not even you, *Mokèlé-mbèmbé.*"

Tom's left hand came up holding a PPA five-franc piece, the size of a U.S. quarter. He flicked it at the Leopard Man. With all his buckle-tank-armor-with-a-punch strength.

The coin cracked as it went hypersonic.

The Leopard Man's body jerked. A darker stain appeared in the front of his dark T. The coin had hit going fast enough to blow through rib cage, heart, and spine. He folded.

A curious *skritching* sound made Tom look up. A vast multilegged blot descended toward him from the roof of the cabin. Just in time, Tom got his hands up to fend off a round furry body.

Thick blunt legs with spiky fur belabored Tom's face. Ayiyi's weight almost toppled Tom over backward. He barely managed to keep his feet. Huge fangs curving from furry bases clawed for his face. He pulled his head backward. The spider-monster hissed at him. All the time Ayiyi's little-boy face stared impassively. A drop of green venom dropped to his left shoulder. It sizzled.

Shouting with pain Tom finally found a grip. He hurled the monstrous spider away. It flew across the water to strike the front of the warehouse, hard. Tom anticipated a gratifying *splat.*

Instead the child ace flipped his spider body in the air, landed using all eight legs to cushion the shock. Then, dropping to the dock, he shot a tendril of web at Tom.

It stuck his bare, painted chest. And clung. He tried to brush it away. His hand stuck to it. "Hey," he shouted. "I didn't know you could do that!"

With a single spring the spider landed on the brass railing. It scuttled quickly behind Tom, then leaped back to the cabin roof.

Tom found the sticky stuff pinning both arms to his sides. He tried to break free. But it had the legendary strength of spider silk, plus monster cross section. And Tom couldn't get decent leverage.

The giant spider reared to fling itself on him. The fangs reached for him. He saw the skin where the poison had struck was blistered. He drew a deep breath.

He was in space. The monster spider floated, tethered to him by webbing that, flash-dehydrated and rapidly freezing, was already losing its adhesiveness and becoming brittle. With a soundless shout of triumph Tom tore free.

The child ace began to turn over as he drifted away. Tom saw his mouth straining open in a scream. He transfixed the monster thorax with a sunbeam. Then he was back on deck, brushing stiff web remnants from his skin.

Candace Sessou, the Darkness, appeared atop the cabin. Flanking her stood a pair of Leopard Men. They raised weapons. Tom blasted each with one hand.

Then he looked at Candi. "Why didn't you help me? Or try to stop me?"

"I'm done being a puppet on a string," she said. "You and he are the same. You don't care who you hurt. Well, you have no more power over me!" She turned her back on him, crossed her arms beneath her tiny breasts.

And she was half hung-up on me, Tom thought. *Ungrateful little bitch.* "You're either with me or against me!" He flung up a hand.

She wrapped herself in Darkness. The sunbeam stabbed through it. He heard a splash near the portside rail. He ran to look. The Darkness spread out across the river like mist. He heard the girl's mocking laughter. Then she was lost. "Hell with her." He thrust through the hatchway.

Lights led him down a stairway. At the bottom little white dogs flooded the corridor, leaping at his legs and yapping. "Jesus!" They relented when he kicked one yipping through the bulkhead and out through the hull. Then they retreated to safe distances behind and ahead of him and growled.

Before him a hatch stood open into the yacht's cargo hold. An unmistakable shape stood before him in a spill of dim amber light. Big head, slight body, uncharacteristically dressed in shirtsleeves. The dull yellow gleam beyond the President-for-Life told all.

"Checking the ballast?" he asked.

Kitengi Nshombo spun. His fine hard features went slack and took on a grey matte tone. "Tom, it isn't what you think. I had nothing to do—"

"Yeah," Tom said. "Yeah, it is. *Exactly* what I think." He nodded toward the gold ingots stacked neatly on a tarpaulin. "You're stealing from the People, *comrade*. That's what you're doing. You're a traitor to the People's Paradise and the Revolution."

"No!" Nshombo cried. Spittle flew from his mouth. "You must listen to me. I did not do this. I received a curious telephone call—from Alicia, I thought—telling me to come to the yacht. When I arrived I found"—he gestured at the piled plunder—"this. I was as surprised as you are. And quite as displeased. Surely you can see I've been set up."

"Sure," Tom said, smiling. The president's taut shoulders relaxed. "Sure, the gold just teleported here *all by its fucking self*!" He shook his head. "You got too rich and powerful, man. You forgot the Revolution. You forgot your *roots*."

"No, no, it's a lie, I've been framed—"

Tom reached out and grabbed that big head with both hands. Lifted the president right up off the deck by it so his legs kicked futilely in the air. "Tom! Put me down! *Please*—"

He tried to say more. It soared into wild screaming as Tom increased the pressure on the sides of his head.

President Nshombo's head burst like a zit.

Wet clumps hit Tom's face and clung.

He wiped his face and spat out something that tasted of salt and iron. "I shoulda known better than to trust the Man. Even when I fucking helped *make* him the Man."

♥

Sunday,
December 27

THE ORGY LASTED ALMOST through the night.

After Alicia left, Michelle faced her chair away from the fire. She was afraid of what Alicia might do to Joey if she left.

Near dawn, it started raining and doused the fire. That seemed to dampen everything else. The drummers disappeared back into the jungle, and some of the new Leopard Men resumed human form and began gathering up their torn clothing as the sun came up.

Michelle stood up and stretched. As she looked at the neat little compound buildings, she jerked back. Staring out of several windows were the faces of children. None of them could have been older than nine.

"Jesus," she whispered. *How long had they been there? What had they seen?*

Alicia strolled into the clearing followed by a little girl. The girl was wrapped in bandages. Her melonlike head was impossibly large for her tiny body, and she didn't walk so much as stagger.

"I know you appreciated my survivor hospitals," Alicia said. "I've been working on many things for my people. I've even been working on a little project for children."

"For children." Michelle was at a loss.

Alicia gave a belly laugh. "These children are building our nation. My project is making us strong. Some of my babies were born of rape, and abandoned in orphanages because they were the product of the mother's shame. Instead of being outcasts they will be the defenders of the People's Paradise. This is a great honor for them."

"What you did last night . . ."

"A sacred rite. The children saw me bestow my gift. I give my Leopard Men power. I give my babies power."

"You give them the virus." Michelle was horrified.

"The gift. Not all of them are worthy, sad to say. But those who are . . ." Alicia beamed at the little girl in the bandages. "This is the Mummy. Would you like to see what she can do?"

A bubble began to form in Michelle's hand. *Take this insane bitch out. The world will be a better place.*

"May I have your answer about Tom, please?"

"If you want him dead, kill him yourself," Michelle answered.

Alicia pouted. "You disappoint me, Michelle. We could have been such friends. Baby, do her for me."

The Mummy ran to Michelle and seized her arm. Her hands were tiny, her fingers wrapped in rags as dry as parchment. *What is this?* Michelle thought.

Then the pain hit.

Her body began to wither. Her throat felt as if it were closing up. And the Mummy's bandages began to fill out, the fabric darkening with moisture, stretching.

Jesus, Michelle thought, suddenly frightened. She tried to yank her arm away, but the little girl held on like a terrier. Michelle kicked backward, sending her chair toppling over. There was a squishy thud as the Mummy hit the ground beside her, but she didn't let go. Michelle grew thinner, weaker. *My precious bodily fluids*, she thought, giggling hysterically. The Mummy was growing as she shrank. *She'll outweigh me soon*, she realized.

Michelle kept shrinking, her precious water draining away into the blobby monster on her arm.

A terrified shriek pierced through her fear.

Michelle sat up, and the world tilted. A corpse came lurching out of the building where Joey was being kept; a child, no older than the Mummy. Two more zombies followed. She recognized the guards who'd been posted at Joey's bedside. Joey appeared in the doorway behind them. She looked wobbly, but her zombies were moving just fine.

Michelle heard Alicia Nshombo scream. She was staring down the road with horror on her face.

Michelle pressed her palm against the Mummy's head. "Let go, kid," she said in French, and then again in English. "I have no intention of dying today. Either we both get up, or I'll be the only one getting up. Got it?"

The Mummy squeezed tighter. Michelle slid a wizened hand down her bandaged cheek and under her chin, then raised her face to look into the child's eyes. They were black, shiny, devoid of any sign of humanity.

"I'm sorry," Michelle said.

Then she loosed a stream of bubbles.

Water, blood, and brains burst over Michelle. She yanked the Mummy's hand from her arm and pushed the tiny corpse away. Where she fell a puddle formed around her.

Alicia Nshombo was still screaming. Michelle struggled to her feet. Joey was staring into space with a beatific smile on her face. Hoodoo Mama was in the house.

Michelle's arms were withered and wrinkled as an old woman's. She was dizzy and shaking from the water loss. All she could do was watch. Shambling into the center of the camp were zombies. All of them were children. Dozens of them, scores of them, hundreds of them, green and grey and rotting. More were coming up around them, little fingers clawing up from the ground like rain lilies after a storm. The earth sprouted small heads and shoulders.

Leopards leapt upon the zombies, snarling, clawing, growling. They ripped the dead children apart, but for every one that fell there were a dozen more. The soldiers were emptying their guns, but bullets can't kill the dead.

Waves of dizziness poured over Michelle. She was so thirsty. Dazed, she had trouble trying to remember what she needed to do now.

Adesina. She staggered to her feet.

Some of the soldiers dropped their guns and fled into the jungle. Michelle held her palms up. She thought about Adesina in the pit. All the dead children. About how horrible it must have been for them to be torn away from their families, dragged to this place, and injected with the virus that would kill most of them, maim some, and leave only a few . . . like her.

And something in Michelle shifted. Something in her broke and her energy surged.

With methodical calm, she created small, extremely dense bubbles and sent them hurling through the air at the nearest soldiers. They screamed and clutched their chests. Blood poured from their wounds. The zombies moved in on the rest, ripping and tearing as they went.

Michelle saw Alicia Nshombo surrounded by zombies. Alicia's face elongated as she dropped to her hands and knees. Her body grew larger, and fur erupted from her skin. Her teeth grew into fangs. She gave a roar that felt to Michelle as if it were echoing in her own chest.

Okay, Michelle thought. *Wasn't expecting that. World's fattest leopard.*

Joey's zombies flowed around her. None looked older than fourteen or fifteen. Most hadn't reached puberty. They surrounded the leopard, piled on top of her, and began tearing and ripping at her with small dead hands. Alicia gave a howl, slashed this way and that. She almost broke free, but one of the zombies grabbed her tail and yanked her back. She screamed again, and this time the sound was almost human. Then she fell silent.

That was when the other leopards vanished. In their places sprawled confused, naked men.

Michelle sat down hard on the ground. It was wet. Mummy. Or what was left of her.

"Jesus, Bubbles, *what did you do?*" Joey ran to Michelle and dropped to her knees. "Wasn't there a kid here? Had hold of your arm?"

The world was spinning crazily again. Michelle closed her eyes. "I tried not to die."

Joey gave a primitive wail. "You fucker! You didn't have to kill her! I was helping you!"

Michelle swallowed. God, she was thirsty. It was worse than waking up from the coma. "I didn't have any choice. It was me or her."

"You didn't have a choice? *You're the Amazing Bubbles!* Nothing can hurt you!"

"She could. She was."

"She was just a kid!" Joey was screaming.

"Not anymore. I looked in her eyes. And you know what, Joey? Shit happens to little kids. Even if they're loved and protected, shit happens. All. The. Time. Welcome to reality." Michelle pushed herself up from the ground. "I told her to stop. Sometimes kids get so broken they aren't really kids anymore. But if you want to hate me, knock yourself out."

Joey slapped Michelle's arm. Then she slapped Michelle's face. It didn't take more than a few slaps for her to wear herself out. "You fucker. You fucker. You fucker," she cried over and over.

"Yep, that's me," Michelle said. Unsteadily, she made her way through the carnage of zombies, leopards, soldiers, and pieces of Alicia Nshombo to one of the compound's buildings.

Inside she found a sink. She opened the tap, leaned over, and put her mouth up to the faucet. Warm water poured into her mouth. She gulped it down until some of the dizziness had passed.

Then she went back outside. She had to find Adesina.

Southwest of Bunia, Congo
People's Paradise of Africa

THE FLATBED TRUCK LURCHED forward with the grinding of gears and a gout of oily, black smoke. Wally shifted his weight, eliciting a creak and groan from the suspension beneath the cargo bed. The truck stank of goat innards. And its best days were long in the past, which reminded Wally quite a bit of Mr. Finch's airplane.

That, in turn, reminded him of Jerusha. He wondered if she got the kids to Tanzania, if she were safe, if he'd ever see her again. He cast a long glance up and down his rust-pitted body, and decided he already knew the answer to that last question.

The truck's oversized tires chewed up the muddy road, leaving ruts the size of small lakes. The mud was a deep, rich brown, and when it splashed on Wally it looked like a rain of caramel or butterscotch. Even in spite of the mud and the constant bouncing, this was the most comfortable he'd been since heading out overland.

One leg burned where the bullet wound had become infected; the dents in his other leg still ached where the crocodile had bit him. His feet were solid orange with rust. Nicks, scratches, and even claw marks covered his arms, legs, and torso. The rust was deep enough in places that when he stuck a fingertip in, he felt something warm and squishy inside.

He pulled out his last S.O.S pad and set to work, doing triage on his crumbling skin. He cast his gaze into the forest while he scrubbed. Sure enough, twenty or thirty feet past the edge of the road, Ghost kept pace with the truck, her toes dangling just inches from the ground. She still clutched the knife handle, though Wally had destroyed the knife.

He hoped the driver wouldn't see her. Getting this ride was the first break he'd had in two days, and he needed the rest. Cripes, did he ever need the rest.

The smaller villages, like this one, had no electricity. No radios. No telephones. He'd eventually figured that out after a long session of intercultural charades; the villagers had spent a lot of time staring at the clanking metal man and his strange gestures. They didn't run from him, though. If anything, he had the sense they knew what he was doing, and secretly approved of his mission. Maybe they'd heard about the Nyunzu lab, and the barge. They seemed to think he was pretty okay. Especially after he pantomimed fighting a Leopard Man. They'd *loved* that. Hence the ride.

He didn't know how far this fella planned to take him—certainly not all the way to Bunia—but every mile Wally didn't have to walk was a small blessing.

Wally scrubbed until there was nothing left of the S.O.S pad but a handful of fuzz. His feet looked a lot better, and he'd buffed out some of the worst pits in his arms, legs, and torso. The spots he couldn't reach, those were what worried him the most. He dozed off . . .

. . . and woke when the truck skidded to a halt. Wally slammed his forehead on the cab of the truck, cracking the rear window. "Ouch. Hey, sorry about your truck, guy."

But the driver had already jumped out, and was running back down the road. *Great.* Wally stood, expecting to find Ghost floating in the middle of the road.

She wasn't. But the road was blocked with an armored personnel carrier and three leopards (two spotted, one black). A fourth Leopard Man stood atop the carrier, in human form, behind a machine gun.

Rats. He should have expected this. The PPA knew where he was; he'd seen a helicopter earlier in the day. By now, they probably had all the roads to Bunia blocked off.

The machine-gunner raked the truck. A line of holes perforated the hood. The windshield shattered. Rounds *pingpingpinged* across Wally's chest. He made a mental note to try to make sure the Committee found the driver somehow and got him a new truck. "You guys again. Don't you leopard folks ever learn?"

He vaulted over the cab. The leopards reared back. Wally hit the ground hard, sending up a spray of mud that drenched the cats. They hissed, shaking their heads to clear their eyes.

Wally took advantage of the momentary distraction to close with the APC, rendering the machine gun useless. The gunner couldn't aim at him as long as he stood next to the vehicle. Wally placed a hand on the armor, ready to disintegrate the whole thing, but then he thought better of it. Why not drive to Bunia in a PPA vehicle?

The leopards surrounded him, one in front and one each to his left and right. The gunner pulled his sidearm. He emptied a magazine on Wally's head, arms, and shoulders. It hurt. A lot. Rivulets of blood trickled down his body, from a dozen different spots.

"Okay, now you're asking for it, pal." Wally gave the APC a violent shove. It tipped up on one set of wheels, just short of flipping over, before landing back upright with a ground-shaking crash. The gunner fell off.

The leopards chose that moment to pounce. One landed on his back, the others raked his arms. Wally jumped and fell backward, body-slamming the leopard on his back. They landed with a splash, a crack, and a yelp.

Wally caught a flash of white in the foliage. Ghost, watching from the sidelines. She looked . . . *terrified*.

But then he was at the center of a maelstrom of fur, claws, and fangs, and couldn't see anything. The remaining leopards dodged his punches and kicks. When he turned to deal with one, the other put new gouges in his rust.

He had finally caught one by the throat and was squeezing hard, when the leopard shimmered into the form of a man. The giant cat scratching at Wally's shoulder also turned into a man. A very confused and very silly-looking man. Wally saw panic in their eyes. He dropped the first guy, who fell to the ground with both hands to his neck, and planted an iron elbow into the second fellow's stomach. They crawled away, past their comrade whose legs Wally had crushed. He, too, had reverted to his human form.

What the heck just happened?

The gunner ran out from behind the APC. Apparently he had reloaded, because he squeezed off a volley of shots while his comrades retreated. Wally charged him, grabbed his hand, and crushed the gun into a useless ball of metal. His opponent fell to his knees, screaming like a banshee.

Wally cuffed him alongside the head, knocking him out. Silence descended over the empty road. Well, it was mostly silent, except for the sobbing.

Sobbing? Did I miss one? Wally looked around, but all the Leopard Men either were unconscious or had retreated. No, the crying came from nearby. From the roadside.

From Ghost.

"It's okay," said Wally. He saw how she stared at the Leopard Men. "You're safe. They can't hurt you now." Her feet, he noticed, were touching the ground.

The knife handle fell from her fingers. She grabbed a fallen branch, ran across the road, and started to beat the guy sprawled at Wally's feet. Her bawling—loud, inconsolable—evoked one of the horrors Wally and Gardener had witnessed in Nyunzu: a Leopard Man handing a syringe to a little boy, forcing him to infect another child with the virus.

"Hey, hey. Don't do that." Wally gently took the branch away. She fell to her knees, hitting the dead man with tiny fists.

He wrapped her in his arms and held her until she cried herself to sleep. It took a long time.

Kisangani, Congo
People's Paradise of Africa

ADESINA WAS IN THE second pit Michelle searched.

At first, Michelle had thought the pit held nothing but body parts. Then she saw something moving in the corner. She started trembling. But then she made herself jump into the pit. Immediately she sank up to her waist in the decaying remains. She waded over to where the movement had been and started digging. Soon she was completely covered in the foul-smelling, rotting flesh.

But what she finally uncovered wasn't a sweet little girl. It wasn't even the feral child who had haunted those dreams. What she found was a hideously repulsive sluglike creature, encased in a shiny filament cocoon.

She knew it was Adesina.

Michelle tried not to think about how she didn't want to touch Adesina now. But when she finally grabbed the thing around its middle, it was as if she'd been flipped into one of her pit dreams.

Adesina is there with her, the dream Adesina, the way she was before the wild card had changed her. Adesina can feel Michelle's revulsion, and in turn Michelle feels Adesina's sorrow. It staggers her for a moment.

Michelle gathered herself and carried Adesina back to the compound, cradled in her arms. Joey glared as she walked up.

"This is Adesina," Michelle said. And then the cocoon began to pulse. A chunk of it fell off and Michelle almost dropped it. "Go get me a towel," she said to Joey. The cocoon moved again. Michelle tried not to be grossed out, but she hated bugs and wormy things.

A few seconds later, a leg emerged from the cocoon—and then another. After that, the head started out. It was covered in a shiny, viscous fluid. Michelle thought it was nasty. Joey was thrusting a towel at her. Michelle plopped on the ground and started dabbing at Adesina's head. Now that she had something productive to do, she could shove her gut reaction aside.

And as she patted away the fluid, she saw that Adesina's face wasn't an insect face at all. It was the face that Michelle knew from her dreams.

A moment later, there was a wet sound and the rest of Adesina's body slid from the cocoon. The husk fell off Michelle's knees and she kicked it away. She kept gently drying Adesina's body. Adesina started shaking and wriggling. A pair of small wings unfurled from her back. She pushed herself up on her legs, wobbly at first. She was the size of a small dog. Michelle didn't know what to do now. Part of her was still not wild about the insecty-ness of Adesina, but then there was that sweet face she knew so well. She was torn.

Adesina raised herself up onto her back legs and put her front legs on either side of Michelle's face. Amazing warmth and happiness spread through Michelle. Then Adesina said, "Thank you."

Tears began to pour down Michelle's face and she reached out and touched Adesina's cheek. "You're welcome," she replied. "I'm so sorry. . . ."

Adesina kissed Michelle's cheek. "You saved me. I held on because I knew you would find me."

Michelle couldn't speak. It felt like there was a golf ball in her throat from the tears. It had been so long since she'd felt . . . since she felt *happy*. She wondered if she had ever really felt happy before.

"Michelle," Adesina said. "Michelle, now you need to go help the others, you need to go to the Red House."

"I don't want to leave you!" Michelle replied, alarmed. "I just found you."

Adesina cocked her head to one side like a praying mantis. "This is the other reason why I brought you here. It wasn't just to help me. It was to help them. I've been in their dreams, too. I know what has been happening to them and so do you. You must go soon. Because I've been in *his* dreams, too."

And then Michelle saw a barrage of new images. A compound in the jungle. Children being rounded up and given shots. Then there were images of Tom Weathers killing people. Lots of people.

She didn't need to see more. She sighed. "Of course I'll go," she said. Adesina removed her front legs and the wonderful warmth and happiness slid from Michelle. And she felt cold inside again.

"What the fuck was that all about?" Joey asked.

Michelle held Adesina up to Joey. "I need you to take care of her for a while. Take care of all of the children here."

Then Michelle got up. She brushed past Joey and went to find someone who knew where the Red House was—and who would take her there.

♣

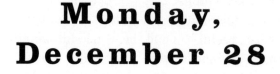

Monday,
December 28

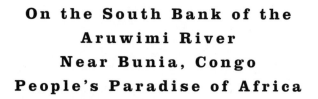

On the South Bank of the
Aruwimi River
Near Bunia, Congo
People's Paradise of Africa

GHOST LOVED PEANUT BUTTER.

She sat behind Wally, on one of the long, low benches that lined the interior of the APC, silently scooping peanut butter out of a jar with her fingers. She still hadn't spoken, but neither had she become insubstantial since letting Wally hug her. If anything, she followed him more closely than ever now.

The APC wasn't the easiest thing Wally had ever driven. He knew how to drive a stick, and even some mining equipment, but this thing had more gears than he was used to. And it handled strangely, too. But he more or less managed to keep it on the bumpy, muddy roads leading to Bunia. They'd passed another roadblock this morning, but the soldiers and Leopard Men had waved the PPA vehicle through without a second glance.

Which suited Wally just fine. The last thing he wanted was to get into a fight while Ghost clung to his side. Also, it gave some of his wounds time to heal.

Wally chanced taking his eyes off the road long enough to glance at the booklet he'd found in the APC. It was a wire-bound booklet of laminated map pages. Together they covered the greater Bunia area, depicting topographic details, roads, power lines, garrisons, military installations, trains . . . everything he might have needed to make a strategic assessment of the area, if only he could read French. *If only Jerusha were here.*

A green "X" had been marked on one map page with a grease pencil, at what appeared to be a compound on the outskirts of town: the central laboratory for the PPA's child-ace project. Wally figured he'd make it there in a few more days. This river road along the Aruwimi would take him most of the way. He was in the homestretch, now.

But with every mile, Ghost became more nervous, more agitated. She inched closer and closer to him. She probably didn't even realize she was doing it. Whatever they'd done to her, Wally guessed it had happened at Bunia.

Wally pulled over for a bathroom break around midafternoon. He parked the APC in the shadow of a trestle bridge that spanned the tall embankments on either side of the river. Ghost followed him into the brush. It took a lot of gesturing before she got the gist of what he was up to, but he finally managed to convey enough that she backed off a little bit to give him privacy.

He'd just finished and was washing his hands when Ghost came running back. She grabbed his hand, pulling frantically toward the APC. Tears glistened on her cheeks, dripping from eyes wide with terror.

Wally knelt, so that she could look at him face-to-face. "Hey, what's wrong? Did you see something?"

With one hand, Ghost gave his arm another panicky tug. With the other, she pointed at the bridge. Wally looked up, suddenly worried they'd been spotted. The bridge was empty.

Somewhere not far away, a train barreled down a set of tracks. The sound echoed faintly across the grassy plains: *tikka-tch-tch-tikka-tch-tch* . . . It goaded Ghost into deeper panic.

"You're afraid of the train? What's on the train?" Wally asked. Maybe she'd been taken to Bunia on a train. He pointed at the bridge, then at Ghost, and shrugged. *Is that how they took you from your family?*

Ghost shook her head. She pointed in the direction of the approaching train—it was louder now—and then curled her lips into a snarl. She held two fingers in front of her mouth, like fangs, then contorted her hands into the semblance of claws.

Leopard Men. There were Leopard Men on that train.

Wally thought about the maps. *Of course. They're pulling reinforcements back to defend Bunia.*

The first smile in many days spread across his face. He laid his hands on Ghost's arms. "Wanna see something neat?" He winked.

First, he backed the APC a ways up the road. Just in case. Then he scrambled up the embankment to the bridge truss and started to climb. The wooden boards creaked precariously under Wally's weight, but they held. By the time he pulled himself atop the rail bed, he could see sunlight glinting off the approaching train.

Wally laid a hand on one rail, concentrating. The steel turned orange beneath his palm. He willed the rust to spread; like a lit fuse, it streaked up the rail past the end of the bridge. Wally stomped his foot, hard enough to shake the bridge. The ruined rail sloughed apart. In a few seconds there was nothing left but flakes of corroded metal wafting down to the river.

The train was close now. It rounded the bend. Wally jumped onto the embankment, then half slid, half tumbled down to the road. He carried Ghost back a safe distance, behind the APC.

The crash was spectacular, if Wally did say so himself.

Cyrene, by the Nile
Old Egypt

THE NILE SIGHED, GURGLED, and whispered as it flowed past. The moonlight coaxed silver from the ripples, and seemed to edge the fronds of the date palms with pale halos. A desert wind rattled in the palms with a sound like castanets.

Noel, pacing along the river, paused and took a deep breath, savoring the scent of dust, dung, river reeds, and dried lemons simmering with lamb. He let the tension leach out of his muscles.

It was done. Nshombo was dead. The Chinese and Indians were pulling out of the PPA, viewing it as a bad bet. The conquered African nations were beginning to exert local control again. Noel had come to Egypt, and still in a manic high, fueled by quarts of whiskey-laced coffee and not enough sleep, he had poured out the entire story to Niobe. She had been appropriately admiring of his cleverness.

The bad news—Weathers was still obsessed with Noel Matthews, and seemed to care not one jot that the PPA was collapsing. Of course Weathers had killed the hero of the Revolution. Perhaps it had occurred to him that he might not be all that popular back in Kongoville.

Noel had slept the entire day. Unable to sit still he had headed out for a walk before dinner. Gravel crunched beneath his soles as he resumed his stroll. He heard voices and recognized Niobe's soft alto and a boy's piping tenor. Noel stepped through flowering hibiscus bushes and found Niobe and Drake seated on a marble bench. A tray with glasses and a pitcher of fruit juice rested on the ground at their feet.

If there was no change in the voice, the year had certainly wrought changes in the boy's body. Drake had shot up and slimmed down. His hair was longer, brushing at the tops of his shoulders. They both looked up at Noel's approach, and he saw the more manifest changes—the lump in Drake's forehead that marked the place where Sekhmet rested, and the age and sorrow that lingered in the back of his eyes. Drake might only be fourteen, but Sekhmet had lived through decades of grief and loss.

But maybe some of that grief is Drake's, Noel thought. The boy had killed (inadvertent though it might have been) his entire family and town, and wiped out thousands of PPA soldiers. He too possessed a lifetime of grief and guilt.

But suddenly he was just a teenage boy. He bounced up, nearly upsetting the tray, and called to Noel, "Hey, Noel, sit next to your sweetie."

Niobe offered him a glass of juice. As their fingers met they had that momentary silent communication that flows between married couples.

Are you all right?

Yes, love.

I'm glad you're here.

So am I.

She came into the circle of his arm, and Noel kissed the top of her head. "Has there been any sign of Weathers?" Noel asked.

Drake nodded. "He scouted once, but I don't think he wanted to tangle with the firepower here. We may be mostly jokers, but there are some aces in the mix and . . . and . . ." He hesitated and suddenly seemed like a child again.

"It's okay, you can say it," Niobe said with a smile. "There's you with the powers of Ra."

Noel took a sip of his drink. It was a mix of peach and pomegranate, sweet and sharp all at the same time.

"Dinner's in an hour. I'll leave you two to snuggle." Drake gave them a teenager's leer, then slumped as he reacted to something only he could hear. "And I've got a ton of algebra homework to do." He walked away.

Noel cocked an eyebrow at Niobe. "Homework?"

"He is only fourteen and he needs to be a wise ruler, not just a powerful one." She smiled. "It was actually Sekhmet who told him he had to find tutors. She puts a lot of emphasis on education." She fiddled with the fringe of the sunset-colored shawl she wore, then walked back to the bench and picked up a folded paper off the tray. She offered it to him mutely.

Noel opened it and looked down at a picture of Weathers raining down death and destruction onto another city.

"This has to stop. He's tearing up cities and killing people because of you."

Noel ran a hand through his hair. "Don't you think I know that? I can't fight Tom Weathers. Or do you just want me to surrender and let him kill me?"

"Of course I'm not suggesting that." Her tone was sharp. "You could work with the Committee."

"They're idiots."

"Then help them not be idiots. You're clever and you know how to do this . . . this sort of thing."

"Kill Weathers. Just say it." She looked distressed and he realized how harsh he must have sounded. "I thought you didn't want me to kill anymore."

"I didn't, but Weathers has to be stopped, and what is happening in the Congo has got to be stopped."

"I got rid of Nshombo."

"They are still torturing and killing children."

"I'll be damned if I'm going to kill these child aces."

"I would never forgive you if you did, but you can help destroy the labs where they're making them."

That pulled a bitter laugh from him. "I thank you for your belief in my abilities, but I'm not that powerful."

"And you're a leader and a planner. The Committee has powerful aces, but no leadership."

"Lohengrin would disagree with that."

Niobe shrugged. "He means well, but he's a dreamer. You're a pragmatist. You'll think of a way to deal with Weathers, but in the meantime at least shut down the labs."

Noel studied her features washed pale by the moonlight. He saw no softening, only determination. He realized this was the woman who had risked everything, faced down the armed might of the American government to save one little boy.

Could he really do less?

But he wanted it to be over.

She seemed to read the thought. She laid a hand on his cheek. "Do this. I think it might be the only way for you to find peace."

On the Road to Bunia, Congo
People's Paradise of Africa

THE INCIDENT WITH THE train brought about another change in Ghost. She started to talk.

Wally couldn't understand what she was saying, any better than she understood him. But she chattered at him in her little-girl voice, and that made him happy. She sounded like a normal little girl. Less like a ghost every day.

And, as they passed through villages on the way to Bunia, she talked to other people, too. About Wally. Based on her gestures and the *boom! boom! boom!* sounds she made, he guessed she was telling them about his fight with the Leopard Men, and the barge he'd sunk, and the train he'd derailed. Especially the train. They loved the part about the train. They clapped him on the back, burbling, offering the strangers food and places to sleep.

Bunia must have been a pretty big city, because Wally started noticing cell phones. Each time Ghost finished her tale, a dozen folks whipped out their phones and began texting. And that's when the story *really* spread.

♠

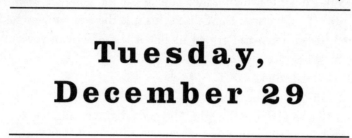

Tuesday, December 29

Bunia, Congo
People's Paradise of Africa

THE SUN ROSE ON columns of oily smoke dotting the horizon, on every point of the compass. But mostly in the direction of Bunia.

Wally and Ghost had acquired an entourage. A small but growing convoy of cars, trucks, motorcycles, and even bicycles trailed their stolen personnel carrier. The people riding them waved shovels, machetes, picks, wooden boards, and anything else they could scrounge.

Wally hated it. These folks would get themselves killed. But he couldn't make them understand.

Ghost refused to leave his side.

More smoke on the horizon.

The radio in the APC came alive with chatter. Wally couldn't understand the actual words, but he didn't need to. He recognized the urgency; the jumble of traffic as people spoke over one another; the plaintive sound of soldiers requesting orders; the barking of harried commanders trying to gather information.

He'd listened to the same kind of chaos on a few Committee ops. It was the sound of things going wrong.

United Nations
Manhattan, New York

NOEL TELEPORTED DIRECTLY INTO Lohengrin's office. The eye patch ought to have made him look rakish and dangerous. Instead the German looked oddly young and vulnerable.

"*Scheisse!* Oh. What do you want?"

"How can I help?"

Bunia, Congo
People's Paradise of Africa

THEY HIT ANOTHER ROADBLOCK about fifty miles outside Bunia. Regular troops patrolled this one; Wally saw no sign of the elite Leopard Men. Not that these soldiers needed the help. They had a tank.

The troops took one look at the line of vehicles strung out on the narrow road behind Wally's APC and raised their weapons. One spoke into a radio handset. The tank turret swiveled, lining up a shot that would kill a hundred people.

Wally was out and charging for the tank in an instant. Bullets ricocheted from his body and from the armor of the personnel carrier. Something wet and warm trickled down his neck. Motors whirred. The tank barrel eased lower.

Wally leapt, hands outstretched. The tank imploded in an orange cloud. Iron fists made short work of the tank crew. Then Wally turned on the other soldiers, but they had dropped their weapons. Hands in the air, they stared behind him.

He turned. A villager had scrambled atop the APC, and was brandishing the machine gun with a wicked grimace. But it didn't matter that the soldiers had surrendered. They were overrun by a wave of angry Congolese, wielding brickbats and hope.

That evening, Wally borrowed a phone. The only number he could remember was Jerusha's. She didn't answer; he left a message on her voice mail.

"Um. Hey, there, Jerusha. This is Wally. You know, from . . . well, you know. Anyway, I figure that by now you must have gotten in touch with the Committee, and you got all them kids safe and sound. Sure hope so. I'm still on my way to Bu—to that place we talked about. I'll get there soon. I just wanted to let you know I'm okay. I hope you are, too. I'm really looking forward to seeing you again." But he knew that was unlikely. So, just in case, he added, "And, Jerusha? Thank you. For everything."

◆

Wednesday,
December 30

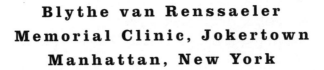

Blythe van Renssaeler
Memorial Clinic, Jokertown
Manhattan, New York

"WHAT THE *HELL* DO you think you're doing?"

Jerusha looked up at the glowering Finn. A nurse—a joker with purple skin and arms and legs that looked like they'd been twisted from balloons—hovered anxiously behind him in the doorway. She straightened, leaving the clothes half stuffed into the garbage bag she had taken from the can. Her seed pouch was lashed to her waist; the belt had gone twice around her cadaverous form. She wiped at her arms, bloodied from where she'd pulled out the IVs. They looked as if they belonged to someone else: skeletal, skin hanging empty from the framework of her bones. She avoided looking at the figure of herself in the glass as she turned. "Figure it out, Doc. You're a smart guy."

"I haven't released you."

"I've decided to release myself."

"Jerusha, you'll die if you leave here."

"That's kind of inevitable, isn't it? On the whole, I'd rather be dying where I might be able to do some good, rather than here in your sterile room. No offense."

"You can't be thinking of going back to Africa."

"Why not? I'm black." When Finn just stared at her, his mouth slightly open, Jerusha laughed drily, the amusement ending in an exhausted, hacking cough that bent her over.

Finn started toward her, and she took a step back from him, straightening. She wiped at her lips—touching her face was always a shock. It didn't feel like *her* face, but some impossibly thin stranger's. She swept a hand over her short hair: the tight curls were dry, brittle, and fragile. "It's a joke, Doc. I need to find Rusty, and I need to find him before"—she stopped, took a breath—"while I *can*. I'm doing exactly that unless you can tell me right now that you can cure whatever that child did to me. Look me in the eyes and tell me you can do that, Doc."

Finn only stared, his gaze almost angry.

"I thought so." Jerusha turned back to the garbage bag, pushing at the clothing and closing the bag. She swung it by the ties around her shoulder. "I have a train and then a plane to catch." She plucked a seed from the pouch and held it up to the centaur. "Get out of my way, or I'll wreck your nice little clinic making sure I'm not stopped."

"They won't let you do this," Finn said. "They won't let you get on that plane."

"What *they?*" she asked. "The Committee? Then they'll have to fight me." She touched the seed pouch. "They'd better send someone good. I'm going, or I swear to you I'll die fighting right there at the airport."

Finn still hadn't moved. "All right. You're an adult. You want to leave, I won't stop you. But let me make a call first. If you're determined to go, then let's make sure you actually *get* there." He held her gaze. "That's not a lie, and that's not a diversion. I'm asking you to let me try to help you."

Jerusha stared at him. She lowered the seed and put it back into the pouch. She swung the garbage bag onto the bed and sat down alongside it, hating how good it felt to be sitting rather than standing. "All right," she told Finn. "I'll wait. For a little bit. But if your phone call doesn't pan out, I'm gone." She looked over Finn's withers to the nurse. "And bring me some food while I'm waiting. Lots of it. I'm famished."

Finn and the nurse fled. Jerusha looked around the room. Her cell phone . . . It was still in the drawer of the stand. She pulled it out. The battery, after days here in the clinic, was dead. She pulled out the cord, plugged it in. The phone beeped; there was a message on her voice mail from a number she didn't know, a sequence that wasn't an American number. She pressed the key to listen.

"Um. Hey there, Jerusha. This is Wally . . ."

The tears then came without volition, huge sobs that wracked her body and brought the purple nurse rushing back into the room. She clutched the phone hard in her thin hand until it hurt, listening to that voice. She looked up at the woman and she smiled.

"Wally's alive," Jerusha said. "He's still alive. . . ."

United Nations
Manhattan, New York

LOHENGRIN STALKED DOWN THE hallway, leaning heavily on the aluminum cane. His head was less gauzed, but a silver medical patch was fixed over his seared eye. His rage radiated like heat from a fire. Bugsy walked on his left, Babel on his right like a cartoon demon/angel pair.

"Investigators," Lohengrin spat. "A month, and we can assemble *investigators* to observe the People's Paradise."

"China is getting most of its oil from the Nshombos," Babel said. "It would be naïve to expect them to abandon their own economic interests."

Lohengrin actually growled. Babel's brow clouded. This was apparently not the first time through the conversation.

"Hi," Bugsy said. "So things are going well, then?"

"The Committee is doing nothing about the child aces of Africa," Lohengrin said. "We are sitting on our hands, because of policy."

"Yeah. Picked up on that."

Lohengrin turned a tight corner and stepped into Gardener's suite. An IV drip was feeding into the woman's arm, but it didn't matter how many calories they pumped into her; Jerusha Carter was starving to death. The sight of her withering body was such a shock, Bugsy didn't immediately register the other two people in the room.

"Jonathan," Ellen said.

She looked beautiful. A deep brown sweater he hadn't seen her in before, and a long black wool overcoat. Her hair was in a new cut, swept back from her eyes. Her smile was almost gentle.

I used to spend time with that body naked, Bugsy thought with a pang of regret. But then he noticed the fedora scrap poking out of her coat pocket.

"Hey, Ellen," he said. "You look great."

"Thanks," she said.

Noel Matthews, sitting by the window, sniffed significantly and raised an eyebrow.

"Oh," Bugsy said. "Noel. Hey. That thing where I blew your cover in Paris?"

"You mean revealing me to the most powerful ace in the world, putting myself and my family at risk, and beginning a global campaign of extortion with my death as its only goal?"

"Yeah, that," Bugsy said. "*Really* sorry."

Gardener laughed, a slow, thick wheeze. Ellen took the clawlike hand. "Bugs," Jerusha said, shaking her head, "you haven't changed a bit."

"This is a mistake," Babel said. "Lohengrin, don't do this."

"Okay," Bugsy said. "Do what? What are we doing? Why am I here? Klaus called me and said that I should come over. . . ."

"Rusty," Jerusha said. "I want to see Rusty again. I promised . . . I said I'd stay alive for him. I don't want that to be a lie."

Bugsy nodded, quickly doing some mental recalculation. Jerusha and Rustbelt? So maybe he and Simoon/Cameo/Nick hadn't been the world's least likely couple after all.

"Rusty's still in Africa," Ellen said. "The best we can tell, he's leading a popular rebellion against the Nshombos' main lab outside Bunia."

"Bubbles is there as well, somewhere," Lohengrin said. "Mr. Matthews has agreed to transport Gardener to the site as a strictly humanitarian gesture of goodwill."

"Careful, old boy," Noel said. "You're starting to sound like an administrator."

"This," Barbara Baden said, "is the most intensely unprofessional, inappropriate plan I have ever seen."

"I'll tell you about Vegas sometime," Bugsy said. "Let me just make sure I've got this all straight. The UN is ignoring this child ace project. We are prohibited from going in to, say, help Rusty lead an unsanctioned vigilante action even though that's *exactly* what he did for us in Egypt. So instead, we're out of the kindness of our hearts shipping Jerusha from her deathbed . . . no offense . . ."

"None taken," Gardener said.

". . . to a war zone. With perhaps the intention that Cameo and I go along 'to help out' and if we should *just happen* to hook up with Bubbles, the world's most unkillable ace, and *accidentally* get involved with Rusty's war to stop these child ace motherfuckers and lose Tom Weathers all his new ace allies . . . Well, it wouldn't be like we went in there *looking* for trouble, right? I mean who could see *that* coming?"

"Yes," Babel said, a note of triumph. Cameo didn't speak. Lohengrin's gaze was challenging. Only Noel seemed as amused by the whole thing as Bugsy was.

"Sure, what the hell," Bugsy said.

"You've got to be joking," Babel said, aghast.

♥

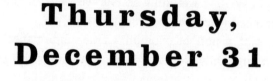

Thursday, December 31

NEW YEAR'S EVE

Bunia
People's Paradise of Africa

BUNIA WAS A FUME of smoke and gunpowder. Bunia was tumbled buildings and burning husks. Bunia was the stench of death and destruction.

Jerusha stumbled as Noel released her, blinking in the sunlight. "Holy fuck," she heard Bugsy comment behind her. Ahead, there were people stumbling through smoke and ruin. There were also several bodies, their outlines fuzzed by clouds of black flies. The husk of a tank sat in the middle of the road leading into the town. There was little left of the vehicle except the caterpillar treads and plastic bits, and the wreckage was half lost in a mound of orange-red powder.

Wally's work. It had to be.

"You're sure this is where you want to be?" Noel asked. She felt him touch her arm and pulled away from him angrily.

"Wally said he'd be here. He *is* here."

"Fine," Noel answered. He pulled off his dark glasses. His eyes were molten gold. "Bugsy, can you send a few wasps out, see if you can find Rustbelt?"

Jerusha was tired of waiting. Tired of half measures when she was so close. "Wally!" she yelled, as loudly as she could, her voice shrill and the effort tearing at her throat.

Noel hissed and looked as if he were about to jump somewhere else, his gaze sweeping around them. Cameo's eyes went round and large, her hand to her mouth. Wasps scattered from Bugsy's neck. "Are you *insane?*" Noel asked. "You have no idea if—"

"*Jerusha?*"

The faint call came from farther up in the town. She saw a crowd of people there dressed in ragtag fashion, some of them brandishing guns. There was a much larger figure in their midst, and Jerusha laughed-sobbed with relief at the sight of him. The rust on his body was terrible and thick, and she could see bandaged wounds and blood on him. But it was Wally. Alive.

She started walking as quickly as she could toward him, hating the old woman's shuffle that was all she could manage, hating that after only a few steps she had to stop to rest. He was staring at her as if she were some apparition, as if he didn't recognize her. There was a child standing alongside, a young girl; he had one arm around her protectively. "Jerusha?" he called again, and now he stirred. "*Cripes, Jerusha!*"

He limbered into motion like a locomotive, gathering speed, wrapped her up in his arms, lifting her, and she was laughing and he was laughing and she didn't care that it hurt. She hugged his massive head, she kissed his hard metal mouth. "Ow," she said finally. "Put me down, Wally. Ow . . . Really. Please."

He seemed to realize how tightly he was holding her, and his eyes went wide. He put her down gently and held her at arm's length. His gaze traveled up and down her skeletal body and settled on her thin face. "Jerusha . . . what's happened to you? How are the kids?"

"It's a long story. But the kids . . . the kids are fine. I got most of them out. Most . . ." She stopped, seeing again the faces of Efia, of Hafiz, of Naadir, of Pili and Chaga. Helplessly, she started to cry, and Rusty folded her into his iron arms again. She sobbed into his chest, then pushed away, wiping at her eyes. "I'm fine," she said. "There's nothing wrong with me that some home-cooked meals can't fix," she told him, hoping that he wouldn't hear the lie.

She glanced back to Noel, at Cameo and Bugsy. Cameo was smiling, and it was impossible to tell what Bugsy might be thinking, but Noel stared at her accusingly. Jerusha realized that her laughter had again morphed into helpless, joyous tears. "Wally, I missed you so much. I've been so scared for you, for both of us. . . ." She could say nothing more, only put her arms around him. She felt his massive hands on her back, holding her as if she were a stick that might break if he pressed too hard. She kissed him again. "You stayed alive for me."

"Yeah," he said. "I did." He sniffed. He seemed to notice the trio behind her then, and the steam-shovel jaw crinkled into a stiff grin. "Hey, Bugsy! Cameo! Noel! You guys came, too? Cool." Then he was looking at Jerusha once more, and the concern was back on his face. "The kids? They're really okay? You're okay?"

"Yes," she told him. "They're okay. Noel helped me get them to the States."

He sniffed again, nodding at Noel. "Good. That's really good. I missed you, Jerusha. I tried everything I could to keep those leopard fellas away from you."

"You did great, Wally." She touched the bandages around his arm and gave a laugh that was a half sob. "We're a heck of a pair, aren't we?"

"We're back together," he said. "That's good, isn't it?" He looked at her as if he were half afraid she was going to say no, and his vulnerability made the tears start again.

"Yeah," she said. "That's good. It's all I ever wanted." Over his shoulder, she saw the little girl coming up to them. Or more precisely, floating toward them; her feet didn't seem to be touching the ground. They were all being watched by the crowd, many of whom were pointing and smiling toward them. "Who's this?" she asked.

Wally craned his head, not letting go of Jerusha. "Oh," he said. "This is Ghost. I found her . . . Well, she found me, actually." Jerusha felt him start under her embrace, as if something had just occurred to him. "Nuts," he said. "Jerusha, the lab—that big one that the files you found talked about—I know where it is. Just outside of the town here. I found it, and I gotta go stop them and get those kids out. I was getting ready to do that, but these fellers over there"—he pointed to the crowd of poorly armed people on the street—"keep following me. If you could talk to them in French, tell them to stay here in town so they don't get hurt, then I can go to the lab . . ."

Fear stabbed her. He looked fragile, the rust nearly covering him, his skin bubbling and crusted with it. She also knew she could not stop him, that he wouldn't stop until he'd done what he came here to do—and that if she wanted to be with him, she had no choice, either.

"I'll go with you," Jerusha told him. "I'll help you."

"You're okay?" Wally asked. "Really?"

♣

Crowds were surging through the streets. Many carried weapons, real and makeshift. Many more carried goods looted from the stores and houses. A pall of smoke hung in the air over the city. The smoke was adding to an already beautiful sunset.

Noel rested his hands on his hips and took a slow 360-degree turn. "Well, word of the events here will certainly be winging its way to Kongoville."

"So, we gotta get going before they send any more soldiers," Rusty said. "We gotta get out to that Red House place right now!" He started away, his metal feet sinking into the soft asphalt road.

Noel leaped after him, and caught him by the wrist. He noticed when he took his hand away his palm was covered with rust. "Half a tic. Rusty, dear fellow. We might do well to talk this out a bit first." Noel paused and surveyed the big iron ace. "The quickest way in will be up the western slope. That will undoubtedly be rigged with motion sensors and cameras. If it were my task to guard this facility I'd also lay down claymore mines for an added surprise. Our best hope is for a two-pronged attack. Bugsy, Cameo, Gardener, and I will slip in from the west and cause enough of a ruckus so the alarm is sounded. Then Rusty will advance down the road and through the front gate. We had best wait for cover of darkness, however. And we will need some chicken wire."

Cameo looked up. She was wearing the battered fedora so it was Nick who looked through her eyes. "Chicken wire?"

"It will handle the RPGs that Rusty can't dodge. Trust me."

"Why am I not reassured?" Bugsy muttered.

"I'm counting on the guards to weigh the relative threats. Given a choice between dealing with gnat stings—"

"*Wasp* stings, please," Bugsy said. "Not that it'll make a damn bit of difference."

"Stop being so damn negative," Nick said with Cameo's voice. Bugsy subsided.

Noel went on. "—or a big iron imperialist at the front gate, they'll vote for dealing with Rusty."

"That puts Rusty in terrible danger," Gardener said.

"I'll be okay. I'm pretty tough." When Rusty looked at her his heart was in his eyes. Noel wondered if he realized that Gardener was dying, and that nothing could be done to prevent that outcome.

He shook off the sudden burst of melancholy and continued. "All of us are going to be in terrible danger. Rustbelt's better able to withstand the attack. You are rather like a tank, Rusty. Gardener, you'll need to deal with the claymores with fast-growing vegetation that will force them to detonate. Will you be able to do that?" She nodded. Noel was worried that the one sentence she had uttered had left her too weak to speak again. "We will then all converge on the Red House. Between Rusty's strength and Gardener's tree roots we ought to be able to crack it open."

"Can we go now?" Rusty asked.

"And what about all those soldiers with guns?" Bugsy asked, ignoring Rusty's plaintive question.

"They'll be focused on Rusty. I can account for a fair number of them, you as bug-boy can certainly discomfit them, Cameo as Will-o'-Wisp will add to the butcher's bill, and when that house starts to come apart I will lay you any odds that most of them will throw down their guns and present us with a charming view of asses and elbows."

"So what's the one big wild card, if you'll forgive the pun?" Nick said.

"Weathers. Our task is to hit fast, hit hard, destroy this final lab and their virus cultures, and get the hell out before the Radical can arrive."

"Will they send for him?" Bugsy asked.

Noel shrugged. "I would. But he's been totally focused on me and the Sudd. I think we'll have time."

"And if we don't?"

"Then it will be our asses and elbows presented. Once the sun has set, Lilith can get you all out, though I'll have to take Rusty separately."

Rusty frowned at the setting sun. "How soon can we go?"

"Soon enough."

"Good. So where do we get this chicken wire?"

♠

The Red House squatted in the darkness, unaware that a hundred thousand wasps were making their way through the brush, past the fences, into the air ducts and hidden trenches and outbuildings. The insects avoided the light, gathered in small clumps on the underside of leaves, followed along behind the soldiers who thought they were alone in the night.

Bugsy's head and part of his torso sat in the backseat of an improbable '67 Cadillac, nestled in the dense underbrush. "Okay, kids," he said. "I'm pulling the trigger."

Inside the compound, two soldiers walked through their patrol, bored and smoking. Then hundreds of small green wasps were crawling under their uniforms, stinging their mouths and eyes. One of the soldiers panicked, and his screams and gunfire brought the camp to life. Through thousands of multifaceted eyes, Bugsy watched the lab's internal security force rush to respond.

He kept on stinking the newcomers until someone dug out a flamethrower. "Okay," he said. "That's as distracted as I can get 'em. I'm pulling back."

"Let's go," Cameo said.

◆

Clangclangclangclangclang . . .

Wally charged down the middle of the road. He carried a wide, hastily built cage of iron rebar. A pair of spotlights followed his every stride. Somewhere, in the darkness outside the lights, automatic weapons chattered, kicking up little puffs of rust and dirt and blood.

Yeah, he had their attention.

He headed straight for the compound. Finally, finally, it was time to break that place. They could have started hours ago, but . . .

Rustbelt, fellow, you're rather like a tank, Noel had said. *Let us consider the possibilities.* And then he'd gone on and on and on about tactics and feints and RPGs for what felt like forever. That's why Wally carried the cage. Something about armor-piercing warheads and liquid copper and other stuff Wally didn't—

ka-RHUMP!

An explosion against the cage knocked Wally off his feet. It splattered him with what felt like lava, like white-hot rain. He heard rust sizzle, felt iron bubble. It hurt bad enough to make him cry out, but the round didn't cut him in half like it was supposed to.

Okay, so maybe Noel was right.

Wally reached the perimeter. Under a hail of grenades and small-arms fire, he grabbed two fistfuls of fence and went to town.

♥

Jerusha found herself crouched in the darkness under the trees, with the fence of the compound a hundred yards away. Wally was on the west side of the compound. She worried about him more than herself. He was all alone out there.

The *ka-RHUMP* of RPGs and the chattering of small-arms fire suddenly erupted on the other side of the compound grounds: Rusty's feint after Bugsy's initial probe on their side. They could hear shouting and see lights swaying and careening over the grass. With an audible *foomp*, two huge searchlights kicked out, their blue-white fury pointed toward the fencing on the far side. "Go!" Lilith hissed at Jerusha. "It's your turn."

Jerusha started to shuffle toward the fence, moving as quickly as she could. It wasn't fast enough for Lilith. She hissed audibly and grabbed her.

After a moment of coldness, they were there. "Can you do this?" Lilith asked. Jerusha nodded, not certain whether she was relieved or angry. She plunged her hand into her seed pouch, feeling for the kudzu seeds: she found them, and tossed them to the ground, opening them as they fell so that leafy vines rippled under the moonlight.

It *was* harder than she'd expected. Her exhaustion and weariness, the hunger that gnawed at her constantly, all made wielding her power more difficult. She rooted the vines hard, then wrapped the tendrils around and through the chain link. She leaned back as she guided the vines, pulling with them in sympathy as they tore at the fence. The smaller vines snapped from the strain, and she thickened them as the fence leaned, groaning, the metal protesting.

A pole snapped from the ground, trailing fencing, then another, and the vines pulled a section of the fence entirely down. Gardener nearly fell herself as the fence went down. Cameo started forward. Lilith waved her back. "Let her finish!"

Bugsy's wasps were hovering over the mines he'd found; Jerusha threw more seeds, this time letting the vines curl out along the ground, thrashing the ground where the wasps indicated. The mines exploded in gouts of black earth and yellow-orange bursts that nearly blinded them.

She staggered. She nearly fell. The edges of her vision had gone black, and she hoped none of them noticed.

"*Now!*" Lilith said. "Go! Gardener, let's get you to that house."

Cameo and a clotted swarm of wasps slid past her. Jerusha shuddered. Lilith came up behind her, dark hair and silver eyes, and folded her arms around her.

♣

Ka-phoom!

"What the hell?" Michelle muttered. The jeep bounced and jumped over the dirt road. Every time Michelle flew up and smacked down hard on the seat, she got a tiny zing of power. Night had fallen and all the shadows had fled. There were muted *pop-pop-pops* of gunfire. The jeep slowed and she noticed that the driver was gripping the wheel like no tomorrow. "It's okay," she said. "Just get me close and I'll walk the rest of the way."

The driver didn't look very relieved. He stopped the jeep and pointed into the jungle. "Take the path and you'll find the main road to the Red House," he said. "But you shouldn't go there. You will die."

Michelle jumped out of the jeep. "That's so sweet of you," she said. "But if there's any dying to be done, it won't be me who does it." He shrugged and jammed the jeep's transmission into reverse and spun around. In moments, he'd vanished down the road.

The path would have been difficult to see in daylight, but now it was almost invisible. But Michelle found it and plunged into the jungle.

It was a shock when she burst from the jungle onto a paved road. She'd expected to be struggling through the bush forever. There were more gunshots. And she started running up the road.

When she reached the top of the hill, she saw the Red House compound. It was chaos. The front gate was busted in. Smoke hung in the air from RPGs. There was a maze of holes blasted into the ground. A gunshot pinged into her. It was impossible to tell where it came from.

Perched above the jungle, the huge brick mansion and its ornate edifice looked out of place here. Fingers of vines were shooting up one side of the house, moving crazy fast. *Jesus Christ*, Michelle thought. *What the hell is Gardener doing here?*

Then she saw Rusty running around the other side of the building, grabbing weapons and hitting anyone he could get his hands on. The rage in his expression shocked Michelle. He was a sweet kid from Minnesota. He had no business having a look like that on his face.

But at least she had some help. She wasn't alone. And even in the midst of the smoke, gunshots, and screaming, that cheered her up some.

People's Palace
Kongoville, Congo
People's Paradise of Africa

SUN HEI-LIAN SAT ON the edge of the bed in her room in the vast People's Palace in Kongoville.

The only thing that moved about her was her eyes. They tracked Tom's every move as he paced back and forth in front of her. His tennis shoes made overlapping red tracks on the hardwood floor and throw rug. "I knew it all along," he said. He was talking so fast he was tripping over the words. "Okay. Okay. Not all along. Not when we were, like, squatting out in the bush together. But I knew he was going bad for a long time."

Hei-lian still said nothing. That was righteous. He had more than enough to say. She was just a woman, after all. And hadn't Brother Stokeley said, back when he was righteous, that the only place for a woman in the movement was prone?

A knock at the door made him jump and yell, "Shit!" Hei-lian jumped, too, going very pale. He wondered why she was so tightly wrapped.

"What the fuck do you want?" he hollered.

The door opened tentatively. A youthful aide wearing a colorful dashiki leaned in. "I beg your problem, Comrade Field Marshal," he said. "There . . . there is a problem at the Red House."

The Red House
Bunia, Congo
People's Paradise of Africa

LILITH HAD TELEPORTED THEM up the steep slope to the house, then vanished again, saying she was going to check on Rusty. Jerusha was so tired. So hungry. So empty of energy. But she had no choice, not if she wanted Wally to be safe.

She took a long, shuddering breath, trying to dredge up the will to remain standing. She could still hear the firing to the west, where he was. Around the corner of the massive structure of the estate house, she could see bright lights flaring where the main entrance must be. "Lots of soldiers there," Bugsy said. There was only his head and torso on the ground near her. "They're not liking the wasps much, though." He grinned.

"It's all yours, Gardener," Cameo said. She was still panting a bit from the climb. "Get us in there."

Jerusha could only see what was directly in front of her; all the rest was gone. Her hand slid again into the seed pouch, her fingers finding the two large baobab seeds she had left. She took one in her hands. "Back up," she told Cameo. Bugsy had already dissolved into a stream of wasps curling around the side of the house. "This is going to be messy."

She glanced up at the red brick walls—it was a shame, to tear down a grand, rambling Victorian edifice like this, and for a moment she felt regret at what she had to do.

So tired. She closed her eyes. *But you have to do it. For Rusty.* Jerusha took another slow breath. Tossed the seed to the ground at the base of the house. She could feel the life inside, feel it wanting release. She gave it permission.

The baobab tore roots into the ground and erupted upward, the trunk growing more massive by the second. She could feel the roots, plunging down and under the house, tearing into concrete, splintering supports.

The Red House moaned under the assault, and Jerusha moaned with it, the roots of the baobab seeming to tear at her own soul. Jerusha pushed the tree, forcing decades of growth in the space of a few seconds. A fissure opened in the foundation, running in a wild zigzag through the mortar of the bricks and climbing. Jerusha changed the direction of the baobab's growth: a crack appeared around the mass of the baobab's trunk. The house visibly lifted, and a mass of bricks fell from the second story to the ground, walls opening as the branches of the baobab tore at the wreckage. She could see inside: offices, desks, workers running wilding away from the destruction; people in lab coats, one in full biological hazard gear.

Jerusha stepped forward, still directing the tree's growth, making the hole in the side of the mansion large and easier to traverse. She was standing alongside the tree, her eyes slitted, her hand on the trunk so she could feel its life. Leaning against it because if she didn't, she would fall.

So tired.

♠

Wally set off a couple of mines as he barreled through the perimeter; they blew shrapnel up into his feet, cratering the rust. He'd let the pain take over later. After he smashed this place to rubble.

The defenders let up on the RPGs when Wally closed with the Red House—a sprawling, brick mansion. It was a relief to dispense with the cage.

The spotlights followed his every move, making him an easy target. Gunfire raked him from half a dozen directions. A few at first, then more and more bullets found their mark. They ripped through his corroded skin with little explosions of rust chips. Something hot grazed his waist. A shot dented his temple, blurred his vision, and left his ears ringing.

He made a big show of tearing through the defenders. Punching them, kicking them, smacking them with a length of rebar he'd pulled from the cage. And he disintegrated every weapon he could touch.

Wally didn't discriminate between the people in uniforms and people in lab coats. They were all part of this. They had all killed Lucien.

The house shook. It lurched, like something huge had grabbed and lifted it. Wally heard a momentous crash, like ten tons of crumbling brick. It came from around back, where Noel had taken Jerusha and the others.

All right, Jerusha!

She'd done her part. Now he just had to get her safe. Wally started working his way around the house.

♦

Gardener's vines had pulled down one side of the house. It had happened so fast, Michelle couldn't believe it for a moment. Then she started running toward the collapsing side. Gardener was bound to be close by.

Michelle wanted to know what the plans were. And she wanted to know how the hell Gardener and Rusty had ended up *here*. It was too damn dangerous for them.

Bullets hit her and RPGs exploded close by. That just plumped her up more. She released a barrage of bubbles as she ran. There were screams and some of the guards went down. They weren't dead—at least they shouldn't be. The bubbles were hard but rubbery. She didn't want to accidentally kill someone friendly. She had no idea who might be here with Rusty and Gardener.

As she got closer to the house, Michelle saw a shrunken, emaciated figure leaning against a massive tree trunk. The tree was still growing up into the air. *No,* she thought. *It can't be.* But in her gut she knew. She felt a chill run through her.

She stopped in front of Jerusha. The person leaning against the tree didn't look like Gardener anymore. Even in the gathering gloom, Michelle could see her sunken cheeks, the gauntness of her body, and the faraway look in her hollowed eyes.

Michelle knew that look. Jerusha was dying.

"Terrible, isn't it? One of the child aces bit her. She's been wasting away ever since."

It was Lilith. She was hidden by the shadows, but Michelle knew that voice. "Why am I not surprised you're in the middle of this," Michelle replied. "Why is she here? She should be in a hospital."

"She was. She wanted to come. For Rustbelt."

"Stop." Gardener opened her eyes and said in a whispery voice, "Stop. Please. Just destroy the lab."

"I'm sorry, Jerusha." Michelle gave Lilith one last hard stare, then ran into the Red House through the gaping hole that Gardener's tree had torn.

Inside, she stumbled over bricks and debris, past desks and fallen filing cabinets. A fluorescent light swung by a long electrical cord, unmoored from the ceiling. A guard appeared in the doorway and started firing at her with an automatic weapon. Most of the bullets hit her. She threw a bubble at him and he went down with a whimper.

Two more guards appeared, and shot her as well. She threw bubbles at them, too. Then she struggled through the rubble until she came to the staircase. She'd seen some labs on the second level.

The staircase had broken apart. A big gap separated the two sections. Michelle wasn't sure she could jump it at her current size. She wasn't sure she could have jumped it when she was skinny. But she had to get to the labs, so she gave a grunt and leapt across.

Her foot hit, then slipped. She went down hard on her knees. Another zing of energy. The banister groaned as she grabbed it. She pulled herself up and then ran to the top of the stairs.

A sheet of fire met her.

The heat. The light. Memories of New Orleans washed over her, and for a moment she could not move.

But what had happened with Drake hadn't hurt her. It had changed her. Michelle walked through the fire, curling her hand, forming a bubble in her palm.

When she emerged beyond the flames, she saw a small boy blowing a stream of fire from his mouth as if he were blowing soap bubbles. When he saw her, his jaw dropped and the fire stopped. Standing next to the boy was a man in a lab coat. He looked as surprised as the boy did. She released her bubble and it exploded on the floor in front of them. They were thrown back by the impact. She fired more rubbery bubbles to keep them down.

The doctor began to scramble to his feet, but the boy started crying and fire shot from his mouth again. The doctor shrieked. His lab coat caught fire and there was a nauseating smell as his hair began to burn. He started running, past her and down the stairs. But he didn't make the gap. There was another scream and a sickening crack as he landed on the floor below.

Michelle turned back to the boy. She said in French, "I'm not going to hurt you." But he started screaming. Flames shot out of his mouth again and the wallpaper in the hall caught on fire.

"Great," Michelle muttered. "Just great." She hopped over the hole in the floor, crouched down next to the boy, and grabbed his arms. She began to form a bubble around him. In a few seconds, he was encased. The bubble wasn't going to last long, but if he started breathing fire again, he'd use up the oxygen inside and knock himself out. She needed him out of the way while she destroyed the lab.

The first door she tried was stuck. Michelle blew it to pieces and stepped through the hole. Inside the room were lab tables and various pieces of equipment she didn't recognize. In one corner, three men wearing lab coats cowered. They began begging her for mercy.

"Get out," she said. They scrambled to their feet and ran past her. Michelle blasted everything in sight. Pieces of metal and glass flew into the air and rained down on her. Instead of going back out into the hall, she just blew a hole into the next room.

This room was like the last one. Tables, equipment, glass, cowering men in lab coats. Rinse. Repeat.

She worked her way through the labs on this side of the hallway. When she got to the end of this row of rooms, she went back into the hallway and checked on Fire Boy. He was sitting quietly in the bubble. He turned and looked at her quizzically. The bubble wouldn't hold much longer, so she needed to finish up quick. She bubbled and blew a hole in the door across the hall, and then went through it.

This lab was different. There were cots lining one wall. On the walls were brightly colored pictures of smiling children. It reminded Michelle of the lab she and Joey had found in the jungle. She felt sick.

She worked her way through the room, destroying the beds, the pretty pictures, the cabinets filled with syringes and bottles of the virus. Then she bubbled her way into the next room. More beds. More smiling pictures. It felt good to blow them up.

The last room contained rows of built-in refrigerated cabinets. They didn't last long. Room by room she systematically obliterated everything she found. She was thinner when she came back into the hallway.

Fire Boy was still in the bubble. Smoke was filling the hallway. Flames licked up the walls. Michelle touched the bubble and popped it. The boy looked up at her, giving her a small smile. She smiled back. He opened his mouth as if to speak, and a wave of fire enveloped her. He clamped his hands over his mouth.

Michelle squatted next to him and said, "You can't hurt me, but you should try not to open your mouth when there are other people around. At least until you figure out how to control your power."

He nodded. Then he smiled at her again. She smiled back. She couldn't help it. Then she said, "Come with me."

♥

Battle flashed and crackled all around the rambling Red House with its complicated compound roof.

Tom landed on well-tended lawn before the front portico. The first thing he saw was a sheet-lightning flicker of muzzle flashes beyond the prefab barracks between the main house and the gate. The rattle of automatic fire was near continuous.

Eyes beginning to water from the smoke that twined around him, he started to trot in that direction. A brilliant blue-white flash seemed to light the whole night sky ahead of him, accompanied by a nasty crack like the sound of lightning striking nearby. An RPG had gone off nearby. As he passed between two of the lightweight wood structures a window with a wall in it exploded outward toward him. A huge figure loomed there, misshapen and dark, like a hybrid of man and steel drum. A vast arm swung toward him, trailing wood splinters.

He bent his will to going insubstantial, to allow the powerful blow to pass right through him.

He didn't go insubstantial.

Fury spiked in him. *That bastard Meadows stole Cosmic Traveler!* Then a fist like a medieval mace clipped the side of his head and sent sparks bouncing off the inside of his skull. Tom spun down hard on his face on dirt worn bare by passing boots and compacted hard. The world reeled crazily about him. His stomach lurched.

Sheer anger drove him to push off from the merciless ground, snapping himself upright with unnatural strength. He found himself facing his attacker. The dude looked like the Tin Woodman on steroids. He had a lower jaw like a steam shovel. "So you're the fella they call the Radical, huh?" the metal man said in a loopy Minnesota accent. "Tough guy. Well, it's high time you picked on somebody your own size."

Tom tasted blood, turned his face to spit out a tooth. Then he slammed an uppercut into the rusted-over steel plate that covered the metal dude's gut. Iron groaned and buckled.

The metal man oofed and bent over. "Felt that one," he said.

Tom slammed an overhand right into the bucket jaw. The metal man flew backward through the corner of the same wall he'd just burst through. A corner of the barracks slumped on top of him.

Tom turned to look for new enemies. There was a terrific commotion coming from the far side of the Red House, toward the west. By the light of flames he saw what looked like the branches of a huge tree looming above the high-pitched slate roof.

I don't remember a great big tree there when I was here before, he was just thinking muzzily, when something like the steel jaws of a trap closed on either biceps.

He jerked his right arm forward. Skin beneath rust-roughened steel fingers. Tom slammed his elbow back against thick metal plate, felt it give. The iron man gasped in pain. The grip on Tom's left arm slacked.

He ripped free, spun to begin trip-hammering punches into the metal monster. The armor began to dent in on itself, the steel man to sag.

Then suddenly there were wasps whining around his ears, stinging his arms and neck and cheeks, and trying for his eyes.

♣

Bursts of automatic gunfire erupted to the south as the local soldiers regrouped. Cameo and Bugsy crouched behind the ruins of a jeep, its front wheels still gently spinning. "This is not going according to plan," Bugsy noted.

"The earring," Cameo said.

"What?"

"Ali's earring. Simoon can force them all into cover."

Bugsy took the chance of peering over the jeep's fender. A bullet hissed by, and he ducked back down. "It's in Central Park somewhere," he said.

"It's what?"

"Well . . . we broke up, you know?"

Ellen said something under her breath. She fumbled with something in her pocket, then the ruins of the fedora appeared. Nick lobbed a ball of lightning at the attackers, following it with ten or twelve marble-sized shockers as the first detonation was still rumbling. *"Go!"* Nick shouted. "Distract them, at least."

"I'm on it." Bugsy dissolved into an angry, living cloud. He flew in a funnel toward Weathers, weaving through the air in tight spirals, dropping low and racing to the sky, no tendril of wasps so dense that their loss would be crippling.

Tom Weathers's fists rose and fell, Rustbelt shuddering with every blow. A lightning ball exploded just to the Radical's left, illuminating him like a flashbulb—hair plastered to him by sweat, lips drawn back in an expression of inhuman rage.

Bugsy went in for the kill . . . or if not the kill, the serious annoyance. Fifty, maybe sixty wasps got in close enough to sting.

The Radical turned, shouting. Beams of terrible power leapt from his hands, sweeping the air, driving Bugsy back.

One beam hit Cameo.

♠

Michelle came out of the Red House with Fire Boy in tow. Rusty was lying facedown in the dirt next to the front stairs. A blast of light came from Tom

Weathers and streaked across the open lawn. She saw Cameo collapse. Bugsy was beside her, surrounded by wasps. *Oh, God,* Michelle thought, horrified. *They shouldn't be here.*

And she was scared. Scared for them, and scared for herself. After what had happened in New Orleans, she knew Tom Weathers was capable of doing anything.

She ran down the steps and knelt beside Rusty, dropping Fire Boy's hand. "Wally," she said, gently touching his shoulder. Rust flaked off beneath her fingers. "Can you hear me?"

He opened one eye, sort of. His metal skin was cracked and red with rust, and leaking blood. "Bubbles," he said. "How'd you get here?" His voice was weak.

"Oh, the usual," she said, trying to keep her voice light. "Teleported to Africa with Noel. Came up the Congo. Found some remote labs. Killed Alicia Nshombo. Heard there was a party going on here."

He tried to smile, but it came out as a wince. He rolled onto his side. "We gotta get rid of the lab. And Gardener . . ."

"The lab is done." She wasn't going to tell him about Jerusha. Not any more than he probably already knew. "Now you stay down and let me take care of Weathers."

"You betcha," he said with a groan.

Fire Boy tugged on her pants leg and then pointed to Rusty. "Friend?" he asked and he managed not to set anyone, or anything, on fire.

She nodded. The boy sat down on the steps near Rusty. Michelle wanted him to be in a safer place, but there was no safe place here.

She ran toward Weathers, releasing a barrage of bubbles. As they hit, his flesh ripped open. *Ha!* Michelle thought. An angry scream came from Weathers. It was frustration and fear. And it made Michelle smile. *Now you're scared, too. You bastard.*

She hurled more bubbles. She made them heavy and fast. Weathers dodged the first few, but then one caught him and propelled him backward. He looked like a cartoon character, his legs splayed out, body doubled over. He landed in the shredded lawn and rolled. The next bubble exploded by his ear, and half of his pretty face was stripped to muscle and bone.

He popped up like a jack-in-the-box. "You *bitch!*" he screamed. A nimbus of yellow light surrounded him, bright as the sun. The beam that flew from his fingers was blinding, too bright to look upon. It hit her, threw her back, and made her fatter.

She lumbered to her feet and released another round of bubbles at him. "Why is it when a man is getting his ass kicked by a woman he has to call her a bitch? I mean, can't you use some imagination, Weathers?" *Anyone else would have been down. Anyone else would be dead.* She didn't know if she could stop him. And if she couldn't, what would happen to everyone else?

Her bubbles threw him back again. He gave another shriek of frustration. "You slut! That hurt!" Then he hurled a light bolt at her. It lit Michelle up like Christmas. She blobbed out a little, and felt herself get denser. The power was fire in her veins again.

"*Again!*" She fired a huge, heavy explosive bubble at him. "*With!*" Another bubble. "*The!*" Another bubble. "*Lame-ass!*" Another bubble. "*Remarks!*" Another bubble. His face was hamburger, his clothes were rags, his lean torso sheeted in blood, but still the light poured from him. He would not go down.

"Great," she said. "I'm going to have to keep listening to your blather even longer." Her hands trembled. She kept bubbling. She had to stop him.

"You fat whore!" Another bolt of light. Michelle rolled her eyes as it hit. Her clothes were smoking.

"That's horizontally challenged American to you," she yelled. "And I'm not a whore. I'm just popular!"

God, I hate this guy. She hated him for what he'd done to Drake. She hated him for what he'd done to her. Hated him for helping turn children into jokers, killers, freaks. Hated herself for failing. For always failing everyone. She couldn't be a hero. She didn't even know how.

She put all the hatred into a bubble and let it go.

◆

There was movement inside: someone coming toward her, not fleeing from the destruction. Jerusha opened her eyes wide, alarmed.

It was a child.

They'd talked about this, as they'd planned the assault. Jerusha had warned them. "They'll have child aces, kids that they've subverted and twisted, with God knows what abilities. They're dangerous, all of them. You may have to be ready to kill a child to save yourself."

She'd warned them.

But seeing the boy, Jerusha hesitated for a breath: with uncertainty, with weariness. For all she knew this could be one of the kids on which they'd been experimenting, an innocent. One of those they'd come to save. "I won't hurt you," she said. "Do you speak English?"

The child did not move, did not answer. He stood and stared at her, his face a mask. He was skinny, homely, an ungainly boy with a bush of unkempt hair. "Do you have a name?" she asked him. "What do they call you?"

"Wrecker." His accent was British, his smile cold. The sudden twist of his lips, the satisfaction and rage in the expression, told her that no, she was wrong. This was something dangerous. This was another one like Leucrotta, like the Hunger who had bitten her.

Jerusha started to reach for her seed pouch again, but it was already too late. The child was holding a red brick from the rubble of the wall in his hand. With a smile, he underhanded it in her direction, softly.

A foot from her, the brick exploded, suddenly and violently, the concussion tossing her backward, and Jerusha felt terrible, white pain rip across her abdomen. Her hands reaching into the seed pouch were suddenly slick and heavy, and there was blood—far too much of it—pouring from her, and she was falling, her seeds spilling to the ground below her, her red, red blood drowning them, and Wally was shouting but his voice came from a world away and night was coming and . . .

"Wally," she cried into the darkness. "I'm sorry . . ."

♥

The flares and flickering glares of battle iridesced across the surface of the bubble as it swelled toward him. For a moment he saw his distorted reflection: face huge and swollen, small body dwindling to tiny legs, like a caricature drawn by a drunk Ren Faire artist. He looked beat to shit, one eye swollen shut, lips puffed, blood dripping over the war paint he still wore from the long-ago ritual in the Bahr al-Ghazal.

Moving faster than it seemed, the bubble clipped him. Tom screamed as it released its energy in an explosion that whited out his vision and consumed his right shoulder and side in shattering pain.

And then he was caught in a swirling blackness. It seemed to bear him up and up, like a drain spiraling him into the sky. He felt the shattered ribs and the bones of his shoulder joint knit themselves back together with a healing agony worse than the pain of the bubble's destruction.

He had an impression of floating several stories above the world, buoyed by a black anger, a volcanic rage that dwarfed the passion that had consumed him so long. It was as if his consciousness were a tiny chip afloat on a sea of black lava, of elemental fury and mindless malice.

As from a very great height he saw a black-taloned hand the size of a minivan rise into his field of vision. A blue nimbus crackled about the crooked tips of its fingers, then leaped away toward the fat woman who stood on the ground glaring up at him. The lightning struck her, lit her like the filament of an incandescent bulb. Yet when the discharge died away to smolder on the ground around her, she still stood, apparently unharmed. She had only gotten fatter.

She raised her own hand, snapped it forward. A bubble swelled from it, zipped toward him. He took it in the gut like a slam from a sledgehammer mated to a cattle prod.

Pain exploded through him. He heard a voice that wasn't his—or anything human—bellow from a throat that wasn't human, either. Through the dazzling agony he felt strength surge into him like a hit of the strongest speed ever. Felt himself *grow*.

He had a sense of a vast tumescence surging from his loins, a quivering hard-on for everything that lived. And then he was swirled down into the blackness, the pit of rage that was the consciousness of the monster he had become.

♣

"Wow," Michelle said softly. "Didn't expect *that*."

Weathers was growing. Surging up into the air like Gardener's baobab tree. His flesh turned the color of rotten plums. Horns sprouted on his head. Long white teeth like knives filled his mouth. His hands curled into claws. His eyes turned into burning yellow slits. He was ten feet tall, twenty, thirty. And an impossibly enormous erection grew from his crotch, pointing at her like an accusing finger.

"You should really put that thing away before something happens to it," she said.

The thing in front of her bellowed. It was a mindless sound: harsh, ear-splitting, filled with rage. Michelle had a moment of panic. She'd never seen anything like this. She had no idea what it was. But it didn't matter. She was going to do her best until she couldn't do anything at all.

The thing—the monster—bellowed again. Then it started toward her, Fire Boy, and Rusty.

"Hey!" Michelle hurled a medicine-ball-sized bubble at it as she led it from her friends. "I'm the one you want. Come on, big boy. Here's where the action is."

The monster howled in pain and staggered as the bubble exploded on its thigh. Lightning danced across its claws and crackled from its horns, blue-white against the night sky. A bolt stabbed down at her, just missing as she leapt aside. The earth smoked where it hit.

Michelle let a stream of bubbles go, aiming for the ground below the creature. A crater opened up and the monster gave a frustrated scream as it tumbled down into the pit. Michelle tried to bulldozer earth on top of it with a stream of bubbles, but it roared again and jumped out of the hole. It landed hard on its hooves, making the earth shake all around her. A turret on the Red House came crashing down behind them.

"Crap," Michelle said as it ran toward her. The monster leapt into the air, and then landed on top of her.

Her body blossomed as she was squished into the ground. She bubbled, forcing the monster off balance. It staggered and slipped off her.

As Michelle climbed out of the monster's footprint, she started bubbling again. She was beginning to think there was no way she could defeat this thing. On the other hand, it didn't appear as if he could hurt her, either.

♠

"See what you've done now?" said Mark Meadows.

The hippie floated in what seemed like midair. He sat in full lotus, naked but for the long grey-blond hair streaming down around his skinny shoulders. The space Tom found himself sharing with his nemesis seemed lit by a violet glow. Behind Mark glowed, for want of a better word, a backdrop that looked like a sort of great big Rorschach blot tie-dyed in a gaudy rainbow of colors. The bright golden sunburst ball in the middle surrounded Mark like a full-body halo from a medieval painting of a saint.

"Fuck me," Tom said. "You've got me trapped in a fucking *hippie poster*. And you're quoting Oliver Hardy at me." He shook his head. "All it's missing is bad sitar music and dope barely masked by sandalwood fucking incense."

Mark raised two fingers. Marijuana and sandalwood filled the air. Sitar music began to play. "Welcome to my subconscious. Or should I say, welcome *back*."

"What happened?"

"You got really, badly hurt. The trauma shock was enough to kick Monster free. Now neither of us is in control. Happy?"

"Oh, I'm fucking overjoyed. *You hippie piece of shit!*" Tom launched himself at Mark. The cross-legged man simply receded before him. As if he were chasing his own image in a mirror. Screaming with rage Tom raised his hands and willed forth sunbeams. They did not shine. "Your powers don't work here," Mark said, shaking his head half sadly, half in seeming gentle amusement. "The few that you have left."

Tom launched a flying kick. But the floating man turned sideways. Tom flew past. Then, somehow, was facing him again. He tried throwing punches. Kicks. Spitting.

All had the same effect on his enemy.

At last Tom felt himself hunched over, clutching his thighs and panting. "Don't think you've won," he wheezed. "You can't beat me. You're nothing! I'm everything you could ever hope to be in your miserable pencil-necked life. I'm *more!*"

To his surprise Mark nodded. "That's true," he said. "I tried to bring you back for years. Dedicated my life, my whole existence, to that holy quest. Neglected my job, neglected myself. Neglected my family, even though I loved them desperately. I did it because I wanted to do right. Wanted to save the world. And because I wanted the girl. But mostly because I wanted to *belong.*"

"What are you rattling on about?"

"I never did. Never *belonged.* I was always the odd kid out at school. Always had my nose in a book. At home, too. My dad was a good man, in his way. I found that out later when we got to really know each other, like, as adults—back when I was first on the run with Sprout, and he swallowed a lot of his prejudices and preconceptions to help us because he thought that was the right thing to do. But back when I was a boy he was supercompetitive. Never could figure out why I wasn't interested in athletics or following him into the military."

Tom tried to say something. But Mark wasn't paying him any attention. Tom lunged at his nemesis. And ran right through him as if he were less than shadow.

"I wanted to belong," Mark said. "To be part of something. To have a sense of purpose. Have shape, you know? Then later, after I got you, got to be you for just one night, that wasn't what I wanted anymore. Oh, I wanted those things too—got them all, too, in their own ways—and wasn't always happy with how that turned out. But I found what I really wanted was something else."

"So you turned out to be just a fucking adrenaline junkie? Just did it for the rush?"

"No. Well, maybe a little. But after I'd had a taste of being you—the Spirit of Revolution—I wanted that certainty. That wild, pure conviction of knowing you were right, and being able to act without doubt or compromise. Of being certain. That most of all. To get rid of my confusion. And that was the cause of my greatest sin: the hunger for the one thing I *couldn't* have. *Certainty.*"

"So you want to fucking *atone* for me. For *me*. The only thing in your life you ever got right."

Mark smiled gently. "You see it the way you see it. I see you as the greatest mistake of my life. I did some good along the way, man. I helped people. It cost me a lot of pain. Along the way I made mistakes that cost others pain. But it was all just trying to do the right thing.

"And it turns out . . . that's no excuse. Intention doesn't matter. Results matter. If you hurt people, it doesn't mean a thing that you thought you were doing it for your own good."

"That's why you're such a loser, Meadows," Tom said. "You were never willing to do what it took."

"Ah, no. I was too willing. In that I was like you. That was what gave rise to you. And if you're going to tell me you can't make an omelet without breaking eggs—that metaphor only makes sense if you're a cannibal."

Tom could feel titanic forces surging around them: electricity and explosions and equally palpable eruptions of rage and triumph and lust. "This can't last," he said. "Monster will run out of rage eventually. And then I snap back in charge. And you'll still be nowhere, man."

Mark shook his head. "No. There are too many of them. You've done too much damage—to them as well as others. You've made it personal. If you return to the world of form they'll simply kill you."

"That'll kill you too, you stupid cocksucker."

"Yes. We're trapped in a burning house, you and I. If my death is the only way to stop you, and I believe it is, then I'm happy to die." He shrugged. "That's the way of the world anyway, isn't it? No one here gets out alive. Did you think your ace powers made you any different?"

Tom's thoughts had cleared. "They won't kill me," he said. "Not if I'm helpless. Their bourgeois sensibilities won't let them. And if I'm not help-less—"

He grinned.

◆

Wally felt like a sack of broken bones rattling around inside an iron whiffle ball. Except whiffle balls didn't have as many holes as he did.

The Radical had hurt him bad. His ribs were broken. Maybe even shat-tered. If he weren't a joker, they'd be sticking through his side right now. As it was, he could feel bone scraping on iron every time he moved, like finger-nails on a blackboard. The pain spiked with every breath. It took everything he had not to pass out.

He tried to stand, to push himself to his feet. But a rivet on the inside of his shoulder caught something squishy, like a tendon or a flap of mus-cle. It pinched a nerve, chewed it, mangled it. White-hot pain surged up his neck and into his brain. Wally staggered, but he grabbed hold of a branch of the tree that had exploded through the Red House, and made himself keep going.

He had to get to Jerusha. She could still get out of this. They'd find a way to cure her. He'd failed to save Lucien, but he sure as heck would save Jerusha. Nothing mattered but that. The Radical fella had turned into a gi-ant monster. Bubbles was fighting him, but that did not matter now. There was no more he could do to help. All that mattered was Jerusha.

A bullet pierced a weak spot behind his shoulder. It ripped through the meaty part of his bicep, but ricocheted back inside when it hit solid iron on the way out. It sliced through something else on the rebound. His arm went numb. It didn't move right anymore.

Wally came around the corner just in time to see a boy emerge from the wreckage of the house, toward Jerusha.

"Jerusha! Look out!"

She didn't hear him. She was watching the boy. It was too dark and chaotic to see what he lobbed at her.

But not so dark that Wally couldn't see the fear flash across Jerusha's face.

Not so dark that Wally couldn't see the explosion.

Not so dark that Wally couldn't see the concussion fling Jerusha back-ward. Not so dark that he couldn't see her land, crumpled, like a rag doll.

Not so dark that he couldn't see the seeds pouring out of her pouch . . . the blood pouring out of her belly, black as ink. Then lightning flashed from the talons of the giant monster, and turned it red for an instant. So much red.

He staggered to her. "Jerusha!"

She called his name. "Wally. I'm sorry."

And then he was kneeling over her, cradling her, stroking her hair, calling to her again and again. "Please don't go," he cried. "You're the best friend I ever had."

But she was gone.

The boy who'd killed her watched it all with a cold smile. His eyes were just as dark, just as soulless, as Ghost's had been that first night she appeared to Wally.

Wally stood. "You killed my girlfriend."

Something inside him screamed in rage, called for justice, demanded revenge. One punch is all it would take.

But something else inside him spoke with Jerusha's voice, the voice of reason. *He's just a little boy.*

If Ghost could be fixed, so could he.

Whatever the boy saw in Wally's eyes, he turned and ran deeper into the ruined mansion. Wally caught him in a few strides. He pushed the boy down, pinned him face-first to a shattered tile floor with one foot on his back. Wally looped the rebar around the kid's wrists and ankles.

It was difficult because he couldn't use one arm. But when he finished, the boy who'd killed Jerusha was stuck hog-tied in an iron lariat.

Wally collapsed.

♥

Ellen lay on the ground, staring up at the night sky as if in surprise. Her skin all down the right side was black where it wasn't bloody. The fedora—Nick— lay five or six feet away, the last low flames smoldering in the ruined felt.

"Are you okay?" Bugsy said, but he knew that she wasn't. That she wasn't going to be. *"Medic!"* he shouted. He was standing naked in the middle of a battlefield. The roaring detonations of Monster and Bubbles drowned his voice, but he kept shouting.

Lilith appeared at his side. "Get down, you idiot," she hissed, but Bugsy ignored her.

"She needs help," Bugsy said. "She's hurt!"

Lilith bent down and looked at Cameo's ruined body with a passionless eye, and then shook her head.

"You can get her to a hospital," Bugsy said. "Something."

"I have an idea," she said, and a moment later was gone.

"Bugsy," Ellen gasped. Her voice was thick.

"I'm here," he said, taking her hand.

"It hurts," she said.

♣

All around, people screamed and died. But the only thing Wally heard was Jerusha's final words. *I'm sorry.* They echoed through his head, over and over again.

He'd failed Jerusha. He'd failed Lucien. He'd failed Simoon and Hardhat and King Cobalt. He'd let down everybody who had ever cared about him. *Good old Rustbelt.*

Wally rolled onto his side, on the arm that didn't make him pass out. He teetered to one knee. A charred body—*Cameo?*—lay sprawled on the earth, curled in on itself, barely moving. Bugsy cradled her, crying. His tears glistened with flashes of lightning and the light of explosions as Bubbles battled the gigantic *thing* that Tom Weathers had become.

Lilith—Noel—surveyed the carnage with a strange expression on her face. From across the smoking battlefield, she looked Wally in the eye. Then a flash of lightning made her silver eyes blaze bright, and she was gone. Bugsy saw her vanish, too. He swore. Michelle was the only person still fighting, and she was losing.

Wally steeled himself against the pain. He gritted his teeth, but a moan still escaped his lips when he pushed himself upright. If killing Wally could occupy the monster for even a few seconds, maybe it would help Michelle, or give Bugsy time to get some help for Cameo.

I'm sorry, Ghost. Guess I failed you, too.

♠

Chernabog, Michelle thought as she flew through the air. *That's what he looks like. That damn big demon from Fantasia. And I look like one of those dancing hippos. Only filthier and less graceful.*

She smashed into a small grove of trees, flattening them as she landed.

The monster had grown tired of lighting her up with bolts of electricity and starlight. Now it was tossing her around like a rag doll.

Michelle groaned as she got up. She was terribly heavy now, despite bubbling at him as fast as she could. As she moved toward the monster again, her feet sank into the ground. The monster roared at her. Its massive erection waggled.

"You have *got* to be kidding me," she said. "A huge, tumescent penis? That is one ginormous cliché, dude." While she was talking, she formed bubbles in her palm: tiny, almost invisible, but extremely dense bubbles. Then she streamed them at the monster.

When they struck, it howled in pain and rage. Its hideous purple-black skin peeled back, exposing pulpy red muscle and bone, but the damage didn't seem to slow it down at all. It dashed toward her again, trailing blood. Where the blood fell on the ground, the grass hissed and burned.

Michelle tried to run away, but the monster's stride was too long. It grabbed her as if she weighed no more than a sparrow and hurled her at one of the smaller buildings. She went through the concrete walls as if they were paper. Her body blobbed out again. Dust, mortar, and cement block bits and pieces covered her as she rolled to a stop.

Michelle saw that Rusty and Fire Boy were no longer on the steps. As she glanced around, she saw Cameo, Bugsy, and Lilith. They were huddled together. At least Lilith could teleport them out if things got too bad.

As she pushed herself up, she glanced over her shoulder. The monster was bearing down on her again. She bubbled and blasted holes in its knees. That only pissed it off more. It grabbed her, hoisted her thirty feet into the air, and swung her around and around its head.

Then it released her.

Michelle saw the Red House coming at her at breakneck speed. It was burning now. When she landed, she would be buried in fire and brick. How the hell were the others going to fight against that thing while she bubbled her way out? And she was afraid again.

She hit with a deafening crash, scattering bricks in all directions and sending fire and ash into the sky. Walls crumbled as her body smashed into them. Weakened floorboards cracked beneath her weight. She smashed down through one floor, then another. As she came to a stop in what must have been the cellar, the roof collapsed above her. A moment later what was left of the Red House came down on top of her.

"Crap," she said.

Kongoville, Congo
People's Paradise of Africa

THE GLASS COFFIN WAS thick. A sledgehammer would take too long, might not work, and the good citizens of Kongoville would come and tear him apart for desecrating their heroine's grave.

Noel stood in the door of the mausoleum and looked up and down the street. Things were oddly quiet, though he could see some broken windows in shops where looting had broken out as the country coped with the idea that the Nshombos were dead.

At one of the construction sites the cranes stood idle, but a lone backhoe was moving the remains of the building that had been demolished to make room for another grandiose monument to the People's Paradise of Africa.

He didn't like teleporting into moving objects, but he didn't want to take the time to run down the street. And that might draw the attention of the nervous policeman who stood ready to direct traffic if there had been any to direct.

Just like shooting. Lead the target. And he made the jump.

The driver yelled in terror as Lilith appeared, standing on his lap. He tried to eel out the door so Noel lost his precarious balance and fell sideways banging his head hard on the side of the cab. He managed to snag the back of the man's shirt with one hand while with the other he drew his gun.

He drove the barrel into the base of the driver's skull. "Drive or I'll kill you," he said in French.

The man's head nodded with the speed of a needle on a sewing machine, and he resumed his place behind the controls.

"Drive to the mausoleum." The man rolled a terrified eye at him. "Do it!"

As they rumbled down the street the traffic cop gaped at them and began pawing for his radio.

They reached the mausoleum. "Knock down the wall."

"Sir, please . . ."

Noel fired a shot right by the man's ear. He screeched, put the backhoe in motion. The wall came down.

Some of the debris fell onto the coffin. Noel saw a few cracks. "Move that crap and break the glass," he ordered.

It seemed to be taking forever, manipulating the hydraulics, lifting the front bucket, using it to push aside the fallen stones. Finally the glass was exposed.

The driver's hands were trembling. "Sir, she is our hero. To desecrate—"

"She's going to live again and save—" His inventiveness failed him. Noel could hear sirens drawing ever closer. "You remember how she saved Tom Weathers, brought him back from the dead?" The man nodded. "Well, her power still lives and she's going to bring Dr. Nshombo back."

The man enthusiastically obeyed. On the second blow the glass broke. Noel leaped from the cab. Cops were clawing their way over the rubble. Bullets began to snap and whine around him. Noel snatched the medal off the corpse's neck, then staggered as a bullet took him in the shoulder. For an instant he felt only extreme heat at the point of impact. He knew the pain was coming.

He made the jump back to the Red House.

The Red House
Bunia, Congo
People's Paradise of Africa

ELLEN'S BREATH WAS SHALLOW, her eyes fluttering. Lilith pressed the golden medallion into her good hand. Bugsy held his breath. Behind them, Monster roared, a sheet of lightning turning the night to day.

Ellen closed her eyes. Someone he'd never met opened them. He was suddenly very aware of being naked. "Hi," he said. "I know this is going to seem a little weird, but the thing is, you're dead? And I kind of need your help."

"I know what I am," the new woman said. Her voice had an African accent.

"Great," Bugsy said. "Really that's great. I was thinking if you could just patch Ellen back up, that would be really, really cool. Then we could—"

The woman sat up slowly. Ellen's skin cracked and split, blood rolling down her side in a crimson stream. "No," the woman said. "The time has passed for that. Help me stand."

Bugsy took her good arm and lifted. She seemed lighter than Ellen. Less substantial. The Lady of Pain turned her head as if no terrible injuries had disfigured her. Her expression was frank and evaluating. Bugsy turned with her, and saw what she saw.

Bodies. Dozens of them. Men in the tattered uniforms of soldiers or the white smocks of nurse attendants. Children lying flat on the ground to avoid the violence all around them, or already dead. And beyond them, in the ruins of the Red House, Bubbles and Monster trading terrible blows.

With every strike that Monster landed, Bubbles grew, and with every exploding bubble that detonated against Monster, the creature became larger, its claws and penis waving in the African air. Each incapable of harming the other, and both wreaking terrible damage all around them. Monster howled at the moon above them.

It struck Bugsy that both the combatants were white, and the dead around them black.

"You do not know the pain I have carried," the Lady of Pain said. He thought at first she was looking at the dead, but when he followed her gaze, it was on the charred remnant of Nick's fedora. She turned to look at him. Cameo's good eye narrowed. The burned one was too damaged to close. "With every healing gesture, I have carried the pain. Do you understand what I am saying? They call me an ace, and all that I have been given is pain."

Ellen, Bugsy thought. *This isn't the Lady of Pain, whatever the voice sounds like. I'm talking to Ellen.*

"Please," Bugsy said. "Could you just heal—"

"This is no day for healing. This is a day for the ending of things," the Lady of Pain said. "Tom Weathers has killed me. Let him take the pain that I carried."

Something came out of her, a bolt of light that was not light, a heat that froze. The air between the Lady of Pain and the monster writhed and shuddered. Bugsy felt the hair on his arms and the back of his neck rise.

◆

And a world of hurt enveloped Tom Weathers.

It was as if he were being wrenched apart and crushed and suffocated and burned alive. All at once. As if it were happening to each and every nerve ending in his body. Every atom.

He struck out. The pain only grew, impossibly grew. It began to eat at his mind like flame at paper.

"Here's what's happening," Mark said, his words clear through the horrific all-consuming agony. "One of those eggs you broke so cavalierly has been put back together again. Sort of. Just long enough to pay you back for all the pain you caused others. *With* that pain."

Tom tried to say something. He could only scream. Even in his unimaginable torment he knew that Meadows felt every bit of it, as strongly as he did. Yet the old hippie spoke as serenely as ever a martyr did through flames.

"Remember Dolores Michel, Tom?" he asked. "Our Lady of Pain? She couldn't just take on herself the pain of others. She could also give that pain back."

The Radical tried to raise a final fist of defiance. But that emotion crisped and burned to ash as well.

And in that agony, he died.

♥

The quiet seemed unnatural. Noel became aware of the whimpers and cries from the wounded. The medal gleamed against Cameo's chest, her hands still clutched around it.

But the demon was gone. There was a form lying on the ground. Noel got to his feet and tottered toward the body. He had to draw the gun with his left hand. The wound in his shoulder had left his right arm useless.

Shock brought him to a stop. Instead of a powerfully built man in his forties there was an emaciated figure with long grey hair and a beard like the remnants of a torn spiderweb. Blood streaked the body, drawing the insects. Noel holstered his gun and laid two fingers at the base of the man's throat. There was a threadlike pulse. "He's not dead," he said. "Even after all that, the bastard Weathers is still not dead."

"He is," came Bugsy's voice from over his shoulder. "That's Mark Meadows."

♣

Michelle bubbled away the last of the Red House, swearing as she went. When she emerged from the rubble, the monster had vanished. The gunshots had died away too, as had the explosions.

She brushed away ash and cinders as she picked her way through the debris. Bugsy, Rusty, and Lilith stood grouped around a man lying on the ground. Bugsy was naked. She didn't see Cameo or Gardener anywhere and that scared her.

"He should be killed," Lilith was saying, with the matter-of-fact air of a person discussing whether to take the bus or a taxi.

The man on the ground was slight in build, almost emaciated. His face was lined and there was a shock of grey-blond hair on his head. A long, thin, scraggly beard covered what looked like a weak chin. He looked about the same age as Michelle's father.

"But that ain't Tom Weathers," Rusty said, confused. "I dunno who that guy is, but he's some other fella. And he ain't that demon thing neither."

"Yes and no," said Bugsy. "He's Mark Meadows. His ace is to turn into other people when he takes drugs, and he's been on a really long, lousy trip. He's the guy the Radical, I don't know . . . *hijacked*, I guess."

Rusty shook his head. "He's just lying there. Doesn't seem right to kill someone that helpless."

Lilith rolled her silver eyes. "However it happened, it could happen again. Weathers is too dangerous to be allowed to live. And the only way to kill Weathers is to kill Meadows. They're one and the same."

"Well, not exactly," Bugsy said, "but killing him is still the smart move. Even if he's not Weathers now, he might turn back into Weathers when he wakes up."

"I'll do it," said Lilith. "What's one more death in the midst of . . ." She gestured at the carnage around them.

Michelle stepped closer. She wondered again how Niobe could have fallen in love with this man. "There's been enough killing here."

"This is Tom Weathers," Lilith said. "I will not allow him to simply walk away."

"You don't get to choose," said Michelle. "You're an assassin. You murder people in cold blood for money. And as far as I can tell, you feel no remorse for what you've done. That makes you a sociopath. You can cut the crusts off it all day long and you'll never make *that* anything but a shit sandwich. Yes, I've killed people too, but I've never killed anyone who wasn't trying to kill me. I've never killed anyone in cold blood. I've never befriended someone so I could sneak in their room later and slit their throat. And just so we're clear, I have never felt good about killing anyone, even when the choice was me or them. You can't wash off what you've done with tea and crumpets and pretty clothes, Noel. That's the biggest difference between us. There isn't a day that goes by where I don't mourn and regret what I've done."

"I had no idea you were the only one among us who possessed such moral clarity and purity," said Lilith. "By all means hug that close, Bubbles. As for Weathers . . . do whatever you want. It's on your heads." She walked away into the darkness.

Then Meadows groaned and opened his eyes. He sat up and looked up at them, dazed.

"Time to shit or get off the pot," said Bugsy. "He fucking killed Cameo. In Paris he killed Garou and the owl guy and a bunch of security. He almost killed Klaus. If it weren't for him and the Nshombos, Gardener would be alive. And how many more? Hundreds? Thousands? Mark Meadows may not be Tom Weathers, but he created him."

"I did," Mark Meadows said softly. There were tears in his big blue eyes.

"Seriously," Michelle told him. "Don't contribute."

"If things were reversed," Bugsy went on, "if it was us sitting there crying, Weathers would be peeling our brains open, scooping out the innards, and pissing down our necks while he laughed his ass off. He would have killed all of us as soon as look at us."

"Yes," said Michelle, "and if we kill him now, we might as well be Weathers. If we kill him now, it will be revenge, pure and simple."

"Fine with me," Bugsy snapped back. "What do you suggest, Bubbles?"

"Mercy," she said. She looked at Rusty. He was holding his arm, which hung at an odd angle. Tears ran down his cheeks, leaving streaks of brown. His pain was naked and raw. So was Bugsy's. And Michelle had no power to fix that. "Rusty," she said, "how do you vote?"

♠

Friday,
January 1
NEW YEAR'S DAY

The Red House
Bunia, Congo
People's Paradise of Africa

"YOU'RE STILL NAKED," BUBBLES said.

"Yeah," Bugsy said. "I keep meaning to go get my pants, but . . . I'll get to it."

Ellen lay where she had fallen, the golden medallion of the Lady of Pain in the grass at her side. The ruins of Nick's hat rested under her head like a pillow. Her ruined face was peaceful. Like she was asleep. He kept expecting her to shudder the way she had when a chill touched her.

"She did it," Bugsy said. "She broke the fucking Radical. None of us could have, and she . . . she did it."

They were silent.

"We should leave," Bubbles said.

"I will," Bugsy said. "I'll go. Just . . . just give us a minute."

"You need a hospital," said Noel, "now." Under his breath, but not so quietly Wally couldn't hear, he added, "And a sodding blacksmith, for all the good it will do."

"Wait," said Wally. It came out more like a gurgle. He shambled toward the garden and its pair of baobab trees, wheezing with the effort of every step. New pain lanced up his side; bone fragments shifting through his innards.

Behind him, Bubbles said, "What is he doing?"

"Saying good-bye," said Noel.

Ghost came running up. She took his hand. He tried not to lean on her, so that he wouldn't hurt her if he fell.

They stopped beneath the baobabs, where the first light of sunrise cast long shadows across the battlefield. Wally tried to reach up to pick seeds, but one arm didn't work at all, and when he raised the other over his head, the pain took his breath away. Ghost saw what he was trying to do. Her feet left the ground. She floated up through the branches like an angel, picking seeds as she went.

To the tree, Wally said, "She's a good kid, Jerusha. I think she's gonna be okay. You woulda liked her. I'll tell her all about you." He looked around, at Noel and Bubbles and the rest. "I'll tell everybody about you."

A stab of pain; the breath caught in his throat. And then the tears came, far too strong to be held back. "Aww, heck, Jerusha. Why'd you have to get bit? It was supposed to be me who died, not you."

He knew people were watching him, but he didn't care. Wally hobbled over to one of the baobab trunks. He leaned against it, put his arms around it. The wood smelled, ever so faintly, of Jerusha. Wally sniffled.

"Thank you for coming to Africa with a big dumb guy," he whispered. "Thank you for being so nice to me. Thank you for being my best friend." He pressed his lips to the tree, careful not to scratch the wood. "I will never, ever forget you, Jerusha. Not if I live to be a million."

A breeze wafted through the baobab. Wally imagined he could hear Jerusha's laughter in the rustling branches. Or was she crying, too?

Ghost descended. She landed next to Wally with an armload of baobab seeds.

Wally called over to Noel. "Okay. We're ready now."

♥

Epilogues

Kisangani, Congo
People's Paradise of Africa

ZOMBIES WERE PATROLLING THE outer edges of Kisangani.

Moto—that was Fire Boy's name—sat beside her in the passenger seat of the jeep. "Don't let them scare you," Michelle told him.

Sitting next to the road—in a very nonzombie state—were a couple of men Michelle recognized, Leopard Men who had been transformed when Alicia Nshombo had died. Michelle preferred them in their nonfeline state. She slowed the jeep and yelled, "Joey, I've got someone here who needs to meet Adesina. And maybe even you."

"What the fuck do I care about that, Bubbles?" gurgled one of the zombies.

Moto's mouth dropped open, and a blast of fire engulfed the zombie.

"God-fucking-damn-it," came Joey's voice through the mouth of the burning corpse. "That little fucker just barbecued up my favorite."

"Oh, please." Michelle bubbled and blew the flaming zombie into a sloppy mess of bones and rags and blackened meat. "I'm coming in." She ground the jeep into first and drove into the compound.

The place was looking far better than Michelle had expected. Between Joey's zombies, the captives, and the staff, they'd cleared away the remains

of Alicia Nshombo and her followers. The blood was gone and there was the
scent of fresh paint in the air.

Michelle parked the jeep and got out. Joey came out of one of the small
houses. A phalanx of zombies immediately surrounded her. "What the fuck
do you want?" she asked.

"World peace, an end to hunger, and a frothy cappuccino," Michelle
replied. "Doesn't look like I'm getting any of it."

"Who's the little fucker with the bad breath?"

Moto had scurried out of the jeep to stay close to Michelle. He grabbed her
hand and gave Joey a frightened look. "This is Moto," Michelle said. "Moto,
this is Joey."

"Hello," he said. There was a little burp of fire, but no more. Michelle
gave his hand a squeeze.

Joey shot Michelle a nasty look—something Michelle was used to. Then
Joey looked at Moto. She gave him a small smile. He gripped Michelle's
hand tighter, but he smiled back at Joey.

"Where's Adesina?" Michelle asked.

"Michelle!" Adesina came running up the main path. Well, she skittered.
Her pretty face looked strange attached to her insect body. She launched herself into the air and flew awkwardly at Michelle. *She's not used to her wings
yet*, Michelle thought. She opened her arms, caught Adesina, and embraced
her gently.

Adesina touched Michelle's face with her front legs. A wave of warmth
and happiness filled Michelle. *This is Moto*, Michelle thought. Adesina
pulled away and Michelle let her go. A wave of sadness came over Michelle.

Adesina flitted in front of Moto. There was a moment when Michelle
was afraid he might accidentally open his mouth and set her on fire. Instead
he held out his arm and Adesina landed. He brought her close to his face
and she put her legs on his face as she had with Michelle. His anxious expression was replaced with a beatific smile.

"When the fuck are you leavin'?" Joey asked.

Michelle watched Adesina and Moto. It was good. She'd done the right
thing bringing him here.

"I'm not sure." Michelle smiled at Joey. A cheerful Michelle annoyed
Joey to no end. "I thought I'd call Juliet and see if she'd like to come join us
in this lovely vacation spot."

Joey's zombies gave an angry growl. "Why the fuck would you do that?"
Joey asked.

"Because the three of us need to sort some stuff out." Michelle looked back at Adesina and Moto. They seemed to be getting along just fine. "And I'm going to stay here for a while to help out."

"No fucking way," Joey said. Her voice was harsh. And she poked Michelle in the back. "Not after what you did to that little fucker—the Mummy."

"Especially after what happened with her."

"You fucking killed her," Joey spat out. "You were supposed to be some kind of hero, and you killed a kid. What the fuck does that make you?"

"Human." Michelle felt a terrible sadness. "Just like you. Just like everybody else."

"I'm never going to forgive you," Joey said.

"That's okay." Michelle touched Joey's cheek, wiping away a tear. "I'm not going to, either."

"Fucker."

"Indeed."

Blythe van Renssaeler
Memorial Clinic Jokertown
Manhattan, New York

AS FINN CAME TROTTING into the waiting room, the rubber booties that covered his hooves squeaked with every step. "You have a fine healthy baby boy, seven pounds three ounces."

Noel handed the joker doctor a cigar. He couldn't quite trust himself to speak just yet.

"More the traditional type, are you? No helping her breathe and count contractions. No video of the blessed event."

"God no," said Noel.

Finn laughed at his horrified tone. "Can't say I blame you. Usually the wife is cussing out the husband, and I have had more than a few of them faint. Men just don't handle blood as well as women."

Never was a problem for me. But pray God I'm done with all that now and forever.

"What are you naming him?" Finn asked

"Jasper, after my father. May I see . . ." Noel's voice trailed away.

"Niobe's back in her room and your son is with her. Come on." Finn led him out of the waiting room and down the hall.

Niobe was in a white lace nightgown she'd brought from home, and a nurse with antennae for eyebrows and faceted eyes like a bumblebee was brushing Niobe's hair over her shoulders. Noel could see where the hair at her temples was still sweat-dampened. A bundle in a soft blue blanket was in her arms.

She raised her eyes to his, and he'd never seen such an expression of sheer joy, triumph, and love before. "Say hello to your son," she said.

He crossed the room in three long strides and kissed her. Then he looked down at the wrinkled, red face of his child. At least the urchin had a lush head of chestnut-colored hair and eyes that were almost aquamarine, because otherwise he was astoundingly ugly.

Niobe pushed the bundle into his arms. For an instant it felt awkward, and then the little warm body found its position in the crook of his arm. The tiny budlike mouth worked in a sucking movement, and a surprisingly adult sigh emerged from between his lips. There was a smell from the baby that was indescribable, but it evoked memories of freshly baked bread, and baking cookies, and wood smoke on a cold evening. It was everything good and safe and loving.

Noel's arms tightened around the baby, and a feeling of such protective love washed through his body like an electric current. He knew he would lay down his life for this child.

He looked at Niobe who smiled at him, but there was a serious look in her green eyes.

"I love you," Noel said.

She didn't give the usual response. Instead she asked, "Are you home now?"

"Yes." And he added, "Now, and forever."

"Good."

United Nations
Manhattan, New York

LOHENGRIN'S OFFICE NEVER CHANGED. The phones were always ringing. The little chiming noise that meant new e-mail had come through was still on its way to nervous collapse. Klaus himself was a little more worn, a little more tired. But he also had the small cut-in laugh lines that came from winning a few. So that was all right.

Lohengrin leaned back in his chair. His smile was softer than Bugsy had expected. His voice was gentle. "You look good, my friend."

"You make a boy blush," Bugsy said. "You're looking pretty spiffy yourself. The eye patch works for you. Very Dread Pirate Odin."

Klaus didn't even look pained. That fact alone told Bugsy just how rough he seemed. He thought he'd been hiding it better. "I'm sorry. For what happened," Lohengrin said.

"Don't be," Bugsy said. "We all knew the risks."

There was a pause. It was the invitation to spill it all out. Bugsy thought about telling him what it had been like, going back to Ellen's apartment to get his things and seeing everything still there. The accumulated artifacts of maybe a hundred ended lives. All the last chances were gone now. All the voices silenced. The dead were dead again.

He let the silence speak for itself.

Lohengrin nodded. "What are you going to do now?"

Bugsy raised his eyebrows in feigned confusion. "Well," he said. "I was thinking lunch. And there's an entomology conference going on at NYU. I was thinking I'd maybe go hang out at the bars and seem interesting. It's Lyme disease mostly, but I can hope for a cute grad student who's into wasps."

Lohengrin did look just a little pained that time. So that was good. "You don't always have to make a joke of it, Jonathan."

"Oh, but I do," Bugsy said with a grin. "Oh, yes, I do."

"I meant, will you remain with the Committee?" Lohengrin said.

"Will I keep putting myself in a position to get killed or watch my friends suffer and die while the whole fucking prospect slowly sinks into the permanent cesspool of bureaucracy?"

"Yes," Lohengrin said.

"I don't know," Bugsy said. Then a moment later, "I will if you will. Or we could strike out on our own. Roam the earth meting out justice, overthrowing bad guys according to our own personal values, making time with the cute girls."

The phone rang. Lohengrin let it. "You make it sound tempting," he said with a grin.

"Yeah, until you remember that was the Radical's job description, too. Didn't work out too well."

"It could have been worse," Lohengrin said.

"Words to live by."

The Jerusha Carter Childhood Development Institute Jokertown, Manhattan, New York

"ANY PAIN WHEN I do this?" Dr. Finn asked. He pulled Wally's arm straight ahead, then gently raised it.

"Nope. Not at all, Doc." The dull ache throbbed through Wally's shoulder. "Uh, maybe a little."

Finn released Wally's arm. "That bullet did a great deal of damage when it shattered inside your shoulder. I'd be lying if I said I wasn't shocked that you didn't suffer permanent loss of function in this arm." He marked something on Wally's chart. "You're lucky you didn't lose your leg, too," he added absently.

"Which one?"

Finn peered at him over his eyeglasses. "After getting attacked by a crocodile? Both of them." His tone was stern, but his eyes gleamed. "You can button your shirt now."

Wally hopped down, gingerly, from the exam table. The bullet wound in his leg had become badly infected during the long trek across the Congo; Finn had said something about river parasites, too. They had it under control now, but after six months of antibiotic treatments, his leg still wasn't back to full strength.

His other leg, the one the croc had chomped, still had teeth marks in it. Finn speculated it probably always would, though he readily admitted he knew very little about healing processes in iron.

Wally's side still ached, too, from where they'd opened him up to fix his broken ribs. They'd removed a big chunk of iron to do that. Most of his skin had grown back, thick and heavy as ever, but he still had tender spots.

Finn jotted something on a prescription pad. He tore off the sheet and handed it to Wally. "One last set of treatments. After this you'll be in the clear."

"Thanks." Wally tucked the prescription into the breast pocket of his overalls. "Let's go check on the kids," he said.

Finn led him down the corridor and through a sheet of construction plastic draped over the doorway where his clinic abutted the new school. The hallways here stank of fresh paint. Finn's hooves left little dimples in the linoleum; the carpet layers weren't finished. And judging by the rolls of carpeting stacked everywhere—all in bright, kid-friendly colors—they wouldn't be for a while.

The Jerusha Carter Childhood Development Institute—or the "Carter School," as people had already begun to call it—was built around a large interior courtyard. A baobab tree grew in the center of the space, shading the playground where Ghost played alongside the dozens of children Jerusha had rescued from Nyunzu. A few of the children had already been adopted; most would need years of counseling.

Wally and Finn strolled along one of the cloisters lining the courtyard. Ghost saw them. (Her name was Yerodin, but Wally still thought of her as Ghost; he probably always would.) She waved, grinning widely.

"*Wallywally!*" she called. "Come play!" That's what she called him. Wallywally.

Wally waved back. He recognized her playmates: Cesar, the little boy who had translated for him and Jerusha back at the Nyunzu lab, and the joker girl covered with extra fingers. It made him feel good, somehow, that Ghost had made friends with somebody who had known Lucien.

The trio started up a little chant. "Wallywally play! Wallywally play!"

Wally wiped his eyes and grinned. "I'll be there in a sec, you guys."

Finn nodded toward the children. "How is she?"

Wally sighed. "She still has the nightmares. Bad nights, once in a while. Sometimes I wake up and find her standing over me." He shrugged. "But you know what, Doc? Sometimes I think she's stronger than I am. Honest."

Finn gave him a funny look. He turned his attention back to the children on the playground. "Don't sell yourself short, Wally." They stood, watching the kids, in amicable silence for a minute or two. "Well," said Finn, looking at his watch, "I need to do my rounds."

"See ya, Doc."

Finn trotted back to his clinic.

Wally tromped across the sandbox, to where Ghost and Cesar were digging a hole with a yellow plastic pail. He sat cross-legged in the sand. Ghost climbed on his lap.

"So. What do you want for lunch today, kiddo?"

"PBM," she said. That was their special shorthand: peanut butter and mango.

Wally glanced up at the baobab. Sunlight shone through the boughs. He imagined Gardener listening to this, imagined her laughing, imagined her tucking a lock of hair behind her ear. He gathered up Ghost, and smiled.

"Yeah. Me, too."

White Sands National Monument
White Sands, New Mexico

"**WHAT THE FUCK,**" **SAID** Jay Ackroyd, biting into an apple, "is that?"

That was a baby triceratops, its colors mottled but otherwise indecipherable in the moonlight that silvered the great white dunes, which stood behind Sprout Meadows in a red Flexible Flyer mired to its hubs in soft sand.

"Kota the Baby Triceratops," Mark Meadows said, bundled up against a biting winter wind. "It was, like, a popular toy last year, I guess."

It turned its grinning head with the three little plush horns and the frill toward the sound of his voice and rolled its eyes fetchingly. Jay Ackroyd recoiled from the robot toy as if afraid it would go for his throat. He was as deliberately unremarkable as possible, wearing a bulky brown coat, a muffler, and a wool hat crammed down over his ears. "And you're dragging it along why?" he asked.

Mark shrugged. "Sprout loves it."

"Even though *he* gave it to her," added Sun Hei-lian.

Ackroyd shivered ostentatiously. "Jesus," he said. "I thought New Mexico was supposed to be desert. It's colder than a bail bondsman's heart out here."

"You should see the Gobi this time of year," Sun Hei-lian said.

"Nah, I'll pass." The detective dug his free hand into the pocket of his slacks.

"It was good of you to come and say good-bye, Jay," Mark Meadows said.

Ackroyd shrugged. "Might as well. Can't dance. You folks sure you want to do this? This is a one-way ticket you're buying, here."

"Well, let's see," Hei-lian said. "Mark's wanted for all of the Radical's crimes. The country I served all my life has a price on my head. We've got no family beyond each other. There's just *so much* to hold us here."

Jay looked at Mark. "Did you tell her she's gonna be spending the rest of her life on a whole planet full of people who make the Borgias look like the Huxtables?"

"I was a Chinese spy, Mr. Ackroyd," Hei-lian said. "Intrigue I can handle."

"I remember Takis as well as you do, Jay," Mark said. "But don't forget, I was already on the run from the law long before the Radical took over. I can be an actual research scientist again. I can do science." He felt himself fill with warmth. "And they can cure Sprout."

"But, Daddy," she said, "nothing's wrong with me."

He stroked her cheek. "Of course not, honey. And they can help you . . . learn to do a lot of fun new things."

"You sure of that?" Jay asked.

Mark shrugged. "If not, I'll do the work myself. Maybe that's what I should have been doing all along, rather than chasing a dream that turned into nightmare for the whole world to share."

Hei-lian's mittened hand squeezed his. "You did many good things," she said. "You helped a lot of people."

"But it doesn't make the other stuff right."

"No. But remembering the good helps us to keep going. The world's beginning anew for all three of us. Don't throw that gift away, lover; it isn't offered to very many people."

"No kidding," Jay said. "So, no more Cap'n Trips?"

Mark shook his head firmly. "Those days are gone forever. I'm hanging the purple top hat up for good. I learned my lesson way too well. Nobody should have that kind of power, man. I sure couldn't handle it."

Ackroyd looked at Hei-lian. "Just one thing puzzles me, Colonel. All respect to my old bud Mark, here, he's a skinny old geek. You're a glamorous lady spy. What's the attraction, anyway?"

She took hold of Mark's arm and nestled against him. "He's both a kind man and a good one. Since he's the first of those I've ever met, I decided it'd be foolish to let go of him. Also, thank you for the compliment, Mr. Ackroyd, but I'm no youngster, either. And unequivocally retired from the spy trade."

Jay shrugged. Taking a final bite of the apple, he hurled it far off over a nearby dune.

"You shouldn't litter, Mr. Popinjay," Sprout said severely.

"It's biodegradable, kid." Jay Ackroyd looked up at the clear star-crusted sky. "So it ends here where it all began. White Sands, New Mexico." He held up a forefinger. "I could just pop you there. Save a lot of travel time. Cut to the chase."

"Thanks, no," Mark said. "I figure the trip'll give Sprout a while to get acclimated. All of us, really."

"Look, Daddy, look!" Sprout said, jumping up and down and pointing at the sky. "A falling star! Make a wish!"

Mark glanced up as the light grew suddenly to the glowing, spiky pink and ochre conch shape of a Takisian living starship descending from above. "I made my wishes, sweetie," he said, "and they're all coming true."

Bunia
The Congo

THERE IS A GROVE near Bunia, on the grounds of the old estate and around the ruins of the house there: a garden of many strange plants and trees, many of them not native to Africa but all of them blooming impossibly here in apparent ease. There are orange trees, apple trees, mango trees; there are flowers of every description; there are cacti and Joshua trees and palms. Marvelous flowering vines wrap around many of them, blankets of gentle green punctuated with blossoms of vibrant red and electric blue and oranges so bright the color hurts the eye.

In the midst of that grove, at its very center where the house foundations can still be seen, there are two giant, intertwined baobabs, each with a trunk one hundred fifty feet or more around—savannah trees out of place here in the jungle, yet both healthy and thriving, so massive and huge that they could have been growing there for centuries.

The locals call the baobabs "The Lovers." They lean upon each other, branches wrapping around the trunk of their partner as if in embrace, their crowns entirely woven together. Monkey fruit hangs heavy on their branches; eagles, vultures, and storks have made their twig nests in the Lovers' tangled, sleepy heads; owls huddle in the crevices of their trunks; squirrels and lizards, snakes and tree frogs, and thousands of varieties of insects make their home there.

The locals come here for the grove's wild beauty, but they are drawn also, they say, by its magic. Couples are married here under the shade of the baobabs, and at the end of the ritual they take a seed from the monkey fruit with them to plant in front of their own homes—because then the luck of the grove will follow them through their lives. They bring their sick here, to feed them *kuka* and *bungha* made from the trees' bounty; it is said that the blessing of the Lovers comes sometimes to those who eat from the trees, and those with the worst illnesses might be cured, even when the doctors have given up hope.

They also say that if one stays here at night and listens very carefully in the black stillness, that you might hear a voice whispering among the branches and through the grove. A woman's voice, calling eternally for someone.

To hear the woman's voice is the best magic of all. If you listen closely to her, they say, you will hear the name of the person who is destined to be your own lover. The skeptics say it is only the wind, but those who know the grove best will only smile at that, and shake their heads. No, they will say. There *is* magic here. All you have to do is allow yourself to feel it.

And that magic will never die.

♣

Closing Credits

FEATURING	created by
Niobe (the Genetrix) Matthews	Ian Tregillis
Dr. Bradley Finn	Melinda M. Snodgrass
Klaus (Lohengrin) Hausser	George R. R. Martin
Barbara (Babel) Baden	S. L. Farrell
Nick (Will-o'-Wisp) Williams	Kevin Andrew Murphy
Prince Siraj of Jordan	Melinda M. Snodgrass
Leucrotta	Kevin Andrew Murphy
The Hunger	Kevin Andrew Murphy
Charles (Wrecker) Abidimi	Victor Milán
Candace (the Darkness) Sessou	Victor Milán
The Mummy	Victor Milán
Ayiyi	Victor Milán
Moto	Victor Milán
G. C. Jayewardene	Walton Simons
Jay (Popinjay) Ackroyd	George R. R. Martin
Simone (Snowblind) Duplaix	Walton Simons
Cesar	Ian Tregillis
Waikili, Eason, Abagbe, and Naadir	S. L. Farrell
Jaako (Broadcast) Kuusi	Melinda M. Snodgrass
Ffodor (Blackhole) Mathias	Melinda M. Snodgrass
Robert (The Signal on Port 950)Cumming	Daniel Abraham

WITH	created by
Denys Finch	S. L. Farrell
Billy	Daniel Abraham
Gataen and Kengo	Caroline Spector
Japhet	Caroline Spector
Kimberly Ann Cordayne	Victor Milán
Ira and Sharon LaFleur	Caroline Spector
Thomas (Digger) Downs	Steve Perrin
Sister Julie	S. L. Farrell
Mrs. Clark	Victor Milán
Devlin (Ha'penny) Pearl	Melinda M. Snodgrass
Dr. Washikala	Victor Milán
Ibada	S. L. Farrell
Makemba	Caroline Spector
Garou	Victor Milán
Nikolaas (Burrowing Owl) Buxtehude	Victor Milán
Wilma Mankiller	Daniel Abraham

WITH	*created by*
Buford (Toad Man) Calhoun	Royce Wideman
Donatien (Tricolor) Racine	George R. R. Martin
Tom (Brave Hawk) Diedrich	Steve Perrin
Michael (Drummer Boy) Vogali	S. L. Farrell
Drake (Ra) Thomas	Walton Simons

Editor's Afterword

Wild Cards is fiction, but the child soldiers of Africa are a grim reality. The People's Paradise of Africa is a frightening place in our alternate world, but no more frightening than the real-world Congo. The Second Congo War began in 1998 and officially ended in 2003, but sporadic slaughter continues to this day. More than five and a half million people have died in the fighting, making it the bloodiest conflict since World War II. And that's without adding in the casualties from the First Congo War, which ran from 1996 to 1997.

Many of the slain have been children.

Their slayers have often been children as well. You do not need a superpower to kill. A gun will do. Leucrotta, the Hunger, Ghost, the Wrecker, and the rest of our kid aces are fictional characters, but there are real children out there whose own stories are not so very different.

In Joseph Conrad's day it was rubber and ivory that drew men down into the heart of darkness. Today it is gold, coltan, diamonds, and uranium. The darkness remains unchanged. The Western media does an admirable job of covering the conflicts in Iraq, Afghanistan, Gaza, and other familiar global hot spots, yet the death of millions of Congolese does not get so much as a mention on the evening news. In Africa the ignorant armies still clash by night, yet the horror goes unseen and unremarked.

But not by everyone. There are organizations and dedicated individuals working to help the victims of these wars and put an end to the practice of turning children into soldiers. Go up on the Internet and Google "Child Soldiers" and you will find them. Read about their work and help if you can . . . with a donation, or just by spreading the word.

There are no superheroes in the real world, alas.

There's only us.

GEORGE R. R. MARTIN